Home Fires

Judith Kirscht

New Libri Press

All rights reserved under International and Pan-American Copyright Conventions. No part of this book may be reproduced, transmitted, downloaded, decompiled, reverse engineered, or stored in or introduced into any information storage and retrieval system, in any form or by any means, whether electronic or mechanical, now known or hereinafter invented, without the express written permission of the publisher.

This is a work of fiction. Nothing is in it that has not been imagined.

Copyright © 2013 by Judith Kirscht

Cover Art by Miriam Kirscht and Megan Kenyon,
Cover Copyright © 2013 by New Libri Press

ISBN: 978-1-61469-043-6

Published in 2013 by New Libri Press
Mercer Island, WA 98040
www.newlibri.com

New Libri Press is a small independent press dedicated to publishing new authors and independent authors in both eBook and traditional formats.

Home Fires

Acknowledgments

First, my appreciation to Miriam Kirscht and Megan Kenyon for the cover of this book and many thanks to my critique group, Serena DuBois, Helen Nopson, Norma Johnson, and Pat Cowgill, who weathered several drafts.

Chapter 1

Early September.

Myra Benning stood on the patio and watched as the orange of poppies emerged from the fog, then the shadowy forms on the ridge became eucalyptus, and finally the sea appeared. The fennel dotting the meadow that ran between house and sea was ripening, adding its licorice smell to the salt air. She inhaled and inhaled again as she waited for Santa Cruz Island to appear across the Santa Barbara Channel. Every morning she did this, marveling that it was really so, that she, the towering girl from the clapboard house sitting naked on the Minnesota prairie could have ended up in such a place.

For most, paradise was Santa Barbara itself, where palm and bougainvillea vied with the blue, blue sea beyond groomed beaches. Not her. She was far happier with this untended meadow and untamed beach tucked away in Goleta, Santa Barbara's ne'er-do-well second cousin to the north. Here she and her family could search for salamanders, encounter skunks, muck about in tide pools. Here bluebirds, swallows, meadowlarks, and cedar waxwings marked the changing seasons. They sank into it, became a part of it. Her morning ritual never failed to erase rumblings of anxiety and unease over the years, returning her to that moment, almost twenty years ago, when she and Derek first discovered this stretch of coast and rented the bungalow behind her.

The sharp tone of a teenage retort drew her back into the house.

"You tell her, Mom," Peter called as he spotted her. He unwound his six-foot length from the chair and headed for the sink with his cereal dish. Blond and blue-eyed, he'd inherited her Minnesota complexion, but otherwise looked like his father. "She needs to get with it."

"With what?" She poured a cup of coffee and went to the table.

"Guys. I see them looking, trying to ... you know ... get her interested, and she's just ... like they're invisible." He flicked at his sister with the last word and headed for his sneakers. He'd begun to grow into his height in the last year and move with his father's easy grace.

"I see what I want to see, thanks." Susan bent her coppery head and scowled into her cereal bowl.

Peter knew nothing at all about being fourteen, a girl, and a head taller than the boys. Susan was already as tall as Myra, who well remembered the torture of those days, though some part of her worried about the cocoon that enveloped Susan at the mention of the opposite sex.

"But why?" cried her brother. "You're going to miss out on ... all the fun!" He stomped a foot into his shoe and rose.

"Everybody doesn't have to be like you," Susan retorted, "with a new girl every month."

"Ease up, Peter," Myra urged, gazing from one to the other. She never tired of gazing at the happy blend of genes they had produced. "You only know the boy's side of the scene and you're a senior." She spoke with certainty, though she couldn't remember a time Peter hadn't been at ease in any social scene. That, too, he shared with his father. "But right now you need to move it along, Susan."

Susan raised her brown eyes to the clock, pushed her half-eaten cereal away, and rose as though being dragged to her feet.

She watched them pull their bikes from the front porch and disappear up the street just as the sun broke through the haze. For a moment, they were a pair again, in sync, pedaling off to some childhood adventure. She breathed in the beauty of them and the too-soon-to-be-adult energy they left in the room, forever amazed that she had produced such children.

Only one more boy to send on his way, she thought, smiling. Derek was still the boy who had beamed at her, astonished, on the Southern California beach. "You surf!"

She'd been as surprised as he was, if truth were told. She'd fled the Minnesota prairie to be an art student, never dreaming that the body trained to basketball and track would convert to sea sport, much less attract a man like Derek, who could have any girl. "Pretties gone in the blink of an eye," he'd said of the girls who hung about him like gnats. She, he declared, as they made love on a La Jolla beach, was a piece of ass you could get hold of.

She turned from the door and saw that the message light was blinking on the phone. Derek hadn't checked it when he came in last night. Let him do it. He was still a product of the Sixties, rebelling against boundaries—holding seminars at home, printing this phone number on his syllabi. Every year, it was the same when his graduate students arrived on campus—sweet, breathy voices whispering through her house. She scoffed at herself for wanting the boundaries they'd both rejected back in their college days, but every year they ate a little further into her peace of mind. She didn't want to hear them. She turned away, then turned back. Maybe it was her mother; maybe Dad had fallen again. She jabbed the button.

"Derek—Professor Benning. This is Gina. Call me."

The nervous young voice clicked off, leaving Myra staring at nothing. The only motion was the drifting fog, the only sound her own breathing; if she stood here long enough, the fog and the sea would lift all else away; gradually all would grow faint, diaphanous and vanish. But it didn't. Not this time. The mistaken use of his first name—the urgency, even anger, in her voice. The breathy intimacy of the tone. Gina with no last name or phone number. Like rocks, damning lumps crashed through her barriers and lay inert.

Then anger burst through, galvanizing her to action. She turned, marched to the bedroom door and stared at the muscular back of her husband, creator of her beautiful children, flung face down across the bed. He could still make her blood tingle, just looking at him. The feel of his hands running across her breasts was always new. The way he crossed the room as though there was no one else present remained as fresh as her morning coffee. He wanted her. If love-making had lost some of its adventure after twenty years, become more reassuring comfort than fire—so what? His body still gave the same message, and his boyish charm hadn't aged.

So when had she become his jolly mother, here to wake him up, smack him on the butt, and send him on his way? Earth mother. His favorite term of endearment turned on her. When, exactly, had she begun accepting that role, even become comfortable in it? Fooling herself that if she didn't listen to the answering machine, didn't attend department parties to meet the understanding smiles of other faculty wives, her dream world would never slide out from under her to dash her on the rocks.

Rage shifted to self-loathing, and humiliation swelled her veins, seared behind her eyes as it hadn't since the days her father had sneered at her size. Then she raged at the return of self-loathing. He wasn't going to return her to that place. Never.

She didn't wake him. She would not. That dutiful dunce was no more. She turned from the sight of him, marched up to her tower studio and sat there, fists clenched. On the easel was a half-finished watercolor of the fog-shrouded mesa beyond her window. On her work table, a carved wood block of a heron waited to be printed. On the wall above her desk, a watercolor of the Serendipity—the sailboat that had come down through three generations of her husband's family, marking the depths of their roots on this shore, beckoned, its sails billowing against the hills of Anacapa Island. All part of the delusion she'd spun around herself.

A half hour later, she heard him curse.

"Myra? Where the hell are you? I've got a seminar, damn it!"

She didn't answer. Fifteen minutes later, the old Jag he'd inherited from a rich uncle and restored with loving care roared out of the drive, its exhaust tainting the sea air.

Myra sat on in the tower they'd built so she could see the sea, anger then shame then anger twisting her gut. She could hear her mother chatting with her friends, condemning women who couldn't keep their men from wandering.

But he wanted her. She knew that in a place nothing could reach. She couldn't be that wrong about him. That much of a fool. She was overreacting. The call was just about some urgent student issue. She was upset about nothing. She hated women who forever pried into their husbands' papers, drawers, and day planners. But the weight that had dropped as she listened to the message wouldn't budge. Her head throbbed. She needed air.

"Skittles!" she called, heading down the stairs. The old beagle who had accompanied her children's growing up scrambled to his feet, knowing from her tone of voice what lay ahead. She stopped only long enough to put on the tar-specked running shoes that lived outside the back door then took off across the open meadow toward the sea, aware only of the anger that drove her feet to the edge of the cliffs and down the path to the beach. Finally, as she strode along the water's edge, the rhythm of her feet calmed her. She began to throw sticks for Skittles, whose amble was a pale imitation of his once-upon-a-time bounding gait, and let the motion of the water return her to herself. The sea still stretched before her, unruffled by her shock; driftwood still blocked her way; the incoming tide still forced her into the water and finally stopped her. She turned and gazed back down the empty beach toward the distant point. The specks in the water were surfers, newly-arrived college students trying out the waves. Like the meadowlarks and poppies, they appeared and disappeared with the turning of the seasons.

The very inevitability of their recurring appearance, like the rotation of the earth, had lulled her into blindness. Derek lived by the rhythms of the sea creatures—they were both his love and his profession. They'd met on a surfing beach, but she'd fallen in love with the rapt attention of the man bent over a tide pool. The voices of graduate students were simply an adjunct to his central passion. And if she'd been startled by the intimacy of a voice or a glance, she'd cast it off, sustained by that belief. Her mind brought up the faces of the men and women—she'd always called them boys and girls—who flowed in and out of her living room for seminars—fresh, bright, inquiring—then vanished like the outgoing tide. Marine biologists took students on field trips. Who would question that? Who would want to?

Myra started back down the beach, the sun warming her shoulders. Gulls rose in irritation at their approach, though Skittles no longer chased them, and the air smelled of warm sand and salt. She turned and walked into the lapping waves until they reached her knees, then stood watching the minnows circle her feet.

When she reached the path back up the cliff, she didn't take it. Instead she went on all the way to the point and stood watching the surfers as they floated, waiting for a wave. She loved re-entering that mindset where nothing existed but the water and the sun, where change was the motion of the waves. In the years they'd taught Peter and Susan to ride, she'd regained her ability to predict the movement that told her the moment to mount her board.

By the time she turned toward home, she'd become as legitimate an occupant of her world as the hound who ambled ahead of her nosing out the inhabitants of the driftwood-strewn shore. She climbed the path up to the mesa and crossed it to the house, her body and mind drained, then sank down on a chaise. She was crying. All the last hour had done was dissolve her defenses. She clenched her teeth, hearing her father's voice jeering that she was too big to cry, but still the tears ran. Exasperated, she got up and went to the shower, rinsing her salt-encrusted legs and letting the tears disappear into the river of hot water.

When she emerged, she stood at the mirror looking at the six-foot blond who stared back. For years she'd seen a statuesque woman whose figure had matured but still passed muster, a woman at her best without make-up or jewelry. Now her father's giant daughter gazed back at her, and she turned away in disgust. Damn him. Damn them both. She would not go back there. She wouldn't. She'd get to work.

Dressed in the jeans and sweater that were her habit, she returned to her tower. She sat down and pulled a drawing pad toward her, but her pen would not move. After an hour, she gave it up, set up the press for the woodblock and began to stamp. Each plunge of the press gave a satisfying jolt. Burying herself in attention to every speck and blurry line, she ticked and stamped the hours of the day away.

Myra was in the kitchen getting dinner when she heard his car.

She watched him come in and toss his jacket into a chair, tall, still lithe, at home in his skin, he defied the stereotype of a professor. His dark hair was graying at the temples now and the adolescent tension had quieted to self assurance over the years. She turned back to the stove before he turned and halloed his usual greeting.

"You have a message on the answering machine."

If he was confused by the frost in her response, she couldn't see it. As the message filled the room, she pared potatoes with sharp clean strokes.

"Saw her at the office." His voice tried for offhand, but missed by a beat.

"Who is she?" Myra put down her knife, then turned around and gazed at his face, made more attractive by traces of the out of doors, the dark curls spiced with gray, the strongly muscled arms showing below the rolled up sleeves of his sport shirt—and hated the virility she so loved.

"A student ... from last quarter," he added too quickly, startled by whatever he saw in her face. "She wants an incomplete."

Myra frowned. "Why don't I believe you?"

"I don't know ... what's wrong?" He sounded bewildered, but the dark eyes that met hers had lost their usual attentiveness and depth.

He approached for his usual embrace, but she put a hand up. "She sounds too young. For a grad student."

"Ah." He smiled, reassured. "She does. But she is." He reached again.

She pushed him back. "She calls you by your first name."

His arm dropped. "Some do." He shrugged. "I don't mind." He gave her his boyish grin and reached for her yet again.

"Don't." She put a hand on his chest. Even Derek drew a line at first names—told his students to call him Professor or Doctor. She'd heard him. "She doesn't leave a last name or phone number. You're lying to me!"

He let his arms fall to his sides, then gave a dismissive wave. "All right, all right." He turned away. "So we had lunch. She was having trouble with a lab experiment, and I was hungry. Look …" He turned and met her eyes again. "Sometimes students get the wrong idea. You know that."

The front door banged, cutting off their conversation.

"Mom? Are you down here?" Susan rushed into the kitchen followed by Peter. "I got moved to advanced English!" Delight had broken through her too-shy daughter's usual mask.

"Mrs. Elliott," Peter added, clearly impressed. "She's the best."

"Well, great!" She held out her arms. "Terrific, in fact!"

"All because she showed her a bunch of stories." Peter's tone was tinged with incredulity. He shared his father's love of science. Susan's stories, though he'd played along with them once, were the stuff of childhood.

"Mrs. Elliott says I should publish them. Can you believe it?" Susan cried. "It turns out she writes children's stories." She plopped her books on the table and spun, flicking Peter with her finger tips as she went. "You're looking at the next Newberry Award winner."

"Huh." Peter was unimpressed. "Too bad you have to take biology." He caught a flying arm and twisted it behind her back.

Susan pulled her arms free and headed for the patio door. "Names, names, names. Nailing everything down with names. Who needs them?" She sailed out onto the meadow.

Peter shook his head and followed.

As Myra watched, her spirits soared. Her queen-of-the-world little girl was back.

She felt Derek watching her. The fragile moment popped. How dare he ruin this? "So. Lunch." She turned. "That's what I'm supposed to believe."

"That's right. It doesn't mean anything ..."

She swung around. "Doesn't mean anything to whom, exactly? Me? Susan? Peter?"

"Come on, Myra ..." His tone cajoled as he reached for her again. "Students get crushes. In fact, if I remember rightly, you had one on ..."

"Leave it, Derek."

He gave a sigh of exasperation and followed the children out onto the meadow. She gazed over the kitchen counter at the now deserted great room with its stone fireplace flanked by casement windows open to the autumn air. The worn couch where Peter had spent a spring with a broken ankle, the dent in the oak mantle where they'd dropped it during their usual do-it-yourself installation, the framed watercolors she'd painted long ago of heron and porpoise. She stood motionless as history wrapped itself around her. She couldn't, wouldn't imagine it disintegrating into shouting matches, lies, suspicion. She had to find another way to think about this day.

She turned back to dinner preparations. A crush. High school stuff. Graduate students were too old for that word. A student conference. Without boundaries. A kindness—without boundaries. The repeated word began to spin. Stop, she told herself. Lunch is not an affair. She tore at lettuce. So why did he lie?

She was still trying to find some trivial name for the whole thing when she went to the patio to ring the dinner bell. They sat down to eat, and Peter diverted Derek's attention, regaling him with the trip to Santa Cruz Island his marine biology class was scheduled to take.

"Where I found my purple star," Susan interjected, pointing to the watercolor that decorated the dining area wall.

"Ochre Star," Peter corrected. "And it's shinier than that."

"In your dumb science book. In the water, that's how you see it, blurred up and dreamy."

Myra smiled, happy to let familiar rivalry between science and art dissipate the days' tension. Sometimes it seemed to her they were raising duplicates of themselves at their best. Derek couldn't resist correcting her descriptions of bird or beast but never sought to replace her vision with his own. He, like his son, put that purple star under the microscope, but at home he wanted art on his wall. An odd mix they were, but it worked.

Or so she'd thought. The words stabbed memory in the heart. She clutched her fork and returned to the present. Conversation had moved on.

"You have to get Schultz, Susan. Whittier makes biology a bore."

"Schultz's class is full. And anyway, I don't care. Science is just endless facts, facts, facts …"

Derek was watching Myra as the subject switched to fencing and drama coaches, but there seemed no truth in the old adage that children sense trouble at home.

"How about a camping trip this weekend?" Derek asked. "Before we all get buried in the school year."

Myra raised her head in surprise. Camping trips had become a rarity in recent years. This was a man making amends. Showing her how much he loved his family. But if he'd done nothing, if she was just overreacting, why so anxious to put it right?

"Cool!" Peter agreed. "Kings Canyon, maybe?"

"That's a little far, don't you think, Myra? We can just go back into the San Rafaels." Derek passed the salad as he spoke, not really waiting for her response.

Myra sat silent. She couldn't spend a weekend in a tent filled with the aphrodisiac mixture of pine and cinnamon aftershave, his body within inches of hers.

"I have to write an essay for English," Susan objected.

"You can write it up there, dummy," her brother rejoined.

The rest of the dinner was spent in planning. If either child noticed that Myra wasn't participating, they gave no sign.

It wasn't until the pair was occupied washing dishes in the kitchen that Myra and Derek were left to face each other again. "I'm not going, Derek."

"Myra …"

"I have to work." She looked at her watch. "I'm in the middle of a print run. Rena needs prints for Sunday's art fair." She turned and headed into the kitchen, where she kissed her children. "The queen has to return to her tower," she explained.

They hugged her back out of habit, barely hearing her, and went back to a discussion of the geeky computer teacher.

The sun was sinking as she closed her studio door. She leaned against it and watched the sea until it was no more.

Chapter 2

Myra turned on the light, finally, and stared at the print run, which was, in fact, complete, and she was in no mood to mat either prints or watercolors of sea lions playing in the surf, tide pool creatures, clouds of silver-winged plover—scenes from a life that had vanished. Instead, she taped fresh paper to her drawing board, and soon an oversized hen with disheveled feathers and long scrawny neck appeared from the point of her pen.

"Matilda. That's surely your name." She smiled, as she cast the day's shame and humiliation onto the paper. If Matilda wasn't art, so what? She brought laugher. "You need company." She laid the chicken aside and took a fresh sheet. A porcupine. Eyes narrowed, he was calculating the distance to a heron who stood nearby, his long beak in the air. Alphonse. That was the heron. And the porcupine? Rufus. That would do nicely.

Feeling blood flow through vessels that had been numb since morning, Myra drew out still another sheet. Quills flew, striking not only Alphonse but a gull who had the misfortune to fly by. The gull tilted and crashed, giving out a long drawn-out screech. Eustasia, Myra named her, as the gull's squawking brought Matilda's head, at the end of her long neck, into the picture, and Alphonse flapped his wings, knocking Rufus over as he took off.

"You're the clumsiest heron I've ever seen," Matilda remarked.
"Bad knees," Alphonse answered.

So there they were. An overgrown chicken with too much neck, a porcupine with lousy aim, a gull bristling with quills, and a heron with bad knees. "I think you're going to be great company," she told them, taping them in a row above her desk. She sat back and looked at them, her body released from the day.

Below her, the house was silent. A coyote howled from across the mesa. She looked at her watch. After midnight. On stocking-clad feet, she went down to look in on her children, because she had to make this like every other night. Peter, as long as his father now, lay on his face, one arm dropped over the side of the bed. His laptop lay on the floor beside his hand, the planets of its screensaver rotating unattended. The glow of the streetlight turned the singers on his posters into hovering phantoms and hugely magnified sea life into monsters whose tentacles reached out into the room, effects that Susan hated, but never bothered Peter. All was as usual.

Susan, far less the master of her life, lay with her knees pulled to her chin, but for the first time since school started she hadn't pulled Doby, her raggedy hound, from the shelf above. Maybe the English teacher had redeemed a year that had loomed as unceasing misery. Sleeping, Susan looked far too young for the high school social scene—ten maybe—watercolors of sea life decorated her walls rather than the magnified photos on her brother's, and they hadn't yet been replaced by posters of rock groups. Susan cried out in her sleep and flung an arm up. Myra laid the arm gently back over her chest, then brushed a hand across her daughter's forehead.

Her intensity hadn't fared well in public school. Myra remembered Susan chasing a boy who ran off with her hat, falling on top of him and beating him with her fists—until she noticed the group of laughing urchins around her. And she remembered Susan's clear voice ringing out too loudly in the class chorus on Parents' Day—and the child's mortification at the teacher's remonstrance. Myra had cringed. The experiences brought back the child Myra had been, with the humiliation of those days. So she wasn't surprised when Susan turned to writing or reading, preferring the company of a few good friends. "Subdued," her teachers remarked with satisfaction. But for Myra, it was as though Susan had lowered a glass dome over herself to hide if not smother the flames.

Now, the peace of the sleeping face gave hope that they would get past all of that. She went out and shut the door quietly. The closed door of the master bedroom faced her. Where was she going to sleep? Was she going in there and curl up beside him, accepting his version of Gina?

Her body refused to budge.

A light showed beneath the door. He was waiting for her. To make love. There had been other nights when, watered by those student voices, the seeds of unease had sprouted, and he, as though sensing it, had folded himself around her drowning them in a flood of desire. And she'd happily sunk into bliss. Shame-fed anger rose. She marched forward and opened the door.

Derek sat on the bed. The orange and bronze stripes of his pajamas overwhelmed his face, which lacked its usual high color. The lines beside his mouth, barely perceptible yesterday, cut deeply, and the scar on the back of his hand, left by a sea urchin long ago, stood out against the pallor of his skin.

She stared at him. "Tell me the truth."

He spread his hands helplessly. A man misunderstood. His face was as open and guileless as it had been the day he'd approached her across a crowded dance floor. The face of a man whose sincerity she'd never doubted.

She walked past him to her dressing room without speaking, took her nightgown from its hook, added sweats for her morning walk, then returned to the bedroom for clean underwear and socks.

"Myra ..." His voice was drained of its usual confidence.

"It's not going to work, Derek. I'm not buying." She stood, arms folded over her bundle, glaring, and watched the last of the smile fade from his face, then his eyes.

"All right," he said, finally. "I admit it went too far. I'm sorry ..."

"How far?" She was as shaken by the force of her voice as he was.

"Believe me, Myra ..."

"Did you sleep with her?"

His dark eyes stilled. "Yes, but ..."

Fighting the rush of tears that threatened, she turned and went to the bathroom. Well, she'd asked for it, hadn't she? Demanded it. Gotten what she feared. She made her hands reach for her tooth and hair brushes and stared at the unfamiliar woman in the mirror until she regained control.

Then she turned and went back to the bedroom. "How long?"

"Just ... since spring. But it's over, Myra. You have to believe ..." He broke off and took a breath. "That's why she called the house. She was upset. Not thinking." Blood had returned to his face, timbre to his voice, as though released from deception.

It sucked the breath from her. She turned for the door, then turned back. "How many? How many others?" She couldn't remember a time when those voices hadn't floated through her house.

"Oh, no, Myra. Not ..." his voice faded out under her stare.

"Don't lie, Derek! It's too late for that." For the first time since she'd known him, she read fear in his eyes.

"Only ... a couple." His eyes, stripped of confidence, met her gaze.

"Others? Besides ... Gina?" Her flesh shrank, as though with another blow.

"But it has nothing to do with the way I love you—need you." His voice was husky with an urgency that was new. "Believe that!"

"Just pretties, gone in a flash." The words he'd so often uttered, curled her tongue. She stared at his face, despising its fresh-washed candor and saw only the "I hate to put you through this" apology with which he'd persuaded her to endure years of faculty dinners and departmental teas. The faces of other wives rose in her mind. The understanding she'd always read as sympathy for a fellow academic spouse was pity. She clenched her teeth as humiliation flooded anew. A hundred questions knocked for attention. When? Which of the polite indulgent young faces that smiled at her when she served them cookies in her living room was "the one"? How long did the affairs go on? But she couldn't swallow any more right now. She turned and left without another word and climbed the stairs to the tower.

Myra swept the room with her eyes, taking in every detail of her self-delusion. She stripped the watercolor from the easel in self-revulsion. The Serendipity came off the wall. She turned and there was Derek in charcoal, grinning from the other wall. Carefully, she took him down, and tore him into strips. She reached for the next picture and stopped.

No, not the children. She took a deep breath and sat down, remembering Susan's new elation. She heard again their breakfast and dinner talk, sunk deep into the problems of adolescence. Sleeping now, oblivious to the fact that she was in the tower, tearing apart their lives.

She drew a breath then exhaled, her strength escaping with the air, then collapsed on the daybed wracked with pain. She held her head until, energy spent, she laid back, too weak to undress, to turn the light off.

She only wanted this numbness to take her into sleep. She forced one shoe off, then another, then her jeans, before she gave up the effort, rolled herself in a comforter and gave herself to oblivion. But it didn't come. The small effort of undressing had broken the anesthetic left by tears, and, despite herself, the years of her marriage rolled behind her closed eyelids.

She felt his presence close beside her as she held new babies, saw him rocking them, and felt him reach over in the bed to draw her to him. Felt his sympathetic gaze on her at faculty dinners, making her smile. Listened to him sing with the children on road trips. Saw him kneeling with two small heads over tide pools. She could not be wrong about the love she'd felt—couldn't call that false. But there were other times. Periods when he was impatient with them all, given to insomnia. He put it to the academic politics or the frustrations of research—ruined samples, unproductive eggs—complications that required extra field trips. The department secretary sometimes called looking for him, surprised he'd forgotten to tell her he was going.

Myra rolled over and stared through the skylight at the glow cast by the fog-shrouded moon. Her marriage was a sham. Had been a sham for how long she didn't know—a half dozen years at least. Like a patient receiving a feared diagnosis, the tension of the unknown dropped from her, and she sank into unconsciousness.

When she wakened, it was dawn. Some detached ghost of herself rose and put on sweats, then descended to call the dog for their walk. Skittles emerged from the now open master bedroom door where he'd undoubtedly been sprawled on the bed, relishing the unaccustomed treat. Had Derek enjoyed her replacement? The question came from some remote part of herself that laughed at it all from afar.

Myra set out across the meadow, the dog at her side. She couldn't stay here. How could she leave? Her mind had snagged on a hook and was swinging in the wind, finding no purchase. She drew the old tennis ball from her pocket for the old dog to chase. The arch of her throw carried the ball toward the eucalyptus along the ridge, and as she followed the motion of the dog, she froze. A coyote stood in the shadow of the trees.

She blew the bobby-whistle she kept on a lanyard around her neck and was relieved to see the dog stop. "Skittles! Come!"

He picked up the ball and came back, and she scratched his ears in praise. The small emergency returned her sense of belonging to this place. Familiar with its inhabitants and its dangers. Peter had been sprayed by a skunk here, had turned every indentation into a pirate's cave. Susan had chased Skittles into a hole where he'd gotten stuck, created princes of every distant figure. Derek was never happier than in the shallows of the Channel, but she was the one who brought the dog out every dawn to greet the day alone. She centered her art in this place, felt her body thank her for the exercise. Her union with this piece of country was no sham. She was not going to be the one to leave.

What then? She tried to imagine telling Susan and Peter that their life as a family was over. Busted. Shredded and scattered on the floor to be collected and recycled into someone else's marriage. A void spread around her. How could one simply destroy the stability so essential, particularly in their adolescence?

No, she couldn't do that, could she? "I have no choice," she could hear Martha, her best friend until a year ago, insisting. "How can I stay? Accept being a used-up wife?" Myra'd watched Martha's children start failing in school, shoplifting, driving drunk. For teenagers, chaos was always one calamity away. And Martha herself had disappeared into some other world where single mothers lived. It damned well is a choice, Myra had told herself as she watched Martha's children struggle to regain a foothold. And still is. The words settled, a truth that wouldn't dissolve in the fog. But she couldn't choose. Not yet.

She looked at her watch. "Come on, time to wake the troops." She glanced at the ridge. "We don't want those beasts trailing us, anyway."

By the time she returned to the house, the bedroom wing was alive with banging bathroom doors and complaints.

"Susan! Move it. It's getting late." Derek's tone sounded just like her own. He'd roused the pair and gotten them out of bed for her. Making amends.

"I'm not going. Where's Mom?" Susan whined.

Myra walked back to her daughter's bedroom and found her sitting on the bed in her nightgown, yesterday's elation a phantom memory. "What's the problem?"

"Let me skip, today. I have cramps." She turned and rolled onto her bed.

"She's afraid of history, I betcha," Peter offered, emerging from his room fully dressed and brushed. "First period, and she's got Mr. Feingold. A real bear."

"I don't like man teachers," Susan mumbled.

"Don't worry," her brother told her. "He's easier on girls than on boys."

"Aren't your drama tryouts today?" Myra asked.

"Yeah ..." Susan looked up, remembering.

"You don't want to miss those, Drama Queen." Peter took off down the hall to breakfast.

"Right," Myra agreed. "So move it."

Fifteen minutes later, she watched them pull their bikes from the porch and realized she'd managed not to look at Derek since he joined them for breakfast. It hadn't even been hard. She'd just edited him out. She glanced at the calendar and realized that it was Friday. They were going camping tonight. A wave of relief passed over her. She need do nothing. Not today. Then she would have two days to deal with the battle going on in her head.

She turned and walked away toward the bathroom for her shower, leaving Derek sitting at the table, his graceful body looking gangly and out of place.

"I'll be late, today. I have a field trip!" he yelled through the bathroom door fifteen minutes later, his voice resentful at her continued hostility.

She closed her eyes, the soothing effect of hot water vanishing. "Indeed." Never again would the words "field trip" mean anemones and snails. And she was to live like this? She turned on the blow-dryer so she wouldn't hear him shuffling outside the door.

When she emerged, the house was silent. She leaned against the wall in relief, then opened her eyes and took in the master bedroom they'd added to the house after Susan was born. The little bungalow was to be their temporary home until they could afford a house in Santa Barbara, where Derek's parents lived. Instead, it had sprouted additions—a wing, a patio, a stone fireplace, and finally her tower studio. They'd worked alongside each other, hammering beams, sanding drywall, painting, laying bricks and tile, and in the end acknowledged they had no wish to leave. How could a man who cared that much about his house and home ... her mind turned blank. Fishing for a word that would express the irrational, illogical, inconsistent, incongruous, nonsensical ... it simply wasn't the man she knew. Thought she knew.

A man who spent his weekends taking his family on camping trips. Except they hadn't, for a long time, and she hadn't even missed it. Why was that? When had things changed? The years slipped through her memory without catching or shifting course in any perceptible way. She gave it up and went to dress, then climbed the stairs to the tower.

Above her drafting table, Matilda, Rufus, Eustasia, and Alphonse hung in a row like marionettes awaiting their puppeteer. Myra taped a fresh sheet of paper onto the board and began to draw.

> Eustasia, her wing spiked with Rufus's quills, hopped about yowling that she'd been ruined. Rufus, striped of his half his quills, crouched in a corner, covering his ears. Matilda's long neck appeared in the upper corner to find out what the fuss was about. Only Alphonse's legs with their swollen knees were visible, but his hoarse croak of laughter came from above.
>
> "What a sorry lot you are," Matilda said.
>
> "And who are you to talk?" Eustasia snapped back. "Look at that neck! It's sunburned! You think you're a heron?"
>
> "And have to stand in one place for hours? Look at those knees!" Matilda poked at the Alphonse's bulges with her beak. "What happened here, anyway?"

The morning was gone by the time the energy that drove her pen was spent, and she sat back in wonder, trying to give it a name. Rebellion. Striking back. Whenever her emotions had become a knotted ball in the pit of her stomach, the pen had released them. The child she'd been doodled during class, turned teachers into pelicans and ostriches. She'd long since packed that girl away with the other sins of childhood. She'd been caught. She hadn't noticed the boy behind her gazing over her shoulder, giggling in appreciation, or seen that he'd been joined by the teacher who was less amused. Now that mortified child seemed to be rising to pluck grief and pain and somersault them into laughter.

She put away her pencils, feeling as though she'd reclaimed some part of herself. She stretched and went downstairs, ready to make the shopping list—her part of every camping trip—and went through the grocery store with an odd sense of detachment—half of a split earthworm discovering it can move. Then Peter and Susan came home, and she became whole for a bit—unearthing the camping gear from the shed, hosing off the tent and laying it in the sun, washing the cooking pots.

By the time Derek came home, the van was loaded. As he inspected it, she backed away, and felt something inside her snap all over again.

At dinner Derek glanced at her between bites. He put his fork down long before he'd finished.. "Are you sure you won't come?" His tone was soft, even gentle, but edged with a plea.

"Quite sure." Sitting at the dinner table with him was bad enough.

"Why not, Mom?" Susan asked. "You always come."

"I promised Rena she'd have some new prints for Sunday's fair, and they aren't matted." It was only half a lie. Rena Ballard had been selling Myra's work at Santa Barbara's every-Sunday waterfront fair for years, but she wasn't dependent on weekly contributions. Rena already had a collection to display along with her own jewelry, and certainly the tourists who were the fair's main customers would never notice there were no new ones. Maybe she'd spend this Sunday at the fair. She hadn't done that for years and had no love for tourists, but a day away from home seemed essential.

"Can we go tonight, Dad?" Peter asked. "Everything's ready."

"Good idea." Derek burst with relief. "If we go right away, we can get set up before dark."

A half hour later, they'd checked their gear and supplies and were gone. The evening breeze off the ocean washed through the house. She stood in the open patio door until she was chilled.

Dusk and dawn were her favorite times of day to walk, but they were also the times of day coyotes took over the mesa. She opted to read before the fire, but when she was settled, her rage burst forth, making concentration impossible. His remorse did nothing to dampen the fires, but bolting from him, as she longed to do, brought up images of friends whose divorces had opened seams of vicious retaliation, oblivious to the effect on their children. Her own rage was still simmering under the surface, making such blindness all too understandable.

She went to the shower and the rage drained away, leaving her exhausted. She let out a sigh. At least she could sleep in her own bed tonight. She stared at the tumbled mess of covers Derek had left, and then yanked the sheets from the bed to rid it of the sickening lure of soap and aftershave.

Ten minutes later, she lay between cold clean sheets, staring at the ceiling. The need to retaliate alternated with the need to protect, and the impossible alternatives rotated endlessly in her head. Finally she got up and invited Skittles in with her, then dozed between the jabbing of elbows, and the push of his cold, wet nose.

Saturday, like most mornings by the sea, dawned foggy. Myra gazed out the window at the blurred shapes, listened to the refrigerator hum in the empty house and felt her body relax. No one was here. Her mind expanded and filled the space. She donned her jeans, called the dog, and walked out into the chill, willing her body to dissipate into the air. Only the distant slap of water on sand broke the silence. Even the dog seemed muted, his nosing halfhearted. She returned to the house damp and cold, but a long hot shower wrapped her in a half-present gauzy state she welcomed.

In her studio, the unmated prints and paintings confronted her. Some compulsive, dutiful part of her set to work, taking out the drafter's square, protractor, and knives. She welcomed the demand of detail that closed out all else. The sun emerged to splash across the watercolor on the board, illuminating the tide-pool with its anemone and hermit crabs, barnacles and waving sea grass. It was good, she decided, and that was enough for this day.

Sunday dawned without fog. The dolphins of the fountain at the entrance to the wharf glistened, and skaters already glided along the bike path under the palms that bordered the sand. Myra was early, as she knew she had to be to find a parking place.

"Myra! Bless you!" Rena threw her arms around her. "Don't tell me you're going to keep me company."

"I am." She handed the tiny artist her portfolio. "The family's off camping, and this is just what I need." She stretched, spreading her arms wide. "No wind today."

"Hush. Don't talk about it. Oh, I like these." Rena leafed through the stack. "You need to hang some of them."

Myra looked around the booth. Watercolors of seascapes alternated with portraits of old seamen or the Serendipity. They looked like the work of a stranger; the vision of an artist who had vanished. She spun away from them to the rack of woodblock prints. Harsher, sharper of line and image, they seemed closer to the truth now—her truth—but she didn't really want to look at any of them. She hung the watercolor of the tide pool, another of driftwood, and a third of a sea lion, then gave the stack to Rena to finish and looked at her jewelry instead. Unlike the cheap, souvenir baubles that filled too many booths along the walk, Rena worked in metals—bronze, copper, and silver. Her works was graceful, thought provoking, and held the eye.

The noise level rose as tourists began to fill the long wharf, with its restaurants and shops, and the beach walk lined with artists' gazebos. Bicycle carts pulled families down the path behind the booths, weaving their way among cyclists, skaters and walkers. Beyond them the beach was dotted with sunbathers, and beyond that, sightseeing boats loaded and unloaded at the pier. Out in the channel, sailboats hoisted sail, and yachts headed for the open sea. The sidewalk in front of the booths became crowded with strollers munching hot dogs, tacos, and the cinnamon rolls for which the waterfront was famous. Nothing in the scene spoke of any reality whatsoever.

Much to her surprise, Myra sold two watercolors and a half-dozen prints in the course of the next four hours.

"Your stuff always sells," Rena said, protesting Myra's surprise. "It's time you came to see for yourself."

"I guess. I admire your willingness to give every Sunday to this." After her first year or so in this paradise by the sea, she'd grown weary of tourists and the souvenir art in too many of the booths. The carnival atmosphere of it all had turned stale.

Rena had shrugged. "It's a living."

Myra nodded, embarrassed by her own attitude. Rena had no mate. She eked out her rent and food going from fair to fair all over the state. She'd sold one pendant and several sets of earrings, so far. Never a lot. Her pieces cost more than the usual tourist fare. "I know. You're a saint to take my stuff too."

"No, I'm not. I'm just a good business woman. Your paintings attract people to the booth."

Myra smiled at passing families, found herself talking to those who paused, and, in fact, started to enjoy herself. Vacationing faces demanding nothing, open to everything. She'd sold a pair of Rena's earrings and a bracelet and Rena had sold three of Myra's prints.

The chill late afternoon breeze began to billow the canvas sides of the booth, and like an aging helium balloon, the scene deflated. Sunbathers hurried away and the passing crowd thinned. Artists began to pack up. Soon the sun would set on the beach and the night life would begin. Time to go home.

"Thank you, Rena, for a lovely day." Myra gave her a hug. "I think I'll come more often—it's sort of a fairy tale, if you don't notice all of the junk along here." She waved to the line of booths.

"Wear blinders," Rena urged. "Some of us meet for supper at Amigo's. Why don't you join us?"

Myra smiled. She'd love to turn up missing—give Derek a jolt he more than deserved. But she didn't want to give out any signals to the kids. Not yet. She wasn't ready. "Thank you, but my family's due home. I'd love to another time," she added, realizing that Rena was giving an invitation into an inner circle of artists. She'd been a serious student once, bent on becoming a professional. Long submerged in family, she'd come to treat her art as an indulgence. "Next Sunday. Promise."

Myra drove north, feeling light. Her day of escape had shifted her to another place. Somewhere inside her, buried in shock, was the woman who had painted those pictures, carved those blocks. She was an antidote worth hanging onto.

The van was in the drive when she arrived at the Goleta house, and Peter and Susan were full of tales of the rattlesnake they'd encountered on the path, the mountain lion seen from afar, and the strange cries that filled the night in the mountains that rose behind the coastal towns.

As they talked, Myra marveled as she often did that that desert wilderness could exist so close to a tourist destination, with its palm trees and bougainvillea. She listened, content to be an outsider, to Peter's account of rock climbing, Susan's pride at her ability to keep up with him. She was aware of Derek, eyeing her from across the room and blotted him out.

Chapter 3

The narrow bed in her studio was hard, telling her that her self-imposed eviction was exactly the wrong response. She should be kicking him out of their bed. In the morning, she rose short on sleep and once again filled with a self-hatred she hadn't known in years. A few moments later, clad in sweats, she stood at the closed bedroom door, ready to put a stop to this impossible situation. No sound came from beyond the door.

An alarm jangled from Peter's room, then another from Susan's. She'd been going to tell him to get out of her life. Despite the children? She took a deep breath, getting control of an impulse that would carry everything out of her control. She set herself to the task of activating teenagers. Her own voice grated in her ears, harsh and impatient.

"Are you sick, Mom?" Peter asked as he sat over his cereal.

"Sick? No, why?"

"You act funny—as though you don't feel good."

"A headache is all."

As Susan and Peter headed out, Derek appeared in her peripheral vision, collected his keys, bent to give Skittles a rub, then followed them without a word. She stared after him, half-shaken, half-relieved that his departure had stalled her. *Get your clothes and get to work.* Let the shock wear off before you decide.

She spent the first hour in her studio digging out sketches from old portfolios to hang on the bare white walls. A wheat field. The campus tower at UC San Diego. A dolphin. Pictures that brought back to life the person she'd been before submerging herself in marriage.

It helped. She heard Peter come in and realized the day had passed. On the easel before her was a barn viewed from across fields, a windmill rising behind it. The picture had none of the lift and motion of her usual sketches—nor had the girl who had grown up in the small town surrounded by such scenes. Except she'd had the gumption to escape. And now, somehow, she had to do it again.

She rose and went downstairs. "Where's Susan?" she asked her son, who was spreading peanut butter on a slice of bread.

"Drama Club." He sank his teeth into the sandwich. "Soccer practice was called off. Coach is sick."

She nodded and went out to the patio to stretch. The phone rang, and she heard Peter pick it up.

"Dad's going to be late!" he called a few minutes later.

Tension went out of her. "Okay!" she answered, stopping the "good!" that had almost escaped.

She had long since retired to her tower, this time with the foresight to take fresh clothes, when she heard his car. Anger was rapidly driving away the numbness of shock. Another day without his presence, and she would be able to act. What act, she didn't yet know. Time, she told herself, twisting to find a comfortable position.

Halfway through the next day, the doorbell rang.

Derek's mother stood on her doorstep, a strained smile on her face. Her white hair was smoothly coifed in a soft bun at the nape of her neck as always, but her hands were clasped in uncharacteristic tension. "We need to talk, dear."

Myra opened her mouth to answer, then closed it again. "Hello, Eleanor. Come in."

Eleanor Benning, who managed to look dignified in a corduroy skirt and loose cardigan, surveyed the living room in appreciation. "You've done such lovely things to this house. I couldn't have imagined you could do this with such a plain little place."

Myra smiled. Eleanor had seen their renovations and additions often enough. Surely she didn't come for that. "Thank you. Would you like coffee?"

"I'd love some, thank you. Black." She went over to the open French doors. "So peaceful. I understand now why you love it so."

Myra watched her from the other side of the breakfast bar that separated the kitchen from the dining area and living room. Why on earth was she here? Though the Bennings' Santa Barbara villa was only fifteen minutes away, her mother-in-law lived by a code that discouraged dropping in unannounced. Myra carried the coffee into the living room and set it on the oak table in front of the couch.

"Roger did this, didn't he?" Eleanor crossed the room and fingered the driftwood and metal sculpture that sat at one end of the coffee table. Eleanor's usual polite reserve was touched with sadness. Roger, Derek's brother, was an artist and preferred life in South America, according to the Bennings. He'd appeared only a couple of times since they'd moved to Goleta.

"Yes. It was a Christmas gift—years ago." Myra's memory of the man—a face like Derek's only softer, a slightly rotund form playing with her children—was vague. But she'd always loved the sculpture—a heron with its wing spread over its young. "Do you hear from him?"

Eleanor raised her shoulders and let them drop. "A post card, occasionally. Roger likes his privacy—lack of distraction, I guess you'd say. You would know what he means, being an artist." She picked up her cup.

Myra smiled. "It's hard to imagine really wanting that—for me. I need distraction. And I don't think I could do without family." Even as she said the words, she realized that yesterday she'd discovered what it meant to use art as a sanctuary rather than a hobby.

"Good. I'm glad." Eleanor put her cup down. "That what I want to talk about. Family."

Myra waited, holding her breath.

"You see—Derek confessed his—misbehavior to me—us." She clasped her hands in her lap and looked at them, then up at Myra, her cobalt eyes remorseful, as though taking the blame for her son.

"Did he." Myra managed to reply. It wasn't a question.

"He did. And I know you must be feeling terrible, Myra. Angry and hurt."

Myra saw no need to answer.

"Yes. Well, I more than understand." Her weighted tone sharpened Myra's attention. "And I wanted you to know you have lots of company."

"Company?" She studied her mother-in-law.

"Many—far too many—academic wives have gone through this." She picked up her cup and took another sip. "It's just a fact of life, my dear. The men are surrounded by these lovely young men and women

28

who adore them. And at home—well, we become a bit old hat, I'm afraid."

"I don't understand." Myra fought to regain her voice. "Are you saying they all just put up with it? The wives?"

"I'm afraid so, my dear. Yes. Because to do otherwise would wreck their husbands' careers, Myra. You must see that. And the families, too. So much rests with us, Myra."

The too-blue eyes had lost their remorse. They drilled into her now. "With us. The women. Not with them?"

"Ah, Myra. They are ..." Her hands fluttered. "... what they are."

Myra cleared her throat. "Misbehaving little boys?" How often had she clenched her teeth when she heard faculty wives describe their husbands in those terms? She pictured her father-in-law, the silver-haired professor of history, on his sailboat, a lovely grad student snuggled away in the cabin as he waved to his wife on the dock.

Eleanor laughed. "Exactly, I'm afraid." Her voice expressed nothing but relief at the return of their usual easy friendship.

Myra rose from the couch and went to the French doors, taking gulps of sea air to unclog her lungs. "Eleanor ..." She turned. "That's outrageous."

"My dear—it's life."

They stared at each other wordlessly.

"Just promise me you'll think about it." Eleanor put her cup down. "We have a club. We call it the 'Women-in-Waiting.' Because they do come back, you know. We're the real women in their lives—the substance."

"The substance." She looked down the length of her body. "Indeed."

Eleanor rose and put a hand on hers. "You must bear up, Myra. You must."

"He said it wouldn't happen again." She wasn't sure whether her response was a concession or merely irrelevant. It simply came out.

Eleanor sighed and patted her shoulder as she headed for the door. "God willing."

Myra watched Eleanor's little BMW disappear up the street then collapsed on the couch to stare at nothing. The world of the Bennings returned as fresh as it had been the day she arrived on the arm of her new husband. They'd driven along the road that wove up into the hills.

Rounding a curve, they'd come upon the town of Santa Barbara spread out below them—a Spanish-tiled fantasy village with its long pier and the many-spired marina framed by a crystal blue sea. The morning mist was gone, and Santa Cruz Island rose gray-blue against the sky, framing the whole. The day came back.

***

"Good grief, Derek—it's not real. It's a picture, right? Something to fool the tourists."

Derek laughed. "That's what they all say. But we just came up from there. See …" He pointed to the valley, "That's the Mission … and the Courthouse …"

Myra took a deep breath and let it out slowly. She felt as intimidated by this scene as she had when she traveled from Minnesota to San Diego for college, sure that such a place could not be inhabited by normal people. The man she'd fallen in love with lived with three other students in an ordinary student flat furnished with Salvation Army couches and dented pans. His idea of a meal, like every other student's, was macaroni and cheese or tuna casserole. He wore nothing but T-shirts and cargo shorts, never anything that didn't stand up to tide-pooling or surfing. He had no use for fraternities or the party scene. The only bit that jarred with that picture was the old Jag coupe he'd inherited from an uncle, but that he treated as a joke on the world even as he nursed its every squeak. She'd known his father was a professor of history, felt the aura of wealth carried in the name "Santa Barbara," but it had all seemed disconnected from Derek, not a world she herself would ever enter. "All right. So now you're taking me to the castle. Lead on."

Derek leaned over and kissed her cheek. "You'll love them. Promise." He led the way back to the dust-covered Jag. It had brought them up the coast with not much more than the clothes on their backs, but brought them, nevertheless, and looked more at home in this place than she was sure she would ever be. Now it took them around two more curves to an arcaded, Spanish tiled stucco ranch perched on the edge of the cliff.

Derek made a deft left turn that made her catch her breath—right off the cliff down into the drive. "Here we are!"

It's not huge, Myra noted with relief, and not gated like the La Jolla mansions. It was only … perfect.

The carved wooden door of the house opened and out rushed a lovely woman with snow-white hair and startlingly blue eyes. Her arms were outstretched and soon engulfed Derek. "At last, at last!" She laughed, then released him and turned to Myra, who stood feeling sticky and disheveled, brushing stray hairs from her cheek. "And you're Myra." She reached out and took Myra's hand in both of hers. "Welcome to Santa Barbara."

"It's breathtaking." Myra smiled, glad her voice sounded more solid than she felt. "And you're Mrs. Benning."

"No, no—Eleanor, please. You must call me Eleanor. Come …" She took a hand of each of them and turned them toward the door where a tall, lean, white-haired man stood, hands in pockets, viewing the scene from afar. He looked, Myra thought, more like a model from a yacht commercial than anyone's father-in-law.

"Ah, there you are!" Eleanor exclaimed. "They're here!"

The man came forward and gave Derek the perfunctory sort of hug men reserve for each other, then turned to Myra and held out his hand. "Cornelius Benning. They call me Conny, if you can imagine that. Welcome."

Myra smiled at the warmth and humor in his voice, though she certainly wasn't going to try "Conny." "Thank you. What a lovely house."

"Well, come on in and make yourselves comfortable. You've had a long drive."

When they entered the house, she gasped a second time, for directly across from the entrance, French doors stood open to the deck beyond and framed the same view they'd gazed at from the road. The room, warmed by the glow of wood beams and soft white walls hung with woven rugs and art works, seemed designed to frame the city below and the sea beyond it. To her right was a great stone fireplace flanked by bookcases full to overflowing. The low slung leather chairs and couches looked well worn and the tables beside them were laden with books and magazines. If the view struck awe, the room enfolded. It spoke of age and use.

Myra took a second look at her imposing in-laws and was reassured to see that Eleanor was comfortably broadened, her skirt denim, and her feet clad in well-worn loafers. Even Cornelius looked a little more paunchy than he had at first glance. She felt her tension unraveling. "What a wonderful room."

"Thank you. Well lived in, too," Eleanor remarked, picking up a pair of slippers and handing them to her husband. "So—what can I get you to drink? Iced tea? Soda? Something stronger?"

"Iced tea would be lovely," Myra responded.

"Beer for me," Derek declared. "Wow, it's good to be here." He collapsed onto a couch, kicking off his shoes, then patted the place beside him and held out his arm for her. "That drive through LA is a bitch."

"And smoggy," Myra added, sinking to the couch. "You're so clear here."

"Well, it's not LA, that's for sure," Cornelius agreed. "When you get settled, we'll go sailing on the Serendipity, and you'll fall in love with it—guaranteed."

"Ah, God," Derek broke in, "you mean she's still seaworthy? The Serendipity," he explained, turning to Myra, "was my grandfather's boat. It's a sailboat—thirty five feet—but he used it mostly for fishing by the time I knew him, and what I remember most about it, when I was a little kid, was the way it stank."

"Now Derek, she hasn't stunk in years. And she's still a grand old girl."

"Dad remodeled her, fitted her out with paneling and new brass, but I can still remember that stench."

"You won't smell anything but varnish and the sea," Cornelius assured her. "So. You were an art student at San Diego, Derek tells us. What are you planning to do with that up here?"

"Oh, I haven't had a chance to think about it, what with the move and everything."

Cornelius's stiff smile told her he was reading "everything" as their city-hall marriage announced after the fact to Derek's parents. Well, it wasn't what he thought. She wasn't pregnant. She just didn't want to be married in Minnesota. She couldn't ask her parents to foot the bill—including bringing the Bennings from Santa Barbara. Derek had assured her his parents would be happy to pay their own way, but she was relieved now that she'd insisted. She couldn't imagine these people sitting in the living room of the clapboard bungalow, looking out at the baking Minnesota prairie. She could picture her father, coughing with lung disease, becoming belligerent in defense and her mother weeping in the kitchen in shame.

She'd be trapped, clenching her teeth to keep her mouth shut. She'd earned her own way through college with the help of scholarships. It hadn't cost him a dime. But he was a spent, sick, disappointed man. For her mother's sake, she wouldn't crush him further. She'd have to bear his ridicule in silence, as she always had. Any protest would only bring a retort about her size—that she was threatening him. No, this room, to say nothing of the view beyond the window, told her their decision had been right.

She looked around the room at the art and smiled, remembering her father's favorite jeer. "She chose art, for God's sake. Can you imagine? Has a chance to go to college and make something of herself, and she chooses art!" She needn't fear that response here. "This looks like a wonderful place for an artist," she answered, pointing out the window, "though I imagine everyone paints that scene."

He nodded. "Afraid so, but there's plenty else to paint, and there are lots of artists around. Go down to the wharf on Sundays—they all display their wares. You'll not be short of company."

He made being an artist sound perfectly ordinary. Myra relaxed further and smiled at Derek. "I feel at home already."

He grinned, knowing she'd been terrified of meeting his father and sociologist mother. The "emeritus" after their titles made them no less intimidating. She'd been sure her own simple master's degree would crumble into nothing in face of that combination.

"Have you been to campus yet, Derek?" Cornelius asked, as Eleanor returned with a tray of drinks.

Derek laughed. "We just drove into town, Dad. Haven't even seen our digs, yet."

"Ah, of course."

"Tricia found them a little rental out beyond campus," Eleanor reminded him. "Derek's sister, Patricia" she explained, turning to Myra. "I'm sure it will do until you have a chance to look around and find out where you want to be."

"Out beyond campus. Not Isle Vista, I hope?" Cornelius frowned.

"The student ghetto," Derek explained, turning to Myra. "No, beyond IV, Dad. In Goleta." He took Myra's hand. "I'm sure it's fine."

"For now," Eleanor added.

"We'll invite you to see it, once we're in. Myra's brother is driving up with our stuff. He should be here tomorrow."

"We thought we were going to have to sell the Jag and buy something that would pull a trailer," Myra explained. "But Jonathan jumped at the chance to see California. So he's pulling a rented trailer. We lost him somewhere in Anaheim, but he phoned that he's okay. Just had to replace wipers. He's going to stay with a friend and come up tomorrow."

"Well, then, you'll have to stay here for the night," Eleanor exclaimed. "Wonderful."

***

Myra emerged slowly from memory. So that welcoming room had been purchased at a price. If it had been ostentatious or showy, she'd understand more easily Eleanor's insistence on keeping up appearances. But there was nothing false, nothing artificial in that scene or in Eleanor, which made Myra's shock more profound. She gazed around the "little rental that would do." It had done very well. Once upon a time she'd assumed they would move into the Bennings' world, but the dream had lost its appeal along with departmental parties and student receptions. Now, Eleanor's visit reminded her that she was the wife of a professor rising fast in his field. Derek's first book was being hailed as fresh and evocative. For Eleanor, she supposed, it was unthinkable that Myra would to do anything but celebrate his new eminence. She shook herself free and rose, then fled up the stairs to her tower.

> A pair of clogs appeared before the misbegotten group of animals. Hands reached from above to wrap a fancy scarf around Matilda's sunburned neck, tie up Eustasia's dragging wing and put a bow on it. Then they put ace bandages on Alphonse's knees and shook Rufus's remaining quills until they stood at attention. "There," the massive clogs announced. "You're a club."
> "What's that?" Matilda asked.
> "Sort of a collection."
> "Yeah? Who's collecting us?" Rufus, always on guard, demanded.
> "Good question," the clogs answered. "Go find someone—that's your mission. Find a collector of animals well-used by life. Shoo!"

Myra named the clogs "Boots," then stared at the strip wondering at the capacity of the quartet to release her from the vise of Eleanor's demand. The troop needed a name. The Rabbleville Varmints. The name wrote itself on the screen and she saved and printed it, then pinned it above the original strip, and took her headache to the daybed.

An hour later, when the sound of Derek's car wakened her, she was amazed that she'd actually managed to sleep. The gaze of the woman in the mirror was steady. She didn't yet know when, but she knew what—she wasn't going to become a patient, all-enduring wife.

Derek opened the door like a wire-walker testing his stance. Gone was the easy warmth that had made twenty years fly by.

"I'm not joining the club," she told him.

He looked startled, and she realized she hadn't addressed him directly in days. "Club?"

"Your mother's club. She came to see me."

"Oh." The word dropped and silence formed around it.

She glanced at him. Had he hoped that her love for his mother would fix it all, cause her to soften? Educate Myra on the expectations of academia? She turned back to the sink without gratifying him.

"I didn't know she had a club," he managed, finally.

"They call it the 'Women-in-Waiting.' For their philandering husbands to come home." She heard the venom in her voice and felt nothing but relief. "I'm not joining."

"What—are you going to do?" He sounded like a pupil on the verge of expulsion. "I need you, Myra." It was almost a bleat.

"So she said. For your career."

"Look—I know how you must feel ..." His voice went soft—gentle.

"No you don't, Derek. You've no idea."

"Mom?" The front door banged and Peter charged in, followed by Susan. "Guess what? Susan got the part of Laura in *The Glass Menagerie*."

"You did!" Myra, saved from answering Derek, threw her arms around Susan. "Wonderful!"

"That's great," Derek said, taking his turn. "That's quite a part."

"Fits her perfectly," her brother quipped and dodged Myra's smack as she remembered the crippled girl in Williams' play who lived among her glass animals. Peter's goading was no help in getting Susan beyond her aversion to boys—Peter and her father excepted. The strength of that aversion had caught her by surprise. She simply hadn't expected it from a Daddy's girl whose favorite playmate was her brother. "When she's on stage, she's wonderful."

Susan curtsied in acknowledgment, sticking her tongue out at her brother.

Myra laughed, and they vanished a moment later, leaving only Derek, waiting for an answer.

She turned to the sink, her fists clenched. "Stop looking at me like a little boy waiting for his punishment."

"No, no." He crossed and put his hands on her shoulders. "If I could undo it, Myra …"

"Undo. As though we can go back …" She swung to face him, twisting out from under his hands. "Just erase it. Is that what your mother did, Derek?"

His face flushed and he stepped back, his eyes dark. "Leave her out of it! This is about …"

"Dad?" Peter burst back into the kitchen, holding up a stack of college applications. "These don't make sense." Like his father, Peter's enthusiasm for life was quick to turn into impatience at the fussy roadblocks of forms and procedures.

Derek let out his pent up breath and turned to his son. "Let's take a look." He took Peter's arm and led the way back to the study where Peter had been working.

Myra, grateful for the reprieve, turned to dinner preparation. "This is about you and me," she muttered, finishing his sentence. But was it? Everything in his demeanor—and his mother's—suggested they were waiting for her to learn the steps of a dance familiar to them both. She jabbed her finger with the paring knife and yelped. Tears sprung and ran down her cheeks. *Stop it!* She clamped her jaw and headed for the bathroom and a Band-Aid. She stood breathing at the face in the mirror until control returned, then went to call her family to dinner.

Susan was curled up on the couch muttering lines from the play. Derek's and Peter's dark heads were bent over the papers, plunging through and swearing at the forms. Even at rest, they were spring loaded, their arms and feet seeking freedom of the sea. A scene from the past.

"Is this what I'm to do, Eleanor?" She asked silently as she interrupted them. Just keep alive a past that is imaginary?

But the adolescent chatter that carried dinner along wasn't imaginary. Peter, freed from forms, was once again deep in his first great adventure—leaving home. Derek fell eagerly into his son's interest in oceanography programs. Susan engaged Myra in explaining lines of Tennessee Williams' play. Were adolescents that oblivious to anything but their own crises, she wondered? An hour later, they disappeared into their rooms to study.

"We have a lot," Derek said, behind her. "Too much to throw away."

She turned. "Maybe you should have thought of that."

The light faded from his eyes. He raised his hands and let them fall. "What's done is done. I can't change it, but … look. You need space, right now. I'm going to the office for a while."

He picked up his keys and headed for the garage, leaving Myra with the distinct sense she was supposed to call him back. She didn't, though some irrepressible urge from the past protested his departure.

Myra stood in the empty kitchen whose counters had turned cold to the touch, then turned and climbed the stairs to her tower. When she closed the door, her anger collapsed into a sense of impending disaster.

> Rufus appeared, dragging his quills behind him.
>
> "What happened to you?" Matilda craned her long neck down to examine them.
>
> "I don't know. Something I ate. Or maybe my shampoo," he mourned.
>
> "Alphonse laughed at him," Eustasia pronounced, entering the square. "Feed him some vitamins. Or steroids, maybe. Better yet, some Vi …" She jumped away from Rufus's bared teeth.
>
> Alphonse limped into the next square, rubbing his behind with one wing.
>
> "And what's wrong with you?" Matilda demanded.
>
> "Trying to fish while sitting down—thinks he's a swan, he does." Eustasia dodged Alphonse's beak.
>
> The clogs appeared. "Doesn't look like you've gotten very far."

Myra put her pen down. The animals had not caught hold, wouldn't carry her away. Voices floated from below from a situation she could neither tolerate nor change. Spent, she gazed at the night fog.

Chapter 4

The next day Myra woke to a pounding on her studio door.

"What are you doing up here?" Peter demanded.

With a groan, she looked at her clock. She'd overslept. "I worked late and didn't want to disturb your father," she mumbled.

"Oh."

That was it. Just "oh," and he went back down to his room. Myra lay back, disconcerted that it had been so easy.

The sounds from below were reassuringly normal. And the next time he found her here? And the next? How long before they guessed the truth? She pulled on her sweats and went downstairs, rousing Susan as she passed her door on the way to the kitchen. Deprived of her morning walk, she was thick-headed and disinclined to conversation. Peter looked at her bemused, but said nothing and soon the kitchen was empty.

"Damned near eight-thirty again, damn it!"

Derek's voice swung her around.

"Buy an alarm clock."

The word brought him to a halt, and she watched sleep fall from his face. "What?"

"Buy an alarm clock. And there's the calendar." She pointed. "It has your dentist appointments, school conferences, and such. Keep track."

He muttered an obscenity and turned away, his shoulders hunched, his scowl bewildered. He was a man who had worked hard, treated the world kindly and been treated kindly in return. Slammed doors were new—and inexplicable.

She was staring at her work table, the memory of the morning grating on her nerves, when Derek's sister, Tricia, called and insisted she meet her for their weekly lunch. Myra almost put her off, then, having accepted, dreaded the date. She'd always considered Patricia a friend, but Derek was her brother, after all, and the whole family seemed dangerous territory now. Seated across the café table, Myra felt Patricia's dark eyes, so much like her brother's, examining her as she studied the menu.

"I need to tell you I know about Derek's screw-up."

"Oh." Myra looked up from the menu. "From your mother?"

Patricia nodded. "She said she visited you."

Myra was unsure how to respond. Patricia, after all, was a Benning.

"I also know what she asked of you, so I want to tell you I think my brother is a bastard. And you don't have to follow my mother's advice." She reached over and put a hand on Myra's. "You can raise hell, swear at him, kick him out—anything you damn well please. I won't defend him, I promise you."

Myra felt tears well up, mortifying her. She squeezed Patricia's hand. "Thank you for that. I didn't know how you'd feel …"

"I know. And I was afraid you were avoiding all of us—which I wouldn't blame you for. Don't be afraid to cry." She looked around the restaurant. "No one will notice."

Myra took a deep breath. "Most of the time, I'm too angry to cry."

"I imagine." Patricia signaled the waiter, and they ordered their salads before continuing.

When the waiter had taken their order and departed, Myra studied her sister-in-law. "Have you been through this, too? Had a lesson from your mother?"

"While I was growing up, yes indeed. I've been spared the need since then, thank God. Unless I'm very very blind. Conrad calls Derek's behavior stupid, and I believe he means it. And since I don't have children, it's hard for me to tell you what to do."

Myra nodded. "Peter's about to leave for college. Susan's trying to adjust to high school and adolescence. I just can't pretend that kicking Derek out wouldn't be disastrous for them." She gave a laugh. "More than for Derek, in fact—or me."

Patricia frowned. "Children know, though, sooner or later."

Myra was sure she was talking about her own childhood, but was hesitant to pry—or maybe she didn't want to be further disillusioned about the family that had enfolded her. "I just pray it's later," she said instead. "Susan's having a tough enough time as it is with the high school social scene, and Peter and his dad are so close—just let him go off to college before I blow the place up." Myra heard herself say the words and felt the jolt of a decision made.

"Can you put off blowing up that long? I'm not sure I could." Tricia reached for a roll and tore it in two.

"I don't know. Right now, I'm a landmine, ready to go off if anyone takes a false step. But there's another part that's numb—as though I'm growing a shell."

The waiter arrived with their salads, and they ate in silence for a few minutes.

"Well at least come to lunch with me—don't cut me off, okay?" Patricia's dark eyes commanded her attention.

Myra smiled. "You're setting yourself up as a relief valve, you know."

"Good. It will counteract my mother, anyway, if not Derek."

"Thank you for that." Myra felt the high tension wires in her head go slack and her limbs warm. Then she bit her lip and speared a piece of tomato as the pain she'd buried threatened to burst forth. She felt Patricia gazing at her, but she didn't speak.

Instead, they let the lunch-hour clamor of the café flow in and return them to normal, spending the rest of the hour talking of other things—the lack of rain, the welfare of Patricia's cats, Myra's dog, and Myra's art, until they'd returned to their light and easy friendship.

The blood was flowing more normally in Myra's veins when she arrived home, and she set to work in the patio garden as though her home mattered again. One friend. One place to be. It was enough. She could do this. The pain would cease to crush her; she would grow the muscles of endurance. Did Eleanor have such a friend? Her mother-in-law was always talking about her fellow wives, but Myra sensed that with them she kept her quiet reserve intact. Poor woman. No, she had her club. That's how she survived, then. Myra returned to her digging, her view of Eleanor transformed once again.

She finished transplanting an azalea and was washing her trowel when she heard Derek's car pull in. She dried her hands, finished putting the tools away, then picked up the broom.

He came to the door and watched, an uncertain smile of hope on his face as he viewed the freshly groomed containers. "You're gardening!"

She stopped sweeping, leaned the broom against the side of the house, and straightened, mentally checking out the whereabouts of the children. "I'm going to hold this family together until Peter leaves for college and Susan gets used to high school. I won't tear their lives apart right now."

He nodded, eagerness fading from his eyes at the coolness of her voice. "Good."

"But I don't want you near me." She picked up her broom. "You keep your distance, and I'll keep my cool." She started to sweep, punctuating her words.

"That sounds like punishment." His voice was cold.

"Punishment." She stopped and considered. When had she given herself the right to give orders? Set conditions. They had never operated this way, nor did she relish the role of a bitch. "Maybe. It doesn't matter. I'm telling you what I have to do to survive. That's all." She started to sweep again with her back to him, so he wouldn't see the tears pushing against her eyelids.

He didn't move from the doorway. "That's a long time to stay away from someone you love." His words argued, but his tone conceded. "But you need time to heal … I understand that."

She didn't answer.

"Maybe then we can go back …"

"Go back …" She heard her voice rise and cut it off. Then she stopped her sweeping and turned to face him. "How, Derek? How do you put Humpty Dumpty together again?"

Tears ran down her cheeks in spite of herself, and she saw his eyes soften. She turned away before she could respond to that.

"Time. Only time. Thank you for giving us that."

"I'm not. I'm giving the children that."

"Right." He turned away.

Five minutes later, he appeared in shorts and went to the shed to get out the lawn mower. At the roar of the motor, Peter stuck his head out of his room window. "You doing that?"

"Yep," Derek yelled. "You get a day off. Sweep the patio for your mother."

Myra winced at the too obvious gesture and wasn't moved to respond.

Days and then weeks passed uncounted. New habits grew unbidden. Myra left the kitchen when she heard Derek's car, so he wouldn't pass her when he came in. He didn't call her name. Instead he changed his clothes and invited whichever child he came across to go beachcombing. She rang the bell to call them for dinner, where they addressed the children. Then she tended Susan's homework while he tended Peter's. Myra grew used to numbness and let it spread, grateful for the relief from pain. She listened to him explode in impatience at Peter and winced. A mutter of apology always followed, along with an invitation to a walk on the beach, but Peter soon began rejecting his father's help.

She was left to her tower and the Rabbleville Varmints who approached benefactor after benefactor only to fall into quarrelling and be sent on their way.

Her shell thickened, reality pierced it only in snatches.

"Dammit, Peter, ask your mother or do it yourself!"
The slamming of doors.
Peter yelling. "You treat him like a piece of furniture!"

Thanksgiving passed and December arrived, habit carrying them through. The foyer of the high school glittered with the lights of Christmas and filled with the buzz of parents pierced by the calls of excited offspring. Opening night of *The Glass Menagerie.* Laura, so at home in her fragile world, so without will or motivation to be elsewhere, received a standing ovation. Susan had vanished into the part. Myra stood listening to her husband and son shout "bravos." She was in tears, which her family misread as joy.

Later, at home Derek watched as she changed her clothes. "She was wonderful."

Myra, hearing the invitation to celebrate in his voice, could only bite her lip and head for the stairs.

"Do you have to do that? Go up there? Even after such a wonderful evening?"

She felt the magnetic pull, the power of children to draw parents back to the force that had created them. In a flash she understood their friends' wish—even need—to make elaborate post-divorce arrangements for their children. But that was not what Derek was asking. She shook her head, the evening soured by his request.

An hour later, she was sitting sleepless in the kitchen over hot cocoa when Susan and Peter arrived home from the cast party, which Peter, who'd hauled scenery and costumes, had been invited to attend.

"They were all drinking." Susan was white-faced. "The boys—they just want to paw ..." She broke off with a shudder and raced up the stairs to her room.

"Peter?" Myra turned to her son. "Do you know what happened? Did she tell you?"

"Nothing, Mom! Just ... nothing. They're guys, for crap sake. You'd think they were trying to rape her. She's such a damned ..." he smothered the last word as he went down the hall.

She stared after him. The impatience—even contempt—of his sister ringing in her ears, memory of another boy flooding her body. From over the years she heard him scream from the cliffs. "Mama! She fell!"

Three minutes later, she was staring down at Susan, motionless some fifteen feet below, Skittles, beside her, alternating between licking her face and howling.

In the endless confusion that followed, Myra had had no eyes or ears for anything but the paramedics raising the litter and the first sign of life from her daughter. It was an hour, at least, before she remembered Peter's "I didn't mean to!" that had floated across the grass, or noticed rescue worker leaning over her blue-lipped son, who sat huddled under the chaparral.

"Shock," the man pronounced.

They'd loaded him into the ambulance with Susan, but more hours passed before a kind-faced deputy named Larson got the story out of him.

"It was one of Susan's silly games," Peter'd begun, then stopped.

Myra had remembered then and recounted the game to Deputy Larson, whose face still stood out clearly in her mind. Susan had decided that the wisps of fog against the mountains were the fires of giants watching over the valley. And assigned her brother the role of giant—good giant, she'd insisted.

"I got tired of being the good giant—I jumped out at her." Peter's voice stumbled on the last words.

"And she slipped," Myra finished for him.

Susan, with a broken arm and a concussion, had recovered more quickly than Peter, who dragged around the house, spending hours in front of the television. Derek took him out to Santa Cruz Island, just the two of them, to explore the sea caves on the far side. Peter had come home ecstatic about the sea life they'd seen, but his mood faded at the sight of his bandaged sister. He didn't return to his usual good spirits until Susan's arm came out of the cast.

Where had that boy vanished to? She pressed her fingers to her eyelids, then rose and went to Susan, who sat fingering the ceramic beasties she'd used in practicing for her part.

"I just don't want them near me. That's all." Her voice brooked no objection.

"That's okay." Myra was going to suggest that that might change, but knew that would only intensify Susan's rejection. "Don't let the party ruin the beautiful job you did tonight."

"It was fun." Her face lightened. "Like fairytales, where frogs turn into princes. I just slipped out of Susan!"

Myra went over and dropped a kiss on the top of her head. "Well, don't lose Susan altogether, will you? I'm rather fond of her."

The next week, Eleanor called. "I just called to set the time for Christmas dinner, dear." Her voice tried for its usual cheery warmth.

Myra sat down. She'd managed to avoid the knowledge that she was expected to join the Bennings as though nothing had happened. That was too much. Way too much. But what choice was there? She closed her eyes as the vision of Eleanor's face, alight with the gathering of family, rose in her mind. To refuse would cause a furor that would collapse everything. "What time would you like, Eleanor?" Her voice sounded flat, without air.

"How about two, then? Is that too early? We could make it three, if you like."

"Three would be better," Myra responded, only because it was later and would shorten the visit. Why hadn't she prepared herself for this?

"Fine. Three, then. You'll bring your wonderful pies and a salad, as usual?" Eleanor's voice sang with relief.

"As usual." The words felt like a prison sentence. What made her think going on this way until Peter left was possible?

"Wonderful. Patricia will bring her sweet potatoes of course—that marvelous recipe of hers."

Patricia. She hadn't called for lunch since … When? Panic struck as she reached back into fuzzy time, remembering a lunch, maybe two, when, unwilling to risk breaking through the numb blanket of her days, she had avoided all mention of her family. The escape valve she had promised had proved too dangerous to open. Eruption would destroy the ruts carved by endurance and even the pact she had made. Memory returned of the disappointment in Tricia's eyes as she said goodbye. She had watched the expectation of friendship fade and done nothing.

Christmas day dawned gray. By the time Myra slipped down from her tower hideout, rain was splattering the patio. She turned on the tree lights and built a fire in the fireplace to drive out the chill, then went to the kitchen and started the coffee. She was in no hurry for the family to waken, nor would she take her coffee into the living room, as in earlier years, to gaze at the waiting tree. The warmth of the past threatened her equanimity as surely as the disintegration of the present or the absence of a future.

"Anyone up?"

Myra winced at the stiff, artificial imitation of Derek's usual Christmas rousing.

Myra watched her children emerge from their rooms, groggy. They moved too carefully, as though afraid of bumping into some fragile, if invisible structure.

Somewhere in the past months, she'd given up the belief that the family could continue unchanged, but every time she asked herself if it would be better to call off her pact, the answer was no.

But today, something had to give. She would wrap herself in past Christmases and make this day, at least, good.

She took her coffee to the recliner, where she always presided over the opening of gifts, ready to glow with maternal pride as her children presented her with this year's Christmas blouse or sweater or jacket. She had a whole rack of them now. They marked the years from Santa-capped teddy bears, through spangled Rudolphs to snowflakes. Opening their package first, she lifted out a boiled wool jacket—green—with gold and burgundy ornaments down either side of its zipper. Its sophistication surprised her. A sign they were all but grown. She gave them each a teary hug, which gave them permission to plunge into their gifts.

She used the flurry of activity for cover and opened Derek's gift. A violet velour robe with matching lacy negligee in shiny lavender satin. Her hands dropped to her sides as good intention fell away. She raised her eyes and found him looking at her. The appeal could hardly be clearer. Fortunately, Susan and Peter were still buried in gift boxes and packing foam. They didn't notice as she rose and went to the kitchen to make the pies.

In mid-afternoon, they drove to Santa Barbara in a downpour, and the pounding of rain on the Benning s' deck accompanied their greetings, but the house smelled of roasting turkey, and flames danced in the fireplace. Eleanor emerged from the kitchen, her arms outstretched for her grandchildren. Behind her, Patricia stood in the doorway, searching Myra's eyes for the answer to some question. What was she doing here? Was she settling for this life?

Myra joined the women in the kitchen. Eleanor's arms came around her to tie an apron. "You girls don't bother with these, I know," she said, "but I'm old-fashioned." She turned away and unwrapped the pies. "Perfect as usual, Myra. I don't know how you do it." She turned her attention to the salad. "And you'll make your wonderful dressing for this?"

"Of course." The words felt like capitulation, and Myra could find no force to combat it. She busied herself with selecting spices, listening to Patricia complain to Eleanor about Conrad's increasing resistance to his ulcer diet, Eleanor's predictable chatter about hers. This is how women survived, she told herself. In the warmth of community kitchens, buffered from their menfolk by custom, they filled their heads with rich smells or rising bread and roasting meats. And talk. Her tension softened and she gave in to ease.

Derek strode into the kitchen and threw an arm around Myra's shoulders. "I'm after ice. Can you find me a bucket?"

Myra stiffened, then remembered her vow to erase strain for this one day and forced a smile. "No, but I'll fill it, if your mother can find you one."

Across the kitchen, Eleanor beamed, then reached into a cupboard and produced a pewter bucket.

Derek hovered over Myra's shoulder as she filled it and gave her a kiss as she rose. He wanted her to meet his eyes, she knew, but she managed to hand him the bucket without doing so. Myra saw Patricia give them a sidelong glance as she chopped radishes for salad.

"Derek, before you go, would you take the bird out of the oven for me?" Eleanor asked.

Patricia and Myra exchanged a look and smiled. They were perfectly capable of handling the turkey. This was Eleanor, rejoicing in the healing power of the male role in holiday rituals. It was impossible not to join in the admiration of the bird, the inhaling of its rich smell, as Derek held it aloft, as though offering the queen her crown.

Myra closed her eyes. This was a celebration of her re-entrance into the family—her forgiving the past. There was no doubting it, no questioning it, and the wrongness caused her to spin on her heel and seek the refuge of the bathroom. She stared at the pale woman in the mirror and condemned her even as she ached to join the bustle of last minute activity in the kitchen.

At the table, Myra found there was little need to participate in the talk of boats and planned excursions. She let her being retreat once again into her buffered half-presence. Endure, she told herself.

As they left for home, Eleanor pulled her aside. "I'm so glad you've forgiven him, Myra, and come back to us. You'll see it's the right thing to do."

Myra could only open her mouth, wordless. She glanced at Derek. He was laughing at his father's joke, relaxed and vibrant—forgiven and free of the tension of these last months.

She turned and met a perplexed question in Patricia's eyes. Outrage and protest rose in her throat. She gave her mother-in-law a perfunctory kiss then fled outside, where the cold rain dissolved the spell cast by her in-laws. She hadn't forgiven him. She had no business letting that charade go on. She ducked into the car and stared at the water beating on the windshield. But was it a day off or was she, in fact, forgiving him? Pain and shock had dulled with time. She ached for the warmth of his arms, the family inside this lovely house her children were reluctant to leave. Somewhere deep inside, a voice whispered that she had stayed too long. She would be lured into the state that they asked.

The thunk of wipers and the pounding of water on the roof of the car covered the lack of conversation in the front seat, and Myra's determination gave way to relief that the day was done. The radio blared warnings of sliding hillsides and overflowing canyon creeks—the usual stuff of a state that had earthquake, fire, and flood instead of weather. In a month, daffodils and tulips would spring forth in her garden, persuading her that it was spring. Another illusion in California's chief industry—

fantasy-making. Myra sunk into a pool of self-revulsion she knew she should fight but could find no strength to do so.

Days passed and left no memories. Derek, when he was home, patrolled the house, from shed to kitchen to living room and out again, as though looking for something lost. On good days, he'd come upon Susan or Peter, and his face burst into a smile of relief. Together they'd vanish toward the beach. On bad days, he found no one and would be standing at their bedroom door, arms folded over his chest, waiting for her when she came out of the bathroom. She had to pass him to the tower stairs, keeping her rejection ever present even as his infidelity faded into the past. On such nights, she often heard him pacing as she lay in her tower bed, waiting for sleep. Some part of her was enraged that he could consider himself the wronged party, another wondered how long it would be before it worked, and she returned to his bed.

Patricia didn't call for lunch. The recurring realization dawned and dawned again as days passed, fading a little each time. The urge to call her weakened as the sense of futility grew stronger. She didn't want Tricia to tell her what she was doing to herself.

Derek gave it up. No longer stood waiting for her, and the desire which rose unbidden in his presence faded, too. They walked past each other like strangers at a supermarket. Unless the children required them both, they were rarely in the same room.

One spring morning, Peter burst into the kitchen waving his acceptance letter from UC San Diego. Myra cheered but felt strangely removed from the promise of release from perdition that beckoned. As though the vow to endure had been made by some Myra she'd lost. She shook free of the sensation and held out her arms to her son, then beckoned to Susan who stood at the door, her face a concoction of excitement and loss. They were standing like that, holding on to each other, shaken free of the shackles that had bound their days, when Derek arrived.

He stared, astonished and confused.

"Hey!" Peter yelled breaking free to wave the letter again.

For one brief moment they were all laughing. Then one by one broke off, as though realizing how absent such moments had been from their lives.

"So, where should we go to celebrate?" Myra asked, to revive the scene.

"Beachside." Peter's tone left nothing to be discussed.

They laughed again, and again laughter returned them to an earlier state of being. Myra breathed great gulps and felt her veins expand, her muscles take life. This was what she'd been determined to preserve. This.

September arrived, shaking her loose from the months of numb blankness that had resettled over the summer. Peter was packing. Myra joined in. This was a signal for her to change her life, but as she folded shirts, she realized she had no idea how to do so. The months had withered her, distance had become a habit. The Myra she'd been had retreated to a place she couldn't reach. She was a shadow without will or purpose.

When the day came for his departure, Myra felt as though she was swimming in space, dislodged from her robotic state, but unable to make contact with herself or her family. They piled his stuff into a trailer and drove south. She opened her laptop and tried to make Matilda, Rufus, Eustasia, and Alphonse come alive. But they remained lifeless as they had for months now, outlines without speech, not even worth filling in. Her only relief was when she begged turn at the wheel where she could seek diversion in the jumble of Los Angeles interchanges.

When they had unpacked his things and were ready to say goodbye, Peter's hug was perfunctory, as though she'd become someone he wasn't sure he knew. The pain of that brought her to life, and she wanted to cry out in denial of the naked truth. Her withdrawal had driven them closer to their father. Her reward for "bearing up" was her exclusion.

Chapter 5

Screams sat her up in bed. They came again. And again. Leaping up, she raced down the stairs, reaching the bottom just as the Derek's shape emerged from Susan's bedroom. Behind him their daughter's screams still rent the night.

"Derek?"

"What …?" He jerked around at the sound of her voice, his face frozen in an expression the light was far too dim to read.

"I don't know!" Derek flung his hand into the air. "She just started to scream …"

Myra brushed past him to find Susan, bolt upright in bed, the whites of her dark eyes reflecting the moonlight that streamed through her window.

"Bodies! All over me!" She began pushing air with her hands, screaming again. "Get him off!"

Myra flicked on the bedside lamp. "It's a nightmare, Susan!" She grasped the flying hands. "You're awake now. It's Mommy." Susan had had nightmares for years—being buried in bodies or covered with worms. Derek must have interrupted one, or become part of it. "Look at me, Susan. Wake up." Myra released her hands and took hold of her shoulders, pulling her around face to face.

"No! I'm awake. I'm awake!" Susan's face was rigid with terror. "It's him!"

"Who? What …" Myra looked around at a loss and saw only Derek, standing in the doorway. "It was Daddy, Susan, just Daddy."

"Get him away!" Susan cried. She yanked from Myra's grip and flung herself onto the pillow, sobbing.

Myra stared at her crumpled form in bewilderment, then looked for an answer in Derek's face, its angles oddly stark in the lamplight.

"No!" Derek yelled, against whatever he saw in her eyes. "I was just—she started screaming. One of her nightmares, Myra …"

At the sound of his voice, Susan began to shake. She and Derek were making it worse. She had to calm herself, so she could calm Susan. She pushed away the suspicion that was pounding the sides of her skull. "Go," she told him. "Leave us alone."

He disappeared from the doorway without a word.

She turned Susan on her stomach and started to rub her back. After a while, she began to sing—murmur, really—a lullaby Susan had loved as a small child. She reached up and took Doby from his shelf, putting him in her daughter's arms as though to wipe out the night and start the hazardous trip through adolescence all over again. Then she lay down next to her, concentrating everything she had on the Susan's breathing, matching its rhythm to her own.

She had no idea how long she lay there. The act of quieting Susan brought back some semblance of rationality, but a terrible suspicion kept rumbling beneath it. "Susan?"

There was a murmur from the pillow.

"Tell me what happened." The back beneath her hand began to shake again. "It's okay now, Susan. It's over. Just tell me."

Susan rolled to her side and pulled her knees to her chin. "I don't know—I was asleep. Then there was a weight, and I woke up. I couldn't get it off! Fingers like worms all over me …" She broke off, running her hands up and down her body.

"Okay, that's enough. It's gone." Unable to watch, Myra took the clawing hands in hers. "Just rest. I'll be back." She got up, went out, and was microwaving a cup of cocoa when a puff of air blew her gown against her knees. She turned and stared at the open patio door. Derek's dim figure was outlined against the fog, familiar and suddenly terrible. He must have heard her, but he didn't turn. She grabbed the cup and returned to Susan. "Here, drink this."

Susan's hands shook as she took the cup. That was all wrong. When nightmares dissolved, they left her calm. Not like this.

"Where is he?" Her daughter's voice was full of fear, as though her home and everyone in it was now dangerous.

"It's just your Dad, Susan. Somehow he must have gotten mixed up with a dream."

But Susan's head began to move back and forth and a deep sob shook her body. Myra grabbed the cup before its contents splashed onto the bed. She put it on the nightstand, then took her daughter in her arms. "All right. It's all right. We won't talk anymore now. Just drink your cocoa." When the shaking subsided, Myra picked up the cup.

After a moment that stretched into the silence of the night, Susan pulled away and took the cocoa from her, clasping it to her chest the way she'd done as a small child.

Myra watched, holding her tongue but desperate to shake the truth out of her—some explanation of the words "a weight, worms all over me" that curdled her gut.

But instead, Susan stared into her cup and wouldn't raise her head. Her body quieted, but instead of reaching out to Myra, she withdrew into the cocoon that had become all too familiar. When the cup was empty she handed it to Myra without a word, turned away and lay back, clutching her pillow.

Myra turned off the lamp and sat beside the bed with her hand on her daughter's back and, for another endless time, waited for her breathing to become even and shallow. She watched the moonlit shape of Susan's body rise and fall beneath the light coverlet. The child she'd comforted had become a fully formed adolescent. The images of other young women rose in Myra's mind, the breathy voices on the telephone. She clenched her teeth as red-hot lava rose from depths she didn't know she had.

No. She shut her brain down. No. He'd simply heard her whimper and call out in her dreams and come in to quiet her. That's all.

But the half-formed conviction knotted in her throat and refused to dissolve. The bedside clock read three AM. What was he doing up?

He heard her cry out, the other side of her brain insisted.

But it had always been she who responded to her daughter's cries.

Not always, replied the other side, determined to stop the stone in her gut that was hardening by the minute. You might not hear her from the tower room.

Her daughter's body seemed to shine in the moonlight, defenseless and inviting. Myra shook her head to drive away the image, then stood up and went down the hall to the kitchen.

The patio door was closed. Derek, in rumpled striped pajamas, his dark hair rising in disheveled spikes, was sitting at the table in the dining ell in the glare of the overhead light—the accused prisoner. She caught her breath. He watched her approach, but instead of the usual parental question in his eyes—which she needed to dispel her impossible suspicion—his face was masked. Frozen. Or afraid.

She stared at him, her sense of wrongness solidifying, and could find no words.

"Myra, don't look at me like that. I swear, I simply leaned down to give her a hug—that's all." He spoke through lips stiffened—by fear?

"What were you doing up this time of night?" She fought to make the words sound merely curious.

"Couldn't sleep. Came down and had a couple of drinks—the usual." He shrugged. "Then she started crying out—one of her dreams."

She stared at the empty glass on the breakfast bar that confirmed his account and nodded, feeling her shoulders relax a little. She sat and put her hands in her lap where they lay quiet. "Some dream," she breathed, letting her body soften. "It's never been so hard to wake her from one."

"Scared me half to death," he agreed. The mask dropped from his face, and he gave her a boyish smile.

Something in that smile banished her relief. It was too like the smile he gave when he begged forgiveness. Forgiveness for what?

She stared at her hands, which were now clenched. "You heard her cry out, you say?" She would have wakened. Yes, she'd slept in the tower, but Susan's screams had sat her upright.

"Thought I did. I was getting myself a sleeping pill from the bathroom. When I went in she was quiet, though." He smiled. "She looked so beautiful, laying there in the moonlight ..." His voice faded as he read the expression on her face. "What's wrong?"

She couldn't speak. His words were wrong. They brought forth the fully developed girl she'd just left.

"She said there was a weight— a body on her." Her stomach clenched as the deadly certainty rose again.

"I gave her a hug!" His voice was almost shrill with outrage and defense.

She tried imagining a hug that put her weight on a child. And couldn't. Her head was pounding now, her tongue dry. "Fingers like worms ..."

"Stop! That's crazy. You can't believe I'd ..." He broke off and waved his hands. "God. She ..."

"Made it up?" The words were bitter on her tongue. Her head pounded. "She's been a Daddy's girl all her life, and now she's making up this awful story? That's what you're saying, Derek?"

He put his hands flat on the table. "Because she was in the middle of some nightmare!"

"Don't." She held up a hand to stop him. In her mind, she saw Susan's eyes as she cried out, "It's him!" Those eyes were awake. Conscious. Focused on hers. She got up to stop the scream of rage and opened the patio door to get her breath. The night was quiet. "Get out!" The words came like hot coals. "Get your things and leave."

"Myra ... believe me ..."

"You haven't given me a single goddamned reason to believe you in years!" She fought for control as she realized her words had been flung out into the night. But she couldn't turn to face him. "This—I want to believe you—I'd rather die than think what I'm thinking, but ..."

"Myra, look at me." His voice held a plea she'd heard once too often.

"No. I can't have you here! Do you hear me? Every time I look at you, I'll ..." She put her hands to her pounding head, imagining it. "Leave now!" She slipped into her beach shoes and walked out into the pitch black of open country. She was in her nightgown, had no light, and didn't care. She had to have space. She walked to the edge of the cliff and stood staring out to sea.

Part of her, disarmed by that penitent smile, rose to say it couldn't be. Daughters occupy a different universe than other women. But the other, larger part, raged at her for believing that. For letting him stay. She looked down at the body that had gained pounds every month of humiliation she'd endured under the illusion that she was the only one who was paying his price. Where had she been this last year? What had her brain and heart been doing? Now Susan would bear the indelible mark of her cowardice.

Back across the mesa, an engine roared to life as the coupe shot out of the drive. Myra returned to the house, numb and cold, operating on an automatic pilot she didn't recognize, but obeyed. A sheriff deputy's card hung on her bulletin board; it had been there since that long ago day Susan had fallen from the cliff. Kept for the phone number in case they were robbed, she supposed.

No. Not Yet. She had to find out more from Susan. Had to be sure.

She went down the hall and looked at her sleeping daughter. The clock said four thirty. She stood warming her cold hands in her armpits, arguing with the newly awakened Myra who had to know right now, then went to lie down next to Susan.

At her touch, Susan bolted upright, her eyes wide.

"It's just me, Susan!"

Susan turned her head, her stare still fixed, then sank back against her pillow. Myra reached a hand out and put it on her daughter's. She lay there and let minutes pass until her daughter's breathing quieted.

"Talk to me, Susan. Tell me what happened."

Susan shook her head and rolled away.

"Honey, you have to." She reached an arm over and rolled Susan toward her. "You said you woke up with someone—were you dreaming? Before that? Do you know?"

Susan shook her head and tried to roll away.

"No, you weren't dreaming or no, you don't want to talk?"

"Wasn't dreaming and don't want to talk. Please, Mommy …"

Myra reached around to put a hand on her daughter's forehead. "I know. But it won't go away, Susan …"

"Yes, it will! It will!" She started to sob.

Myra rolled over and put her arms around her. "If he hurt you, I'll …"

"He loves me!"

The words, muffled by her pillow, shook Myra to the core. She closed her eyes and long minutes passed before she could go on. "Yes, I know. So … did he lie on top of you?"

"He loves me! Go away!"

Myra's blood turned to ice. "What else, Susan. Tell me!"

Her daughter shook her head, refusing.

There was no denying her daughter's desperation. No way to explain the episode into a nightmare. She stood up and went back to the kitchen where she stared at the phone for a long minute before picking it up.

She was amazed when the night officer said Randy Larson was still working there, nine years after Susan's accident. He'd come on duty at seven. She left a message for him to call her, then curled up on the couch to wait.

Chapter 6

The rapping on the front door jarred her back to consciousness. She pulled on a robe and ran to the door.

Randy Larson stood there, cap in hand, looking much as she remembered, except for a few lines forming around his jaw and a receding hairline. He smiled in recognition, and she found herself returning it.

"Come in." She tightened the belt on her robe and stepped back. "You remembered me."

"Sure. Your little girl fell off the cliff. I always remember happy endings—and nice people. They keep me going. What's up?"

She remembered now, that low-keyed casual voice and the reassurance it brought. Nice people. Was she really going to do this? She had a choice, didn't she? "The little girl is fourteen now. Her brother is in college."

He frowned. "Seriously? Is that possible?"

Myra nodded. "As for happy endings …" she clenched her fists. "My husband molested Susan last night." The words came in a rush, unstoppable once they started. She turned and walked to the French doors, so he couldn't see her face. Morning mist obscured the scene of that long-ago accident. Rigging tackle littered the table where Derek, determined to keep the Serendipity sailing, had been working yesterday. His beach shoes were kicked against the low wall that separated the patio from open country. She heard Randy clear his throat and turned.

"I'm sorry."

She examined his face. The pleasure had vanished, leaving the lines more marked than before. His eyes looked pained, but there was no shock. "I thought we were nice people, too." She sank into a chair then leaped up again. "No, damn it, that's not true! He slept with other women—his graduate students—and I knew it. I knew it and lived with it and didn't do a damned thing!" She swung her arm and cracked her knuckle against the mantle, doubling her over in pain.

Next thing she knew, he was standing over her, his hand on her shoulder. "Hey, slow down. You're way ahead of me. Tell me what happened."

His quiet firm tone quieted her. She understood now, why he'd stuck in her memory. She gestured toward a chair. "Susan screamed. I woke up. I went downstairs and there was Derek—her father—coming out of her room. He shook his head as though he didn't know what was wrong—damn him!" Her voice rose and she reined it in. "Susan was in her bed screaming that she had bodies on her—weighing her down. I thought it was a nightmare, too, but then she cried out, 'It's him! It's him!'" Myra cut herself off as the words sank in. "My God," she whispered. "Does that mean he's done it before, but she didn't know who it was?" The thought took her breath, and she collapsed into a chair.

Randy Larson looked at her, his expression unreadable. "Possibly. Was it dark when this happened?"

"Not really. The moon was shining in."

"Do you know what time all of this was?" He drew out his notebook and began to write.

"The bedside clock said three."

He nodded. "What did you do?"

"I quieted Susan as best I could—got her to sleep—then I came down and ..." She stood up again, clasped her arms around her middle, and went to the front windows to look out into the street. Did she expect to see him there? Waiting to be taken back? "He said he couldn't sleep, that he went in and gave her a hug—that it interrupted a nightmare."

"You thought so, too. Does she have nightmares?"

"Yes—sometimes. But a hug doesn't weigh you down, and she was awake—I know she was—when she said 'It's him.'" She raised her arms and slapped them to her sides. "I kicked him out." She turned to face him. "I couldn't—can't—believe him. Trust him. Ever again."

He nodded. "We'll find him. Do you have a picture?" He looked around the room and spied a family photo sitting on a corner table. "Ah. I remember him." He walked over and picked it up. "Can I take this? I'll bring it back."

"Oh, God ..." She stared at the happy family. "Not that one. I'll give you another." She crossed the room and opened a cabinet next to the fireplace, then pulled out a box of loose shots. Quickly she gave him one of Derek alone, standing in front of their tent up at El Capitan State Park, and took the family photo back.

Larson shot her a look of understanding, then went back at his notes. "All right. I'll have to talk to Susan."

"Oh." She frowned. She hadn't thought this through at all. "You have to, don't you? I'll see if she's awake."

But when she went down the hall, she heard the shower running.

"Susan?" She opened the bathroom door. "Are you all right?"

"I just need to get warm."

Myra leaned against the wall, closing her eyes. She, too, felt chilled to the bone. "All right," she said as calmly as she could. "That's fine. When you're finished, Lieutenant Larson is here waiting to talk to you."

"Who? Why?" Susan's voice was shrill.

"Lieutenant Larson. The man who helped you when you fell off the cliff, remember?"

"No. What's he doing here?" Her voice was sharp with suspicion, and the shower went off.

"I want you to tell him what happened." Myra said it as quietly as she could, but the shower door opened with a bang.

"What? No!" Susan stood naked, dripping water and staring at her, outraged. "I can't do that! He's my Dad! That's—no!" She grabbed a towel from the rack and pulled it around her.

"Susan ..."

"You mean you called him here? I can't believe you'd do that. Where's Dad? Where did he go?"

"I don't know, Susan." She stared at her daughter's towel-wrapped figure and wanted to yell, "He's not living in the same house with you ever again!" Instead, she locked her jaw and said simply, "I told him to leave."

"No!"

Susan's eyes widened in a mixture of terror, confusion, and shame that took Myra's breath, but she persisted. "Yes. What he did was criminal, Susan. Do you understand that?"

Susan shook her head and raced past Myra out the door to her bedroom where she threw herself on the bed, her body wracked with sobs.

Myra laid a hand on her back, helpless, trying to imagine her daughter's gut-ripping pain. How could she have let this happen? How? "All right. We can wait."

She stood up slowly, feeling every pound she'd gained in denial, and went back to the living room. "It's too soon," she told Randy, who sat with his arms on his knees, staring at the rug. "It's her Dad and …" she broke off, spreading her hands in a gesture of helplessness.

He nodded. "I know. It happens a lot," he said, rising.

"A lot? This is a usual thing?" Her voice squeaked.

He gave a rueful smile. "More than you want to know, I'm afraid. And more often than not, the victims won't file charges."

"Oh, God. You mean it just goes on?" Well, she'd let his infidelity go on, hadn't she?

"Sometimes. And sometimes the wife kicks him out—the way you did." He put a hand on her arm.

Myra stared at him, unable to speak. Were these the parents she stood behind in the grocery line? Girls who caught the school bus every day? Played beach volleyball on Saturday?

"Look. Like you say, it's too soon. Let her recover a bit, then we'll try again." He hesitated, his quiet brown eyes studying her. "Then we'll need an examination, you know."

She didn't know. The idea made Myra cringe. "I don't think—it was just a hug …" How did she know that? What would an examination do to Susan? What madness had she pitched herself into? But she wasn't going to turn away, not again ever. She nodded.

"Meanwhile, we'll look for him. Question him. Do you know where he might have gone?"

Myra stared at him, visualizing the places of Derek's life. "His office—Department of Marine Biology. His parents, Eleanor and Cornelius Benning." She gave the address, every word dropping like a stone on her husband's life—on all of their lives. "His boat—the Serendipity—docked at the Santa Barbara Marina." She turned away as though the whole affair would vanish if she weren't looking at his officer's uniform.

"What does he drive?" The question came softly.

"An '86 Jag coupe. Black." She swallowed and gave the license number.

"Okay, thanks. That should do it. I'll let you know when we pick him up."

She winced at the words.

"Look. You did the right thing. You need to know that."

"But too late. Way too late."

She watched him go down the drive, then went and sat on the patio, staring out onto the mesa, watching it take shape now as the fog cleared. Her daily habit. But in her mind, nothing took shape; she was sitting in a void. An endless time later, she cleared Derek's litter off the patio table and shoved it into the shed where she wouldn't have to look at it. Then she went into the kitchen and put the coffee on—to assure herself that she could still put one foot ahead of the other.

She went down the hall to their bedroom to dress, but stopped at the door. She couldn't go into that room. It was Derek's. Had been for months. She needed to tend to Susan, whose door still stood open as she'd left it. "All right," she said to the silent form on the bed, wrapped in a robe. "He's gone. Don't worry about it now, okay? Just rest."

Susan didn't answer, but Myra saw the muscles in her shoulders relax. "You're well-loved. Remember that," she said softly. "And this whole mess is not your fault." She stood looking at her daughter for a long moment, needing to know how far Derek had gotten, how much damage he'd done, knowing she couldn't push further right now.

Finally, she stretched out on the bed next to her and stared at the ceiling. Susan's breath became even and shallow, and Myra tried and failed to follow her into sleep. Finally, unable to lie still any longer, she rose and dressed.

She dare not walk on the mesa, lest Susan wake again, so she found herself pacing. She stopped at the coffee pot, dimly remembered turning it on, poured a cup, and made herself sit down. No. This was where Derek had sat. The scene came back. She jumped up, taking her coffee to the living room where she stared at the cold black hole of the fireplace.

Halfway through her coffee, she realized she was waiting for the phone to ring—the call that would say they'd found him and carry her into the next stage. Charging him. Could she? She resisted even visualizing his face, much less saying his name, facing him, or having him in the same house. Would Susan do it? Did she have to? The unanswered questions drove her to her feet to pace again.

She glanced at the clock. Nine. What day was it? Tuesday? A school day. Myra shook her head, impatient with the fog, and called the school. Susan was sick, she told the secretary. The very normalcy of the excuse, so easily given, put her derailed brain back on track.

She went to their bedroom and stripped the sheets from the bed she hadn't slept in for a year, took the sheets and hamper to the laundry, returned to the bedroom and began to pack the clothes he hadn't taken.

When three boxes sat by the door, she started to clean the bathroom, ridding it of his distinct but unnamable smell. The exercise cleared her head and strengthened her resolve. Derek wasn't coming back.

She went to Susan's door and watched her daughter sleep. If Susan wouldn't—or couldn't—charge him, she would. If she couldn't charge him with—her mind balked at the word. If he only touched … no, damn it, laid on her … She gagged. Don't back off, she told herself. Say it. Incest. And if it wasn't—hadn't gone that far—she'd sue him for divorce. She'd been going to do that anyway. But hadn't. Now, he'd opened a yawning pit of possibilities that couldn't be shut again.

She went to his study and began putting his papers in boxes. It was noon when she looked up to see Susan, wrapped in a fuzzy pink robe, standing at the door, watching her. She rose and took her in her arms. "Come. Let's get you something to eat."

Susan shook her head, staring at the boxes. "What are you doing?"

Myra turned and looked at the torn-apart room. It was perfectly obvious what she was doing. "What has to be done, Susan."

She's head moved back and forth. "No … no …"

Myra caught her shoulders and turned her away. "Don't think about it. Come on …" She led Susan toward the living room, sat her on the couch and threw an afghan over her legs.

Susan clasped her hands hard in her lap.

Myra went to the fireplace and built a fire, though the fog had dissipated, and the September day was warming. "There," she said, as the flames rose.

"You can't send Daddy away!" Her voice verged on hysteria.

Myra went to the couch, knelt before her and took her clasped hands in hers. "And if he walked in the door right now, Susan, how would you feel?"

Susan jerked back at the words and began to shake.

Myra took her in her arms. "All right. It's all right. This is not your fault, Susan. But I won't let him do that to you. Do you understand? It's wrong."

Susan's shoulders began to shake in soundless wracking sobs, and Myra simply held her, convinced that trying to stop the spasms would only make things worse.

A moment later, Susan shoved her away and flopped sideways onto the couch, pulling her knees to her chin.

"Did he do it before, Susan? You need to tell me."

Susan put her hands over her ears.

Myra pulled them away. "I need to know."

"I don't know!" Susan pulled her hands from Myra's grasp and began to sob again. "I don't … I don't … just stop it!"

"The whole thing is terribly wrong, Susan. But you have to leave it to me, now."

Susan lay staring at the fire without words.

The phone rang, and Myra jumped for it. "Hello?"

"Lieutenant Larson here. We haven't found him yet, Mrs. Benning. I called to see whether you have any more ideas about where he might be."

"No. He likes to camp, but he doesn't have anything with him … I don't know."

"The manager at the marina thinks he saw him this morning, and there are footprints on the deck of the boat. Could he have gotten camping gear from there, do you think?"

"Maybe. Yes. We keep sleeping bags there. And a tent."

"Food?"

"Yes. There's always food on board in the summer. We keep it stocked."

"Where might he camp?"

"El Capitan, Refugio, or anywhere back in the mountains, really."

"Okay, we'll check. Is Susan awake? How is she?"

"Not good." She looked at her daughter. "Confused."

"Understandable. Look, I'm going to send a woman deputy, Sergeant Sanders, over to talk to her and take her in for an exam."

"Oh, God …"

"I know, but we have to do it. Make her understand that, will you? And you can go with her, of course."

Not yet, not yet, she wanted to cry, but held her tongue. "All right," she said instead, forcing her brain to concur. She hung up and went to get Susan's clothes. When she returned, Susan's eyes were closed, though Myra doubted she was asleep. "You need to get dressed, Susan. A woman deputy is coming to talk to you."

"No! I don't want to. It's over, Mom. Can't you see that?"

"Just get dressed, okay? You'll feel better." She sank into an easy chair and waited until Susan sat up, muttering under her breath, and untied her robe.

By the time the deputy arrived, Susan was dressed, sitting washed, combed, and sullen in front of a bowl of cereal.

"Susan? I'm Carrie Sanders. I want you to tell me what happened last night." She was young and petite, sandy-haired and as fresh-faced as a coed.

"Nothing. I don't want to talk about it. It's over." Susan's voice threatened tears.

"Susan, that isn't going to work," Myra told her. "It simply isn't going to go away."

"Your mother says your father came into your room."

Susan began to tremble. "Don't ... he's my Dad ..."

Myra took a breath. "Did he lie on you, Susan?"

Susan wrapped her arms around herself, rocking back and forth. "Stop talking about it!"

"Susan, I'm sorry," the deputy said softly. "I know you don't want to remember, but we have to know. Do you understand? Just tell us and get it over with, can you? Then it will be done, and you won't have to say it again."

Susan shook her head. "She made him go away!"

Myra closed her eyes at the ten-year-old voice emerging from her daughter. When she opened them, the deputy had her hand on Susan's arm.

"Okay, Susan, we'll leave it for now." She rose and turned to Myra. "We have a psychiatrist, Dr. Garvitz, who sees cases like this for us. He's good." She seemed unperturbed by Susan's obduracy. "We do have to take you to the doctor, though, to be sure he didn't hurt you."

Susan's head whipped back and forth. Her eyes sought Myra's in a desperate plea for support.

Myra put her hand on Susan's shoulder. "We have to. Now, Susan." She used that tone rarely with her children, but when she did, it never failed to work.

Susan rose.

The ride to the hospital was silent. Sergeant Sanders began to chat about the weather and the flood of students and traffic that marked the opening of the university's school year. Susan stared ahead of her, unmoving.

When they arrived, she walked into the examining room like a zombie. The antiseptic soaked air seemed to make her withdraw even further from her surroundings. Myra stayed with her during the exam, mortifying at any age, but Susan remained like a stone throughout.

"I don't see any sign of penetration," the resident reported when they were done, and Susan sat, dressed and immobile.

Myra swallowed in relief. "Thank you." Maybe it was the first time, then. Susan's shock and hysteria said that it was. But in that case, what did "It's him!" mean?

"He didn't get that far," she said to the deputy when they were back in the car. "Thank God for that."

Carrie Sanders nodded. "You're sure about all of this?"

"Yes. She woke up and screamed at his weight—she said she couldn't get him off."

"Right. Well, something clearly happened. We'll see if Dr. Garvitz can get to the bottom of it." She reached for a folder sitting beside her on the front seat and drew out a card. "Here. I'll tell him you'll be calling to make an appointment."

There was no message from Randy Larson waiting for her when she got back to the house. They hadn't found Derek. Where had he gone? She went upstairs, booted her computer, and discovered a thousand dollar withdrawal from their bank account. Her hands went cold. Surely, he couldn't disappear for long. Classes started next week. Wherever he was, he would return for that.

She gazed at her drawing board where Matilda and her friends sat waiting for their next adventure. How criminal, diddling away her time—poking fun at herself and the world instead of paying attention. What had she missed? Had he watched Susan with the eyes of a man not a father? Starting when? She didn't know. She'd simply ignored her husband—stayed away from him. He'd been restless since they took Peter to college, but he frequently was in the last weeks before classes started. Before the grad students arrived, she told herself. Peter wasn't around to distract him with college preparations, Susan was at school, and Myra had shut him out.

She gave it up and went downstairs to call the sheriff's department with the news about the bank account. Lieutenant Larson wasn't there. There were no developments.

Chapter 7

Two days passed. Susan went back to school. There was still no sign of Derek.

Myra took Susan to Dr. Garvitz, a rotund, bespectacled man shorter than she was by three inches or so, with a relaxed cheerfulness that set her at ease.

When Susan emerged an hour later, some of the tension had gone out of her face. The frozen sullenness had melted away.

"She's clearly suffered trauma," Dr. Garvitz told her privately, as Susan waited in the outer office. "She's resisting talking about it—not unusual—but I'd say her father is involved. She started to tremble when I suggested bringing him into a session."

"Did she say … has he done it before?"

"That's not clear. The extent of her upset suggests not, but …" Dr. Garvitz shook his head. "Other things suggest some prior event. It's just too soon to tell."

"What can you do to help her?"

"I'd like to see her at least once a week—more if possible. I think we can ease her through it."

"That would—that would be great. Right now, she's just so angry at me for kicking him out …"

"I know. But it's best she doesn't see him—for a while, at least. We'll leave the future open. It's easier that way."

She nodded though she could see no future with Derek. "All right. If it helps." She rose to go. "Thank you again, Dr. Garvitz. She looks better, having talked to you."

"Give her time." He patted her arm "With help, she'll recover." He patted her arm.

"What are you going to tell Peter?" Susan asked as they drove home.

Myra blinked. "I don't know. I haven't thought about it." But she was going to tell him the truth. She had no choice.

"He's going to be mad. Really mad."

Yes, thought Myra, he surely would. She glanced at Susan, who stared, stony-eyed, out the windshield. "Susan, you need to get past the idea that you started this. You didn't."

"Yes, I did. And it's like … I can't get hold of stuff … of what happened. It's always there, but the more I try to grab it, the further it goes … maybe it *was* a dream."

"No. It wasn't." Myra's voice carried a certainty she didn't feel. "Give it time. Things come back as our brains let them, Susan."

"Peter's going to say I'm crazy. Really nuts. You know that." She folded her arms over her chest, protecting herself.

"Let's not worry about Peter right now." She reached over and laid a hand on Susan's leg. Peter was in the middle of his first term. She remembered her own first semester away from home—the crises of first mid-term grades, the roommate fights, drunken parties, disastrous dates. "I'm not calling him right away. This is your time …to heal."

Susan fell silent, but Myra's dread did not. Peter's brazen adolescent self-confidence was rooted in his father's pride. They were constant companions at the tide pools, on the bike paths and hiking trails. She pulled into the garage, turned the engine off and sat.

"You have to let him come back. For Peter."

Myra closed her eyes, remembering Dr. Garvitz's advice. "Let it rest, for now, Susan. Let's just—live for a few days, okay?"

"Okay." She opened the door and climbed out. "But I'm not going to charge him, Mom. I can't." She went into the house, leaving the jagged edge of the last words behind.

She followed her daughter into the kitchen and punched the blinking answering machine.

"Lieutenant Larson calling. Please give me a call."

Her hands went cold. They must have found him. She was going to have to keep going now. She couldn't let herself stop.

"Hi." The lieutenant's voice was warm. "I'm afraid he's taken off. No sign of him anywhere."

"School starts next week. He has classes."

"He called his department and asked for a personal leave. Told them to cover his classes or cancel them."

"Good grief." She sat down. "Did he tell them why?"

"I'm not sure. I've only talked with the department secretary at this point. Professor Benning talked to the Chair."

Myra remained silent, letting the news sink in.

"Has Susan seen Dr. Garvitz yet?"

"We just came from there. He says she was traumatized and shakes at the mention of her father. But she still refuses to talk about it—or charge him. "

"There's time for that."

"Can't I charge him?"

There was a silence. "She's fourteen. It would be better if she cooperated, Mrs. Benning."

"Myra, please."

"Myra. Since the physical exam didn't show anything …"

"You're saying it's my uncorroborated word." The word of a hysterical over-protective mother angry at a philandering husband. She felt herself spinning away from everyone.

"No, Dr. Garvitz's diagnosis is listened to. Something happened. I have Sergeant Sanders' report—she believes you, and so do I."

"Thank you." But that wasn't enough for the courts, she said to herself, finishing his thought. "All right. I guess we just wait, then."

"Right. Try to get back to normal, and we'll keep looking for him. Let me know if you see him or find out anything."

Myra stared at the dead phone. Normal. The shower went on again down the hall, as it had at least twice a day since that night. She tried to imagine this waiting state as permanent, his belongings sitting on the bedroom floor in boxes.

At her elbow, the phone jangled, making her jump.

"Hi, it's me." Peter's voice startled her out of limbo.

"Hi. How're you doing up there?" Her pleasure at hearing his voice concealed, for a moment, her dread of having to speak to him.

"Cool. I have a ride home for the weekend."

Her heart sank, and she started shaking her head. "So soon, Peter. What's the matter, are you homesick already?"

"Ha. No way. I'm having a blast, but I need some stuff, and I need

Dad to put more virus protection on my computer. This place is crawling with bugs—everyone's crashing."

"Your dad's not here, Peter." She heard the words, uttered without her will.

"What do you mean? School hasn't started yet up there, has it?"

"I told him to leave." She heard her voice go on, telling him the rest of it, quietly, deliberately.

"That's crazy!" Peter's cut her off, his voice breaking on the words. "He'd never do that! It's another of Susan's damned nightmares!"

"You weren't here, Peter." She made her voice far firmer than she felt. "And it was not a bad dream. Susan knows perfectly well when she's been dreaming."

"Well, I don't believe her. Or you! And I don't believe you'd have him arrested!" He slammed down the phone.

Myra listened to the buzz of a clear line, then put it down and sat with her hands pressed to her face. Peter wouldn't be bounding in with his friends for the weekend, now. Something in that slammed phone said she wouldn't be seeing her son for a long time.

She raised her head to find Susan, wrapped in a robe again, staring at her from the doorway.

"I told you!" her daughter yelled, outraged, and disappeared down the hall to her bedroom.

So she'd been standing there the whole time.

An hour later, the phone at her elbow jangled again. Myra eyed it with trepidation. She was beginning to feel besieged.

"What is this about?" Eleanor's strident question jarred her eardrums.

"It's about Derek molesting Susan." Myra put all of the strength she had left into her voice and was glad of the anger she heard. This was the price she'd paid for being a good faculty wife. She was rewarded with silence.

"That's absurd," Eleanor said, finally. "Susan's disturbed. We all know that."

Myra's brows shot up at this news. "Do we? I don't think so, Eleanor." She was amazed at her own determination to defend herself and Susan, a strength so absent when talking with her son.

"You mean you'd do this to Derek on her word alone?" Eleanor's calm control had disintegrated.

Myra began to tell her what she'd seen.

"Don't tell me such trash …" Eleanor interrupted. "You're talking about my son."

"Eleanor, I'm not going to argue with you," Myra told her finally. "He molested her—and that's that."

"Well, I … you're a family wrecker, that's what you are!" The voice was one Myra had never heard, raw and engorged like cyst about to burst. Then the phone line went dead once again.

Beyond the patio doors, a sundowner wind picked up the leaves and threw them against the glass. The wind chimes sounded. Someone far down the mesa called a dog.

No sound came from Susan's bedroom. She knocked at the door.

"Go away."

"Susan …" Myra opened the door.

Susan was standing by her window, her arms folded over her chest. "I don't want to talk. I wish I'd never told you anything." Her voice broke and she began to cry.

Myra crossed the room and took her in her arms. She felt the tension go out of her daughter, felt her body quiver in sobs. "It's a mess, Susie, but I had to know. That kind of secret makes you sick. Can you understand that?"

Susan's sobs died, and she turned away to sit on the edge of her bed. She put her head in her hands. "I'm so tired."

Myra went to the bathroom and returned with a warm, wet washcloth. Gently she washed her daughter's face. "That's no wonder. Can you sleep?"

Susan kicked her shoes off and lay down, pulling her knees to her chest.

Myra took the afghan from the foot of the bed and covered her, then sat holding her hand.

A half hour later, she climbed to her studio and stood staring at the long inert Varmints, then picked up her pen and, without thought or intent began to draw.

> The oversized chicken had tigers on her mind. She was certain she'd seen one at sunset. On the beach, she came upon Alphonse, the heron, who was dancing with Eustasia, the gull. They scoffed at her, as usual, assuring her there were no tigers in this part of the world.
>
> "You're dreaming again, Matilda, like the time you chased zombies around all day." Alphonse scoffed.

> Matilda set off for the woods to find Rufus, the porcupine. He would take her seriously. Rufus took everything seriously.
> "Never saw one," Rufus said when she shared her tale with him. "But I've always wanted to go on a tiger hunt."
> "I'll give him a drilling," Rufus boasted, rattling his quills as they set off together.
> And so they set off through the woods, Matilda stretching her long neck this way and that, sniffing, Rufus with his nose to the ground, searching for tracks.

Myra's pen flew as though some relief valve had been opened.

> A rabbit jumped into their path, startling Rufus who let loose his quills. A fox, a mole, and a snake met the same fate. No tiger.
> Then Matilda spotted its stripes in the shadows at the edge of the garden.
> "Aha!" Rufus fired in exultation.
> The beast gave a yell and jumped. But when it rose to full height, it had only two legs, at the end of which were garden clogs.
> "We thought you were a tiger," Rufus mumbled, as Boots' eyes drilled into him from above.
> "A tiger. Really!" Boots cried.
> Rufus nodded. "Matilda's idea."

Myra raised her eyes to the sea beyond her window. Her hand was at rest, her shoulders limp, the nagging pain gone from her neck. Her pen anchored her mind and gave her relief from the relentless sameness of the open water. This was the way it was and would be. She and Susan exiled to this place outside the walls, seeking to find a foothold in this endless space between question and answer. Between knowing and certainty. This suspension. Everything was gone but that and Susan and whatever confused place between nightmare and reality her daughter occupied. Randy Larson had provided the solidity of action to their days, but that would fade in this perpetual limbo. There would be no closure. Only Dr. Garvitz would be their touch point with reality. The daily hours of school would provide the momentum for Susan's days, the misadventures of the Varmints for hers.

Myra took a deep breath to settle the new reality, then turned to her drawing board in earnest.

Chapter 8

The open mesa beyond the eucalyptus grove was just emerging from the night, the sea beyond it still shrouded in fog. Myra breathed in the unchanging opening of the day. Nowhere was there evidence that twelve years had passed. Meadow and sea remained untouched by the changes in her life. Once the limbo had terrified her; then, the unlikely happened. A newspaper gave her a contract for *The Rableville Varmints* and her escape became her livelihood. Another life took form, and the rhythm of weekly deadlines anchored her. But now she stopped, struck by the silence, uneasy. Rex and Lily, the hounds that had been her sole companions these last years, bounded over the plain, sensing nothing more than the possibility of mice in the golden-brown grass.

"Nonsense," she scolded herself. There was no one on the broad flat above the cliffs. She took off on her morning circuit, driving her feet forward in her usual self-derision. When she reached the edge of the cliff, she looked down at the beach but saw nothing but the wet, kelp-coated rocks of low tide. What was she looking for, for heaven's sake? She'd been in this state of mind since Susan's call yesterday.

"Mom? Dad's back!" Her daughter's voice, half-afraid, half-excited rang in her ears. "I saw his Jag up at El Capitan."

Myra shook herself free, called the dogs again, and headed down the path to the sand below.

Surely, Susan was mistaken. The Jag must have become some kid's pet project long ago. Even if she was right and Derek had returned from whatever place he'd vanished to a dozen years ago, both of them had moved too far to change course now.

"No!" She swung her stick to get the dogs away from a seagull corpse and continued to swing it at the driftwood that littered the beach. It made a satisfying crack, expressing exactly her reaction to any mention of her ex-husband. His name brought back the faces of the young woman who crowded around him, and worse—Susan's face in the middle of that night, a memory that never aged. Her mind balked as always, and she stopped to take a deep breath of the fog-laden sea air to cool her brain.

"It's over, Susan. You're a married woman, now, with a new baby," she'd told her daughter. "You've put a whole life between you and the past. He can't bring it back. Think of Doug—of his love."

Now Myra brought up the picture of Doug and Susan holding her first grandchild. She'd been afraid it couldn't happen, that Susan would be forever too terrified by men to form a relationship. But there she was, beaming and easy beneath Doug's arm. She'd beaten the terror of that night. Her mercurial little girl was stronger than any of them would have thought.

She whistled to the dogs and set off again, hanging onto that thought, brushing off the confusion that had returned to her daughter's voice. "If he really does show up," she'd told Susan, "it'll be to ask your forgiveness."

She whacked at the chaparral next to the path, seeing all too clearly that remorseful-boy look. She'd wanted to add, "Don't be taken in the way I was," but had bitten her tongue. Nasty cracks about Derek were taboo, especially for Peter, but for Susan, too. Even twelve years of silence hadn't changed that.

The dogs bounded up the hill with a grace that had never ceased to awe her. Then she saw that they'd stopped to circle a campfire, still smoldering above the rotting seawall. "Leave it!"

But they kept sniffing as though the scent was fresh. Myra's fingertips turned cold. She tucked them into her armpits and scanned the slope. Nothing. She pulled out her cell phone and called the sheriff's office. Fires on the chaparral-covered slopes were outlawed at any time, particularly in the middle of a California drought.

"Santa Barbara County Sheriff," the voice answered. "Lieutenant Larson speaking."

She stopped in surprise at the voice she hadn't heard it in twelve years. "Hi Randy, Myra Benning."

"Well, hello! How're you doing?"

Myra grinned. He sounded as though he really recognized her voice.

"Fine. But it looks as though we've got vagrants on the mesa again. There's a smoking fire on the south-end path to the beach."

"Okay, thanks, we'll get right on it."

"Just above the seawall. It's probably nothing, but this summer's given me a case of nerves." She scanned the chaparral-covered mountains in the distance.

"I know. We're all seeing arsonists behind every bush. I'll stop by after we've had a look around."

She flipped her phone shut and surveyed the hillside, telling herself that the devastating fire season was all that was bothering her. After climbing up the slope, she stood gazing out across the mesa again toward the rim of eucalyptus that separated the open country from the town. Nothing but crows. A lone blue heron rose from the distant slough. She smiled. Just another morning by the sea.

When she reached the house, she turned and looked back for the peace of mind the place always gave, then whistled to Rex and Lily. A half hour later, the dogs fed, she settled before her drawing table, the Rabbleville Varmints, and their eternal quest that carried her through monthly bills. A month's strips were due, and her agent had called to say another new outlet was in the works.

She pulled yesterday's strip toward her. Matilda, the old hen, stretched her overly long neck, cackling at Rufus. The porcupine had developed chronic wilt. The hen had been about to utter some suitable comment when Susan had called. But the words were lost. She sketched in Eustasia, the crippled gull, hoping she would join the conversation, but she just stared at Rufus, tongue-tied as she never was. Alphonse, the heron with bad knees, cocked his head at her, mocking her unproductive state of mind.

She pulled a fresh sheet of paper toward her, but her pencil remained motionless. Susan's voice, far too like the fourteen-year-old, had quashed the caustic humor that had carried Myra through the years. She took a deep breath, half-cursing her daughter's ability to shatter her best and only defense. All right, she told herself, spinning away on her stool. She wasn't going to get the call off her mind, so she'd better go see Susan.

She went down to her bedroom to change out of her sweats. The woman in the mirror was taller than she ought to be, as usual, but less bulky than she'd been twelve years ago. She'd started putting on those pounds on a day she'd schooled herself to forget, and only with her first signed contract for The Rabbleville Varmints had she begun to shed them—and the past.

She'd descended to the kitchen to pick up her car keys, when the tall, lean figure of Randy Larson crossed her patio and knocked at the French doors. The lines alongside his mouth, just forming when she'd seen him last, were firmly embedded now, and most of his hair was gone. But the penetrating brown eyes were the same.

"Hi," she said, opening the door. "You're going to tell me I'm a silly old woman."

"No, no." He grinned and stooped to give Lily's head a rub. "That I'd never do. You were leaving?"

"No rush. Come in." She was flattered by the quickness of his response to her call, and amazed at how glad she was to see him again. Affable and understated, he never threw up his official function as a barrier. He'd been an anchoring presence, that night, in a world that was spinning out of control. "What did you find?"

"Only the campfire. But keep your eyes peeled for smoke in case whoever it was comes again. We're still looking for the arsonist who set the last one."

"You're sure it was set?"

"We're never sure, but the investigators think so."

"Well, thanks for checking it out, Randy. I confess, I wasn't thinking about arsonists when I called you. My daughter thinks she saw her father in the area."

"Oh yeah? No kidding. After all of this time?"

Myra could see he was remembering those now-distant days after Derek had disappeared.

"I don't know why he'd come here, really. He'd be more likely to go to Susan, if he knows where she is. Which I doubt. So you see, I am a silly old woman. But thanks for not saying so." She liked this man. He'd never treated her as a "case."

"What makes her think he's around?" Randy asked.

"She says she saw his Jag up at El Capitan."

"Ah." He relaxed.

"I know. That doesn't mean much. I'm on my way to her house—to see if there's anything else." She was embarrassed by the trivial sound of her fears when voiced.

"How *is* your daughter—Susan, is it?"

Myra smiled, pleased that he remembered. "Wonderful, actually. She's married and a new mother! She and Doug are starting a landscaping business over off Patterson."

"And your son—what was his name?"

"Peter. He's a lawyer, now, would you believe it? That delinquent son of mine?" She could laugh now about the boy who had refused to return home between college terms and instead spent his breaks in Isla Vista, drinking and tearing the place up with the local student body.

Randy shook his head. "Not delinquent by our standards, Myra. Just upset by the whole thing, and who can blame him?"

Myra sighed. Who, indeed? But Peter had never forgiven her. Anger had faded to dutiful politeness and then to a more casual friendliness as years passed, but the barrier had only hardened into permanence. "We've survived. Which amazes me, when I stop to think about it—which I try not to. I just don't want it to start in again."

He nodded. "Amen to that. Well, I'll let you go. Let me know if you see anything else out there."

Myra watched him head out across the mesa, absurdly pleased at his reappearance in her life. Calmed by his visit, she drove south past the university and turned toward the sea again, past the rows of greenhouses to the piece of cliff-side land where Douglas and Susan were starting their own landscaping business.

"Mom!" Susan cried in surprise. Her face was pale and her coppery hair roughly combed. "What …?"

"Am I doing here?" Myra smiled. "I just came to see how you are. After yesterday's call."

"Does that mean you believe me?"

Myra winced as that haunting question reared its ugly head again. "I believe you saw an old Jag, and it could be your dad's." She smiled. "Will that do?"

Susan's shoulders settled in relief. "Thank you. I'm not sure Doug does." She turned her attention to the almost-grown golden retriever whose tail was knocking against the floorboard, waiting for permission to say hello.

At a word from Susan, the dog bounded over to be embraced. "How're you doing, Stacy?" Both she and Doug raised puppies for service dog training, and Stacy was their latest foster child.

"Wonderfully," Susan answered for him. "He's the smartest we've had."

"Really? Is that true?" she asked the dog who wagged his tail in agreement.

"Okay Stacy," Susan ordered. "Go lie down."

Myra could have petted him for far longer, but she knew the rules. He was to be a working dog, not a pet. And she liked the quiet authority of Susan's command. She could only admire what Doug and Susan did with these animals, and there was no question that working with them, and with Doug, done more to release Susan from her emotional prison than years of therapy had been able to accomplish.

Cries of their four-month-old son came from the bedroom.

"Let's see that baby."

Little Billy was round and blue eyed—and hungry. Susan settled herself in the rocker and began to nurse him. Myra lay back on the bed and watched, her whole being relaxing into the scene. Billy was going to look like his dad, she was sure. Big, blond, and brawny—not dark and slim like Derek. Myra had been worried, during Susan's pregnancy, that Susan would have a son who brought back her father every time she looked at him, but the baby's eyes showed no signs of darkening and the few wisps of hair on the small bald head were light.

"Where's Doug?" she asked.

"Out working on the new greenhouse. He'll be in for lunch soon." Susan drew her sleeping babe from the breast and laid him back into his crib. Putting a finger to her lips, she led the way back to the kitchen. "You'll stay for a sandwich, won't you?"

"Sure."

Susan opened the refrigerator and drew out meat and cheese. "He thinks I'm seeing things."

"Well, maybe he's right, Susan. There are a lot of old Jags around."

"I know, I know." Susan opened the bread. "I keep telling myself that. But …" She swung back to the refrigerator. "I just knew, that's all. Just knew."

"Did you see anything else?"

Susan shook her head. "I didn't look. It threw me back … I just wanted to get out of there." Susan spread mayonnaise with more energy than the job required. "And since then I've been wondering what would happen if I just … ran into him." She put meat on the bread and shook her head. "What would I do? Why haven't I prepared myself for that?" She clasped her arms around herself as though cold.

The kitchen door opened and Doug came in, bringing the morning air with him. "Hi, Myra." He walked over and hugged his wife. "Any lunch around here?"

As usual, Myra's whole being warmed in the presence of this big man. She hadn't believed such a blessing could fall upon them. Years of therapy had helped return Susan's life to a semblance of normality, but the damage remained. Susan, at twenty-three, still froze at the approach of men.

But then Douglas had appeared in her therapy group. He'd spent his youth caring for younger siblings in place of largely absent parents. Protectiveness was in his blood, and when he was there, according to the therapist, Susan quieted and began to open. He was a miracle.

"Good to see you, Myra," he said now, turning. He looked tired.

"I've been driving him crazy," Susan confessed, running a hand through her curls. "The sight of that car … I've been fourteen all over again." She gave her husband a kiss on his cheek, then turned to put sandwiches on the table.

"Sometimes I wish he would come back," Myra exclaimed as they sat down, "so your adult eyes could see what he is. Very charming, actually …" At the expression on her daughter's face, she stopped. Susan was as afraid of her love for her father as she was of his love for her, a love that had turned in the middle of the night. When Doug had appeared in her life, she's seemed to wipe her father from her consciousness, a development the psychiatrist said was a natural defense against unmanageable emotions. "You're a woman now. You can handle it. Bring him back and look at him for what he is. He's just—his mother's darling, I guess you'd call it. Raised to believe …"

"Don't!" Susan cried, then visibly restrained herself. "Don't blame Grandma and Grandpa," she went on more quietly. "They are wonderful, loving people."

Myra closed her eyes. Cornelius and Eleanor were untouchable for both of her children. The perfect grandparents even though they'd shut Susan out of their lives since their son's disappearance. "All right. All

I'm trying to say is if you saw him, you'd lose this fear."

Susan held up a hand as though to stop the conversation. "I don't know. I have trouble … even thinking about it. All the confusion comes back …" She shook her head.

Myra frowned, and the table fell silent. It was a long time since she'd seen this volatile Susan, calm then explosive by turn, like a ship riding a rough sea.

"Look," Doug said finally, as they finished. "Listen to your Mom, Susan." He picked up an apple from the fruit bowl on the table. "The past won't come back if you stay focused on the present. And if he's really here, well … you concentrate on what he is now. It works."

Myra gazed at him gratefully. He should know. His alcoholic mother appeared and disappeared periodically, a different man on her arm each time.

"Speaking of which, they're bringing lumber for the new greenhouse this afternoon." He pushed back his chair.

"I'd like to see that project," she told Susan. "I'll be right back." She followed Doug outside. "How're you doing?" she asked as they went down the path.

"Okay. She's been edgy since the baby, and I guess put it to that …" He led the way toward the greenhouse.

"Motherhood does that, Doug—the first time around especially."

"Yeah. And I don't want her thinking I don't believe her—that business with her father is huge. I know." He began moving equipment out of the way to make room for the lumber.

"Did you see the Jag?" She joined him in moving planters and hoses.

"Sure, but I never met Derek. I don't know his car." He straightened and surveyed the area next to the drive that he'd cleared.

"True," Myra realized.

"This is good enough. Thanks." He turned back toward the house. "We went out for a drive because the baby was fussy. Susan was getting weepy—exhausted. We both were." He stopped to pull a hose out of the way. "And now … since she saw that car, it's like there's a volcano in there … I don't know when to expect it, is all."

"It's opened the past, I'm afraid," Myra responded. "And the timing—to have him come back just as she's adjusting to motherhood."

He nodded, but his shoulders were tense as he coiled the hose.

"But I guess you grew up with that—not knowing when things were going to blow up."

Doug turned in surprise, then smiled. "Yeah. But Susan's not like … it's not that bad." He stretched. "We're just short on sleep these days. The little fella keeps us hopping." He opened the back gate. "But thanks. I just wanted to know what you thought about it."

Myra nodded. "Let things settle down for a few days." She turned and stood staring at the herb garden that occupied the front yard.

"Well?" Susan's voice came from the path near the house. "It's a mess, isn't it?"

"No. Just needs weeding—not something a mother nursing a new baby should fret about."

Susan turned and walked back to the stoop. "Come on, let's go sit down."

Once they were seated over fresh coffee, she studied her daughter's gaunt, fine-boned face. "Have you started beating yourself up again, Susan?"

Susan slumped. "I don't know." She took a drink. "Doug says I'm a good mother, but sometimes when Billy won't stop crying, the shame comes back …" Her voice broke off. "I thought I was past all that."

Myra put a hand over hers. "New babies do that, Susan. They cry, and we feel we've failed somehow, which brings back all of the bad stuff. His crying has nothing to do with any of it. Keep reminding yourself of that."

"I suppose. Part of me knows it doesn't make sense, but it feels the same. And now I'm afraid no one's going to believe me, again. About the car. It's going to be like before."

"It won't be, Susan. You're strong enough to take control of the past now. You can do that."

Susan turned her hand over and grasped Myra's. "Thanks, Mom. I wish I was more like you."

Myra laughed. "You are more like me than you'll ever know, my dear." Like Susan, she'd discovered early that intensity upset people. In her case, it wasn't fitting—was shocking in fact—for such intensity to come from her large frame. She was supposed to be a stolid Swede. The shame of those childhood humiliations still burned. She'd become a master at concealing her emotions—releasing them only onto the drawing pad or canvas. "Which is not something I wished on you, believe me. And I'm going to go see if I can find your father, so you—we—can write the end to whole struggle and go on."

Susan gave a faint smile. "You think I can?"

"I know it."

She rose and drew Susan to her feet, enclosing her in her ample embrace. "Take care. I love you."

Then she sat in the car, wondering what to do next, though a part of her knew exactly what she must do. Find the Jag. Make it real. Derek's or not.

Chapter 9

Myra turned the car north on US 101, remembering camping trips that started this way, the van stuffed with coolers, tent, sleeping and cooking gear. Listening to Susan and Peter play "Simon Says" or sing endless verses of "Ninety-Nine Bottles of Beer on the Wall." On her left, the sea rolled by, revealed then hidden, then revealed and hidden again as she covered the ten-mile drive to El Capitan State Park. Away. Away was wonderful, still.

"Just checking it out," she told the ranger at the gatehouse, as though she didn't know the park by heart. She spent the next hour driving the curving roads past the campsites. Nothing. She stopped at a grassy area and watched a family enjoying these last days before school, remembering weekends spent here before the explosion that disintegrated all family bonds. Was it the same for Derek? Did he come here to remember?

She jerked away from the question and drove on. No Jag. Finally, she parked in the day-use lot and walked down the path to the beach, then took off her shoes to let the warmth of summer sand bleed between her toes until her limbs softened and her head lightened. The vastness of the open sea here, north of the Channel Islands, overwhelmed and returned her to her home perspective. The absurdity of a middle-aged man still driving the Jag of his teenage years. The ridiculous middle-aged woman out looking for a man whose self-indulgence had wrecked their lives. So what if he came back, for goodness sake? She was a strong woman now, a successful cartoonist with a house on the beach—almost. She'd plastered a life over the forever unresolved crime and Derek's disappearance—as had Susan. How dare he bring it all back? She had to find him and put it to rest for good.

An hour later, restored, she returned to the car, ready to make the visit she'd avoided by driving north. She regained the highway and headed back to town, past her own Goleta turnoff, past the university, to the road that would take her into the foothills above Santa Barbara. It had been easy to avoid her in-laws these past years. Their house was on a side road. One of many short shoots off the Alameda Sierra Padre as it wound up from the valley.

Would the Bennings house look as it had then, despite the trouble she'd dumped into their orderly lives? She rounded the last curve and turned into the drive. The adobe house looked just as it had thirty years ago. The scarlet bougainvillea on the trellis that framed the garage doors had wandered over to the front door, but Birds of Paradise lining the walkway still stood out against the blue of Nile lilies. She raised the knocker and let it fall.

"Myra!" Eleanor's face went blank in surprise. "Why—what—come in! Goodness, it's been so long." She stepped back, stiff with shock.

She was dressed as she always had been, managing to look stylish in a denim skirt and baggy sweater. She was thinner than Myra remembered, and her face was lined now, its perfect complexion less rosy. But her hair was the same beautiful snow-white cloud pulled into a soft bun.

"Hello, Eleanor." Myra looked out over the deck and felt tears rise, remembering Derek there, teaching Peter to sail paper airplanes from the rail. "I came to find out whether you've seen Derek."

She watched Eleanor's face close and her eyes become those of a stranger. "Why?" The word was sharp.

"Because …" She stopped, then backed away from mentioning Susan's name. "Because I thought I saw his car."

"Where? I mean—I don't understand why it matters—to you, anymore." Eleanor's voice was stiff.

The response stopped Myra cold. She could only stare. How could she have forgotten? Nothing had happened as far as the Bennings were concerned except that Susan's fantasies, which Myra refused to recognize as such, had destroyed their son's career and robbed them of their grandchild. Still the answer was wrong. If it didn't matter to Eleanor, then she must already know where he is. Her forehead throbbed. "It matters, Eleanor. And I have a right to know if he's around."

Eleanor sighed and closed the door behind them. "It's best to leave the past alone, Myra." She raised her hands and let them fall. Her face had lost its rigidity and softened to sadness. "Such a waste of lives."

She shook her head. "But you still believe her—those hysterical accusations." It was half question, half statement.

Myra stood immobile, not answering.

"Susan needs help, Myra. Surely you see that. Even as a little girl—don't you remember? She saw ghosts out on the cliffs—in the rolling fog."

"Stop, Eleanor. This is going nowhere. She and Peter made up stories together all of the time."

"Oh, yes, but they were so real to Susan, don't you see?"

Myra felt her teeth clench at the woman's patronizing tone. "Is Cornelius here?"

"What? Oh, you don't want to talk to Conny." She raised her hands in protest. "No. He's never forgiven you. Derek had such a brilliant future. You don't want to ask him."

Myra turned on her heel and left, backing out of the driveway with a roar that caused a delivery truck to come to a squealing halt.

It wasn't until she was halfway down the hill that Myra realized Eleanor had never answered her question. Was Derek around or not? She pounded her fist on the wheel in frustration. There was no point in going back. Eleanor had put up a wall around the family to keep her out. Her accusations had wrecked Derek's career—or his disappearance had. Eleanor's words came back as Myra took the ramp onto 101. "It's best to leave the past alone …" Pretend it never happened was more like it.

She felt nauseated and slammed the door on threatening memories, concentrating on the freeway ahead. Ten minutes later, she reached the last Goleta exit and turned toward the sea and the house she'd held onto through the chaos.

She dropped her keys on the table by the door and went to the kitchen, where she stared at the blinking message light on the phone. A moment later a pleasant secretary's voice reminded her that her monthly batch of cartoon strips was due. Good. Back to routine. That's what she needed. A couple of hours in the tower usually served to fill the holes in her life.

She climbed the stairs, spun around three times on her drawing stool—a ritual she'd practiced for years to clear her head—and got to work.

Matilda stood as she'd left her, gazing at Rufus's limp quills. Eustasia the gull was, as usual, smirking behind her wing. It was a state her group had returned to after every misadventure, a state her fans had come to count on.

"So what happened to you this time?" Matilda asked.

"It's these birds," Rufus complained, aiming a kick in Eustasia's direction. "So high and mighty—as though having wings makes them some kind of nobility."

"He needs some starch in his spine," Eustasia suggested. "Or a good dose of ..." She jumped as Rufus, who couldn't throw his quills, nipped at her sore wing.

"We've no time for this." Matilda put her wings on her hips. "We're late already."

"Late for what?" asked Eustasia.

"We're off to see the Queen." Matilda picked up a pile of signs.

"Couldn't possibly," Rufus protested. "Not like this."

"Sure you can," Eustasia grinned, patting the limp quills with her wing. "You add to the pathos."

In the next strip they met Alphonse limping toward them, one wing covering his rear.

Rufus guffawed in delight. "Trying to fish while sitting down, again, eh?"

Alphonse thrust his bill into the air, insulted. "Scruffy little beasts like you don't *need* knees."

Matilda sighed, grabbed a towel from a clothesline and tied it around him, diaper fashion, then handed him a sign, and they headed off the strip.

Myra signed off and pulled another blank from the pile.

Matilda stood before a pair of enormous feet in gardening clogs, her pathetic entourage behind her carrying signs protesting the queen's neglect. "Look at us," Matilda demanded. "We're hungry. Our ink is fading. We've gone limp. Look at Rufus!"

A giant hand turned them about, poked at them, making them giggle. In the next box, Matilda and Eustasia were hanging on hooks in a steaming stall labeled "Inking Station," Alphonse was sitting with his backside in a tub of antiseptic, his knees swathed in liniment-soaked rags, while Rufus was strung up upside down, his quills in a tub of starch.

"Big mouth," he muttered. "Bright idea."

85

Myra signed off again and stared at the blank squares of the next strip. Her brief spurt of inspiration spent, memory of the morning flowed into the vacuum. A muzzle nudged her hip. And Rex gave a bark to gain her attention.

"Good idea."

She changed into jeans and went to the back patio; the mesa was gold in the late afternoon sun. The dogs darted ahead then came back to her side, urging her to speed it up, but today, she was more in the past than the present. The ghosts of her small children pranced with the now dead Skittles—Susan begging to go see the butterflies. When she reached the eucalyptus grove on the ridge and gazed toward town, the questions that had plagued her for twelve years rose up. Why hadn't she left? Right then. Before he was dressed or out of bed. Before she'd had a day to let the shock sink in, or the weeks and months she'd done nothing. For the sake of the children, she'd told herself. The night she'd wakened to her daughter's screams came back with terrible clarity.

She turned away from the view, but it didn't help. Whacking the trunk of the nearest eucalyptus didn't help either. She stomped back down the path toward home, engulfed by the rage that had consumed her that morning. At Derek or at herself? She'd never bothered to sort that one out because it didn't matter. They both wore that night around their necks.

Myra shook off the memory of that endless year that followed and went to find herself some supper. She stared at the meager offerings in her refrigerator, then ordered a pizza.

When the doorbell rang a half hour later, she opened it to find Randy Larson, rather than the pizza man, on her doorstep.

"Hi." He smiled at her surprised face. "Just thought I'd stop by to check whether you've seen any more signs of him—your husband."

"Ex-husband. I divorced him. Come in." She stepped back. "No. The fire's dead—nothing else. Have a seat, why don't you? I was just going to have a beer. Will you join me, or are you on duty?"

"Just got off, and I'd love one, thanks." He reached over to stroke Rex and Lily. "You had a beagle back then, didn't you?"

"Oh, yes. For years. Skittles lived to be an old man. These are his replacements." She brought two beers and sat down. "I went up to El Capitan and found no sign of him."

The doorbell rang again, and this time it was the pizza man. She returned with the box warming her palms. "Do you have dinner plans or will you join me in a pizza? Pepperoni, olive, and mushroom."

"Great. No, no plans. Kids are grown, and the wife found a replacement." He spoke in an offhand tone, but his lean figure sagged, giving him away. Suddenly the lines around his mouth deepened.

"Really. That sounds familiar." She put the pizza down on the coffee table and went for plates. "How long ago?" she asked when she returned.

"A while. Eight years, almost. That smells great. My favorite meal."

She put a two pieces on a paper plate and handed it to him. "Bachelor food?"

He laughed. "Right." He raised his piece high to escape Rex's muzzle.

"Rex! Lily! Go lie down. Now." She pointed to the hearth rug. "So how many children do you have?" she asked when the dogs had obeyed.

"Three. A boy in the Coast Guard and two girls—both married. Two grand kiddies. They're all in the Bay Area, though. I don't see much of them."

They ate in silence for a bit.

"How's Susan doing?"

She was warmed by the concern in his voice. "All right—marginally. She thinks no one believes her, but she's okay. Motherhood is a great distraction from almost anything."

He laughed. "I guess. I wish she'd filed charges, though, so we could have at least kept looking for him. Would she now, do you think, if he does show up again? She can still do that until she's twenty-six, you know. She's not ... how old is she now, anyway?"

"Twenty-five. Twenty-six in August." Myra remembered the agony and confusion on Susan's face when she'd been urged to do so twelve years ago and cringed at the idea of bringing the subject up again. "Doubtful. She really slammed the door on that. But thanks for what you have already done," she assured him.

"I think if I'd been in your position—if it were one of my daughters—I would have killed him." He finished off the piece of pizza in his hand.

"Policemen aren't supposed to talk that way. You're supposed to be hardened, aren't you? Beyond surprise?" She served him another slice.

"Beyond surprise, maybe, but not hardened. Not when families get torn apart."

"My mother-in-law would say it's a woman's job to see that never happens." She remembered Eleanor's frozen face. "I went to see her this afternoon—she thinks it all in the past—and to be left there. I never did find out whether she's seen him."

"If I remember rightly, she insisted nothing had happened anyway, didn't she?"

"Right." Myra bit off a piece of pepperoni.

"People like that really piss me off. They protect these guys. Eight out of ten families won't report that stuff." He put his beer down. "Do you think she's protecting him now? Knows he's around?"

Myra raised her shoulders and let them fall. "A good question. Her first response when I asked her if she'd seen him was 'Why does it matter to you?' Which makes me think she does. You know, Derek had a brother who took off—long ago. He lives in Argentina and hardly ever comes back. I keep wondering whether he got into trouble, too. They rarely talk about him." Again she saw Roger's kindly face and balding head, but an unpleasant aura returned with the memory.

"Silence is wonderful, isn't it? Erases ugly truths. Well, thanks for having guts, Myra."

"Except that I don't—didn't." Myra put her plate down and wiped her mouth. "I didn't kick him out soon enough." She rose to rid herself of the weight that had descended at Susan's phone call. "Another beer?"

"No thanks. You couldn't have known he'd do that—go for his own daughter. That's ... well, not unheard of, I'm afraid, but not usual."

"Thanks, Randy. I appreciate your defense, but ... the irony is I was trying to protect the family! Hold it together." She gave a bitter laugh. "I didn't want to be the bad guy ... the accuser."

He nodded. "How's Peter? Is he on speaking terms with you, yet?"

"More or less." She reached for another piece of pizza, reluctant to elaborate.

"You should call him, you know. Ask him whether he's seen his dad."

"I suppose." She let her voice fade. She was tired and had no wish to encounter the cool distance in her son's voice—coolness that was sure to turn to hostility at the mention of his father. "How did your children take your break-up? Did they take sides?"

"For a while. I was the bad guy. If I'd let her do her own thing— hadn't yelled at her when she came in at three o'clock in the morning—

she wouldn't have left." His tone was matter of fact, holding little heat or pain. These were wounds long healed.

Quiet fell as they watched the shadows grow long as the sun sank behind the headlands to the north.

"I'd better be off," he said after a while, and stood up. "I go on duty early in the morning." He picked up his hat. "Get that boy of yours to look around. Is Derek the sort to hang about, hoping you'll take him back?"

"Good God. I hadn't thought about that. No—I don't know." She wanted to say "no" absolutely, but the memory of those months when he'd tried to show her he'd be good came back, along with the hang-dog expression he'd worn most of the time, reminding her of her rejection. He'd won Peter over—and even Susan. Memory of Peter's outrage, echoed by Eleanor filled her mind. Then Susan's "I can't believe you'd do that?" completed the chorus that often woke her in the night.

"What are you thinking?" Randy was standing very close to her.

"Just remembering—being the bad guy." She gave him a rueful smile.

He put a hand on her shoulder and gave it a squeeze. "Take care, okay?"

And he was gone, leaving the warmth of his company behind in the darkening room.

Chapter 10

The next morning, Myra called Peter and got his answering machine. As always, Peter screened his calls. She wouldn't have gotten an answer until evening when he got home anyway, and maybe it was just the habit of the next generation, but her heart always sank a little when she went through this procedure. The machine was symbolic of their relationship.

She climbed to her tower room and sat down at her desk, resigned to filling what promised to be an empty day with the necessary drudgery of bank statements, tax reports, and marketing. At noon, she swung her chair away from the desk, put on her beach shoes, whistled to the dogs, and took off across the mesa, stretching her legs to counteract the morning's inactivity. At the edge of the cliffs, she turned to look back at the house. She'd never thought of it as exposed, but this morning its windows seemed to invite a stranger's gaze. Remembering Randy's advice, she scanned the open country for unusual visitors. The mesa had a peculiar talent for looking alive and empty at the same time. Bicyclists, runners, dog walkers, kite flyers, and model airplane pilots flowed through without passing each other within greeting distance or crowding the coyotes and skunks, rodents and deer, who were its native inhabitants. If occasionally she came across the campsite of some passing biker or homeless person, she'd treated it as expected, scarcely giving it more thought than a distant figure crossing the grass. How easy it would be to blend into this scene.

Her tour turned up a lost neckerchief, two beer cans, and a T-shirt, all bleached by the summer sun. The dogs fared a little better, scaring up two of the mesa's ample supply of rats and mice and rousing a night heron from his perch. When they descended to the beach, there were more signs of human habitation—clothing, shoes, plastic jugs, Styrofoam floats washed in by the tide. A sea lion's head appeared just beyond the rolling breakers and accompanied them for a while, barking at the dogs, then disappearing when they lunged into the water after it. A practiced tease.

When they were about to climb up to the cliff again, a pod of dolphins appeared. Myra collared the dogs and watched the black fins circle. Dolphins playing in open water put one into the eternal stretch of time that absorbed all else, reducing problems to bubbles popping along the beach. The presence of dolphins blessed the day.

When they disappeared, she quit her search for oddities and climbed the cliff path at peace with the mesa once again. The fire above the old seawall showed no signs of recent use. The house no longer looked exposed. She'd spend the rest of the afternoon repotting plants and trimming the exuberant bougainvillea that covered the lattice over the patio.

When Peter returned her call at six, she came back to reality with difficulty.

"Hello, Mom. What's up?" Peter's voice was friendly enough, casually interested. Only she would notice any lack of connection.

"Peter. Thanks for calling. I just wanted to ask—have you seen your dad?" She hadn't meant to sound so abrupt, but could think of no chatty way of putting it.

"Dad? Why? I mean, why would I?" There was no doubting the edge to his voice.

"Because Susan saw his Jag at El Capitan, and I was wondering if he was back."

"Oh, for … Mom, that's just Susan." Over the years, his attitude toward his sister had shifted from anger to a tolerance tinged with impatience. Now, his exasperation was tinged with warning.

"Don't patronize us, Peter," she snapped. This was not a subject they could bring up without conflict, so they'd learned to avoid it. His "wiser than you girls" tone always set her teeth on edge.

"I'm not—or I don't mean to, but Susan's imagination …" He cut himself off.

Broke up the family, ruined his father's career, and—worst of all for Peter—cost him his father, she said silently, finishing his thought.

"She never confused reality with fiction. You know that."

"All right, but dragging it all up again …" There was no doubting his anger now.

"I know, but I'm trying to find out whether she's mistaken—not crazy."

"Okay. Sorry if I was short. It's just …"

"I know," she conceded. "Let it go. If you'll come help me move planters this weekend, I'll feed you enchiladas. If you don't have other plans, that is," she added. Peter's social life, the little she knew of it, was as active as it had been in high school. His ease in making friends had been his salvation during his college years when he had refused to come home at all, and still felt like a barricade between them.

There was a pause as he considered the peace offering. "All right. Tomorrow?"

Was tomorrow Saturday? "Sure. Anytime after nine."

"Okay. See you then." He sounded recovered. His tone even had a tinge of the affectionate teasing that had marked his relationship with her before it all blew apart. But talking to him never failed to bring back the memory of his fury that day she told him she'd kicked his father out of the house.

The refrigerator came on beside her; the wind chimes on the patio sent faint tones across the living room, a beam creaked. She felt as though she'd been lost in time and was reentering the world where she'd left it twelve years ago.

***

Peter arrived with his pick-up truck the next morning, just after Myra returned from the farmer's market. He never knew what a jolt he gave her every time he appeared. He was a carbon copy of his father when she'd met him.

"You caught me off guard, Mom. Threw me back." He was still on edge, she could tell, but contrite.

"I understand," Myra assured him. "None of us wants to go back, believe me. But …" She shrugged, "life happens." Despite the rift between them, they both took care, in recent years, to stay shy of another break. "Ready to move planters?"

"Right." He pulled a sweatshirt and work gloves out of the cab. "What do you want done?"

"There are a couple of new boxes in the garage to replace these." She pointed to two long redwood containers that framed the front entrance.

"We'll need to empty those. I'll get the wheelbarrow." She went around back to the shed to find gloves and shovels, loaded them into the barrow, then wheeled it around the house.

Peter took a shovel from her, and they spent the next two hours moving dirt. Once the new boxes were in place, he helped plant them with fresh evergreens. His conversation, limited as it was to the disposal and placement of boxes, soil and plants, was affable but without intimacy. When he left to haul the rotted boxes to the dump, she retired to the kitchen to make the promised enchiladas. As she worked, she tried to imagine a future without barriers.

"How are you doing?" Peter came into the kitchen. "I'm starving."

"Take these …" Myra handed him the plates and silver, "and get out some beer. Let's eat on the patio." She pulled salsa out of the refrigerator. Once upon a time she'd prided herself in making everything from scratch—a determination that had faded away during her years alone. "I'll bring the food in a couple of minutes."

When she arrived on the patio, Peter was leaning back in a lawn chair, watching a group of kite flyers out on the mesa. His face was a boy's again, without the mask he presented to her.

"A great place to grow up," she said softly, putting the food on the table.

"I really miss it."

Myra's heart lurched. He hadn't known, when he went off to college, that he'd never return to this house. "I know. But it's always here for you, Peter."

He made a noise of assent. "Too damned busy." He turned his attention to the steaming food.

As she gazed at her son's face, a movement in eucalyptus on the distant ridge caught her attention. She watched, expecting a person or dog to emerge into the open. It was the weekend; the place was full of cyclists, hikers and pets. Nothing moved, now, and she returned her attention to lunch and her son. "What's the latest?"

"Couple of embezzlements and a bunch of civil cases," he muttered between bites. "It never stops."

He sounded weary. Myra wondered when he would burn out, when his childhood fascination with sea life would resurface. She'd been astounded and dismayed when he switched from science to law, joining the current trend, the lemmings marching to the sea. Science reminded him of his father, she'd guessed, though she hadn't dared suggest it. But she never heard the fascination for law that he'd had for science, and he turned to an ever-changing series of sports—and women—for diversion. "And what are you doing for fun?"

"Mountain biking." He looked at his watch. "There's a bunch going out around three." He continued to inhale his enchilada.

Again, she spied movement in the trees. The afternoon wind hadn't yet come up.

"What do you see?" Peter turning his head toward the ridge.

"I don't know. Movement." Myra took a breath and let it out in exasperation. She had no patience with the Nervous Nellie she was becoming, and she resented her change in attitude toward the open country around her. This was her refuge, her balm. She wasn't going to become paranoid about every motion in the distance.

"Probably a coyote," Peter mumbled, his mouth full. "But I'll check it out."

"In the middle of the day? I don't think so," Myra retorted, knowing full well that her son was just making fun of her vigilance. "But don't bother. Whatever it was will be gone by the time you get there—particularly since who or whatever it was has a full view of anyone approaching."

Peter studied the trees, then turned back. "Let's walk off that lunch. Do we have any more boxes to move?"

"No, we're done. And thanks. A walk would be great."

Together they carried their dishes inside and took off toward the kite-flyers. The dogs leapt for meadowlarks as they went.

Once they reached the path that went along the top of the cliff, Peter paused to explore every enclave made by the California oaks that clustered along the path.

"That was your favorite hideout," she remarked the first time.

"Yeah." Peter withdrew too quickly and went on, as though hastening away from the past.

"And that's where you insisted on sliding down to the beach." She pointed, unwilling to let the subject go so easily. "I think you made a couple of girlfriends do the same."

Peter laughed at the memory in spite of himself. "Bet I still could."

"Peter! You aren't seven. You'll tear up the cliff face or yourself, or both." She turned at the proper path, aching for her son, torn between reliving and running from his childhood in this place. She heard him on the path behind her, talking to the dogs.

"Low tide!" Peter exclaimed when they reached the bottom. There was no masking his delight as he surveyed the families that dotted the beach, exploring the tide pools.

Breathing the keen-edged smell of kelp and salt water, they spent the next hour among anemones, limpets, and empty sea-urchin shells. Peter spied an infant octopus and Myra simply watched the transformation as the lawyer disappeared and the boy returned. She dared say nothing for fear of reminding him she was there.

Finally, Peter rose up and looked at his watch. "Need to go."

"Are you sure?"

"Yeah. I have a new girl I'm meeting." He worked his way back over the kelp-coated rocks to shore.

Their skin tingling with salt and sun, they climbed the cliff path. "She's a mountain biker?" Myra asked.

"So she says." He headed across the meadow without amplifying.

Myra frowned at the lack of enthusiasm in his voice. Was he tiring of the succession of women in his life? She'd wondered more than once over the years why he never found the right one, and whether he was even looking for that one and only.

They reached the house and kicked off their wet shoes.

"You have time for strawberries, don't you?"

He smiled. "Yeah. I'll take time for that. He sank into a chaise lounge.

Myra turned the hose on their salt-crusted feet, legs, and hands, then put the hose away and headed for the house, reveling in an afternoon spent in the past—the good past.

She was on her way out with the berries before she noticed that her desk was open, its contents scattered across the surface and littering the floor. Her hands went cold as she scanned the room. The door of the cupboard to the left of the fireplace—the one that stuck—was ajar. She put the tray down and crossed the room, yanking it open. Its contents were tumbled.

She raced upstairs to her studio. The contents of the desk in her studio had been turned out. She'd locked the doors, hadn't she? She always

95

did out of habit, before she walked away from the house. Yes, she'd unlocked the patio door on the way in.

"Mom?" Peter's voice came from below.

She turned and went back down the stairs. "Someone's been here." She checked the front door. It was locked.

"What?"

"Someone's been in the house," she repeated impatiently, going to the patio door. It showed no signs of being forced. "Every desk has been ransacked."

Peter frowned and looked around the room. "Was anything taken? Your computer, stereo, jewelry? Stuff like that?"

"Nothing's been touched except the desks. And the doors were locked. Unless you think it was Susan, your father's the only other person with a key."

"You mean ... aw, come on, Mom. Don't go balmy on me." He crossed the room to check the front door again. "You probably just didn't lock it."

"Whether I locked it or not doesn't change the fact that someone's been here looking for something."

"No, but it doesn't mean—you've just let Susan's imagination ..."

"Don't start."

He looked at her for a long time, but decided not to push his luck. "Okay. Let's have strawberries. Then I'll help you look around for what's missing."

She should call Randy, not eat strawberries, but she let it go in favor of accepting her son's concession.

They ate without further talk, the break-in having wiped all topics from their minds. When they were done, Peter excused himself and went inside.

Disturbed by something in his attitude, Myra followed a minute later and found him closing his cell phone.

"Had to check on a case," he muttered.

"Peter. Tell me you weren't calling your father."

"What?"

Peter had never been able to lie to her no matter how he tried.

"To see if he's home," she continued. "Was he?"

"No." Her son let out his breath and slapped his hands to his sides.

"Which doesn't mean a damned thing."

"But you have a phone number. You know where he is."

"I do." He regained his poise and looked her directly in the eye. "He *is* my father."

"Tell me, Peter."

"No." He turned away. "You're going to start it all up again."

"He's breaking into my house. I have a right to know."

Peter looked at her. "You don't know it was him." His eyes were dark with determination. "He's made a new life. He has a job teaching. You can't—tear everything apart again!"

"Believe me, Peter, there's nothing I want to do less. I've made a new life, too—as has Susan. But this …" she waved at the desk. "I need to know. That's all."

"I'll ask him."

She sighed. "Peter that won't do. I have to talk to him."

"You'll charge him."

She opened her mouth and closed it again. "That thought never entered my mind." She spoke the truth, and they stared at each other in silence for a full minute. "Look," she said finally. "I suspect that's up to Susan, at this stage of the game, not me. I only want to know whether he's breaking into my house and why."

He stood frowning at his cell phone without answering.

"Peter, this is a crime. If you'd rather, I'll call Deputy Larson and have him ask you for it."

In his eyes, as he raised them, she saw the afternoon die and betrayal return. Without a word, he pulled a notepad from beside the telephone and jotted an address.

"The phone number too, please."

He glanced up and then down again. When he finished writing the number, he flicked the paper to the middle of the table, turned and left. The sound of his truck roaring out of the drive brought back the day his father had done the same.

Chapter 11

Myra watched Peter drive off, then returned to the house and stood looking down at Derek's address. So Peter had been in contact with his father all along. She felt betrayed, too, but knew that wasn't fair. As he said, the man was his father. Derek had shown him the mysteries of the sea, the creatures hidden beneath the chaparral of the mountainsides, flown kites above the mesa. That such a man had molested Susan was beyond possibility, much less acceptance.

And if Peter had been in contact, so had the senior Bennings, she was sure. The family had simply sealed off the place where she'd been—she and Susan—and gone on. The idea brought a rough laugh to her lips and sat her down in the nearest chair, which happened to be in front of the disheveled desk. She'd known this utter aloneness after she'd kicked Derek out and Peter had slammed the phone down. She'd known the silence, but never had she felt that a huge and ugly joke was being played on her. Which probably wasn't fair, either. Derek was the Bennings' son. She was, after all, the in-law, no matter how successfully she'd fooled herself that she'd become a member of the family. She laid her head back in the chair and closed her eyes.

Come on, Myra, snap out of it. You're not a baby cast out of the nest. Leave that act to the Varmints. She sat up and stared at the mess in front of her, the rumblings of rage mounting. Bad enough to be shunned, this tearing apart of her privacy … Derek. It had to be.

But what was he looking for?

She went to the phone, then halted. Peter was right; there were no charges against Derek. Even if there had been, Susan was unlikely to charge him after all this time. What justification then, did she have for calling Randy? She'd been robbed. That's what. And Randy would come. That was enough.

He wasn't on duty. She sat down, deflated once again. She had his home number. He'd left it for her on a slip of paper she'd found on her counter the night she'd fed him pizza. She was calling as a friend anyway, wasn't she? She rose and took his card from the wall and turned it over. Yes, she'd jotted it there. She dialed.

He answered on the fourth ring. "Hello, Randy here." His voice was foggy.

"This is Myra. Did I wake you?"

"Mmm. Guess so. Napping in the sun. What's going on?"

"Derek's been here." She went on to tell him of her rifled desks. "And what's more, Peter has been in contact with him. He gave me Derek's address. He's in Pismo Beach …"

"Whoa! Let me catch up. Look. I'll come over."

Forty minutes later, Randy was circling her living room, examining it for other evidence of disturbance and looking every bit the policeman. "What was he looking for, do you think … if it was him? And I suspect you're right about that. The place doesn't show any other signs of burglary."

"I don't know." Then she froze. "Susan's address?"

He frowned. "Why would he have to go through all your stuff for that? Don't you have an address book? I assume Susan's in there."

Myra nodded. She pointed to it, lying on top of the mess. "Dear God, he's got it." She quelled the panic in her voice. "I'd better call her." She headed for the phone.

"Wait …" He put a hand on her arm. "Let's think this through." The policeman vanished; his voice was that of a friend again.

Myra sank into a chair.

"Do you have any reason to think he's … would do her harm?"

The change of tone and language mid-sentence almost made her smile. "No. But seeing his car brought it all back. Seeing him without any forewarning would be a real shock."

"Right. So I'd tell her husband, not her. Just tell him to be on the lookout."

Myra let out her breath. She wished Randy would send his men out to guard her daughter, but with no charges against him, Randy couldn't, she knew. "What the devil does he want with her?"

"Well—she's his daughter, after all. Maybe he just wants to see her."

"I suppose. But if he found the address book lying there, why did he go through the rest of my stuff?"

"Why, indeed? Money? Maybe he's broke."

"Peter says he's teaching at a community college."

"Full time? Most community college teachers are part-timers—they don't earn peanuts."

"True. But I don't keep money in the house, anyway. He knows that."

"Papers, then. Birth certificates, insurance policies—a will? Did you make a new will after he left?"

"I did. He doesn't know that, of course. Maybe divorce papers? He was never served because they couldn't find him. In the end, I divorced him by public notice."

"Ah. So if he didn't see the notice, he might not even know?"

"Peter would have told him."

"Ah. Well, I guess we need to go have a talk with him."

Myra gave a start. He was a policeman again. His shifts were disconcerting, but there was no mistaking his meaning. She looked down at the piece of paper on the counter. "That's the next thing to do, isn't it? After I call Doug." The discussion of concrete possibilities had calmed her. Why had she been so rattled, anyway? Because the lurking presence on the mesa and the break-in had unnerved her? Furious as she had been and still was at Derek, she'd never feared him. Even knowing what he'd done to Susan—it had disgusted and repelled her—horrified her. Fear just wasn't part of the mix.

She went to the phone, trying to think of what to say if Susan picked it up. But she didn't. Doug did. A piece of luck.

"Susan's out in the kennels," he told her.

"Good. Listen. Susan was right. Derek is around."

"Really? How do you know?"

"Because someone came into my house this afternoon while I was at the beach and went through all of my papers."

"And you think it was him?"

"I know it. Who else would know every desk and drawer where I keep such things? And nothing else was disturbed. Nothing taken. Peter was here. It turns out he knows where his father is."

Doug made a sound she couldn't read.

"I know now, too. He's in Pismo Beach, and I'm going to talk to him and find out what he's up to. I just want you to keep an eye out in case I don't find him."

"Sure. You think he'd come here? Does he know where we are?" His voice acquired an edge, and Myra realized that to Doug, Derek was a specter without substance.

"Probably. My address book was lying on my desk."

"Well, I hope you do find him up there. Maybe if he becomes real, it will be good for Susan as you said—settle the past, somehow." His voice had quieted again, back to the calming presence his life as eldest child of alcoholic parents had taught him.

"That would be great. But don't tell Susan about the break-in, okay?"

He laughed. "Not to worry. We're off to a dog-training session when she comes in, anyway. So we won't be home."

"Good. Susan says Stacy's doing really well." Myra looked up and watched Randy wander out to the patio.

"He's a whiz. We aren't going to have him much longer."

"Well, have fun," she said in closing.

"Good luck. And keep me posted."

"Will do." She hung up and stood for a moment appreciating Doug's restorative powers. Susan had found a jewel, no question about it.

Randy was on the patio admiring a row of shells left to dry on the low wall. Had she really been beachcombing with her son an hour ago? "The daily catch—Peter and I were out earlier," she said, coming up.

"A good one," he said. "I was down there myself earlier. I collect these." He picked up a turban and admired it.

"Take it," she said. "I have cartloads."

"Peter was here, you said."

She nodded. "He hadn't been here in a long time—still avoids me, ordinarily. But today ... it was sort of like old times, until ..." She cut herself off as tears threatened.

"Ready to go?" His look was gentle. He missed nothing.

"Ready." She looked at her watch. "We can make it before dark, I guess." As she walked down the front walk, she eyed the Sheriff's car at the curb. "My car," she declared.

As they drove north along the coast, the reality of what she was about to do hit her. She was going to have to speak to this man who still had the power, she was sure, to twist her guts and blur her mind. "Have your kids forgiven you and your ex? For splitting up the family?" she asked to get her mind off the coming encounter.

"More or less. You can't put it together again, which is what they really want. It was hardest on my boy; he was the youngest—only fourteen at the time. I think that's why he went into the Coast Guard—to get away from the mess."

Myra looked at him and saw his jaw tighten. He was still angry, behind the sadness of his tone. "It's always a mess, isn't it?" She gazed at the car ahead of them, its top rack loaded with camping gear. Its blinker went on, signaling for the exit at El Capitan State Park. Some family living the days of contentment. "Did your kids take sides?"

His shoulders went up, then down. "At first. The girls sided with their mom, but she's married twice since then—and they're married themselves—so they've changed their tune a bit." He smiled a little, "Jeannie, the oldest, said last year—out of nowhere—'Mom's never satisfied, is she?'" He broke off to pass a truck.

"True?"

He pulled back into the lane. "Seems like. She wants her men to be heroes. I was, once—I was a dashing young firefighter when I met her." He smiled ruefully.

Myra gazed through the windshield, remembering the naive girl from Minnesota standing spellbound beside her tall handsome hero, his lovely academic family welcoming her, the fairytale city spread below.

"Then I became a deputy—that was okay for a while, but the novelty wore off. She fell for a Navy Captain.

"She likes uniforms."

"Liked. She divorced the last one—a forest ranger—last year and is rapidly becoming a drunk." He ripped off the sentence as though he was shredding paper.

"Sounds like she doesn't manage disillusionment too well. I think I could have started drinking the day I discovered that all of those sweet voices on the telephone weren't just devoted grad students."

He glanced at her, then back to the road. "What did you do instead?"

"Became a cartoonist."

He laughed. "That's a new one. What do you draw?"

"A strip called the Rabbleville Varmints. Full of misshapen, time-worn animals who perpetually douse themselves with trouble."

"I've seen it! You draw that?" His faced lit up. "I'll be damned. I love that strip."

"Beats drinking, anyway. And earns me a decent living." She found herself tingling from his praise.

"So that's you," he mused, clearly fitting her with the caustic humor of her motley group. "What did you do before?"

"Real art. Watercolors and prints—that sort of thing. It doesn't lend itself to vengeance."

He looked at her, then shook his head. "Not vengeance. Something else."

"Self-derision?" She'd never stopped to analyze her motives.

"Maybe. Just shrinking us all down to size, I guess—making us laugh at ourselves."

"Mm. True. Well, I guess I needed some shrinking." Myra looked down her length.

"What? Why?" He sounded genuinely surprised. Then grinned. "I always liked substantial women."

"Really. You're a minority. Is your ex … 'substantial'?"

"No. Well, not tall but round. I guess, according to the girls, she's gotten really heavy now. Dousing herself with trouble, like your characters."

Myra smiled in sympathy with the woman.

"Have you ever gone back to the art?"

She gazed at the sea, which was close to the road at this point. "From time to time. I was about to get back to it when this came up. Painting takes a certain state of mind—a calmness. At the moment, I need the strip—for more than the income, that is. It's like a safety valve."

He nodded. "I fish. Clears out all the garbage."

"It does, for sure. We sailed for years. Derek took over keeping his parents boat in working order. The Serendipity." Her voice faded as she remembered the wind in her hair, the prow slicing the water of the Channel.

"What happened to it?"

"Mm?" She came back to the present. "Oh. I gave it back to his parents. For all I know it's still sailing. I used to watch for it; then I decided that wasn't healthy."

"I'll take you out in the Lucky LuLu. She's a fishing boat. Twenty years old, but a war horse."

"I'd really love that," Myra burst without giving herself time to think. "I miss boating—particularly at this time of day." The islands stood out darkly against the reddish glow of the late-afternoon sun.

They drove on along the sea without talk, then made the turn at Gaviota to head inland through the cut in the hills. The tang of the sea was replaced by the smell of sun-dried grass. Myra breathed deeply. "I love this country. Did you grow up around here?"

"Ojai, when I was little, then Carpinteria. My father actually was a carpenter, which let me in for a certain amount of joshing."

"Good little towns to grow up in, though." She'd always felt comfortable in the unpretentious seaside village south of Santa Barbara. "I lobbied to move there, once. Derek wanted to move to Santa Barbara, near his parents."

"What's the matter with where you are?"

"That's what we asked ourselves, finally, and remodeled the house. It was a tougher decision for Derek than for me. He wanted a Santa Barbara address, but finally decided he loved the shore more."

"Mm. You won't find that stretch of wild beach in Santa Barbara."

"I almost left it, after I kicked him out, but then I decided it was my salvation—the beach, the Varmints, and the dogs make everything okay." She leaned back and watched the hills pass, letting the warm sun work its magic.

In Santa Maria they stopped for gas, and Myra went to wash her face. "Shape up, lady. You can't blow this," she told the face in the mirror, then took a brush from her purse and flattened her dark blonde frizz. Wavy flying hair had come into fashion long after her youth and appalled her.

Randy was still filling the tank when she returned. "Your soda's in the car," he told her.

When they regained the freeway, she could see nothing but the straight flat road up the valley—unstoppable progress toward their destination.

"What's wrong?" Randy asked after a while.

"I'm trying to think what I'm going to say to him. What exactly I'm trying to accomplish by this."

"Well, what he was doing in your house, for one thing."

"Indeed. Thanks." He'd jogged her mind out of stasis. "And what he wants in general."

"And whether he's still driving that black Jag," he added as the road turned toward the ocean again. He glanced at her. "You're really a very gutsy lady, you know. You'll be okay."

"Right. Just fine."

"You still love the guy?" He was watching her as much as the traffic.

"What? How could I? After what he's done."

"Stranger things have happened, believe me. It's a hard switch to turn off, for some people." His face had sagged.

So he was one of those people. Was that why she'd put up with Derek's infidelities for so long? "I don't remember being anything but furious." But her answer was only half true. She'd been hurt by his infidelity, but she'd never known the depth of anger she'd felt when he molested Susan.

"You never asked yourself whether you still love him?"

"No. Only whether he still loved me. That's ridiculous, isn't it?" She folded her arms around her chest to quiet the shiver of apprehension. Surely, she didn't. Surely.

The exit for Pismo Beach came into view and she closed her eyes as the car slowed on the exit ramp.

Chapter 12

It was twilight when they pulled to the curb in front of a row of weather-beaten bungalows. The sea shanties lining the street differed from each other only in their shape, color, and yard decorations. Pismo Beach, unlike the coastal towns of Santa Barbara County, wasn't protected by the Channel Islands, and their faces paid the toll of the open sea.

"I guess that's it." Randy pointed down the street to a yellow clapboard cottage beyond a yard littered with driftwood, shells, and dried starfish. The dusty black Jag sat in front.

Myra stared at the house. Beside her, Randy turned the engine off and opened the door. She laid a hand on his arm. "Wait."

He turned, a question in his eyes.

"I have to do this alone."

"No, no." His tone was definite.

"It has to be between the two of us, Randy, and he's not dangerous. Really." As she spoke, the door of the bungalow opened, and a young girl appeared. Even as Myra stiffened, the girl was joined by another and another. A boy appeared. Then Derek came out onto the porch, shaking their hands and bidding them farewell. Myra's breath went out with a whistle as she viewed this reincarnation of the past. "A seminar." Derek looked no different at this distance. Tall, dark, his rugged face relaxed in an easy grin. Was that a beard?

"Seminar?" Randy's tone was bewildered. "At a community college? I thought seminars were for graduate students."

"Well, a class, then. He loved having students gather at home. They'd go tramping down to the beach—not that the department didn't have its own beach on campus, mind you." She cut short her spitefulness. "Sorry. I'm not being fair. He hated the institutional classroom setting, and I never minded, really. Lots of professors did it. We were children of the Sixties—break down boundaries, be friends with your students ..." She broke off again as she registered Randy's skeptical gaze. "All right, so he loved entertaining young girls at home. Boys were fine, too. He was one of them."

"Those look very young."

"Undergrads. Which makes sense. As you said, he's teaching at a community college." The last of the students left the porch and Derek disappeared inside. The door closed.

Myra sat back and recollected herself, then touched his arm again. "I appreciate your concern, but I have to go alone. Okay?"

His jaw clamped.

"I have my cell phone. I'll call if he gets too angry."

"Okay, go ahead, but don't take chances."

"Thanks." She got out of the car and headed down the sidewalk, pushed open the rickety gate and went up the gray wooden steps to the porch.

He opened the door quickly, probably assuming she was a student who had forgotten something. His eager welcome died on his lips and his dark eyes went still. "Myra." His lips barely moved.

"Hello, Derek." It was almost a relief to utter the words, as though they'd been ready-formed and waiting all of the missing years.

He gave a slight nod, but stood immobile in the doorway, his hand frozen to the knob.

She foundered for a moment, searching a way to move the scene forward. "May I come in?"

He stepped back without a word.

She went past him into a small living room. Beyond it, a large deck, far newer than the house, faced the sea. The room itself, though smaller than the one in their Goleta house, was so similar, it made Myra blink. The same sea urchin lamps, books, the leather sling chairs. The mixture of sea air and leather was so familiar it made her head whirl. The weather-beaten front had given no clue to the comfortable, well-established interior.

"How did you find me?"

A lamp went on behind her, and his voice, full of gravel—some combination of anger and surprise she couldn't read—spun her around. He had changed. New lines had appeared around his mouth, and he *had* grown a scraggly beard. The whole effect was of faded youth—or aging playboy. "Peter." She saw him frown. "Not voluntarily. I walked in while he was phoning you. I confronted him. In fact, I gave him a choice—your address or the police."

He ran a hand through his dark hair, dull except for silver streaks, and walked to a chair. "So." He sat down and studied the floor. When he raised his head, his face looked bleak, and the lamplight accentuated the grooves beside his mouth. He was going to say no more, or he had no more to say. His face had none of the life she'd watched from the car as he bid farewell to the young students.

"So, what were you doing in my house today?" For the first time in twelve years, it felt strange to Myra—maybe even insulting—to call it her house instead of theirs, and his eyes kindled at the word.

He opened his mouth, then shut it and instead rose and walked across the room to close the doors to the deck, shutting out the chilly evening breeze off the ocean. Then he drew the blinds against the darkening glass, which reflected the pair of them. When he turned, he put his hands into his pockets. "I was looking for my birth certificate and the divorce papers. Peter said you divorced me."

"Why didn't you just call me?"

"I didn't intend you should know where I am. Last time I saw you, you were about to charge me with incest." He disappeared around a corner into what looked like the kitchen.

She followed. "So you were sneaking around up there on the ridge watching me?" For the first time, she noticed how faded his shirt was, how run-over the heels of his boat shoes. One lace had been broken and tied. He'd often worn such clothes if they were working on the boat or beachcombing, but he always put on chinos and a sport shirt for class. My God, he could be taken for one of the homeless men who occasionally found a place to sleep on the mesa.

"Coffee?"

She shook her head.

"All right. The answer is yes." He walked past her, back to his chair.

This time she sat down opposite. "That's—creepy, Derek."

He gave a sardonic smile. "Well—I've been reduced to a creep, haven't I?"

The accusation in his tone was unmistakable. She swallowed and changed course. "So why did you need the divorce papers?"

"To prove who I am." His voice was more tired than harsh. "I had to change my name, since I'd become a wanted man …" He stopped in a visible effort to control his anger. "I'm Donald Baldwin to everyone up here," he finished in a quieter tone.

She waited for him to go on, but apparently he'd said all he intended.

"Donald Baldwin." The name bore no relation to the man in front of her. "And why …? Are you going to change it back?"

"No. Dad's lawyer asked for proof that Donald Baldwin is Derek Benning—his son. He and Mom are revising their wills. That's all." He leaned back, his face lost in the shadows of the room.

"So Eleanor and Cornelius have known where you were all along." Well, she'd suspected as much.

"No. I disappeared for five years. South America, if you want to know. I worked crew on freighters, but my back gave out. I was bumming around the docks looking for work and hanging around the marina. But I still browsed through academic job postings—habit I guess—and saw a job notice for the college. I decided it was safe enough to come back if I changed my name." His mouth twisted. "Fred Schneider had kept the Jag for me, so I had wheels."

Myra stared at him, taking in the world he described, trying to imagine being knocked clear out of one's life. Becoming another person on another continent. "Susan never filed charges, you know," she muttered it into the silence without understanding why the situation required it. It simply did.

"That I found out after I came back." He got up and went to stand at the front window where he looked out into the shabby street. "But it wouldn't have mattered. I'd be done for as soon as the university found out I was under suspicion—which they would have." He turned. "I'd just published a book, remember? I was all over the college paper, and the town relishes a good scandal at the university."

"Stop." She leapt to her feet. "I hear you loud and clear, Derek. You're saying I'm responsible for all of this. Because I kicked you out." She took a calming breath. "Forget it. Just—forget it."

"I did not molest our daughter, Myra." The words carried a flat certainty. He'd stepped forward, and his face was clear in the lamplight. There was no tension in it, no guarded mask.

His words took the air out of her. "Why should I believe that?"

He raised his hands, looked at them, then put them in his pockets. "Maybe you shouldn't, given the rest of my behavior. I acknowledge that. So there is nothing—was nothing—I could say or do but disappear."

"You're really saying you didn't touch her?"

"No. Didn't molest her. It was exactly as I told you. She was sleeping. I reached down to give her a hug … she looked so sweet … and she woke up screaming. End of story."

They gazed at each other across the empty space, dead in the water, in a place Myra realized they could never move from. The words, "she looked so beautiful" came back from the past. The same? No. Not. "And that's all you wanted. Your birth certificate and the divorce papers?"

He spread his hands.

"All right. I'll send them to you." She headed for the door.

"I'd like to see Susan."

The words, spoken with quiet force, stopped her. "Susan."

"I'd like to explain to her—or try—now that she's an adult. I'd like you to give me that chance."

She'd wished for that, two days ago; today it felt very different. "She saw the Jag at El Capitan a couple of days ago, Derek, and she's been thrown back … You're threatening to undo it all. Believe me, you can do nothing but hurt her further."

"I don't want to do that." His tone was genuine.

"Don't, then. Okay? Give me your word."

He lowered his head for a long moment, then raised it. "For now, I guess. If that's the way you want it."

She believed him without understanding why she should. Because he didn't lie? Hadn't lied about his affairs when she confronted him? If concealment wasn't lying, that is. Was that all of the protection she was offering Susan? Trust? In Derek? Ridiculous. He could get Susan's address from his parents, couldn't he? Or Peter? Could have done that long ago. Or he could have taken it while he was ransacking her house. But he hadn't gone to see her. Maybe the Bennings had refused to give him her address? Peter, too? No, he could have charmed it out of them. Was he asking her permission, then? The situation was oddly familiar, and she only wanted to end it. "Goodbye, Derek." She headed for the door again.

He rose and handed her a card. "Here's my phone number in case you change your mind."

She looked down at the card in her hand. "Donald Baldwin, Lecturer," and the name of a community college she didn't recognize.

"It was good to see you." He sounded as surprised by the words as she was.

She turned and looked at him one last time, unable to read the confusion of emotions in his eyes.

She closed the door behind her, then leaned against it. An engine started up. She descended the steps. When she reached the car, she collapsed into the passenger seat, trusting that Randy couldn't read her face, for she had no idea what it said.

"Well?"

"Go, please. I'm sure he's watching." She didn't turn her head as Randy pulled from the curb and didn't say anything until they were safely on the freeway. She had no idea what kept her silent, except she needed to put space between herself and the scene she'd left. She'd been back in her marriage. They both had been. Fused. And it felt like a trap. She watched the jutting rocks of Morro Bay pass, silhouetted against the last of the light.

"Tell me what happened, Myra." Randy's voice was quiet, as though he understood.

"He wanted his birth certificate and the divorce papers. To prove who he really is. He goes by the name Donald Baldwin here. His father's lawyer is drawing up—or revising—his parents' wills. He needs proof."

"I'm not sure I understand what all of that means."

"It means he's been in contact with his parents all along. And with Peter. That's what it means." She struggled to take hold of the important pieces before they floated away. "Not all along, he says. He went to South America, worked on freighters, then saw this job and came back. But for seven years, he's been back, really—having a regular family life with his parents and Peter—while I was living on some other planet. Susan and Doug and I—as though there's some vacuum between that no one could enter." She fell silent, letting this revised sense of her condition become solid.

"So far so good," Randy said, heading south toward Santa Maria. "But it doesn't tell me why you're acting as though you've seen a ghost."

"Because I have. The ghost of a marriage."

He put a hand on hers. "They do stay around, don't they? Waiting for you to walk back through them, come out the other side and wonder what hit you."

She laughed. "That's it, exactly. The strangest part is … he asked me if he could see Susan."

"What did you say?"

"I said no. But he was asking my permission, don't you see? He could have gotten her address anytime. If he wants to see her, why didn't he?"

Randy frowned in thought as the night gathered around them. "Because you can still charge him with incest."

"Ah. If he knows that … knows the law. And if I give him permission, I'm saying I won't?"

"Maybe." Randy frowned into the windshield. "You'd be more likely to if he snuck around behind your back, wouldn't you?"

"For sure. You're right. He wanted me to say it's safe."

"Will you charge him? Now?"

Myra turned her head away and gazed out the windshield, amazed that she hadn't asked herself that question. "He says he didn't molest her."

Randy swerved onto a Santa Maria exit and left the freeway. "We need food. And you need to make some sense of this. McDonald's okay? I'm not in a state of mind to look around for something interesting."

"Fine."

They ordered and sat in a booth with their paper packages. "Now," Randy said. "I can concentrate. Let me tell you what I think I heard you say." He unwrapped his burger and took a bite, followed by a sip of root beer, managing it with the expertise of one who eats like this often. "Forget the stuff about the papers. I guess I understand it, and it doesn't have much to do with the problem of Susan, that I can see." He took another bite and another drink. "Okay. He wants to see Susan."

"Right." She nodded.

"But he wants your permission first. So you won't—can't—charge him."

"You're sounding like a cop."

He let his breath out. "I am a cop. I try to unsnarl things I don't understand."

Myra frowned. "Because she's my daughter, and if I say he can see her, it means ... I trust him not to hurt her."

"Or believe him when he says he didn't do it." He took a drink. "Do you?"

"Could I be wrong, Randy?"

He sat back in the booth. "Oh." He put his burger down. "I don't know. Could you?"

She shook her head. "All of a sudden ... it's like a shadow passed over the whole thing."

"You're asking whether Susan could be wrong, aren't you?"

Myra nodded. She stared at her untouched hamburger and tried to imagine picking it up and eating it.

"He says he didn't touch her?"

"No. Didn't molest her. He leaned down to hug her—because she looked so sweet ..." She shoved the food away. "She said there was a weight on her that she couldn't get off. What kind of a hug is that?" She felt her voice catch and her head began to pound.

Randy reached out and put a hand on her wrist. "Take it easy."

"I'm okay." She straightened. "Just take the food away, okay? The smell is ..." She waved her hand in front of her nose. "... too much."

"We'll talk in the car.'" He gathered up the wrappers and handed her the drinks.

Once they were outside, she began to feel better. "Thank you," she said, when they were seated. "And I'm sorry for that. Not my usual style."

"I more than understand. And I'd say your husband likes the company of young girls, whether he's telling the truth about Susan or not." He started the engine and headed toward the freeway. "The men I've known who molest young teenagers don't pay much attention to birthdays. They end up being charged with statutory rape, if nothing else."

Myra nodded. "That much is true. But there's a difference ..." Her voice faded as the nausea of the restaurant threatened to return. Had the humiliation and hurt she'd lived with for so long merged with the depth of shock in her daughter's eyes to trigger a response?

"And I'd also say you occupy a very different place for him." He turned onto the ramp and accelerated.

"Earth mother." The name shifted the topic to solid ground.

113

"What?" His attention was on traffic as he settled into a lane. "Where did you get that?"

"It came to me on a long ago morning when I first woke up to the fact that he was sleeping with a grad student. He kept pleading that he needed me."

Randy grunted. "I begin to see."

"Can you stand to listen to me a little more? Because I need to keep unraveling it—making sense, as you said."

"Shoot." The headlights of northbound cars flickered over them in an even rhythm.

"Earth mothers give permission. Right?"

"I guess …" He sounded at sea.

"Like today. And back then. I always told myself I was the person of substance. Wonderful word, that. The girls were mere passing flirtations. Eleanor said something like that, too. We were the real women in their lives. Sooner or later they would come back—to mama. Had I been giving him permission to have affairs?"

"I sure hope not. I don't see you as the type, frankly."

"I was different then. I did confront him. But he begged for forgiveness, and Eleanor said to let it be … said faculty wives put up with it. That the men were surrounded all of the time by these doting young women and … never mind, it's too … debasing. Making a fuss would ruin their careers. But above all, the kids—I didn't want to tear apart their lives. So I didn't do anything. That *is* giving permission."

"Well …"

"No, no, don't protest. It is. And I'm still …" She dropped her head into her hands. "He's asking me to be that … all forgiving earth mother again." She raised her head, remembering the expression she'd seen on Derek's face. Need. That's what it was. As though twelve years had vanished. She laughed in disbelief. "Let's go home, Randy. I'm terribly tired."

"We should get you some food." The lights of Buelton and Solvang appeared ahead.

"No we shouldn't. I'm not ready to eat. Really."

He drove on without answering. Not until he slowed for the curves of Gaviota Pass did he speak again. "I guess it makes sense, now."

For a long time, the purring of tires on the pavement was the only sound in the car.

"Randy ..." She sat up as the thought hit her. "Why does he come back now? Because he knows Susan's about to turn twenty-six and after that she can't charge him?"

"Maybe. If he knows the law."

"Well, surely he would, wouldn't he? If you have a charge hanging over your head, that's the first thing you'd do."

"Mm. But you found him. So the question now is ..."

"Will I charge him?" She fell silent and wrapped her arms around herself as the possibility of being wrong struck again. "Or will Susan?"

Chapter 13

It was after eleven when they pulled into Myra's drive. Randy turned off the engine and leaned back. "So, where are you, Myra?"

"Back where I was twelve years ago. Except I never doubted myself—or Susan.

"And you do now?"

"You don't?" She turned, but could only see the shadow of his face in the dark. "Everyone else thought it was Susan's imagination. Eleanor said she was disturbed."

"I didn't. Sergeant Sanders didn't."

"I know. Thank you for that." She paused to collect her thoughts. "Tell me, is there a difference—is it a different sort of man who goes for a fourteen year old? Different from a man who likes his women young? When the fourteen year-old is his daughter?"

She could feel him looking at her, but it was too dark to read his expression. "I don't know," he said finally. "That's a question for a psychiatrist, Myra. We see a lot of men going for girls under eighteen. As to fourteen …" He shrugged. "They're out to get what they want." He sighed. "As for incest—I suspect that for every incest case that comes across our desk, there are ten more out there unreported. Would Derek?" He paused and opened the car door. "I never met the man." He got out and headed around to hand her out.

Randy was very close to her when she stood up. She put a hand on his arm. "Thank you for taking me up there … and listening to my unraveling."

"Let's go make sure your visitor hasn't been back." He took her arm and led her toward the door.

"I'm sure it was Derek—he said as much." She unlocked the door and led the way inside where she turned on the lights, then greeted Rex and Lily who came bounding from the back of the house. Everything was as it had been before.

"It doesn't hurt to check." He vanished down the hallway to the bedrooms, then climbed to her studio.

She followed and found him staring at the strip tacked to the board.

> Alphonse sat in a stream soaking his backside and knees; Matilda stood blinking at him, still wearing the scarf around her scrawny neck.
>
> Rufus appeared to mock the ugly chicken. "Who do you think you're fooling with that silly thing? No wonder we can't find anyone to take us in."
>
> "It looks better on me than on you," Matilda answered, pulling the scarf off.
>
> In the next square, the scarf had gathered his starched quills into a bouquet and was tied in a great bow. Eustasia, the gull appeared holding her belly in laughter. A bad idea.
>
> She reappeared in the next square as a pin cushion for Rufus's newly energized quills. Matilda and Rufus smirked.
>
> A few drops of rain finished the square.
>
> Then it poured, rinsing all of the starch from poor Rufus's quills.

"They were going to see the queen," she told him.

"Amazing. It's really you. I'll never read it the same way again." He shook his head, then leaned forward and gave her a kiss on the cheek, a mere brushing. "You're a very complicated woman."

On reckless impulse, she pulled his head down and kissed him squarely on the mouth.

He pulled her close and returned it. Her veins turned to liquid fire, then he pulled away. "I'd better go."

"Thank you," she called as he headed down the stairs.

He turned at the bottom of the stairs and blew her a kiss. "Until next time."

Myra stood gazing after him, a chuckle rising into a laugh of pleasure. A car door slammed, and he was gone. Rex and Lily had returned to the kitchen and were banging their food dishes. She laughed again and did as she was bade.

Once she'd fed them, she looked around at her disheveled house. It could wait until tomorrow. She didn't want to just shove the papers back without looking to see what was missing, and she wasn't about to dislodge the tenuous peace she felt at this moment.

She slept fitfully and woke at six with the same confusion of emotions she'd taken to bed. Seeing Derek had brought some closure to the years spent in limbo. Put a period at the end of a sentence. Freed her in some way she couldn't put into words. But it was a freedom shadowed by doubt, which she shook off by putting a finger to her lips, remembering Randy's kiss and the fire she'd long since forgotten. A walk would settle her confused emotions and let her think.

The morning mist was lightening, the perfect time of day according to Rex and Lily, who lunged about, chasing the night creatures back into their dens. She stopped at the blackened circle of ashes above the rotting seawall. Maybe it had been Derek, waiting his chance, or building up his courage. And maybe not. Maybe some vagrant in need of warmth. It didn't matter now. She turned and climbed down the steep last section to the beach, and watched the dogs disappear into the gray dimness that stretched ahead.

She was alone. In the chill of the fog, the newborn doubt returned. Again, she felt Susan clinging to her and heard her muffled cries against her breast. Not a nightmare. She'd vanquished many a nightmare, over the years, feeling Susan's tension dissipate into relief when she found herself awake. Not that night.

Certainty regained, Myra peered into the fog. "Rex! Lily!" The dogs appeared, and she headed for the path and the house, but once there, the upheaval around her desk confronted her.

She sighed and set to work, sorting the mess and trying to remember the contents. An hour later, she'd returned order to both desk and cabinet. As far as she could tell, nothing was missing. Her financial and insurance documents were intact; the unmarked envelope of birth, marriage, and divorce papers, which lived in the bottom drawer, had been tossed into the mess unopened.

She undid the clasp and laid the contents out on the table. Ashes of a family that had been. Her flesh shriveled and her hands were cold as she pulled out the needed documents and shoved the rest back into their envelope. She'd have to copy the divorce papers before she mailed them—another hateful job.

She wiped her hands down her jeans and went upstairs to her office desk, knowing now that she would find nothing missing. Only her cartoon and art business papers occupied those drawers. By the time she finished returning tax documents, royalty statements, and contracts to their folders, she was heavy with weariness. She copied the divorce papers and put them into an envelope with the birth certificate, then stared at the address she'd written, seeing again the shabby bungalow, the bachelor's quarters that were a reproduction of his previous home, including the view of the sea. Guilt for his ruined life stopped her breath, and she had to force herself out of it by licking the flap and stamping it. Done. A last act of amputation, but the rage that had triggered that first act returned only in flashes, and she felt none now. Only a flat sadness.

She turned to Matilda and Rufus for relief, but they came before her a rain-sodden bunch.

> Matilda's scarf was sopping wet, her mood sour, and Rufus dragged his quills behind him.
> "I told you to stay out of the rain," said Boots, who was firmly planted before them.
> "It was a dumb idea, anyway." Eustasia stormed into the square, the tails of her untied bow flopping along the ground behind her.
> "Where's Alphonse?" Boots asked.
> "Soaking," Rufus sneered.

Myra's pen stopped. She had nothing to offer them. Certainty spent, doubt retook the stage. If she'd made a mistake, it would follow her forever.

"I'd say he is a hazard around young girls whether he did it or not." Randy's words came back along with the memory of the dispersing seminar on Derek's front porch. She had never thought him a danger to his graduate students. Quite the other way around. She'd watched them flirt with him at department parties; it was all too clear they knew what they were doing. The community college students coming out of his house were younger. Too young to make choices about who to flirt with? Still adolescents believing it was all a game? Maybe all of those things, but Derek was no greenhorn.

Myra put her pens away and went downstairs. She wanted to go see

Susan, as though that would set her fears at rest, but in this mood, she'd only increase her daughter's anxiety. After pacing the living room for several minutes, Myra went to the phone to called Dr. Garvitz, then remembered that it was Sunday.

With a sigh, she put down the phone. What had she hoped to get from him, anyway? Answers to what? She shook her head and turned her attention to fixing herself supper. Then she settled in front of the television to pass an uneventful evening. Here, at least, she'd be able to fall asleep.

At midnight, she dragged herself to bed, only to wake early the next morning, still floating in limbo, unable to grasp any solid handhold that would pull her out of it. She telephoned Dr. Garvitz as soon as the clock said it was reasonable to do so.

"How's Susan?" the doctor asked, when they were connected.

"Pretty good, I think," Myra answered, realizing he hadn't seen Susan in at least three years. "She's a new mother."

"I know." His chuckle was downright jolly. "I got the birth announcement. That's terrific news."

Myra plunged into the topic, and brought him up to date, wondering what exactly she hoped to get out of this call.

"You say spotting the car upset her?" he asked when she'd finished.

"Yes. It brought back all of the confusion."

"Then he should stay away. And you think he will?"

"Yes. For now, anyway."

"Good. Well, I think you did right by telling him to stay away. Tell her you saw him and talked with him. You were always very good at quieting her fears. And tell her to bring the baby to see me." His voice told her he was assuming the conversation was over.

"Dr. Garvitz." She waylaid him.

"Yes?"

"He still says he just bent over to give her a hug, and she woke up screaming. Is that possible?" She was relieved to get the words out.

"What are you asking, Myra? Whether she was molested?"

"Yes. I never doubted it. I still don't. But …"

"I can tell you she was traumatized." He stopped. "It certainly has to do with men, and I don't think a hug would cause it. I can't tell you when that happened, and exploring it only created more confusion, going nowhere. The physical examination didn't show anything, but that certainly doesn't mean nothing happened."

"But it wasn't just her imagination. A nightmare come alive." She needed to put a stake through the heart of this beast.

"No, no. Not a nightmare. Susan's not unbalanced."

Myra sank into a chair in relief. "Thank you. I know that's what you said at the time. I just needed to hear it again."

"Glad to oblige." She heard the smile in his voice and marshaled her courage.

"Another question." She forced the words out. "When that happened … when he molested her … I was already angry at him, because he'd been unfaithful over and over, and I was living with it. So I need to know … did I get carried away by that? Is there a difference between liking younger women and … going for his daughter?"

"Incest is a strong taboo. Thank God. But whether social or instinctive no one can decide, and impulse carries men across that line more often than any of us want to think about. She was post-pubescent. That's the key. If she hadn't been … well, that's a different story."

When she said nothing, he went on. "Don't torment yourself, Myra. You did the right thing. I certainly wouldn't have been comfortable with him in the house if I'd been in your place. And I know I couldn't have treated Susan successfully if her father had still been there."

Myra let out her breath. "All right. Thank you. And I *will* tell her to bring Billy in to see you." She hung up the phone, feeling his reassurance penetrate to her core. Her cells resettled into their normal places.

Then she rose, shut the dogs outside, checked the lock on the gate, collected her keys, and set off for Susan's.

No one answered at the house. She heard hammering down the lane and found them at the half-built greenhouse; Susan was holding boards in place for Doug. Billy sat in an infant's jump chair under a nearby tree, happily waving his arms at the dancing light above him.

"Looks like progress."

They turned at her voice.

"Just in time!" Doug beamed. "We were about to quit for lunch." He straightened and stretched. "Come on, Susie, let's eat."

Myra picked up Billy and followed them into the house. "Where's the pup—Stacy—by the way? He wasn't outside."

121

"No, he's off visiting his owner-to-be." Susan sighed. "That's the really hard part—letting go."

They washed some apples, then Susan put the baby in his chair, and they sat down to lunch. Myra fed Billy applesauce, listening to the conversation centered on the greenhouse and the plants to order for it. She was forever grateful for the enthusiasm they brought to their business, the pleasure they found in their lives.

"I saw your father," she said quietly as they munched cookies.

"What?" Susan's head shot up. "You saw him?"

"I did." The quiet of her tone countered Susan's rising anxiety. "Peter gave me his address."

Susan's hands dropped to the table, startling the baby. "He knew? All along?"

"I don't know for how long, but yes. He knew. Derek's not here, though," she added quickly. "He's up in Pismo Beach. Teaching at a community college."

"Pismo Beach." Doug echoed the words as Susan stared. "So you might have seen his car at El Capitan," he told his wife. "You said he liked to camp."

Susan closed her eyes, took a deep breath and let it out again. "All right. Good. At least I'm not losing my mind." She said it lightly enough but there was a sharp undertone.

"You never were," Myra assured her. "And I told him to stay away. He promised."

Doug gave a short laugh. "How good is that?"

"Pretty good." Myra considered going on to explain herself but rejected the idea. She wasn't going to get into their history of infidelity and confession, nor was she ready to bring up the subject of charging him. She suspected that Peter had had an idea of what was going on, but as far as she knew, Susan was still oblivious to Derek's antics. She put her napkin down and laid a hand on her daughter's arm. "You can believe it," she reassured her. "But if you don't … if you get scared again, go see Dr. Garvitz, will you?"

"Dr. Garvitz. I haven't seen him in ages. Since Doug and I got married, in fact." Her voice wasn't tight. At this point she seemed relieved that she'd been right, or maybe that her father was fixed in place and time rather than a specter who might reappear in the middle of some picnic or birthday party.

"He'd like you to bring Billy to see him."

"What? You've seen him? Why?" Susan was alarmed again.

"I called him. Just to bring him up to date." And to reassure myself, she finished under her breath. "He was delighted with all the good news of you both. As though he was responsible, in fact." Myra smiled at the memory of his voice.

"Well, I suppose in a way, he was," Doug agreed, reaching a hand across the table to put on Susan's.

It was a story Myra knew only second-hand, but loved turning over in her mind. At first, she'd resisted Dr. Garvitz's suggestion that Susan attend a support group for troubled adults, hating the fact that she'd allowed her child to be so damaged. Then Susan began talking about others in the group as though she'd never had such friends before. Myra came to see it as a hole in the fabric of life where people in pain could find each other. There'd been no doubting Susan's surge of energy. The electricity had come back in her smile when she mentioned the man named Doug, another member of the group, and the joy he'd found in training animals.

Then one day she'd come home with Doug and Stacy, a pup he was raising until it was old enough to train. Myra had found herself in tears. She'd felt forgiven. This marriage was as close to redemption as she would ever get.

"Do Grandma and Grandpa know you saw him?" Susan asked, picking up a spoon to feed Billy cereal.

Myra eyed her, unable to read the intent of the question. The only blotch in the memory was Susan's insistence on inviting the Bennings to the wedding, against Myra's advice. Myra had found Susan in the pantry in tears because her grandparents had not arrived. At some level, Susan understood their absence was a result of her accusations against her father, but their rejection had never hit her in the face before. She and Peter had been the only grandchildren, treasured as rare gifts by the lovely couple on the hill. Susan had certainly never realized her screams in the night would cost her Eleanor and Cornelius. "Not yet," she answered, returning to the present, "though I think they know where he is. I think Grandma, at least, would like forget it ever happened."

Doug gave a harsh laugh. "Fat chance."

The intensity of his response was a defense of Susan, but Myra knew that wasn't the whole of it. He'd come to the therapy group, Susan said, after spending a boyhood trying to save his parents, who'd wandered from alcoholism to meth addiction. Occasionally, Myra wondered what had become of the pair without their protective son. Doug never mentioned them. She knew the therapy group talked of forgiving parents, but for the sake of his mental health, she hoped he never saw them again.

Now, her daughter's expression in response to Doug's "fat chance" was a faintly nostalgic sadness. Susan's picture of the Bennings remained that of beloved grandparents who might someday forgive her.

"School time at the kennel," Doug said, rising from the table. "Would you like to see the dogs?"

"Of course!" Their decision to start a kennel of their own was recent. Susan took the chief responsibility, while Doug was getting the landscaping business underway. She was impressed with the care they both took in selecting dogs. Despite their pasts, they were still of an age that believed in perfection.

"We have a new retriever," Susan offered, her voice clearly welcoming the distraction. "Come see." She picked Billy up from his chair and headed for the bedroom. "Time for nap, buddy-boy."

The kennel was in an old shed. Doug had replaced the roof and siding. Myra, who had spent a day painting it, was pleased to see they'd added a tile floor, plumbing, and drains since her last visit. She said hello to the occupants of cages—a shepherd, a black lab, a mutt of many colors, and the new retriever. Susan let them out into the yard, where she lined them up and began commands.

"Do you really think he'll stay away?" Doug asked in a low voice before following her.

"I do. And I'll talk to Peter to get his cooperation. Or try to, anyway."

"Good. Susan and Peter should be better friends." He headed out to the yard.

Myra watched them take the dogs through their routines, perfectly willing to remain part of the group and knowing it was time to go.

Susan brought the new retriever back to her cage, and Myra gave her a kiss on the cheek.

"Are you okay?"

Susan nodded. "I will be. I'm shaken up, but it helps, knowing where he is—that he's not lurking."

"I really can't picture your dad lurking, you know."

"Neither can I, as a matter of fact. If the jitters don't stop, I'll go see Dr. Garvitz. Promise."

"Take Billy, anyway," Myra urged. Then she'd at least visit the man. Maybe they'd get talking.

"Did he really mean that? He wants to see the baby?"

"He means it. Think about it. He counsels people in crisis day in and day out. What a treat to see a victory, once in a while."

Susan laughed. "I get your point. And thanks, Mom, for dealing with this. It's really weird, but when something—like seeing his car—happens, I turn to jelly. I'm just—so damn helpless."

"You're welcome. And I'm taking off—unless you want me to baby-sit Billy so you can get some work done."

"No, no, no need." She took a baby monitor receiver from her pocket. "Modern technology."

"Amazing—being replaced by a gadget." Myra laughed, gave Susan another kiss and departed. A deep satisfaction permeated her limbs, as she drove. Susan had ridden the wave and returned to safe harbor with more ease than Myra had anticipated. She'd grown more muscles than her willowy form made evident. They'd all developed a solidity.

Chapter 14

Myra returned to her empty house and sank into a chair, tired but satisfied that she'd cleared at least one hurdle successfully. Now she wished there was something else to occupy her head besides the ticking clock. At times like this, she usually climbed to her tower studio to work. This afternoon, the stairs looked long, and she was in no mood for the antics of her varmints.

Finally, she rose and went to the kitchen to make a cup of tea. The message light was blinking.

"Hi. I wondered if you'd like to go to dinner." Randy's voice came over the machine. "I get off at six. You can call me on my cell."

She chuckled. He hadn't felt the need to identify himself. That pleased her. She dialed the number and got his voice mail. "I'd love to. See you a little after six."

She sat without moving for long moments, her lips remembering the feel of his. Her kiss seemed bold on recollection, but it had not felt so at the time. Her skin still held the memory of his easy touch on the day Susan had fallen from the cliff. This was like the kindling of a spark from long ago, bringing a new energy. She took the warmth up the stairs to her drawing board to let it flow through her pen.

>Rufus appeared, his quills still limp, rolling mud balls with his forefeet. Then Eustasia and Alphonse flew in, carrying sticks. Finally, Matilda appeared, without her scarf, flapping her wings at a flock of hens who were stacking the sticks and shoving the mud balls in between. She twisted her neck to examine the placement of every stick.
>
>"What on earth are you doing?" Boots asked.
>
>"Building a beauty parlor."

"A spa,"
"A nest."
They answered all at once and continued building happily, unperturbed by the dissonance of their goals.

She put up another strip.

Boots peered down at the finished product. The circular wall had neither roof nor floor. The four reclined in separate holes in the mud, while the hens rubbed ointment into Matilda's chapped neck and Alphonse's knees, brought Rufus cans of sport drink, and massaged Eustasia's perpetually sore wing. No one spoke a word, but a contented humming rose from the nest.

Myra leaned back in her chair and let ease sweep over her. Her mind, turned free, moved from anticipation of the evening ahead to another source of contentment. She was dealing with events she had pushed away for twelve years. She'd lived in stasis, earning a living, walking the beach to relax, eating, sleeping, outwardly a successful independent woman. Inside, walking a treadmill. With that thought, she righted herself, fed the dogs, then took her sense of well-being to the shower to let the hot water soak it in.

She was a woman, not a relic. My God, had she treated herself as a relic? She stared at the image in the mirror. She had—"a used-up wife," as a long-ago friend had put it. She gave an exasperated huff and toweled her dark blond hair roughly to massage the thought away. Then she dried it and coifed it into a soft swirl at her nape the way she'd worn it long ago. She stood in front of her open closet for a long time, looking for something not designed for tide-pooling or sitting at a drawing board. She dug in the back, but found only outfits for posing at academic teas. Finally she chose a pair of black slacks and a blue silk blouse that brought out the gold highlights in her hair and the deep blue of her eyes. The blouse, a shirt, really, was loose fitting enough to wear open over a shell; she studied the effect the mirror, then added a scarf and loop earrings to dress it up a bit. At least she didn't look trussed or as sloppy as she had every other time Randy'd shown up.

Finally, she dug in the drawer of her vanity for make-up that had survived twelve years of neglect. She hated the stuff. Always had. A little base and a touch of lipstick was all she'd ever had the patience for, and the doorbell was ringing.

"Come on in!" she called, then returned to the meager leavings and smeared on a base and lipstick. It would have to do. She grabbed her purse, then laughed. She was topping off her efforts with a scuffed brown leather sack—big and lumpy—that looked every one of its years. Too late now. She'd never quite managed polish, anyway. She remembered Eleanor's kind amusement when she'd forgotten to change her shoes or topped off an outfit with a shabby car coat. "Oh, don't worry about it my dear. Women are too worried about their own outfits to notice anyone else's." Which wasn't true, of course, but Myra had decided there was something vaguely intentional about looking as though she belonged somewhere else. She slung the strap over her shoulder and headed for the door.

Randy was standing in front of one of her watercolors as she came down the hall. His face lit up. "Wow. Where did you come from?"

"I used my magic wand," she retorted. In an open-collared shirt, sport-coat and chinos, he looked younger and oddly vulnerable. "You clean up pretty well, yourself."

"Thank you. You're lovely. Truly." He gestured to the painting. A piece of driftwood at low tide. "Is this one of yours?"

"It is. From once upon a time—back when I had the peace of mind for it."

"I like it. The sort of picture you can look at for a long time." His voice was relaxed, without the tone so often heard when people tried to find something nice to say. He was without pretense, nor did he look intimidated, which brought a genuine smile to her face.

"Where are we going?" she asked.

"Wherever you'd like. Montecito?"

"God, no. Do I look like Montecito?" She'd never been—or intended to be—a tourist, gawking at the movie-star wealth of Santa Barbara's neighbor to the south. "And please don't say yes."

"Yes. But if you'd like something more homey, how about the Beachside?"

"Perfect. Wonderful." Nestled on the edge of the sea between campus and town, the seafood restaurant had been her favorite ever since she arrived. Away from the tourist restaurants of Santa Barbara or the wealth of Montecito, it was content to let the beach and the sea dominate the scene. Behind it, herons studied the slough and nested in the trees of its parking lot.

They got a table on the patio more easily than usual, since it was early. Most of the crowd would wait for sunset. Myra gazed through the Plexiglas, a smile spreading over her face. To her relief and amazement, memories of family dinners here returned without pain. Her gaze wandered over the crowd consisting mostly of locals in open-collared shirts or loose-fitting tops, punctuated by Hawaiian-shirted college students who were its wait staff. Nothing had changed. "This was where we came for birthdays and anniversaries. I think I've avoided it for years."

He nodded. "I know about that. There are places I still won't go. Does it bother you? We don't have to …"

"No, no. It doesn't. To my surprise. Maybe I've finally gotten around to realizing there were good things about our life." She opened the menu. "Especially the fish. I do hope you like fish. I didn't drag you here, did I?"

He looked up from the menu, surprised. "I suggested it, remember?"

She laughed. "Sorry. All right then …" She returned to her study of the menu.

They gave their order, and for the next fifteen minutes sipped wine and nibbled bread, saying little, sinking into the somnambulant tonic of sand, sun, and sea. A waiter brought their salads, then lit the fireplace next to them, completing the scene. Again they let the minutes float away as they ate, as though afraid words might dispel the aura.

"You're glowing tonight—as though something good happened today," Randy commented.

"I do? Yes, I feel that way, actually. I went to see Susan."

"It went well?"

She nodded. "I think so. Oddly, she seems relieved to have Derek fixed in place. I'm afraid he'd become a ghost."

"I imagine he had—especially since he disappeared." He shook his head. "Too bad. I do understand it. I look at my daughter and try to imagine her in that situation. I can't."

"Susan was lucky it didn't destroy her utterly." Myra let silence fall, concentrating on her salad. "But today … it just felt good, being out there, watching her with the baby and their dogs …" She broke off and gazed out at the sea. "Have you ever noticed that the sea from this spot is always dreamy—full of hope?"

He smiled at her. "Is it? And what are you dreaming?"

"Hoping. Believing that some miracle can happen that will restore Susan to the little girl I knew. Just change her back. Dissolve the shell."

"You said it felt good being there. Doesn't that mean she's happy?"

"Yes. With the happiness of someone who's won a battle—content and resting and healing. All of those, and it's good." She looked up as the waiter brought their dinners.

"But?" Randy asked, once they were alone again.

"But I want it all." She poked her sea bass in self-derision. "I want the fire back." She took a bite of fish and smiled. Randy's eyes were soft as he gazed at her. "Eat," she ordered. "It's perfect."

They concentrated on their dinners, and Myra let her mind float. "She had too much fire," she said, letting the words flow. "As though she was born without the proper shielding. She attracted attention without understanding why, and it frightened her. She didn't know what to do with it. But when she was just with family—she was electric with energy."

"Were you like that?"

"Me! Oh, no, I don't think so." Had she been? She'd certainly learned to hide early enough. "I think Derek was, though." She diverted attention out of habit. "From stories Eleanor and Cornelius used to tell, he was wild. And he was used to attracting attention. But that never frightened him. He gloried in it. Maybe boys are just different that way. When Susan started school, it was as though she was a magnet for attention she didn't want. One day a switch turned off, somewhere." Myra became aware she was rambling and let her voice fade off. "I'm sorry. I'm going on. How did we get off into this?"

"That's okay. It's good to talk. Stuff sits and smolders in there. It doesn't sound like she ever was an easy kid."

"No. Not like Peter, who was always on top of it. Control seems to be a part of Peter's genes. He can't imagine being knocked off his horse." She stopped with a bite halfway to her mouth. "Maybe that's why the family breakup was so hard on him. He couldn't believe something had happened he couldn't fix. Something outside his understanding of the way things worked."

"And he still refuses it. That's the way my boy Carson is. The Coast

Guard is a universe unto itself. One he understands. Beyond that—chaos he wants no part of."

"But he survives. It's amazing how children manage to do that, isn't it? And your daughters?"

He took a bite of potato and gazed at the fire. "The younger one's all right, I think. Funny, she was the one I worried about. She was only six, when her mother took off."

"You mean—she left you with the kids?" Mothers didn't do that, in her experience.

"Yeah. Well, she came back for them later—when I filed for divorce—but I didn't give them to her." He wiped his mouth and returned his gaze to his plate.

"That sounds nasty." She tried to read his expression, but he didn't look up.

"Not too bad." He was concentrating far too hard on his half-eaten fish. "She really didn't want them."

"Oh." The word came with a flash of understanding. "I'm glad you kept them in that case."

"Yeah." He looked up, his face lightening. "I was always big on being a father."

"Which is why your kids are okay."

"So far. I'm not so sure about the oldest, though. She was twelve when we broke up and she turned wild—barely finished high school and ended up marrying a security guard." He shook his head. "I always suspected the guy of being a rogue cop—was glad when she dumped him." He reached for a piece of garlic bread. "She's on number two now. A nice enough guy." He took a bite. "But I'm afraid she's too much like her mother—can't settle."

"Peter is like that. I keep waiting for him to—well, get serious—but it's like he's been burned. I wonder if Susan would have been like that, too, if it hadn't been for …" Myra let her voice fade and gazed out at the islands.

"Why?"

"All of that extra energy. And she had a way of flitting from one fascinating thing to the next. I always found it stimulating—exciting, really, but I wonder. Would she have been carried away on its tide?"

"Ruby wasn't carried away. She was just restless, discontented.

Looking for another diversion. Doesn't sound like Susan." He sounded frustrated, irritated even.

The image of a man forever trying to please an unhappy woman rose in Myra's mind. "She needs to find something—not someone—to love. A lot of women are like that," Myra assured him, thinking of her own mother. "Or they were, back when women believed they existed for their husbands and children. It just never occurred to my mother to be interested in anything else. Then, after we'd all left home and my father died, she discovered she loved to play the flute. Can you imagine? I guess she'd played it in her high school orchestra and had forgotten all about it." Myra sat back in her chair. "I went home one winter, and there she was, sitting in the window, her face all lit up in a way I'd never seen, playing that flute." She laughed. "Maybe your daughter will find a flute." There was a luminescence to his gaze again, that made Myra look down.

"A lovely idea," he said softly. "Or her mother will—though Ruby doesn't look in the right places." He shoved his empty plate away. "Dessert?"

"I couldn't. Just coffee."

"This time of day?" He waved for the waitress.

"I'm an addict."

He ordered coffee for both of them, then sat back in his chair. "So, is art your flute?"

"Yes—or was. Maybe I'll get back to it someday."

"Cartooning isn't the same?"

"No, cartooning is—venting, I think. Or a way of twisting self-pity around so I can laugh at it." Their coffee arrived and Randy asked for the bill. "What is your flute?"

"Wood," he answered without hesitation.

"Wood?"

"Wood. It fascinates me—working with the grain. Studying it. So I turn it into bowls and plates and boxes—anything that comes to mind …" he shrugged self-consciously as the waitress arrived with the check. "I have a garage full of tools. I'm also hooked on tools."

He reached an arm around her waist, and she breathed in the lemon spice of his shaving cream.

"How about a walk on the beach?" she asked, as they wound their way out of the restaurant, which was filling now, as the sun headed for the tips of the campus towers.

"Good idea."

At the edge of the parking lot, she slipped her sandals off and stepped out onto the sand. Randy put an arm around her shoulders, and she resisted the impulse to turn and kiss him again. He turned her toward the peninsula where the buildings of campus glinted in the setting sun. "Let's go the other way," she suggested.

"Sure." He turned her back, past the wharf that jutted out from the restaurant and on down the beach toward town. The tide was coming in; they wouldn't be able to go far in this direction.

"Will you show me your woodwork?" she asked, when they'd gone as far as they could. Then she realized how that sounded and burst out laughing. "Someday, I mean."

He drew her to him slowly and kissed her. "I'd love to."

Her arms went around him and her being let go of all resistance. Then they parted and stood gazing at the blood red sky outlining the campus. Only in winter would the sun set over the water, but it commanded silence at any time. Now it seemed to honor them and this moment they'd found.

They headed back through the gusts of wind that arrived with the departing sun. When they left the parking lot, Randy turned the car toward the freeway and Santa Barbara rather than toward Goleta. Toward Carpinteria and his house?

"Am I pushing it?" he asked, glancing at her.

She was far too old to blush. Surely she was. "No." The word came out as a mumble. Where had she left her poise? She sat back and told herself she was no teenager—only a self-possessed mature woman about to shed some rust.

Santa Barbara appeared and slid by. Saturday night traffic was heavy, covering the fact that they seemed to have exhausted conversation.

"Do you live on the beach?" she asked, finally.

"Mm. Almost. But in bachelor quarters, I'm afraid. You'll see."

The wooded hills of Montecito were turning black in the dying day as they rolled by.

"I always thought Carpinteria was a neat town."

He laughed. "You really have a taste for the offbeat, don't you? Most people would describe it as no-place."

"Right. A place no one has 'discovered.'" Her fingers put quotes around the word. "Alice's hole you can slip into and do as you please."

"Is that it?" He grinned into the dark.

"Yep. That's what our piece of shoreline was, when we moved there. Only the people who lived around it or an occasional biker or vagrant knew about it—except for the Monarch grove, of course."

"I guess Carp is a little like that, come to think of it." He left the freeway and drove down its main street of the beach town toward the water. He turned off on one of many side streets of unassuming clapboard and stucco houses, then dodged down a lane and stopped in front of a brown-shingled house that seemed to have been stood on its end—rising three stories on a base that couldn't be bigger than a sizeable garage. A staircase circled its exterior to the top floor, which had a balcony all the way around, like a lighthouse.

"This is yours? It's wonderful!"

"Really, Myra. It's a monstrosity." He opened his door. "But I like it. Come."

She got out of the car and stood gazing upward. "It's The House That Jack Built."

He laughed as he took her arm. "The House the Jack Built, Alice in Wonderland ... I thought you said it was Santa Barbarians who lived in fantasyland."

"Well, reality should be taken in small doses."

They entered a door at the base of the tower, and he flipped on the light. Myra blinked. She stood in the midst of a gleaming array of power saws, drills, and lathes breathing in the smell of wood, sawdust, and oil. "Your shop."

"This is what you came to see, right?" he teased.

"Absolutely." She moved toward the shelves that lined the walls where polished wood gleamed. She picked up a bowl and slid her hands around its silky sides, running her finger along its swirling grain.

"Maple," Randy said from behind her shoulder. "The longer you work it, the more beautiful it becomes."

Myra smiled. Unlike a policeman's life, she thought, dealing with all of the ugliness that lies under the polished surface of things. She picked up a box, its lid inlaid with a geometric design of darker wood. "Oak and walnut?"

"Right. This one …" He picked up a larger box, "is bird's-eye maple and cherry."

Myra gazed at the dimpled grain surrounded by a dark scroll, then stepped back and ran her eye along the full length of the display. "My God, Randy, they're beautiful." She went forward again to pick up a tray with a lily inlaid in the center. "How did you ever learn to do this?"

He shrugged. "Just kept bungling along, messing up wood. There's a guy in town who teaches that …" He pointed to the geometric design. "Marquetry. Here …" He moved off down the shelves and picked up a gracefully curved open bowl of walnut with lines of lighter wood running through its interior. "This is for you."

"Oh, no."

"Oh, yes. It's perfect to hold your shells and sand dollars. I saw them on your mantle."

"Not on a bet, Randy. The sand would ruin it." She ran her hand around the polished interior.

"Well—I want you to take it, in any case." He put it in her hands.

"I don't …" She stopped herself. "Thank you." She raised a hand and brushed his cheek.

He caught it as she lowered it and brought it to his lips. "Good. Come on, let's climb." He put an arm around her shoulders and switched off the lights as he led her out.

Climb they did. Up two stories to the balconied top floor, where Randy opened what was clearly the front door. He turned on a lamp to reveal an overstuffed couch covered with a plaid blanket, two or three leather bean bag chairs, and a low coffee table, with a mixture of driftwood and magazines scattered across it. Across the room was an open bar with a kitchen behind it next to an alcove. It wasn't until he turned on another light that she saw, in the alcove, a round oak table with a scrolled edged of some reddish wood. His handiwork, no doubt.

"Welcome." He waved around the room. "A bachelors den, as I told you."

"No," she responded. "It's cozy. Most bachelor's quarters are cold and stark—and smelly. Not that I've seen that many, you understand." She laughed, then turned toward the front windows and looked out into the black void beyond the winking lights just below. "That's the sea, isn't it?"

"A block away." He came up behind her and nuzzled her hair, then reached around her and pulled the blind. "You can see it in the morning."

She was startled at the disappearance of the diffidence she'd become accustomed to, though the idea of spending the night neither surprised nor distressed her. "Oh, yes?"

"Yes. Early. I have to be on duty at eight." He kissed her neck, and a buzz she'd long forgotten ran down her limbs, her body lost its years. "How about a cognac?"

She nodded, dazed now, with a contentment edged with desire. "Perfect—again." She laughed. "I haven't said that word in years. Now I don't seem to be able to get away from it."

He crossed the room with the aura of a master of his own environment and took a bottle from the kitchen shelf. She felt her blood take fire at the change from polite policeman to self-possessed man.

"Well," he mused, drawing two snifters from the cabinet, "Maybe you're practicing for another life."

She gave a small chuckle as she took her glass. "Now who's living in fantasy land?"

He raised his own in a toast. "You're giving me lessons."

The couch was soft, the cognac warm, the arm around her shoulders gentle. "I think you don't need lessons." She leaned back and closed her eyes.

"Come," he said a few minutes later, taking her glass. "I have a better place to sleep, if that's what you want to do." He pulled her to her feet and led her to a railing set into the corner of the room.

She looked down. "Don't tell me. A spiral staircase."

"Yep. Advanced technology. I don't have to go outside to go to bed." He started down ahead of her, then reached a hand up. "Be careful."

"Not the sort of stairs to manage drunk."

"On a glass of wine and a cognac? Even a policeman wouldn't call you drunk."

She descended into his arms. "No? Then why do I feel as though I'm floating?"

He drew her across the room without answering.

She hadn't been touched in a very long time, and suppressed desire rose in waves as his hands slid down her body, pausing to stroke. Her fingertips tingled with it as she returned caresses that became ever more urgent. She let go of any need to retain her grip on reality and released herself to sensation.

An hour later, she lay sated with her head on his breast, feeling sleep approach. There was something protective and private about this single room without hallways or doors to connect it to the world.

Chapter 15

Myra woke with the sun in her eyes, suffused with a joy whose source she couldn't name. Then the room took shape, and she drew her arms around herself and laughed. The bed beside her was empty, and the sun bounced off a white blanket on a white dresser across the room. Beyond the window was the sea. She shifted away from the beams and sat up, looking at her watch. Six thirty. And Goleta was forty minutes away—an hour in morning traffic. Shaking herself free of her dream state, she hurried to the staircase. "Randy?" she called through the hole in the ceiling.

"Good morning! Bathroom's to the back."

She turned and saw the door next to the head of the bed for the first time. In the closet-sized bathroom, she washed her face. A clean towel lay on top of the toilet tank.

"You should have wakened me," she said five minutes later, as she emerged into the room above.

"I was about to, actually, but the sun usually does the job." He was serving up bacon and toast. "Coffee's over there. How do you like your eggs?"

"You're not bothering ... well, I see you are. All right, sunny-side up, if you please." The oak table was set with two places, complete with orange juice. "You've been up a while."

"Not really. A half hour, maybe." He reached over and gave her a kiss. "You are lovely, asleep."

"I'm sure." She kissed him back.

"Are you always that way?"

"What way?"

"Making fun of yourself ... making a joke of compliments."

138

"Oh." She leaned against the counter. "I guess. I can't imagine doing anything else. Can you?"

He looked surprised. "Never thought about it." He served up the eggs. "Let's eat."

She glanced at her watch again. "Quickly."

When she reentered an hour later, her living room was bright and warmed by the sun. A light-hearted room, she decided as she stood cradling the wooden bowl he'd given her. The dogs, barking and pawing at the patio door, were the only sign that anything was amiss. Clearly they had spent the night in alarm—hopefully not barking to broadcast her absence to the neighbors. She placed the bowl on the mantle, then let them in and succumbed to their tongues and lunging paws.

Fall stretched its long fingers toward winter, but the sun seemed reluctant to leave. The rains didn't arrive, and the danger of fires rose, but Myra didn't share the town's anxiety. Her days, divided between beach and drawing board were punctuated by Randy, who showed up at the odd times of day and night peculiar to a deputy's schedule. She reveled in his unexpected arrivals. They walked on the beach, watched the life of the tide pools, lay on the patio gazing at the moon, and took long car trips in search of wood, or crabs, or canvases.

She started painting again, settling in the sand with her sketchbook while Randy searched the beach for the driftwood that inspired his sculptures. All activities carried the promise of his hands on her flesh, his body pressed against hers in the lovemaking that was the end of any activity.

Her Rabbleville bunch settled into benign amusements she knew she could not sustain for long. Matilda spearheaded a treasure hunt, and they spent a week unearthing heron feathers, a purple rock, crab shells, and empty snake skins to decorate their mud and stick nest-spa-beautyshop. Myra lost the acidity necessary to give their pursuits the usual futility. Surely the rains would come and melt the mud that held the nest together; a live crab would emerge to take hold of Rufus's nose; Matilda's long neck would get her head into somewhere it didn't belong, or Alphonse would wreck a wall with his take-off. But day passed day without mishap.

Thoughts of Derek and Peter, who had not spoken to her since that day, emerged periodically only to float away with the appearance of Randy. On Sundays, Susan and Doug visited more often now, as though the knowledge of Derek's whereabouts had produced a new closeness or dissolved some necessary layer of protection. They introduced Billy to the sea, bouncing him up and down in the rapidly cooling waters of the Channel. Then they took him to the house, dried him off, and watched Rex and Lily nose him as he lay on the rug, struggling to get his legs under him to crawl. Susan's face had lost its tension, and she laughed often, even running across the meadow with her arms outstretched as she had when she was small.

Then one morning, the answering machine was blinking when Myra came in from her morning walk. She expected Randy's voice, telling when he would be off duty or one of the children thanking her for the day.

"Myra, this is Patricia. Would you call me please?"

Patricia. What on earth? Myra knew it was her own doing that had caused their friendship to fade, and in the days after she kicked Derek out, there had been a message from Patricia on her answering machine. "Myra, call me. I need to know this isn't true." She'd sat looking at the phone, knowing she couldn't make that call. Patricia was a Benning. She couldn't ask her to believe it—or to be her friend. After that, there'd been only silence.

Now, she played the message again to catch the number and noticed it had a Los Angeles area code. Had Patricia moved? Her husband, Conrad, commuted to LA. He'd been some sort of manager with Warner Brothers. It had never occurred to her that that might be the reason Patricia had never called again to share lunch. Myra dialed the number, feeling only curious.

"Patricia? This is Myra."

"Ah. Thanks for calling. Can we have lunch tomorrow? I'm going to be in Santa Barbara for the weekend." She sounded urgent, wasting no words. Not as though she was offering a reunion of friends.

"Up? From LA? Have you moved?"

"You didn't know? No, I'm sorry, of course you wouldn't. Yes—not long after …" She broke off. "Can you meet me?"

"Yes. Of course. Where?" Her own eagerness surprised her.

"The Pelican? That okay?"

"Sure." The Brown Pelican, half-way between the tourists of Santa Barbara and the campus crowd, had once been their favorite haunt.

They set the time and Patricia ended the call, as though she had too much on her mind to engage in chit-chat.

Myra frowned, feeling the old unease rising. Whatever was on Patricia's mind would have to do with her visit to the Bennings—with Derek's return.

Forget it, she told herself, rising to empty the dishwasher and tidy the kitchen. She spent the morning pushing worry away with domestic details, then decided the only cure of this uneasiness was to work.

> In Rabbleville, it looked like rain. Matilda and Eustasia eyed the gathering clouds, then, as drops began to fall, began goading each other about the inadequacy of their respective wings.
>
> Alphonse spread his over the nest, knocking Eustasia aside as he demonstrated their magnificence.
>
> "Where's Rufus?" Matilda demanded.
>
> "Right here," Rufus answered from under her wing. "Just stop jumping around, can't you?"
>
> A bolt of lightning and an explosion of thunder filled the square. Matilda and Eustasia ended up peppered with quills and Alphonse, knocked from his throne, wings askew, sat in their midst as rain drenched their nest.

Myra left them in their discomfort and put away her pen. She paid some bills, answered her e-mail, and went shopping for groceries. A phone message awaited on her return. Randy, from Santa Ynez, telling her he was held over on a drug bust and wouldn't get off duty until who knew when. She went for a long walk on the beach with the dogs, working off tension and frustration, then went shopping again, this time for a present for Billy. She didn't believe in spoiling her grandson with continuous gifts, but she could think of nothing else to do with the hours.

By the time she arrived at the Brown Pelican on Saturday, she'd returned to a level of stress she hadn't known since the past had risen to engulf her two months ago. Patricia rose and waved. Then, catching Myra by surprise, Patricia reached out and hugged her.

"You look good, Myra."

"As do you." Patricia, tall and dark like her brother, was as slim as always, and her face seemed untouched by the years.

"It's good to see you." Tricia's voice was full of the old warmth. "I'd forgotten how much I missed you."

Myra smiled, relieved, and sat down. "I wondered what happened to you." She studied Patricia, who took her seat and picked up a menu. "I never called you after … I didn't know how."

Tricia nodded. "That's all right. After I cooled down … I guess I really didn't want to talk about it. Mother—-who never loses her poise—came totally apart. Dad just took off in his boat, leaving her to me. I was so angry at that—and fed up with the antics of the Benning males I just didn't want to know any more." She paused and gazed out the window at the sea. "But now I have to." She shook out her napkin. "First, tell me how you've been. How you're doing."

"Just fine at this moment. Susan's married and is a new mother. And I'm making a living drawing the cartoons I used to create to unleash my frustrations."

Patricia smiled. "I know that. I've seen them. They're wonderful."

"Peter is a lawyer, doing well, and I have a man who I'm seeing also." Myra considered telling her of Derek's reappearance, but decided to let Tricia broach that subject. "The cartoon business is lively enough to feed me—so I guess I'd say life is good."

Patricia smiled. "I always knew you were strong—were Derek's strength in fact, but when I saw those cartoons … it blew me away."

"And what happened to you?" Myra asked. "You disappeared."

"When he heard the latest Benning mess, Conrad said, 'That's it. We're out of here.' He'd been agitating to move to LA for years, but I had my real estate base so well-established here that he always relented. But between Mother's hysterics, Derek's antics, and his commuting …" She cut herself off and picked up the menu. "He came home one day and said he'd found a house in Malibu. I could either move or we'd get a divorce." She looked up from the menu she wasn't reading. "We left."

"Are you still doing real estate at all, then?"

"Oh, sure. It took a while, but I'm settled in now. Let's order, shall we?" She signaled a waitress then turned to the menu.

When they'd ordered and the waitress had disappeared, Patricia put her hands flat on the table, as though to give herself nerve. "Myra," she said after a long pause, "Mother has breast cancer."

"Oh, dear." She wished she could think of something to add or at least feel more than a jolt of surprise for the woman who'd once been a friend.

"She's had it for about three years, actually, but you probably didn't know."

"No."

"How could you, really? Anyway, it hasn't been going well, this past six months."

"Really? I saw her this fall—briefly—but she looked all right." So that explained the slight sag to Eleanor's face and the pallor. "She had a full head of hair, anyway."

"A wig. How did you see her? Or I guess I mean why?"

"Susan thought she saw Derek's car up at El Capitan. I went to see whether Eleanor knew where he was."

Patricia didn't look surprised. She simply nodded. "Did she?"

"I'm sure she did—does—but I didn't wait to find out, I'm afraid. She wanted me to pretend the whole thing never happened, and I walked out. End of story."

Tricia sighed. "She would." She fingered her silverware, looking worn and tired. "Well, Derek is around. You might as well know that."

"I do. Peter told me, as it turns out. And I went to see him."

"You did?" Her hand stopped fidgeting and her eyes widened.

Oddly, Myra remembered the day as something over and done with. With the entrance of Randy into her life, Derek had, once again, been relegated to the past. "He came to the house while I was away and rifled my desk. It turned out he wanted his birth certificate and our divorce papers."

"Good grief. So he was hanging around your house? Why?"

"Something to do with your father's will. Proving who he was. I told him I'd send them. Then he swore he did nothing to Susan and wanted—or wants—to see her. I told him no way." The scene was coming back, now, more fully than she wanted. "He promised he wouldn't until I said he could."

Patricia closed her eyes. "And you believed him?"

"Yes. He's afraid I'll charge him. And he hasn't, so far." Odd, how confident they'd all been, as though the matter was settled, and they could go on with their lives.

"How is Susan? Has she recovered?"

Myra shook her head. "I don't know what recovery means, in her situation. When she thought she saw his car, she threatened to come apart, but she got past it. Over and over again these past years she's proved stronger than I thought."

Their salads arrived, and they dug in. It was a good five minutes before Myra realized Patricia was eating very slowly, looking out the window. "What's the matter?"

Tricia turned her gaze to Myra. "Mother thinks—knows, really—that she won't see another Christmas. She wants the family together one last time."

Myra sat back with a thud. "The family. Not including us, surely?"

Patricia nodded. "She wants to see her great grandchild at least once."

Myra sat remembering Eleanor's words: "I was hoping we could leave all of that behind us." She closed her eyes. "But … you said the whole family. Derek's going to be there?"

"Yes. It's a lot to ask, I know, Myra, but for Mother's sake I have to. Roger's coming from Argentina."

Myra put an elbow on the table and leaned her head on it, without responding,

"I'm sorry, Myra. You've put up with a bellyful of Bennings, and you sound as though you've all recovered marvelously, but …" She broke off and shrugged wearily, turning her gaze to the window. "So has she … survived a lot, I mean."

Myra roused herself from shock. "How so?" It seemed to her, Eleanor had mostly denied anything that might lead to suffering.

"I could always tell when Mother had found out about another of my father's affairs. I'd go into the kitchen, or wherever she was, and she'd turned into a mannequin. Not a zombie, mind you. A mannequin. And Father would mope around with his head hanging to his waist. Life would come back, after awhile, and I'd get another lecture on the strength of women." Tricia gave a wry smile and took a bite of salad. "Then one day when I was about twelve, I came home from school and heard Mom yelling. I'd never heard that. I was terrified, as though our lives were coming apart. They were in the study, and I crept to the door. She'd stopped by then … cut herself off, I guess. I heard her tell him in a very quiet voice to never tell her again. 'As far as I'm concerned, it simply didn't happen,' she said, 'and I'll thank you to respect that.' Then she came out ..." Patricia broke off. "She didn't see me, thank God. She looked ... like a stone."

"And that was what we were all supposed to do," Myra mused.

Patricia's mouth twisted. "My brother certainly learned his lesson well, didn't he? Marry a strong woman, and you can do anything you want." She sighed and reached a hand over to put on Myra's wrist. "I guess I'm the one who lucked out. Ironic, isn't it? Conrad lives his days with movie folk, a notoriously unfaithful bunch, and curses them all for it. He doesn't stray—has never been tempted to, according to him." She sat back and looked out of the window again. "And I never had children. Not so lucky, but at least I never had to watch them take after my father, the way Mother did." She turned back and started to eat again.

Myra had a fleeting image of Peter and his rotation of girls. She shivered and forced her thoughts back to the Bennings. "Roger, too? I only remember him vaguely."

"Oh, yes, indeed. A father came home while Roger was messing with his underage daughter. Threatened statutory rape charges. That was when Roger decided Argentina was a great country."

"I never knew that." Myra felt sick. This was Derek's brother they were talking about, doing virtually the same thing ... was the whole family infected with a fatal weakness? Hers, too?

"No, of course you didn't. No one was allowed to talk about it." Patricia threw her napkin down in disgust. "And I played their game, Myra. For that I owe you an apology."

"We all protect our families, Tricia." Myra saw again the beautiful welcoming living room of the Benning house, remembered the sense of a peaceful den for book lovers and felt again the sense of having found a home. That, not a social image, was what Eleanor fought to preserve. "I did the same thing ... and brought hell down on all of us."

"I was furious with her for putting up with it. Just letting him get away with it."

"Giving him permission," Myra murmured.

"Exactly. And my brothers—it was as though they felt entitled to whatever they wanted from women."

"But even that's not the same as molesting children—their own, in Derek's case."

"No. I couldn't believe that. But I knew you wouldn't make it up—or Susan either. And I knew Mother would deny it. I'm not asking you to forgive her, Myra—well, maybe I am. At least to understand. It was one blow too many. For all her strength—or what she saw as strength—she's become like a shell these past years. As though it's been eating away like the cancer." Patricia picked up her fork, looked at her salad, and put it down again, shoving her plate away. "She just wants to die believing … I don't know what. That we've lived on—gotten past it."

As we have, thought Myra. All of us. But by how much? Enough to have mercy on a dying woman? "And you want Susan to be there, too? With her father? God knows what that will do to her, Tricia." Once again she pulled back from a meeting she had wished and unwished in the past two months.

"Just ask her. Let her decide." Patricia picked up her napkin, wadded it up, and put it down again. "Mother loved Susan so much when she was little—just delighted in her."

Myra remembered Susan's avid defense of her grandparents and knew Patricia spoke the truth. "She's also the one who called Susan disturbed." She tried to imagine such a reunion. Even if they steeled themselves, it was likely to bring the past crashing—an avalanche they'd have to dig themselves out of all over again.

"That was cruel. When she's fighting some reality, she can be. I won't deny that, but …"

"She's dying," Myra finished for her. "We should forgive the dying. And she wasn't the sinner … only protecting them because they were her children." She put down the fork she'd been diddling with. "But you're asking us to recreate the illusion she lived by."

"I know."

"I'll have to think about it, Tricia. It's …" She pushed her plate away as though it was the offender.

"Macabre." Patricia took her wallet from her purse. "Thank you for not refusing outright."

They left their money on the table and headed for the door.

"Was something the matter, ladies?"

They turned and saw the waiter gazing at their half-finished salads.

Chapter 16

Myra drove home, choosing the winding roads of Hope Ranch, another enclave of the wealthy, where everyone was required to have enough land to keep a horse. On these roads, she could let her mind move slowly. Eleanor's face rose in her mind, her skin pasty, less translucent than Myra had remembered, along with her plea to put it all in the past. Myra had read the face as aging, not ill, the plea as an insult, not a cry to relive the past back for a day.

Another day some fifteen years ago came back as she drove, when Eleanor had stood rapt in front of one of Myra's paintings, a water color of a tide pool.

"I'm right there," Eleanor marveled. She turned to Myra, her eyes shining. "However did you manage it?"

Myra glowed at the memory, remembering how she'd hesitated and put off showing Eleanor her work, fearing comparison to the works on their walls. She'd given it to Eleanor for her birthday, and it still hung on the Bennings' wall. She'd seen it on that brief visit last week. At first glance, the painting was of water covering the variegated rocks of a tide-pool. Only when one paused awhile did the anemone, barnacles, and hermit crabs take shape.

Eleanor had sighed that day, she remembered. "I spent hours gazing into those pools with Derek, when he was little." Her voice was dreamy. "It was like losing yourself in another world."

Myra felt as though she'd passed through a curtain to another Eleanor, unguarded and vulnerable.

"I thought I was a photographer once," her mother-in-law had gone on, "but then I went to galleries and saw the work of real camera artists. I had no talent." She'd leafed through a stack of Myra's prints, pulling them out, hands gentle, as though stroking them. "Derek's a fine photographer, though. I settled for at least passing on the love of it to him." She'd smiled, her voice regaining its certainty.

On a later day, Eleanor had confided that she'd once tried to sketch, too. She'd pulled a box from a closet shelf and turned over the contents one by one. "That's Roger," she said, pointing to the dark-eyed cherub with a topknot of black curls, "when he was three. This is Derek." The sketch was of a small boy squatting on the beach, peering into the water.

"You're wonderful with children," Myra had told her.

"You think so?" Eleanor looked surprised and pleased. "But it's the children that are the wonder, don't you think?"

Myra winced at the sound of those words, coming back now, from a far different time. Eleanor had deserved better—far better. She'd condemned her for putting up with Cornelius's affairs—and herself for putting up, in turn, with Derek's. She'd raged inwardly at Eleanor for convincing her to follow in her footsteps, accused her mother-in-law of violating herself to keep up appearances. But that had never been true, or if it was, it was for Cornelius's career.

Cornelius was the one who mattered. Eleanor hadn't doubted that for an instant, and it was Cornelius who'd taught her sons to be the men they were. Her mouth twisted, the irony so heavy she could taste it.

She exited through Hope Ranch's cast-iron gateway and approached the freeway. On impulse, she turned south rather than north toward home. For reasons she couldn't explain, she needed to fix her image of the male side of the Benning family before she tackled the problem of Christmas. She headed for the marina and the Serendipity. Why she expected to find Cornelius there, she didn't know, except that her image of him was always with his boat.

Sure enough, the Serendipity was still in its slip, and Cornelius's head appeared in the cabin gangway when she stepped on board.

"Hello, Cornelius."

"Myra." He was gaunt, his eyes bewildered.

"I just had lunch with Patricia. She told me about Eleanor." Had she come to see his reaction? She felt nothing but compassion for the face in front of her. "I'm terribly sorry."

He sank down on the opposite bulkhead. "It can't be true, can it?" His brown eyes looked opaque and helpless. He ran a hand through his scant gray hair and looked about, as though to discover where she'd gone. "I can't even sail without her crewing."

Myra, who had opened her mouth to respond, closed it again, finding nothing to say.

"I'm the one who's supposed to go. Not Eleanor. My heart's been bad for years." His voice broke and he buried his head.

She stared at him, but the image in her mind was of Derek, pleading his need for her. She'd come to confront him and his overweening sense of entitlement—to find out whether he had any sense of the disasters he'd caused. Instead she saw only a lost soul.

After a few minutes, he raised his head. "Sorry to be a blubbering ass," he muttered, pulling a handkerchief from his pocket. "I guess seeing you here—it's been a long time—brought back the old days." He blew his nose. "Good to see you," he said, trying to recover his usual heartiness.

"Do you know what Patricia asked?"

He sighed and nodded. "Eleanor wants her family back for one last Christmas." He rose and shoved his hands into his pockets. "It doesn't seem real, you know. I've been down here puttering because I don't seem to know anything else to do. It's like I've fallen into a hole."

"I know. Eleanor is a part of us all." She stopped, realizing it was true in spite of the fact that until the other day she hadn't talked to the woman in twelve years.

"Would you go for a sail?"

The request came out of the blue and knocked her back.

He read the shock on her face. "Just for an hour or so. To get my sea legs back. You're going to say that's selfish, and it is. But I wish you would … to make something … less awful of this day."

"You mean—now?"

"Right. Will you?"

She looked down at her slacks and knit top—hardly a sailing outfit, but her shoes had rubber soles. Randy wouldn't be off until eight. If she left a message on his cell phone that she'd gone sailing with Cornelius Benning, he'd think she'd lost her mind. Quite possible. She'd certainly lost her bearings at any rate. "All right. Just a couple of hours, though."

"Good." He looked around. "Wonderful." He patted the roof of the cabin. "Come on, old girl. Get your buns in motion." He opened the bulkhead, took out life jackets and handed her one.

When she'd belted it on, Myra climbed up onto the foredeck. The rest of the family's life might be a tangled mess, but the ropes were neatly coiled.

Cornelius tossed her the mooring lines. Is that how he'd spent these last days? Readying the Serendipity for a phantom sail? She shivered.

The auxiliary motor started up, and she knelt to pull in the bumpers, then slid back into the cockpit, realizing her slacks weren't going to survive this trip. She went below as they motored out of the marina and stood looking around the cabin, which was as shipshape and gleaming as it always had been, the smell of wood and polish competing with the tang of the sea. The triangular forward bunk, where they'd put children to sleep many a night, still wore its red plaid cover; the table that filled the central space gleamed, as did the brass fittings around the portholes. The galley bore the remnants of what must have been lunch—an open can of tuna and a bottle of Scotch. She found a sandwich bag and put the tuna away. The cooler contained nothing but beer and a hunk of cheese.

Returning to the deck, she found they were passing the dredge that marked the entrance to the marina. Cornelius turned toward the Channel, and Myra readied the sails. Tourists watched from the famous wharf alongside them, as though they'd been standing there for the twelve or fourteen years since she'd last done this. Except it had been Derek at the helm. Now, she was Eleanor.

Her system seized up at that thought, and she sat back, appalled. She couldn't be doing this—could she? The tourists waved, sending the pelicans that inhabited the end of the wharf into the air.

"Let's go!" Cornelius cried as they motored into open water.

She began to haul, a reflex without intention, and the mainsail rose above her, flapping as Cornelius headed into the wind. She was out of practice; her shoulders were going to give out long before the sail reached the top of the run. Cornelius came forward, reached up and gave a powerful tug. The sail jerked up the mast.

"Thank you," she muttered, tying it off. How long had it been, she wondered, since Eleanor was able to haul sail? Not lately. She was helping another Benning grab hold of a lost past. Deep inside, something settled into acceptance.

She went forward to the jib line, grateful that it rose more easily.

Cornelius had returned to the wheel and now turned the bow off the wind and killed the motor. The sails filled, and the boat lifted and surged forward. The man at the helm became Cornelius again, a grin of pure pleasure spreading on his face as he gauged the wind.

"Pull her in a little," he called, turning the boat closer to the wind.

Myra did as she was told and shifted her weight as the boat sped up and heeled.

"Coming about!"

Myra released the jib, ducked under the mainsail as it came across the boat, and grabbed the sheet on the other side. Her body moved with the rhythm of the Serendipity, her mind empty now of everything but demands of wind and sail.

"Take her," Cornelius called, falling off until the boat flattened. He stood aside.

The wheel tugged under her hands, and her body responded. She let the boat fall off the wind and slow down, so she could get her breath. Beside her the Channel waters hissed on the hull as they headed on a diagonal course toward Santa Cruz Island, leaving the mainland behind. Far to their right, the campus peninsula grew smaller, and the Goleta shore beyond it was out of sight.

She lashed the wheel to retrieve a windbreaker from the bulkhead beside her, then drew the boat back closer to the wind, ready for the burst of speed. A whale-watching boat came up from behind, dolphins cavorting in its bow waves.

"Look!" she cried to Cornelius, who waved that he had already spotted them. She grabbed the wheel and steadied her so they could watch. Dolphins made one believe that if the world wasn't right, it could be. Cornelius was feasting his eyes on them. She waited as long as she could to come about, falling behind the faster vessel so they could follow them up the Channel. Fifteen minutes later, a commotion on the ship ahead alerted them to the presence of a whale. This time of year, it would be a late blue or an early gray.

"There!" Cornelius pointed ahead, toward shore, and she spotted the end of the blow.

"Falling off!" she cried, and he loosened the sheet.

They crept along, waiting for the long low hump of its back to surface. Instead, the tail fin of the whale flipped into the air. Myra turned the

Serendipity into the wind, stopping her. Around them, the tourist boat and two other pleasure craft lay still. Soon the shiny arc of back rose and water slid off its length—far too long for a gray—then sank again. It was a blue. Orcas in the Channel caused excitement, gray whales admiration, but the presence of the longest beast on earth transfixed. They sat on, waiting, imagining the long sleek body, giant of the invisible world beneath them.

She looked back to see Cornelius in tears. Later, she'd pass judgment on herself. Right now, she sat under the soft flapping of the sails, the sighting of the blue submerging all regrets.

But the surface of the Channel lay undisturbed. The blue's departure was as soundless as its arrival. She looked at her watch and discovered they had been underway for an hour. "Time to turn back," she said quietly.

He nodded and came to take the wheel.

The wind freshened as they headed south, reminding them of how quickly the Channel could turn wicked. Cornelius trimmed the sails for a steady, modest pace, neither challenging the water nor allowing it to take control. He was a good sailor. It wasn't hard, watching him maneuver, to see where Derek had gotten his skill. She'd been an apt enough student, having spent much of her youth sailing Minnesota's lakes, but wet-bottom sailing on those little freshwater ponds required none of the expertise of sailing the Channel. This was a grown-up sport.

Under the demands of the weather, Cornelius regained his composure. By the time they re-entered the harbor next to Stearns Wharf and fired up the motor, he was ready for his usual salute to the tourists. Myra was busy lowering the sails and so was relieved of that expected ritual. They passed the dredge and headed for Serendipity's berth as Myra scrambled onto the foredeck again to lower the bumpers.

Memory of her lunch with Patricia flowed back as Myra stowed gear, and the weight of it dropped her like an anchor. The afternoon sail became an aberration—inexplicable but somehow not inappropriate.

"Thank you," Cornelius said, behind her.

She turned.

He sat hunched over, leaning an elbow on his knee, a man with no inclination to move. "That was a kindness I didn't deserve from you."

She struggled to find some reply.

"No, no, don't answer. No need." He sat up, then stood. "I can go home now." He put out a hand. When she put hers out to shake it, he drew her to him, then released her as quickly. "My son and I, we were cursed with women too good for us." He put his hands on top of the cabin, leaning there, looking up at the hills above the marina. "But if you could give Eleanor, who asks far too little, her one last request …" he broke off. "God, if there is one—or this old man, anyway—would bless you."

She caught her bottom lip in her teeth, unable to voice the promise he wanted. "I'll try," was all she could manage, and that as a mumble.

He smiled and came forward, putting a hand to her cheek. "That's all any of us can do, in the end. Go home, my dear. And thank you for this day."

She stepped forward and kissed his cheek before he could withdraw. "It was a sail to remember …" She turned and leapt to the dock.

A few minutes later, she pulled the expected parking ticket from her windshield and sat in the car looking at her stained slacks and rope-burned hands. What had she done—or meant to do? She had no idea. The afternoon felt like an oracle's gift whose meaning she was meant to puzzle over for years. Central to the puzzle was the long back of the great sea beast, reducing to insignificance the bobbing boats around them—which it could splinter in an instant had it been so inclined. She'd always loved to sail, but never had she been taken so deeply into its heart—playing with the far greater forces of wind and water. Only to end motionless in the presence of that great beast. They'd been engaged in some necessary obeisance to life and death. An experience that had brought Cornelius to acknowledgment and confession.

Fuzzy-headed from the shocks and unexpected exertions of the day, she started the engine and headed for home.

Randy's car was in her drive. "Randy!" she exclaimed as she entered. He sat on the couch, watching the dogs bound around her. "I thought you worked until eight, tonight."

"Got off early. Thought I'd get here in time for a walk. What have you been up to?" He was gazing at her ruined slacks and windblown hair. Her face was probably filthy, too.

"Oh, God, I wish I knew." She went over and sank to the couch next to him. "If you'll get us a glass of wine, I'll tell you."

She was half-dozing by the time he returned to the couch with two glasses of cabernet.

"You're exhausted." He sounded surprised and concerned.

"I'll live. Sit down and listen." Step by step, she told him the story of her afternoon, omitting nothing, and without trying to explain her reactions. "And that's it," she finished. "I hope you can tell me where I am, and what I'm supposed to do, now."

He pulled her to him and kissed her. "Rest. Let it sink in."

"It feels as though I've eaten a huge hunk of the past and haven't a clue how to digest it." She closed her eyes and leaned back.

"Maybe you need to do that before you can go forward."

"Maybe," she murmured, and they fell silent. "And here I thought I'd gone forward." Rex and Lily came and curled at their feet. "I need to shower." She felt no inclination to act on the need. "Cornelius is a different man at the helm. As though he discovers some deeply right part of himself."

Randy nodded, looking a question. "Can you understand that?"

"That power—skill—at dealing with the elements. Manhood." She saw gratification in his eyes.

"Yes."

"The same strength that becomes a weakness on land—that need to satisfy elemental desires."

"Which he acknowledged today."

"He asked forgiveness for his son. That was clear. So … if the family gathers for Eleanor, that is his redemption."

Randy let his breath out slowly. "He surely put you in a hell of a spot, didn't he?" He handed her her wine glass. "Drink up and go shower."

Chapter 17

By the time Myra came back downstairs, the sun had set. Randy had the barbeque going. The smell of cooking beef filled the air.

"You didn't find those in my larder," she commented, eyeing the steaks that sizzled on the grill.

"Picked them up on my way. My skills are limited, so you'll have to put up with these."

"I think I can manage. I'll go make us a salad."

"Good. You can microwave the potatoes and open the wine, too."

"Bossy." She turned and went back inside to do as she was bid.

It wasn't until they were seated, the patio door closed against the chill of the sea-breeze, that her mind returned to the day past. "Thanks for this," she said, picking up her fork. "I might even be able to start thinking straight."

"Wait until you eat," he advised, pouring her a glass of wine. "In fact, wait until you sleep on it. Much wiser." He popped a piece of steak into his mouth.

"Are you planning on helping with that?" She tested the potatoes for temperature.

"I am. I have tomorrow off, too."

"That's the best news I've had all day." She rose enough to kiss him on the cheek.

"Doesn't sound as though I have much competition in that department, but thanks." He took her hand and gave it a squeeze.

They turned their attention to the meal before them, breaking only to watch the pleasure-boats ply the Channel and listen to the sea lions call from the oil rigs that marred the landscape to the south.

"He loves her." She said the words without any volition.

"Mm? Cornelius?"

"Yes. Standing in the shower, the day washed away, and that's what I'm left with. How deeply he loves her. How rotten he feels about his own behavior."

"And where does that leave you? About going?"

"It leaves me wondering what not going would do to them."

"They have it coming." Randy rose to clear the plates.

"Yes. But that suddenly feels like vengeance." She rose and followed him into the kitchen. "Like kicking a man when he's down."

Randy turned from the sink and took her in his arms. "I love you." He shut off any response with his lips.

When she withdrew, she could only breathe "Dear God." She clutched him to her and rested her head on his shoulder.

"What's wrong?" He pushed her away enough to look into her eyes.

She met his gaze. "Wrong? I love you, too." She shook her head in amazement. "I didn't think I'd ever fall in love again." She heard a rumble of laughter in his chest. "Really," she said, stepping away. "I was soured on the whole idea. Derek made love seem very cheap—or very dumb. Something that trapped people because they were weak—or needy." She went back into his arms. "Not like this at all."

"Not even at the beginning?" he asked, his voice muffled by her hair.

"Oh, then it was a miracle—to be chosen." She laughed. "I fell into a swoon, I think." She put a hand up to his cheek. "Which really wasn't like this, either." She pulled back again. "How about you?"

"I thought I was in love." He shrugged. "It was very hot, for a while."

"And for your wife?"

"I don't know that Ruby's ever been in love." His voice was sad, and he seemed disinclined to say more. Instead, he put his lips to hers again. "Not like this."

They stood in each other's arms without motion. Then he led her toward the bedroom.

The birds woke her, chattering away in the evergreen outside her window. The clock said it was not yet five, but beside her, Randy roused also. "Good morning," she said, nudging him. "The finches say you should be up and doing."

He threw an arm over her. "I can do that without being up, thank you." He rolled toward her and put his mouth to hers.

Her body relished his touch, moving slowly around from her back to belly, and he didn't hurry. Making love in the morning, still half-asleep with a whole day free of obligation stretching ahead, was a new experience. Morning space had always belonged to the children. Now fire rose, unrestrained by the distractions of the day. Never had desire seemed so pure. She hadn't known this, even with Derek, where incredulity and need had drowned out all else. Now pure pleasure filled all space.

When they were finished, they lay in each other's arms and fell asleep again, despite the birds. She awoke to find the bed empty and heard the shower running. She closed her eyes, the memory of lovemaking buffering her from the day. Only when thoughts of Eleanor intruded did she rise, pull on sweats, and go down to make coffee. The morning mist had dispersed, leaving only the everyday California sun and a flat, calm sea.

"Good morning again." Randy's kiss on the back of her neck smelled of shaving lotion.

She twisted around and returned it, then leaned against him as long forgotten feelings flooded in.

Finally, she drew away, took a deep breath, and let the day settle into her bones. "Breakfast."

"What do you usually do for Christmas?" she asked, as they ate bagels and cream cheese.

"If I have time off, which is rare, I go up to my younger daughter's in San Jose, but my brother lives in Ojai with his family. I usually spend it with them—and my mother. My father passed away about ten years ago."

"Oh." She felt oddly abandoned, which was ridiculous.

"But that isn't the question, is it?"

She sighed and got up to refill their cups. "No. That isn't the question." She took her seat. "We spend it barbequing salmon on the patio. Susan, Doug, Peter and I. For the first few years, I had to do something outrageous—something that flew in the face of the holiday—stick my tongue out and say I didn't give a damn." She stopped and let her pent-up breath out. "But it's become our tradition, oddly enough—even for Peter and Susan, who lived for their Daddy as little kids, and for Christmas dinner at their grandparents." Myra stopped, her chest filling.

"And—is it something you can do, Myra? Now?"

She sat, remembering her visit to Derek. She had felt the bond that comes with long familiarity and creating children, but had any love remained? No. "I suppose I could, if I had to. And yes, for Eleanor and Cornelius I would do that even if Derek were there. I can manage it. But it isn't me they want, and I can't ask Susan to go."

"Would it be enough if you and Peter went?"

"No. She wants to see her grandchildren ... plural ... and her great grandson." Myra raised her shoulders and let them fall. "Who can blame her?"

"Then I guess it's up to Susan, isn't it?" He leaned back, having put the question they both knew was at the heart of it.

"It's not fair, Randy. To ask her to open up the past that way. I've been doing that, for the last couple of months and believe me, no one needs it. If it was just her grandparents, no problem, but it's confronting Derek ..."

"And the fact that you left the past in pieces, with a lot of unanswered questions."

She nodded. "And opening it up again may be better—might end it, or it might throw us all back to live it all over again—infinitely worse." She got up and took her cup to the kitchen.

"She's an adult, Myra."

"Yes. But it took years, Randy. High school and college were a constant struggle for her. Who am I to tell her she should go back there?" Myra put dishes into the dishwasher. Eleanor's face floated before her, became Cornelius's, then Eleanor's again. If she didn't ask Susan, those faces would haunt her.

Would she let Eleanor die without seeing her granddaughter again? "Eleanor had a terrible time of it when I accused Derek and kicked him out. She adored Susan. Said her imagination was a sign of brilliance ... artistic genius ... you name it." Myra gave a harsh laugh. "She was torn between her precious son and marvelous granddaughter ... so Susan's imagination became madness."

"Nasty." His voice was soft in her ear as he came up behind her and put his arms around her. "That must have been rough on you."

"I looked up to Eleanor in those days ... a sort of a mentor to academic wifehood. Even after she told me to put up with Derek's affairs and suggested she'd gone through the same thing with Cornelius. I didn't like it, but I admired her in a way—before Susan."

"And now?"

"I feel desperately sorry for her. Cornelius is right. She deserved better—from her husband and her sons. And Susan deserves a grandma, too." That hadn't occurred to her. For years Myra had wakened in the night, Eleanor's voice screaming that she was a home-wrecker.

"Does Grandma hate me now?" Susan had asked, her voice thin as a ten-year-old's.

"I'm sure she doesn't, honey." She'd reached for her daughter and pulled her to her. "But Daddy is still a little boy to her, Susan. She can't understand that he could hurt you."

"Neither can I!" Susan had cried and run off.

Myra had found her on her bed, face down, clutching the edge of the mattress with one hand, her pillow with the other. She'd had no explanation or even the hope of one to offer. She could do nothing but lay her hand on Susan's back and wait for the pain to subside on its own.

"Has Eleanor been in contact with Susan at all since then?"

Randy's question brought her back to the present. "No. I'm sure not. But then, I didn't think Peter had either. The whole thing … it's as though I lived behind blinders while another life went by out there."

"Just as well. You broke off and went on. If you hadn't, life would have continued to be hell."

She looked at him. "How long did it take you to figure that out?"

He smiled. "I did a lot of fishing for a year." He turned her toward the patio doors. "Out there, around Anacapa. The only beings you have to talk to are the seals and cormorants."

"God bless the sea," she murmured.

"Amen."

They fell silent.

"I've made a decision," she announced, turning to him. "Thanksgiving is next week. I'm celebrating what I have, first. Sinking into it. Getting to know its bumps and curves. Then I'll know I'm not acting on impulse again."

"I vote for that."

"You'll come help? You don't have to go to Ojai for Thanksgiving, do you?"

He leaned over and kissed her. "I'll come."

Myra, who had dreaded holidays since the family's breakup, poured herself into preparations. She pressed a white tablecloth for the big round table that for years had been a repository for junk, then retrieved her crystal from the back of high shelves and washed it. It wasn't until she was polishing the silver that she realized she was assuming Peter would be part of the celebration. He hadn't spoken to her since she'd forced Derek's address out of him.

She dried her hands and went to the phone. "I don't blame you a bit for being angry at me, Peter," she told his answering machine. "In your place I'd be furious. But I'd like you to come for Thanksgiving, so we can straighten it out." She hung up and stared at the instrument. Short of promising not to charge Derek, that was the best she could do.

She returned to cleaning and preparing, her mind singing with thoughts of Randy Larson, who continued to appear at odd times of day—a continuous surprise. Eleanor came and went from her thoughts, as did Cornelius, Susan, and Derek, but she was content to let them simmer on the back of the stove.

From Peter, she heard nothing.

Then, the day before Thanksgiving, she returned from shopping to a blinking answering machine.

"I'm spending it with Dad ... bye."

That was all. No "Hello, Mom." No acknowledgement of her peace-making. Only the faintly remorseful "bye."

She sat down and put her head in her hands, remembering that one day of closeness she'd ruined. If Susan charged her father with incest, they would never see Peter again. That felt certain.

"What's wrong?" Randy appeared beside her, holding a bouquet of golden chrysanthemums.

"It's Peter. He's not coming."

He pulled her to her feet and let her cry. "Eventually, he'll see it differently," he said when she'd finished and pulled away. "He had no right to stand between you and Derek, and he'll have to deal with that."

She nodded. "And until then, there's nothing I can do."

"Right. Except put away the groceries."

She made a noise that was half sigh, half laugh.

Thanksgiving dawned as balmy as a day in September. By mid-afternoon, the house smelled of turkey and bread, her table was set with a centerpiece of driftwood and gourds, and she took herself to the shower.

Susan and Doug arrived with pumpkin pie and a vegetable tray. Her daughter stopped on her way to the kitchen, gazed at the table, lifted her nose to the fragrance, and burst into tears.

"Whatever is the matter?" Myra asked, following her as she headed for the kitchen.

"It's like it used to be!" Susan turned from the counter where she had deposited her bundles, and threw her arms around her mother.

Myra held her for a long moment before giving her a gentle push. "Good grief, was it that good?"

She gave a snuffling laugh. "Is Peter coming?"

"I'm afraid not …"

"Hello?" The call from the front hall interrupted her, and Randy appeared, bearing wine. "It's not hard to find everyone today—just follow your nose." He came across the kitchen and kissed her.

Myra turned to the astonished faces of her daughter and son-in-law and made introductions. "I'd ask you to build a fire," she told him to give them time to recover. "Then it would be perfect. But I'm afraid it's just too damned warm."

"You're complaining?" Randy asked.

"I am. This time of year I actually miss Minnesota. After all these years, it still feels wrong to wear shorts on Thanksgiving."

"Okay, a fire it is." Randy declared. "Come on, Doug, let's do it."

And so, after moving the table closer to the open patio doors, they had a fire in the fireplace. Randy carved the bird. The clatter of passing dishes took Myra back to the past, when they'd exchanged this day with her in-laws. How strange that it should be the Bennings who were cut off and lonely now.

"I wish Grandma and Grandpa could be here." Susan's voice broke across the thought as though she was in her mother's head.

Myra opened her mouth to answer, but the doorbell interrupted. She excused herself and rose to answer it.

Peter stood on the doorstep, a bottle of wine under his arm.

"Well … hello!" she managed and stepped back for him to enter.

"Dad said I should come." His tone, as he passed her, was a mixture of embarrassment and concession.

"Really." She blinked.

"Peter!" Susan cried. "Mom said you weren't coming."

"Yeah. Changed my mind," he muttered. "'Lo, Sis … Doug …" He paused, staring at Randy, perplexed, as though trying to place him.

"Peter, meet my friend, Randy. Randy, my son Peter."

"Actually, we've met before." Randy rose and stretched out a hand. "When you were about twelve."

"Yeah?" Peter's brows formed a question. "You look familiar, but …"

"Your sister fell off the cliff," Randy added.

"Randy is a sheriff's deputy," Myra explained. "He answered the call that day."

Now Peter's brows rose in surprise. "A … oh, yeah? Really." He seemed at a loss as to how to go on.

"I'll get you a place setting," Myra exclaimed and headed for the kitchen.

Peter followed. "Dad says you had a right to know, and he's sorry he broke in."

Myra looked up from the plate in her hands. "Well, thank him for that."

Peter nodded. "But why … a sheriff's deputy, Mom? You're going to charge Dad?"

"Oh, good grief, no, Peter. It has nothing to do with …" She cut off the words as she realized they weren't true. "We're friends. More than friends, if you want to know. But charging your dad is Susan's business now." She handed him the place setting. "I'll get you a chair."

When Peter was seated, he gave Randy a sharp glance, then gave his food more than the attention it required.

"Where were you?" Susan demanded.

Peter's head shot up. "With Dad." The answer challenged her to object. Silence fell as the two confronted each other.

"At Grandma's and Grandpa's?" Susan's voice held a challenge also, tinged with resentment.

Peter shook his head. "He's going there, but he sent me here." He took a bite of turkey, then looked up at Susan, his hostility gone. "Grandma has cancer."

Susan's fork fell to her plate. "What? How do you know? What kind?"

"Breast." He didn't answer the other questions, and in the silence, no one picked up their forks.

"She's not doing well, Susan," Myra added, realizing the subject, once opened, had to be dealt with.

"How do you know?" Susan swung to her. "Why didn't you tell me?"

"I had lunch with Aunt Tricia just a couple of days ago. I guess they've done everything they can. It's just a matter of time, now."

"She's dying." Susan's voice carried certainty, and no one contradicted her. "I have to go see her, Mom. To find out if she's forgiven me …"

"She has." Peter spoke for the first time. "She wants to see you."

Myra bridled at Susan's idea that she needed forgiveness, from Eleanor or anyone else, but was grateful Peter didn't mentioned a Christmas reunion. If Susan went now, without Derek's presence, maybe they could dodge that bullet. "So go, Susan. Take the baby and Doug. It will do you good to know that fence is mended."

"What if she brings up Dad?" Susan stared at her plate. "She'll want to know if I'm going to charge him."

"Are you?" Peter's question was a shot.

"Let's hope she doesn't bring him up," Myra countered, trying to cut him off.

"I don't know." Susan's tone was calm. "I think I need to see him before I can decide."

Myra wanted to shake her head in a vehement 'no.' Face-to-face with the man she'd loved as a father? That was no time to decide. But Susan's voice said she'd made up her mind, and Myra remembered Randy's, "She's an adult," and kept still. "You have another decision to make, Susan, before you go. If Grandma wants to die believing nothing happened, are you going to let her?"

There was a long silence.

"And I guess I have to think about that, too," Myra added, nailing down one piece of the dilemma.

From his end of the table, Randy smiled and nodded his approval.

"All right." Susan sounded calm. "Will Dad be there?" Her voice was stiff, as though preparing itself for a necessary encounter.

"Your father is teaching in San Luis Obispo," Myra told her. "If you go in the middle of the week during the day, I doubt he'll be there."

Susan didn't answer.

"I'll call Grandpa and make sure. He'll understand," Myra assured her.

"He will? Why? Dad's his son. You mean he believed me?" Susan's voice was incredulous, and she shot Peter a look whose point could not be missed.

In her mind, Myra studied the face of the old man at the helm of the Serendipity and the words he'd spoken. "I think maybe he did." She was appalled at the implication of her own words. "I don't know that, Susan, it's just a guess. But I think he won't blame you for wanting to avoid your father."

"Okay." Susan's voice was less certain than her word.

"Do you want me to call, Susan? Go with you?" Myra was determined to keep hold of the opportunity to at least test Susan's reaction before making a decision about Christmas.

"Would you?"

"Sure." She could manage anything if it avoided a Christmas party, couldn't she? "Now let's eat. The food's getting cold."

Her order was greeted with relief, and the sound of knives and forks returned the table to normal. Conversation took on the extra zest of a hurdle crossed, and the subject didn't come up again until they'd cleared, put away, and washed up evidence of the feast.

"Call them, Mom." Susan's voice sounded taut but determined.

"All right. And you'll talk it through with Doug before you go?"

Her daughter nodded. "Make it soon—like tomorrow. Before I lose my nerve."

Myra turned and dialed the number that once had been part of everyday life.

"Benning residence." Cornelius's voice was as hearty as ever—almost.

"Hello. This is Myra."

"Ah." There was real pleasure in the word. "Happy Thanksgiving! What a lovely chance, sailing with you."

"I enjoyed it, Conny. And Happy Thanksgiving to you both." She paused, then plunged ahead. "I'd like to bring Susan and the baby to see Eleanor."

"Wonderful! That would be ... a great kindness." He struggled with the words.

"Good," she said, relieving him of the need to continue. "Can you tell me when would be a good time?"

"Anytime … but soon, Myra." His voice had become heavy again.

"How about tomorrow, then?" Myra glanced at Susan, who nodded.

"Fine. Perfect. I'll tell her." His energy returned.

"What's her best time of day?"

"Morning. And thank you. She'll bring the baby, you say?"

"Morning?" She mouthed the question at Susan, who nodded again.

"Morning's fine. And yes, she'll bring Billy. And Conny …" She broke off, fishing for some graceful way to put it, "Susan wants to avoid seeing her father. He won't be there, will he?" The last question came in a rush and sounded cruel to her own ears. She wished she could recall it.

His voice, when he answered, had gone dead, robbed of the anticipation she'd generated by the visit. "No. He won't be here. Not in the morning."

"Thank you." She struggled for a way to make it right. "It just makes it easier, this first time." Why did she say that, as though there'd be more than one visit?

"Sure. I know. We'll see you tomorrow."

She hung up. "Done." She rubbed her eyes.

"Bravo." Doug stepped forward and planted a kiss on her cheek. "And now we must be off. We have beasts to feed."

"Thank you, Sis." Peter's tone, for the first time in years, was genuine and warm, without the polite barrier it usually wore. "She really wants to see you."

Myra surprised him with a hug in gratitude for the gesture, for coming, and for not mentioning Christmas. Whether he read its intent didn't matter.

Ten minutes later, she was alone with Randy.

Myra sighed and sank onto the couch. "That felt right. And if she goes now, she doesn't have to go at Christmas."

"True. Except that she said she needs to see Derek to decide about charging him." He walked over to the sidebar and poured them the last of the Thanksgiving wine. "And Christmas would be an opportunity."

"One thing at a time. That's the key, isn't it? The whole thing is a minefield. We'll defuse one bomb at a time."

Randy put a glass of wine in her hand as an answer. "You did well. Just go by what feels right."

"One careful step at time. Not my natural mode, believe me."

"No?"

"No. I act on impulse and go crashing through … or haven't you gotten that picture? This step by step bit …" She broke off with a shudder.

Randy had crossed the room and was looking through her CD collection. "You seem to have lots of music."

"A little bit of everything. That's either great breadth or terminal indecision. Take your pick."

"Great breadth, of course." He chose a disc and put it on.

"Good," she breathed as the Beatles filled the room. "I need them, tonight."

He held out his hand. "Will you dance, Milady?"

"Good grief, Randy." She rose. "I haven't in years."

She felt fifteen and was glad her living room had no mirrors to deny it. Randy's eyes were on her face, not her body anyway.

She wondered, for a moment, whether he was a fresh new life or a refuge from her old, but was in no mood for the question tonight. Randy's offhand humility was the diametric opposite of Derek's ever-gregarious charm. He was protective, which Derek had been with their children, but with her … quite the opposite. Had her husband depended on her to anchor him? Like Cornelius? The weight of responsibility felt the same. Randy was, she decided, a great relief … as though she had, without knowing it, carried Derek's weight all of these years—as well as guilt for sending him away—and was just now casting him off.

She let herself disappear into the dance.

"Now," he said, an hour later, "I have to go home. My uniform is in Carpinteria, and I have to be on duty at seven."

"The end of a beautiful day." She sighed.

"A policeman's way, I'm afraid. Everyone's on duty the night after a holiday."

She gazed at him, her mind shifting from her world to his, where holidays meant families loaded into cars with drunken drivers. She held his face and kissed him. "Stay safe."

Chapter 18

The next morning, she woke up to sunlight. She stretched luxuriously, then remembered her date for the morning and came awake. She was going to have to hurry. By the time Doug drove up, the sun had disappeared behind low clouds. It looked as though the rains, a month late already, were finally arriving. Her day on the water had been a timely gift.

Cornelius welcomed them at the door. He stepped back and beamed at Susan. "Well, well, you've grown as lovely as we always knew you would. Welcome, my dear. And you are Douglas." He held out his hand, as warm and welcoming as he had been to Myra thirty years ago. "Come in, come in. That wind's getting chilly."

As they passed him into the house, he reached over and gave Myra a kiss on the cheek.

"This is Billy," Susan said, holding the baby up.

"Hello, Billy." Cornelius chuckled, beaming at the child. "It never occurred to me I'd ever be old enough to have a great-grandson. William Douglas, is it?"

"Right," Susan said, surprised.

So Cornelius kept track more than they'd known. On the piano in the corner, there was a picture of the baby. Had Peter given them that? And another, more familiar, of Peter and Susan as children. When had that reappeared? Myra could have sworn it hadn't been there on her brief visit to Eleanor.

"Eleanor?" Cornelius called. "They're here!"

The tall woman who came down the hall, her hand on one wall for support, was a specter, bearing the outline of the woman Myra had visited two months ago. Nothing more. Myra laid her hand on her daughter's arm to soften the shock and to cover her own.

"Grandma." The word was hardly a breath. Susan handed Billy to Doug and walked forward to offer her arm as Eleanor cleared the hall and came across the room.

Eleanor put her hand up to Susan's cheek. "Why, you're lovely!" she exclaimed. "Isn't she, Conny?"

Cornelius came to her other side and they led her to a chaise that faced the windows and the sea. It had once been in her bedroom, Myra remembered. When they had her seated with an afghan over her knees, she waved them away impatiently. "Ridiculous to be so weak. Now …" She clasped her hands. "Come round here and let me take a look at you."

"This is Douglas," Susan said, holding out her hand toward Doug.

Doug reached forward and shook her hand. "And this is your great-grandson, Billy." He held out the baby. "Shall I put him on your lap?"

"Oh, please," Eleanor breathed. She reached out her arms and Doug handed her the baby, whose eyes opened wide in surprise but made no sound. Eleanor took the soft hands in hers. "Conny, come see. Isn't he wonderful?"

When he stepped forward, Cornelius had a camera in his hands. He raised it to his face, but not before Myra saw that his eyes were wet.

"Come stand by me," Eleanor cried to Susan, "and Douglas, you come to my other side."

Myra viewed the vignette from across the room, behind Cornelius. Eleanor's eyes were alight as she held up a hand to Susan, the other holding the baby. Susan shot Myra a glance, noticing her exclusion, but Myra waylaid her protest with a gesture. For her to stand behind Eleanor's chair without Derek beside her would ruin the balance Eleanor had created with such joy. Her very presence was the discordant note, she realized, for it pointed to the missing figure. She walked back further and sank into a seat in the shadows where the humiliation of being the wrong note would be less acute.

"Conny, bring everyone a drink." Eleanor's voice had energy now.

"What will you have?" Conny asked. "Coffee … tea? Eleanor will have tea, I know." He gave in with a smile, then collected orders from the rest of them.

"Now tell me, child …" Eleanor turned again to Susan. "What have you been up to all this time? Other than getting married and having a baby, that is."

"Well, I went to college …"

"Yes, to UCSB. Peter told us. He comes to see us once in a while, you know. You studied psychology, I think. Is that right?"

Myra leaned back and closed her eyes. The questions and answers sounded like the conversation of distant relatives. Only she and Susan knew what an achievement that had been, surviving daily advances by boys, even an occasional date and party. Susan had lived at home, in no way ready for a coed dorm or an Isla Vista apartment. With twice-weekly therapy and two quarters off to recover the energy needed to go at it again. She'd finally stood on the lawn above the lagoon and received her degree. For one awful moment that day, Myra thought she saw Derek, half-concealed in the trees. When she looked again he was gone, if he'd ever been there, but the sighting brought back the sense of calamity that rarely left her in those days.

She brought her mind back to half-listen to Susan and Doug tell of their landscaping business and the dogs. Eleanor seemed content to listen, to make their lives part of hers, erasing the calamitous past. And she hadn't mentioned Derek. Myra relaxed further.

"You see Myra," Eleanor's voice brought her to attention. "You had nothing to fear, after all. Here they are back, having a perfectly fine time."

Myra smiled. "I'm glad … for you and for them."

"For all of us." She held the baby's hands and tried to stand him up. "We'll be like you, Sweetie," she said to him. "Practically brand new, with no past at all."

Susan shot Myra a long look.

"Isn't that right, Susan? " Eleanor released one hand from the baby's grasp and reached for Susan's.

Susan froze, then put a hand on her grandmother's. "I always loved you, Grandma."

Myra started to breathe again. Billy began to wriggle and fuss, and Doug reached forward to pick him up. "Nap time," he explained.

Eleanor reached for her cup with a trembling hand.

"I'm afraid you're tiring, my dear," Conny said, crossing the room.

"Like the baby. Such a nuisance. But you came. So wonderful." She took a sip of tea and replaced the cup carefully. "Come, Myra, take my hand."

Myra went forward, willing herself to agree to the illusion as gracefully as Susan had. "I'm glad we came, Eleanor. It's been good."

"Hasn't it?" She reached for Susan's hand as well.

"And now I want only one thing, before I go."

Myra, her hand imprisoned, stiffened in spite of herself.

"What's that?" Susan asked.

"To have my family around me for one more Christmas."

Susan stared at her mother, her face clearly asking if Myra had tricked her into this.

Cornelius, who had disappeared and returned with a wheel chair, broke the long silence. "Your family all loves you, my dear, whether they are all here at once or not."

Myra thanked him with her eyes, but Eleanor was having none of it.

"Oh, I know, I know, but it isn't the same. I want it just once like it was before. They'll give me that, won't you, my dears?" She pushed herself forward in her chair and let Cornelius raise her to her feet without waiting for their reply.

Saved for the moment, they waited for Cornelius to wheel Eleanor to the bedroom and return before departing.

"She would die happy if she had that," he muttered as he bid them goodbye.

"What did she mean, have her family together for Christmas, Mom?" Susan exploded as soon as they pulled out of the drive.

The rain had arrived, and the wipers emphasized the pause between question and answer.

"Exactly what you think she means, I'm afraid." Myra should have anticipated that request—prepared Susan for it—but now that it was out, there was no point in dodging it.

"You mean Susan and her dad there together?" Doug's voice had lost its usual calm.

"Yes. She wants everyone. According to Patricia, Derek's brother Roger is coming from Argentina, too."

"Sounds like a gathering for a funeral." Doug took the curve onto the Alameda Padre Serra too fast, then headed for the Mission.

"Like attending your own … for Eleanor, anyway." Myra looked at the back of Susan's head. "But you don't have to do it."

"No? How can I not?" Her voice rose, then she put a hand to her mouth in a visible effort to control it. "She's dying."

Doug put a hand on her knee. "Don't think about it right now. You went today, and you did a terrific job."

"That's for sure. You were great," Myra agreed. "That's enough."

"She looks so sick. I didn't expect that. I know I should have, but she was always so strong."

"A very single-minded strength," Myra added, wishing that decisions were as simple for her as they were for Eleanor. "Keeping the family intact. Above all and without any doubts—ever."

"Then why did she … banish us?" Susan blurted the last word as though naming her exile for the first time.

"Because I didn't do that—I broke it up." And that act came flowing back unbidden.

"Where's he going?" Susan had cried that day watching the Jag drive off, its engine roaring. "You can't do that! Just send him away—he's us!"

"No, Susan." Myra had tried to take her in her arms.

Susan pushed her away and fled to her bed, flopping face down in bewildered tears. "How can this be happening? Everything breaking apart in a day!"

"No, I did that. It was me." Susan's declaration brought Myra back to the present. "So, I guess it's up to me to …"

"No." Myra's voice was sharp as she cut of the words that echoed from the past—"*Peter's right! It's just me! I'm crazy—I'm always flying off. I'm just ... bring Daddy back! It's me!*" Though her words were no longer shrill, they carried the acceptance of fact. "No it isn't up to you. Don't talk that way. You father did it. Period."

"Did you know, Mom? That that was what she wanted?" There was accusation in Susan's voice.

"Yes. Patricia told me. But I was hoping that if you went today, Eleanor wouldn't push for more. I was wrong."

"I wish you'd forewarned me."

"I should have, but I didn't want to land it on you all at once. If she hadn't mentioned it, you wouldn't have to cope with it at all." How silly she'd been to think she could stop the avalanche of unfinished past.

"I said I had to see him to decide…" Susan cut herself off mid-thought and gazed out into the rain.

"Whether to charge him?" Doug finished for her. "It doesn't have to be now, Susan. Today was good. That's enough."

But Susan fell silent. An old anger rose in Myra. Derek had given Susan a life sentence, and now his parents were asking her to deny it had ever happened. And would she—could she—charge him after eating Christmas dinner with him? It wasn't credible. *Don't do it,* she wanted to yell, *don't satisfy their illusions at the expense of your own mental health.* But the words didn't erase the image of Eleanor's dying face for her any more than they would for Susan. Death's demands didn't fade. Nor would they fade if Susan refused the request.

"I think we all need to put a little distance on this morning," she offered. "We need to get our breaths."

"Let's go train some dogs," Doug said, moving them past the impasse. "They have a way of putting things right."

"Susan reached over and brushed Doug's face. "Good idea. An antidote."

"And you, Myra?" Doug turned his head. "Do you want to join us?"

"Thank you, but Randy's coming over later."

"Ha. That should do it."

Fifteen minutes later, they drew up at Myra's house. She reached over the seat and put a hand on Susan's shoulder. "Call Dr. Garvitz. He'll help you sort it out."

Susan nodded. She put a hand on Myra's. "I will. But it's ... it feels like something that had to happen."

Myra wanted to object, but held back in response to an inner voice that kept repeating, "Let her be."

Once she was inside, she wanted a nap, but when she lay down, the war in her head wouldn't subside. She rolled over and got up in exasperation at her circling mind. She was helpless. That was it. The decision was Susan's, not hers. Susan's face, as she left them was pale, heavy with the weight of the choice, but not hysterical, not begging her mother for help. Myra was left to watch, to reach out only if needed.

She turned to her tried-and-true method of relief—the drawing board.

> Matilda appeared and, floating her scarf above her head, pranced over puddles left by the rain.
>
> "What do you think you're doing?" Alphonse cried, coming in from

the right. "Why aren't you cleaning up this mess?"

"I'm entertaining Rufus. To perk up his quills," Matilda replied.

"He doesn't seem impressed," Eustasia commented, pointing to the curled up ball in the corner. "I think a feather dusting would be more effective." She tickled Rufus with her wing.

Rufus leapt to his feet, his quills flying, causing Matilda to land in a puddle and leaving both Alphonse and Matilda looking like pin cushions. Eustasia laughed at the pair.

"Who ever heard of tickling a porcupine!" Matilda cried.

The Boots appeared and their owner gazed down at Matilda, splashed and quilled, her scarf dragging in the mud, at Alphonse, a quill sealing his beak shut, at Rufus, forelegs wound around himself to cover his nakedness.

"Helping each other again, I see," said Boots.

Myra put her pen down, relieved of some pressure, though she couldn't have said what. Frustration at her own helplessness? The talent of humans to compound their own miseries? Who knew? But she was hungry. She went downstairs to fix herself a sandwich. When Randy arrived an hour later, she was settled enough to look back on the morning without rebelling against the quandary Eleanor had created.

"So how did it go?" He kissed her before she could answer.

She drew back and considered his face. What human messes had he already dealt with this morning? She would have to learn to read the telltale signs. Now she read only the concern in his eyes. "Fine ... and awful."

"That's a start." He frowned. "You look as though you've been run over."

"Thanks. But I'm better than I was. I just need to get out of here. I feel as though I'm trapped in the house I lived in fifteen years ago."

"This *is* the house you lived in fifteen years ago."

"Thanks again. Just take me to your house, will you? Please?"

He took her in his arms. "Sure. Find your raincoat, and let's go. Have you fed the dogs?"

"I have. Let me get my toothbrush this time."

As they rolled south along the freeway, she filled him in. "I'd love to tell Susan not to go, but I can't.

"Which is why you look like someone dragged you behind the Lucky LuLu." He put a hand on her knee.

"Shark bait? I feel like it."

They drove without talk for a while, letting the early dark of a rainy day enclose them.

"It sounds as though your Susan is stronger than you thought." His voice came out of the dark,

Myra heard again Susan's steady voice as she tussled with the dilemma. "Yes, it does. I always thought of her as fragile," Myra confessed. "She was so intense and vulnerable."

"Not like her mother." His voice held the smile she couldn't see.

She shot him a glance. "Meaning what?"

"That you are both of those things—but you hide it well." He reached a hand over and tousled her hair.

"From years of experience." She leaned back and closed her eyes. "But Susan was always off in Neverland, making up plays, stories. A dangling ribbon could become a captive princess ... you never knew."

"Not at all like stories of scrawny chickens and crippled herons," he teased. "House-That-Jack-Built coming up." He swung off at the Carpinteria exit, and they rolled through town toward the sea. "So, Mother Hubbard, are you ready to put it in her hands and give yourself space?"

"Yes. I think that's why I had to get out of the house."

He opened his door. "Subject closed, then. Okay?"

As they climbed the stairs, he stopped at the second level and opened the door to the bedroom. "Dinner can wait." He swept her inside and closed the door, then heated her body with his lips.

She returned the kiss and let herself float into unencumbered space, aware only of his gentle touch as he slid her coat from her shoulders.

Chapter 19

Myra spent the next week distracting herself with the Rabbleville Varmints' Christmas preparations and avoiding her own. The strip she was drawing was, in fact, for next year, but she made a habit of staying parallel with the current season. It made drawing less artificial.

> Matilda knit Eustasia a sweater with one sleeve. Rufus constructed neck-warmers out of plastic pipe covered in sequins for Matilda and Alphonse, and Rufus made ice-skates for everyone. Together they bought a tree that wouldn't stand and had to be hung from a branch. Alphonse snitched a string of lights from a nearby roof; Eustasia scavenged shells from the beach for ornaments. Rufus contributed by shooting his quills into a vat of silver paint. Those they hung from the tree to catch the light.
> "You see?" Matilda gloated, surveying the results. "We don't need any old collector."
> On Christmas day, they appeared decked out in their skates, spinning on a pond. Eustasia wore Matilda's gift sweater, which almost went around her; Matilda and Alphonse spun with their wings around each others' shoulders, their long necks a-glitter, and Rufus wore a cloak that flew in the wind as, with a push from Alphonse, he made a four-footed plunge through the midst, sending them all flying.

But then the strips were scanned and sent off into electronic space, and Myra was left with the calendar staring her in the face. Susan hadn't called. She would have broken her pledge to stay out of Susan's decision three times over if she'd known what advice to give her. Any decision would be better than this void. She was left to imagine Susan confronting her father. Or greeting him? The face her mind brought up veered from the frozen face of shock or terror to the eager anticipation of the child that had been. The transmuting images gave her vertigo.

Three days later, Susan called.

"I'm going, Mom. I've made up my mind." Her voice was tense, but under control.

Myra sat down, "You are. You can manage it?"

"Dr. Garvitz is encouraging me. He says it might be a good thing … slaying the giant under the bed. Bring closure."

Not if she charges him, Myra said to herself. "And you're all right with it?" Myra was amazed that she could find so little to say.

Susan laughed. "Depends on which minute you ask. This minute, I'm jittery—probably only because I'm calling you. Casting it in stone."

"Nothing's ever set in stone." Not true, she responded to herself. Some deeds are. She wanted to tell Susan she was glad she was trying, but she wasn't glad. One whole part of her wanted nothing to do with this charade. Still, telling Susan she could back out was probably a bad idea. "Susan, would it help …" She paused to frame the thought, "… to meet with Derek first? So it's not everyone?"

Susan was silent for a minute. "No, I don't think so, Mom. People—Grandma and Grandpa, anyway—somehow dilute it. If I was alone with him … no, I don't want to do that." The words came in a rush of certainty.

She'd schooled herself for one scenario, Myra realized, and shifting now would only derail it. "This will be a real victory. Keep telling yourself that."

"That's what Doug says. All right. I'm getting off the phone now, before I change my mind."

"I'll call Aunt Tricia."

"Wait! I almost forgot. Will you come here for Christmas Eve? You and Randy? Peter said he'd come. We can have our own Christmas then."

Myra almost protested that she wanted them all at her house, but reconsidered. Preparations would keep Susan busy and avoid memories of Christmases past. "I'd love to. I'll ask Randy—he may have family plans or be on duty, but you can count on me."

"Thanks, Mom." Susan sounded far more grateful and relieved than the occasion called for.

Myra hung up and sat, feeling her muscles relax. The relief, she knew, was for a decision made. The rest, she would just have to live through.

She picked up the phone and called Tricia with the news, but got her answering machine.

Leaving a message to call, Myra hung up the phone and felt her muscles come to life, released from the clamps that had imprisoned them. It was finished.

And she had to shop. Not a job she'd ever relished, but wandering through small shops in old shopping district at least amused her, and this year she could start with Randy and Billy ... new additions to her list. She changed and headed for town.

She was deep into blocks and puzzles far too advanced for her infant grandson, when a long necked, very yellow chicken decked out in scarf and spectacles caught her eye. Surely it was Matilda. She found a dish, cup, and spoon similarly decorated to complete the set and left the store with Matilda's head protruding from the sack. She went on to the hardware store. A woodworking tool would be the right gift for Randy, but when she stood before the array of power tools, she couldn't remember what she'd seen in his shop. Instead, she selected a drill for Doug, who'd been swearing at his cheap version.

And for Randy? A fishing something, maybe. The fishing and hunting store was a rude shock after the gay colors of the children's store. Everything was in camouflage, a monotony guaranteed to deaden the soul. "Something in color," she told the salesman who quickly spotted her bewilderment. He led her to the flies, which tickled her imagination, but she had no idea whether salt-water fishermen used flies. "Perhaps scuba equipment, then," the clerk suggested, clearly as amused by her dingy-lady specifications as she was by his soldier/great-white-hunter store. She selected a torch in orange and goggles in iridescent green, grateful that divers, at least, had no objection to being visible.

She wandered down the street looking into shop windows for the next idea and found herself stopping at a display of scarves—Eleanor's forte—and caps perfect for Cornelius. She stood gazing at the display and stood imagining the day ahead. Derek, she would treat as a distant acquaintance. She'd watched others pull that off at Christmas parties; surely she could manage the same. A little practice was all it took. Were the holidays such a minefield for everyone? An image rose in her mind of Cornelius snapping a picture of Derek and her standing behind Eleanor's chair. She jerked away. Not that. She shook herself free and entered the store before she could retreat from her decision. She bought the scarf and cap quickly, choosing the ones that had first caught her eye.

Once back onto the street, she turned to shopping for Peter as an antidote and found her favorite model shop. Peter still, as he had as a boy, built model ships in his spare time. But she wandered through masses of intricate rigging only to keep returning to the sailboat that looked like the Serendipity, revisiting Cornelius's plea each time. Peter probably already has one like that, she told herself, and the model presented little challenge for an expert. Finally, she went to a display as far away as she could get and bought a Seventeenth Century Spanish galley.

Now for Susan. She stood on State Street, looking up and down as though she'd find the perfect gift in the arms of some passerby. Then she remembered Susan's offhand comment that she couldn't wait until Billy was old enough for stories—she'd like to write them herself, someday. Myra turned and crossed the street to the bookstore. Fifteen minutes later, she emerged with a book on writing for children. Not enough, but a start, and she would supplement it with a donation to their dog-training endeavor.

Time to go home. She was drained. She headed for the parking structure, dumped her packages into the trunk, then wove her way through the throngs of shoppers to the freeway. She flipped on the radio, which brought news of the ever-increasing number of fires, robberies, auto accidents, and suicides that came with the season. Had it always been so, or were they brought close by Randy's jangling telephone? Or was it because she'd become one of those who found celebrating the holidays like playing in a wasps' nest?

Peter's Honda stood in the drive. Surprised and pleased, she parked at the curb, and he appeared at her front door.

"I'll get out of your way," he called and headed for his car.

The jockeying about with cars gave her surprise time to settle. He filled the silence that had spread, encompassing every detail of her life. When she was securely in the garage with her packages retrieved, and he was parked in her drive once again, she invited him to lunch.

"Thanks, I've eaten. I was hoping for an apricot bar, though. Have you done your baking yet?"

She cocked her head at him and put her hands on her hips. "You came all the way out here for a cookie?"

He grinned and headed for the kitchen, where he knew the Christmas baking would be stacked in boxes on the counter.

"And would you like a cup of coffee to go with that?" she asked.

"That would be great." He took his handful of cookies toward the patio.

"Better not go out there unless you want to share," she warned him, as she filled the pot.

He swerved and sat at the breakfast table, watching her and munching. It wasn't until she had the pot dripping and served herself a couple of cookies that he came to the point of his visit.

"When is Susan going to make up her mind?"

"She has. She's going."

"She is!" The words exploded from him, and he sat back in such obvious relief that she frowned.

"She's already been up to see Grandma. Why does it matter so much?"

"For Dad." He took a bite of cookie.

"Peter, do you see your father? Often, I mean?"

He looked at her, then down. "Not too often. But he called me—quite a while ago, now—and asked if I'd go hiking with him. That was the first I'd heard from him." Peter fiddled with a cookie. "So when he calls, which isn't often, I go. Hiking … sailing sometimes. That's all. He asks about you … says the whole thing was a huge mistake, and he wants to work it out with you, somehow." Peter looked up, a plea in his eyes.

"With me? Not with Susan?" She stared, dislocated, her mind shifting back to her lone confrontation with Derek two months ago.

"With both. He told me … what he'd done. Said you'd done what most wives would do when you threw him out. He wanted me to understand that. Take it as a lesson. If he ever caught me cheating on my wife—or my girl, for that matter—he'd give me a thrashing."

"Really. Good for him, then. But Susan … that's a whole different level, Peter. I was hurt. She was damaged. No thrashing will put that right."

Peter stared at the lone cookie on the napkin. "If he did it."

The words revived the nightmare doubt that had risen after that meeting then receded under Randy's reassurances. Now, Peter, staring at the table, waited for her response. "Do you honestly believe Susan made it up then believed it so strongly that she would have nothing to do with boys for years?"

"I don't know what to believe." His fingers traced patterns on the table. "Susan used to be my best friend."

"And now?" She spoke carefully. Peter rarely opened up this way. Confession had freed him.

"She knows I don't believe her—partly. And that I still see Dad." He pushed the napkin away and rose. "I have to go, Mom. Thanks for those …" He pointed to the lone cookie. "And for showing up. Here I was, home for my Christmas cookies, and you weren't here!" His self-derision was a little forced, covering the hole he'd just dug for himself.

"Take some with you."

He drove off and Myra turned to the telephone. She put her hand on it and then withdrew it, the image of the family photo returning. For Peter, she told herself, stepping into Eleanor's shoes and knowing the importance of family full well. She picked up the receiver and dialed. Patricia answered.

"Hi, Patricia, Myra."

"Ah! Thank goodness. I didn't want to rush you, but I was about to call …"

"I know. But it's been tough, but I called to tell you we'll come."

"Susan, too?" Tricia's voice rose a notch in relief.

"Yes. She did go to see your folks, you know."

"Do I. It picked Mom up for the rest of the week. Thank you for that … and Susan, too."

"You're welcome. It felt like the right thing to do."

"A wonderful thing, and that you're coming even more so. Dad will be so relieved."

"I don't know how long I'll stay, but …"

"We'll see how it goes, Myra. I'm not into child or ex-spouse torture, believe me." Her tone was warm with gratitude and understanding. "Okay, that's settled. Myra, when this is over, let's have lunch again."

"Good idea."

"And talk about something besides family. I have a client who's a graphic artists' agent. He had one of your cartoons on his wall. I told him I was related to you—I hope you don't mind—and he'd like to meet you."

"Really. That sounds intimidating."

"Nonsense, Myra. I've never known you to be intimidated. He represents artists who work in animation, too."

"Now you've really whetted my appetite." Only in self-indulgent fantasy had her trio been animated.

"Good. There's life after Christmas. Okay?"

"Amen. Thanks, Patricia." She hung up, her body warmed by the return of a friendship she hadn't realized she missed so much.

"Susan's going," she told Randy when he stopped by that afternoon.

He paused with a cookie halfway to his mouth. "Good for her. Can she do it?"

"I don't know. I'm going to try not to think about it. Speaking of which, she wants the family at her house Christmas Eve—probably to distract herself, which is a good idea. She said to ask you. Can you come or are your kids expecting you?"

"No, they don't have enough time off to come down, and I can never get off this time of year to go up there."

"And your son? John?"

"Is at sea. I'll be on call, but I'd love to."

"That's set, then." Myra sank back, content to have insured one good evening at least. "It'll celebrate the present ... seal it off from the past. We need that."

"That we do. And I'll be happy to give you—and me—a great big dose." He reached over and drew her to him, planting a long kiss on her lips. "How's that for starters?" He released her and looked at his watch. "And now I have to go."

The settling of plans released Myra and let her work for the next days, setting her Rabbleville Varmints to making New Year's resolutions. Matilda was to stop snooping so as to prevent further stretching her neck. Rufus would practice calmness and so avoid accidental quill launchings, Alphonse promised to sit an hour a day to see the world from the same level as the rest of them, and Eustasia swore off the contents of open garbage cans, which gave her gas. Myra was grateful for the illusion that this Christmas was past and the air cleared for sailing into the future.

Each day she walked the mesa and the beach. The sea, like her comic strip, returned perspective and humor to the waiting.

When Christmas Eve arrived, she concentrated on the evening with her family. Peter was already there when she arrived.

"Here," Susan said, handing her Billy. "You can give him a bottle, if you would. Doug and Peter are out in the kennels. Queenie had her puppies this morning, would you believe it? A Christmas present for us." Her face glowed with the excitement of the event.

Myra was grateful to the dog for the additional distraction. She took the baby and sat in a rocking chair, watching Susan in the kitchen preparing clam chowder and Christmas bread, her family's traditional Christmas Eve dinner. A strange mixture of sadness and pleasure flooded her as she watched her carry on the rituals without her.

Doug and Peter, shaking the rain from their slickers, came in to report that the six new puppies were doing fine and mother was doing a good job of taking care of them. They'd set up an extra heater in the kennel. As soon as they'd given the news and hung up their wet coats, they crowded around Susan in the kitchen, smelling the soup.

"Wash your hands and set the table," she ordered them. "We're ready to eat."

"Is Randy coming?" Susan asked, sticking her head around the door.

Myra roused herself from the near-somnambulant state induced by the sleeping child in her arms and looked at her watch. "Yes. He got off an hour ago, I think, but something's always holding him up this time of year. He wouldn't want us to wait."

Susan frowned. "It must be awful, tending bloody traffic accidents while everyone else is feasting around the fire."

Myra stared at her daughter's departing back, realizing how totally she'd been caught up in her family crisis, how little she'd considered Randy's state of mind. Frequently, Randy came in as though escaping the world of gang-bangers, wife-beaters, and all those whose celebrations ended in disaster. As though her crisis was a relief. When this was over she was going ask to ride with him for a few nights.

He arrived when they were halfway through their soup. Myra examined his face, which seemed only warmed by their welcoming presence. Once he'd been served and conversation had resumed, she saw the glow disappear. His face was lined, and when he smiled and responded to a query from Susan, it seemed he was coming from another place. How much of that had she missed?

She let her remorse die in the flurry of presents, the warmth of his body as he sat next to her on the couch, and the Christmas music from the stereo in the corner. They finished the evening with a visit to the kennels, where Queenie lay among the wriggling black balls.

"Merry Christmas," she said, taking Susan in her arms. No one, she realized, had mentioned the coming day.

"Follow me home?" she asked Randy as they went toward their cars.

"Righto. I'm off until tomorrow night."

The pleasure of the evening and the promised warmth of the night to come carried Myra down the freeway the short distance to home.

"What held you up?" she asked, holding the door for him.

"Ah …" He took her in his arms. "Nothing you want to know about tonight."

"An accident?"

He looked down at her. "Stubborn, aren't you?"

"Yes."

"A bunch of kids with too much to drink. I'm always grateful when it's no one I know." He kissed her. "Now let's have a nightcap and go to bed."

She took the drink he handed her without a murmur, happy enough to accept release from the day and float into the warmth of the night.

Chapter 20

Christmas day, Myra awoke to blinding sun in her eyes. Already the day attacked. She rolled over. Randy, asleep beside her, reminded her that Christmas Eve, at least, had been good.

Now, the trial was here. She slipped out of bed to shower, then woke Randy to share the Christmas bread.

"Are you all right?" he asked, pulling on his robe.

"I'm numb. Is that a good sign?"

"Could be worse." He took her in his arms and kissed her. "Still numb?"

"No. Can I stay here all day?"

He laughed. "I'm hungry."

An hour later, Randy left for his brother's in Ojai, and she was left staring at her empty house. She took the dogs and headed out across the mesa toward the water, walking quickly to work her muscles. Once on the beach, she strode all the way to the surfers' spot at the campus point, then turned and paced to the oil processing plant at the north end. By the time she returned home, she was blessedly emptied out. Tired. And it was time to dress and go.

Susan, Doug, and the baby were waiting for her when she arrived to pick them up.

"You probably won't believe it, but I've been ready for an hour," Susan said as she secured Billy's car seat.

"Whatever for?" Myra searched her daughter's face.

"To get it over with. Go quickly, please." She took the seat next to Myra, then closed her eyes, waiting for Doug to put the bag of presents into the trunk. "This is crazy-making. One minute, I think it's twenty years ago, and I'm going to Grandma's for Christmas, the next I'm shaking like a leaf in the middle of a nightmare I can't even name."

Myra put a hand on Susan's knee. "Remember what Dr. Garvitz used to say when things got rough."

Susan smiled. "Just slow it down, Susan."

"Ready." Doug climbed into the seat beside Billy.

"We ate Christmas dinner on Grandma's deck, once, when it was this warm," Susan reminisced as they drove toward the freeway. "Remember? We opened presents out there too, and the paper kept blowing away. Grandpa gave us kites and took us down to the beach to fly them. Peter and Daddy even went off to surf ..." She cut herself off as though her words were carrying her beyond her depth.

"Those were good days," Myra said softly. Was it possible today would give them back? But Susan, beside her, sat motionless, her eyes focused on some distant place.

The car fell silent. Myra made a half-hearted attempt at conversation about landscaping and Christmas sales, then gave it up and let the quiet wrap each in their thoughts until they pulled into the Benning driveway.

Cornelius met them at the door, his arms outstretched. Susan went into them immediately. Their entrance was far easier, this second time. Eleanor sat in a wheelchair by the open door to the deck. She wore a crimson blouse and a green and gold velvet turban sporting a gold-filigree star. Her legs were covered with a snow-white blanket strewn with gold snowflakes. The only shock was her face. Eleanor was an artist at subdued make-up, but today red patches of rouge glowed against her parchment skin, and her mouth was a wound across her face.

"You're here!" she cried, raising her arms for their embraces.

"Hello all!" Patricia's voice boomed from the kitchen, turning it into a party.

Myra looked around the room quickly. He wasn't here yet. Nor was Roger. The balding man on the couch with his laptop was Patricia's husband, Conrad.

"Cheers," he said, lifting his hand.

"Cheers, Conrad," she responded and headed for the kitchen. She'd always liked the man. Far shyer than she'd expected for anyone in the movie industry, he still managed to convey warmth and sympathy in a gesture.

"What can I do?"

"Nothing at all …" Tricia began, then turned to look at her. "Sorry. Mistake. You can peel potatoes. Will that do?"

"Perfect."

Through the door, they could see Eleanor trying to bounce the baby on her lap again. Susan stood beside her chair, her expression alternating between distress and joy. "It's really done wonders for her, seeing that baby—and Susan, too. I guess it must become vital in a basic sort of way, when you're dying, to see some part of yourself continuing." The childless Patricia's voice held more than a hint of sadness.

"Mm. Well, my mother certainly lives on. I hear her voice in my head every day—don't cut the potatoes so small, Myra, they'll turn to mush."

Tricia laughed. "Isn't that the truth?"

Myra continued to watch as Eleanor returned the baby to Susan then leaned back, tired from the exertion. How long would she last, today? Could she survive it at all?

Susan passed Billy to Doug and came toward her, her face a plea. "Can I help in the kitchen?"

"Of course," Myra smiled.

"Come join the great escape," Tricia invited, keeping her voice low. "You can get those green beans on to cook."

"How are you doing?" Myra asked.

"All right, except Grandma's just—so different. I can't get used to it," Susan explained, taking the beans to the sink. "I feel as though … I've cheated her out of time with Billy … all of us."

They heard Peter's voice in the hall. He came directly to the kitchen and kissed both Myra and his sister before going in to Eleanor.

Fifteen minutes later, Patricia glanced at her watch, then at Susan. "They're late."

Susan bit her lip, but was saved by Billy, who they could hear fussing in the living room.

"I have to nurse him." Clearly relieved, Susan dried her hands and disappeared.

"I thought Roger would be staying here," Myra said.

"He is. He and Derek went off to do something with the boat. Let's finish the table. Hopefully they'll show up while the turkey's still fit to eat." She set off for the dining room with cranberry sauce, and Myra followed with the butter and jam. She stopped in the doorway, not knowing whether to laugh or cry. Every member of her family bore a scarlet brand on one cheek.

She put a finger to her own cheek. It came away red. She hurried toward the table. This wasn't a day for thinking too much. She was heading back to the kitchen when the door opened and a softer, paunchier version of her ex-husband entered, followed by Derek, himself.

They stared at each other across empty space.

Myra had a sudden sense of returning to the place where they both belonged. Dangerous waters. "Hello again," she said, cooling her voice to create space. Where was Susan?

Derek gave her a sad, remorseful, and terribly familiar smile.

A plea. Or was it forgiveness? Both? Peter was right. He wanted her back. She recoiled from the thought and half-turned to the man next to him.

"Myra, do you remember Roger?"

"Only vaguely," Myra confessed, putting a hand out.

He pulled the offered hand to his mouth and kissed it. Myra resisted the impulse to jerk it away and hoped her faked smile was not as grotesque as it felt.

She stepped aside and turned as they passed her. Susan stood at the bedroom door rubbing Billy's back. Her eyes, fixed on the pair, were filled with confusion. What did that mean?

Peter stepped into the space between. "'Lo, Dad."

Derek's face relaxed. He beamed and grasped his son's shoulder, giving it a squeeze. "Roger, do you remember Peter?"

Roger shook his hand. "You've grown up to look just like your dad."

The warmth of the interchange lessened the tension enough for Myra to take a breath. The men went forward to embrace Eleanor and greet their father before Derek turned to look for Susan.

She came forward, holding Billy tight to her chest. Her gaze was intense, as though recollecting every line of his face. Tears stood in her eyes. Myra read fear there, too, but not the terror she expected.

"Roger, do you remember Susan?" Derek asked.

A stroke of genius, Myra thought, for Roger stepped forward, deflecting Susan's attention. But then, as Myra watched, a strange look came over her daughter's face that she couldn't read.

"I'm not sure," Susan mumbled.

Roger put his hand out, but Susan gave a little wave instead of gripping it and withdrew her hand to the baby's back. Myra recognized it as a habit from an earlier period when the touch of a man had been abhorrent. Susan's eyes moved from one man to the other.

"It's good to see you, Susan," The quiet of Derek's voice belied the eyes that searched hers and the question there.

Susan nodded. "Hello."

Her daughter had never managed a poker face, and the confusion of emotions that suffused her eyes and choked off the word clutched at Myra's heart.

"This is Billy," Susan managed, turning Billy to face him.

But when Derek reached for the baby, she didn't respond.

"It's time to wash, everyone," Patricia called from the kitchen door. "Dinner's waiting!"

Myra saw Susan sag with relief as the men turned and headed for the powder room. Doug came up and put an arm around his wife. "Shall I put him down for a nap?"

Myra gave a sigh of relief as Susan turned to him and they headed for the bedroom together. She returned to the kitchen to help Patricia carry in the serving dishes.

Her sister-in-law embraced her. "Thank God that's over." She released her and pointed to the side counter. "You can put ice in those glasses."

Myra did so, then filled them and carried the tray to the table. Doug and Susan were in the side hall near the master bedroom. He had her in his arms. She nodded at something he said, then turned toward the living room.

Peter met her and gave her shoulder a squeeze, muttering something Myra couldn't hear, but it made Susan smile. Myra closed her eyes in a prayer of gratitude. She had always lived for moments when compassion broke through her son's macho façade.

Cornelius wheeled Eleanor's chair to the end of the table, then took the head, surveying them as they found places which Patricia had identified with the whimsical pottery markers she'd made years ago for such occasions.

Susan gave a cry of pleasure when she spotted her squirrel, picking it up to show Doug. "And look! She made you a tree for it to sit in," she cried, picking up the piece from the next seat.

Doug was right next to her, putting Susan securely between her husband and grandfather. Perfect. Myra found Matilda across the table, with Patricia, a heron, on one side and Peter's giraffe on the other. Patricia had nestled both Susan and herself safely away from Derek's jaguar, which, along with Roger's bear, flanked Eleanor at the other end of the table. Eleanor's cat and Cornelius's lion sat in splendor at the ends of the table. It was not an Emily Post arrangement, Myra thought, but it was a work of genius. Only the baby, asleep in the bedroom, was unaccounted for.

Patricia brought the turkey and placed it in front of Cornelius, who sat, carving knife and fork in hand, gazing down the table. "This is beautiful."

He rose and took his camera from the sideboard. "Remarkable," he added, looking through the viewfinder. "Merry Christmas, my dear." He clicked the shutter, then beamed down the table at Eleanor as he took his seat and picked up the serving utensils again.

Eleanor leaned back in her chair, already exhausted, with tears in her eyes.

The table fell quiet, watching. Myra prayed that the required photography session was now past.

"All right!" Cornelius recovered his aplomb and stood up. "Ready for orders! One at time, if you please. Susan, you want white meat, isn't that right?"

Susan's face lightened. "You remembered!"

"Of course." He set to work and there was little need to converse as he circled the table, testing his memory.

Passing, commenting, and eating filled the space. Under the talk of weather and the state of the garden, Myra saw Derek glance at Susan, seeking her eyes, but Susan was right. The presence of others, especially the need to keep Eleanor the center, prevented an emotional deluge that could spell disaster. Susan kept her eyes on her plate, but ate little. She raised her head, as though sensing Myra's gaze. Her eyes opaque and unseeing, cleared for a moment and steadied, as though anchoring herself in Myra's presence. She lowered them to her plate almost immediately, and Myra turned her own eyes toward Roger, wondering why she'd always been put off by something in his manner. As she half-listened to Cornelius lead the conversation from sailing to Peter's law practice, she saw Roger's glance move to Susan also. She frowned, unable to place her unease.

Cornelius was asking Doug about the landscaping business, drawing him into the circle. He was an artist at transitions. Eleanor listened intently from the other end of the table, as though this was a symphony Cornelius was conducting for her. Once her lively and often acerbic contributions had balanced her husband's. Together they'd had the capacity to make dinners an adventure. Now she said little and ate less. She simply sat listening, her hands spread out on either side of her as though waiting for her sons to take them.

Myra noticed Cornelius didn't include either Derek or Roger in this family knitting operation. Intentional or merely safe, Myra wondered, and decided on the latter. Today he would avoid topics that cast light on the family's pain—or shame.

Doug asked about the art on the walls, turning conversation first to their travels, though Myra sensed that the company's attention was more on following the surreptitious glances than the conversation. She came alert only when Cornelius turned the subject to Myra's watercolor. Eleanor asked when she would bring her a companion to the one that hung in the entryway. Myra promised her one, carrying the conversation into a pretended future.

Talk then moved to other more probable futures.

"Perhaps Susan will let me get to know my grandson," Derek said casually, as though merely adding it the list of wishes already on the table.

Susan raised her head, fork halfway to her mouth.

Myra's breath paused in her throat. It was as though a chill wind had rippled over the table.

"Oh, yes," Eleanor breathed. "I'm sure she will, now, Derek."

Susan's eyes filled with tears. She struggled for words.

"He's cute as a button." Roger chimed in, as though unaware of the silence that had fallen. "Almost as cute as you were last time I saw you." He grinned, unaware of Derek's sudden frown.

Susan turned to look from her father to Roger, her face a mask of confusion. Myra frowned, trying to remember Roger's visit, but only a vague feeling of distaste emerged.

"You don't remember? No, I don't suppose you do," Roger continued. "You were all decked out in a pink polka-dot pinafore." He grinned.

"You even had polka-dot socks with your patent leather Mary-Janes."

"That was our anniversary!" Eleanor exclaimed. "Our fiftieth. Remember, Conny?"

Myra noticed that Susan was still motionless, her fork now idle on her plate.

"Yes, indeed. Patricia, I think it's time for dessert," Cornelius asserted.

Myra sat back in relief at Cornelius's interception, though she noticed Susan's brow was drawn, as though fishing, as Myra was, for memory.

A general demurring followed, with requests to wait before tackling the pies.

"Very well, let's retire to the living room for a bit. Roger, perhaps you can take orders for brandy and liqueur."

Myra and Patricia collected dirty dishes.

"Trust Derek to rush in where angels fear to tread," Tricia hissed, rinsing the plates. "And Roger never did have the sense of a rhinoceros."

Myra frowned, still trying to understand exactly what had happened. "Your dad was not pleased, I think."

Patricia grunted her agreement. "Derek had no business pushing it. It's enough Susan is here. And Roger …" She broke off and shook her head.

Myra remembered Patricia's story about Roger being charged with statutory rape and wondered what other sordid baggage he carried.

The voices from the living room had resumed their normal level, safely beyond the fissure. By the time the table was clear, Myra began to hope they'd escape without further disaster.

Derek had gone over to sit next to his mother and Doug stood beside them, holding Billy. They were having a quiet conversation on the baby's Benning traits, though none were evident to Myra. Good.

Susan watched from across the room, her face relaxed, even pleased by the scene. Peter was holding a conversation with Conrad on computer programs.

Roger was serving drinks.

Myra was aware that Tricia had come up beside her. "Let's play Santa while all is well, shall we?"

"By all means. Let's." Usually the Santa job had been reserved for the youngest. Tricia was sparing Susan that chore and Myra was grateful. "Your mother looks exhausted," she remarked, looking at Eleanor's sunken face. "Let's make it quick."

They made the process as short and chaotic as they could, handing out all of the gifts at once without waiting for the recipient to identify and thank the giver. She knew neither she nor Susan had gifts for Derek or Roger and only tokens for Conrad and Patricia. Her family had exchanged gifts last night. The ones that mattered were for Cornelius and Eleanor. This was their day.

When the floor was littered with paper and ribbon, they prepared to serve the pie.

"None for me, my dear," Eleanor told her daughter, then gestured to Cornelius. "I believe I'm going to rest now."

"Let's get one more picture," Cornelius said, taking hold of her chair and wheeling it so that she faced the windows. "Come …" He turned to them. "Derek and Roger, stand behind your mother."

"That's it," he continued as they took their places. "Now, Susan, put the baby in Eleanor's lap … that's it." He hesitated only for a moment. "Patricia, next to Roger, Conrad next to Derek … that's fine. Now, Myra, you sit on the floor in front. Peter, Doug, and Susan, on your knees on either side of her."

He hadn't put either her or Susan next to Derek. Myra's smile, as he clicked the shutter, was genuine.

"Now," she said, rising, "Let me take one with you in it, Conny." She placed him behind Eleanor, with his sons on either side.

Then the group broke up, and one by one they bid Eleanor Benning Merry Christmas and good night, then withdrew, shaken by the weakness of her response.

As the pair disappeared down the hall, the family sat silent. Costumed and made up, they were actors left on an abandoned stage.

Myra felt time stretching to eternity. At least they had reached the final act—only pie and cleaning up remained.

Cornelius returned and made an attempt to revive the party, but only Conrad and Roger took pie. Relieved, Myra tapped Susan on the shoulder and they retired to the kitchen. They were loading the dishwasher, when Patricia came in.

"No, no," she admonished them. "You leave this to me. You've been great, both of you. Now, I think you should make your escape."

Myra straightened and looked at her daughter. "I think she's right. Go give Doug the signal, why don't you, and say goodbye to Grandpa."

When she'd left the kitchen, Myra embraced Patricia. "You've been a miracle worker to pull this off. Many thanks."

"Don't thank me. You came. And Susan was a trooper. She's stronger than you think, Myra."

Myra gave her hand a squeeze of thanks and returned to the living room. Susan was tucking Billy into his blanket. When she stood up, her grandfather embraced her. "I thank you, my dear—more than you know," he mumbled into her hair.

Susan smiled up at him, untroubled by his touch, then turned and, in a tight controlled voice, said goodbye to her father.

"I hope," Derek began, his eyes examining hers, "we can meet again."

"I don't know." She stood without tears, her eyes steady. Then she turned away.

Myra was impressed by her courage as well as relieved. The trial was over. She turned to make her rounds, saying goodbye to Derek in the casual voice she'd heard others use.

"We should talk," he said in a soft voice.

"I don't think so," she answered with a smile and moved on toward the spare bedroom where they'd left their coats. She put hers on and joined Doug and the baby in the front hall, while Susan went to collect her things.

The clatter of dishes from the kitchen, the fresh breeze coming in the open doors, the picture-perfect scene beyond, all spelled relief at a trial completed. A job well done. Peter stood on the deck watching the setting sun. In the living room, Cornelius stood chatting with Derek and Conrad.

Susan's scream came from the bedroom, riveting them all.

Chapter 21

Myra and Doug arrived at the bedroom door in time to see Roger backing away, his hands raised in protest.

Susan stood wide-eyed, staring at him, her mouth frozen in the last scream. "You!" Susan's voice was a hoarse whisper, but it carried the same undeniable tone of recognition that had stopped Myra in her tracks twelve years ago.

"What the hell …?" Doug began, then crossed the room to take his wife in his arms.

Myra stared at her daughter's pasty face, another Christmas, long ago, rising in her mind. Susan was eight. The scene came back, rendered static by time but no less clear. She saw Eleanor looking around her gleaming kitchen.

"All done!" She sighed in contentment. "Thank you, ladies for a lovely day. Let's go sit on the deck and have a liqueur."

Myra looked around the living room as they passed through. "Where's Susan?" she asked Conrad and Derek, who were crouched over a new computer game.

"Playing checkers with Roger," Derek mumbled.

The checkerboard was on the coffee table, but there were no players. Susan's new doll lay half-dressed on the couch. Myra turned and went out on the deck. "Cornelius, have you seen Susan?"

"Roger took her to look at Grandma's stone collection," Peter answered from the rail where he was shooting paper airplanes out over the hill. "She always begs to see it."

Myra relaxed. "She does indeed." She took her liqueur glass and went to stand at the rail, where the winter sun was reddening the sea.

Behind her in the deck chairs, Patricia and Conrad were telling Eleanor about their coming cruise to the Sea of Cortez. Ordinarily, Myra would have listened, dreaming of such a cruise, but a restless unease had seized her. She turned and went to the master bedroom, where Eleanor kept her collection of polished stones.

Susan and Roger weren't there. She turned and explored the other two bedrooms, then went downstairs to the recreation room. Conrad and Roger were chalking their cues for a game of pool.

"Have you seen Susan? They said you went to get Eleanor's stone collection for her."

"I left her with it," he assented. "Far as I know, she's still there."

"She's not."

He shrugged.

"Well, help me find her. She's gone!" She turned and raced back up the stairs. "Susan's gone!" She announced, as they went through the living room to the deck.

They found her ten minutes later curled up in the back of Eleanor's walk-in closet, the stone collection scattered around her.

"Susan?"

She didn't answer. She wasn't asleep. She wasn't crying. She was just staring at Myra, mute.

"What are you doing here, honey?" Myra lifted her up, and Susan clung to her. She was shivering. Myra felt her forehead, wondering if she was ill. Her skin was clammy. "What happened, Susan? Tell me. Why did you shut the closet door? Were you hiding?"

Susan just pressed her head harder into Myra's chest. "… tummy hurts," she mumbled. "I want to go home." Her hands, around Myra's neck, clutched so hard, Myra winced.

Paralyzed by the memory, Myra was only dimly aware that Derek had pushed past her and reached for Roger, who backed away shaking his head. "I was saying goodbye," he protested. "… telling her how beautiful she'd become."

The last he addressed to Myra, a plea in his eyes. Past and present fused, and in a rage of revulsion, she swung away and was confronted by Cornelius, his face a frozen mask of suspicion and hatred. Then he disappeared, answering a dim call of alarm from the master bedroom.

The second one, she realized. Patricia and Peter stood in the doorway now, staring at Susan, concerned but mystified.

Susan, shaking in Doug's arms, quieted a little. "Get him away," she mumbled.

"What's this about, Roger?" Derek barked, pushing his brother from the room. "You threw your damned arms around her, didn't you?"

"Can't a man hug his niece?" Roger's plea faded down the hall.

"Let's get out of here," Doug mumbled in her ear, as he passed with Susan.

Patricia squeezed Myra's hand as she left of the room, mumbling something that sounded like "bastard."

Cornelius came toward her from the opposite wing. They met in the entry hall.

"Is Eleanor all right?"

"Yes, yes. I told her Susan burned her hand."

Myra closed her eyes.

"I know, I know." Cornelius patted her hand. "But it's too late for anything else, my dear. Go say goodbye."

Myra turned to make sure Susan and Doug had escaped, then did as she was bid, knowing this was her final farewell.

"Goodbye, Eleanor," she said softly to the face on the bed, its lipstick smeared now across the parchment of her cheek. She should add "Merry Christmas," but knew she wouldn't be able to keep the sarcasm from her voice.

Her mother-in-law's eyes opened and closed again. Her hand came up and took Myra's. "Thank you, my dear. Tell her to put butter on it. She'll be fine."

Myra closed her eyes again and pressed her fingers to the lids. "Right." She laid Eleanor's hand back on her breast and left the room.

As she approached the entry, she heard male voices, muffled but angry, from the lower reaches of the house. She didn't stop. Cornelius stood alone at the deck rail, his figure silhouetted against the setting sun.

She forced her mind to return to the time before Susan's scream and went up behind him. "You gave Eleanor a perfect final gift, Cornelius. She will die satisfied."

He swung around, and she was shocked at the tormented twisting of his face. "Is Susan all right?"

She stopped. What could she say? "I don't know. But we'll take care of her, Cornelius. You tend to Eleanor."

He struggled for a smile, then reached out and hugged her. "Tend to her blindness. Yes. She is blessed, is she not?" He released her. "Go to your family."

Patricia waited for her at the door. Conrad stood behind her, a hand on her shoulder. "Let me know what's happened, Myra. As soon as you find out."

"All right." She stopped and looked at Patricia's face. "This isn't your fault, Tricia. Okay?"

Patricia made a grimace.

"It isn't," Myra insisted. "We all wanted to do this for Eleanor, or we wouldn't have come."

Patricia's smile had a bitter tinge. "For Eleanor. Yes. Hers is a magic power." She reached out a hand and put it to Myra's cheek. "Or your fault, either, okay?"

They exchanged a smile that said neither of them would or could cast aside the weight.

Myra climbed into the car, glanced at Doug, holding a shuddering Susan in the back seat, and roared up out of the drive.

"So—what happened, do you know?" Doug asked when they were halfway down the hill.

"She won't say?"

"It's like her jaw is locked."

"Susan?" Myra was aware her voice was too loud, too demanding, but she was determined to break through the paralysis. "Was it Roger?"

Susan caught her breath.

"Roger?" Doug asked, his tone bewildered.

"Roger. Susan, answer me."

"I don't know," Susan mumbled. "But he—yes! Something—from long ago—he swooped and something came back. A feeling, but more … I can't get hold of it …"

"Okay. That's enough." Myra turned the corner by the Mission and headed for the freeway, feeling everything in her harden. "We're going to see Dr. Garvitz in the morning."

"You know what it's about?" Doug asked.

She opened her mouth to answer, then closed it and shook her head.

The memory returned and a terrible certainty came with it. But she'd felt that certainty before, hadn't she? Heard that gasp of recognition and kicked her husband out of the house. Destroyed her children's family. Had she'd been wrong?

Except for Billy, cooing as he pulled his Christmas boots from his feet, the rest of the drive was silent.

When she pulled up in front of their house, Myra grasped the only truth she trusted. Something terrible had happened to Susan. About that much, she'd been right, and it gave her the courage to speak. "Give her some hot chocolate and climb in bed with her," she said, turning to Doug. "That always did the trick when she was little."

He hesitated, then nodded.

"Call me when she's asleep."

"Right." He looked relieved and turned to unfasten the car seat.

"Here," Myra said, getting out of the car. "I'll take Billy. You get Susan." They stumbled up the now-dark path to the house. Doug turned on the lights, and Myra saw Susan's tension reduce by half as she looked around the familiar room that was home. Myra put Billy in her arms and gave her son-in-law and grandson a kiss apiece. "Merry Christmas."

Fifteen minutes later, Myra reached her own house and found it dark and empty. Half of her had hoped Randy would be there, but the other knew she needed solitude to revisit the memory that had blasted its way from nowhere. She put on the teakettle and lit a fire in the fireplace. Then, warming her hands on a steaming cup of hot chocolate, she sank to the couch and stared at the flames.

She pictured an eight-year-old Susan heading for her grandma's bedroom to look at the polished stones Eleanor had collected from the beach over the years. Then she tried to picture Roger, going after her to reach the box down from the shelf of the walk-in closet where it was kept. That picture was vague. She could see him in the rec room chalking his cue. It wasn't the first time she'd met him. He'd come from Argentina once before, when the children were very young. That was where the polka-dot dress remark had come from, but she remembered little of the visit. The second time, he'd come for Eleanor's and Cornelius's fiftieth wedding anniversary the week before Christmas. Yes. There had been a party—a celebration. He'd come bearing gifts. She stared at the heron sculpture that occupied the place of honor on her coffee table—the bird protecting its young.

He'd thrown his arms around everyone as though he'd known them forever. She hadn't liked it. But then, as though sensing the adults' displeasure, he'd gone to make friends with the children. He was easy with them. Warm. They'd laughed and welcomed him into their games—sailing paper airplanes from the deck. Now she pictured him following Susan into that closet and knew why, if she'd seen them, she'd have thought nothing of it. He was the good uncle.

So had she kicked the innocent brother out of her house? Her skin crawled. Who was innocent? How would they ever know? Susan. Could they trust the memory of an eight-year-old more than the screams of a thirteen-year-old? The image of Roger rose, repelling her.

She put her cup down, picked up the sculpture and shoved it into the cupboard beside the fireplace, then went to the kitchen and left a message for Dr. Garvitz on his answering machine. He wouldn't get it until morning, but she had to take action—any action. When she returned to the fire, her initial revulsion had faded, and she could think again. Was that when Susan had changed? She remembered bringing her home and lying with her in her arms. She trembled for a long time. And after that?

Pictures flashed through her mind of Susan as a little girl—six, maybe?—roughhousing, running pell-mell down the soccer field—older—eight?—pillow fighting with girlfriends at a birthday sleepover. What birthday? When did those other memories start? When Susan shrank from a group of boys in the school hallway? The images refused to fit themselves neatly into chronological order, but a cold certainty was freezing her limbs. The ring of the phone released her.

"Merry Christmas. How did it go?" Randy asked.

"Bearable until the end. Then it flew apart big time."

"What happened?"

"Derek's brother Roger threw his arms around Susan …" she began, then choked on the words.

"His brother?" Randy sounded confused.

"His brother. And I remembered …" she stopped, unwilling to bring the whole story back. "Where are you?"

"Just leaving Ojai. In fact, I was thinking I'd stop on the way home."

She laughed, wondering how Goleta could be considered on the way from Ojai to Carpinteria. "Great. Stay the night."

"Can't. I go on duty at midnight. But we'll have an hour, maybe more."

"That'll do. See you in a while." She hung up and dove into the cabinet beside the fireplace for the family photo albums.

By the time Randy arrived, she'd lined up Susan's elementary school class pictures on the coffee table. She'd found pictures taken at the Bennings' anniversary celebration showing a giggling bright-eyed eight-year-old and was searching for shots taken after that day, cursing her lack of organization.

"Look at the difference," she told Randy when he arrived, "between that picture …" She pointed to the second-grade class, "and that." She picked up the third-grade group. The little girl whose grin lit up the front row of the second grade class was hard to find in the third-grade shot.

"Tell me what happened."

Myra turned her back on the pictures and did so, remembering every detail she could of the day, including the memory that had surged back after Susan's whispered "You!"

"So you think it was Roger who molested her, back then? And Derek?"

"Derek—oh, God. Maybe he was doing what he said he was doing, leaning over to hug her. Waking her brought back memories …" She sat down and put her face in her hands. The saying of it was so much worse than the thinking. "Maybe it wasn't him."

"Hey." He sat down next to her. "Worry about that later, okay? Right now, you need to find out if you're right … that it was Roger."

"The pictures. Look at them. And the snapshots taken later. She's so sober. She became a bookworm. I didn't see anything wrong with that. Lots of children do, after they become good readers … which she was." She stopped her chattering as she laid the shots alongside earlier ones. "It's a different child."

"What did Susan say, Myra? Today."

"That it brought back something from long ago. Feelings without content. I put in a call for Dr. Garvitz."

The telephone rang.

"That's probably Doug. I told him to call when she went to sleep." Myra crossed to the kitchen and picked up the phone.

"Myra? It's me." Doug sounded tired.

"How is she?"

"I gave her a sleeping pill, finally. She kept dropping off then jerking awake."

"Not surprising." When had Susan started having nightmares? "I left a message for Dr. Garvitz to call. If he calls you first, tell him to call me. I think I remember the day it happened."

"You do? What …?"

"She was eight. Roger had come back for Eleanor and Cornelius's fiftieth wedding anniversary. He went to help Susan get a box down from the closet shelf and no one thought anything about it, but later we couldn't find her."

"She didn't scream or anything?" He sounded bewildered.

"No. She was hiding. I never connected it …" She broke off and shook her head. "But today—the way she said 'You!'—just brought it back."

"Maybe she can remember. That would help."

"It would." And if she did remember, would she charge him? Would they ever be certain enough to urge her to? And it has to be now—before he takes off for Argentina. "Let's hope Dr. Garvitz can help her remember. For now I'm just glad she's asleep."

"Right. I need to go check on those puppies."

"Ah." The Christmas Eve puppies belonged in another life. "Do that." When she'd hung up, she turned and leaned against the counter. "I feel as though I'll never be sure again."

"Mm. That's why there are so many pedophiles on the loose, Myra."

"I know. But I was ready to charge Derek—would have if Susan had been willing. I kicked him out—of the family, of his career …" She went to the patio door and stared out. The image of Susan cowering in the corner of the closet returned. "No." The word was in reaction to the years of nightmares, the terror of men. "I won't let Roger get away with it."

The telephone rang again. Myra picked it up, expecting to hear Doug. "Mom?"

"Peter. Hello."

"It wasn't Dad!" He sounded outraged.

"It looks that way. We don't know enough, Peter …"

"I feel like—I don't know—like I've never been this mad. It's so goddamm … Dad's really angry, too. I've never seen him like this. How's Susan?"

"Okay for now. Doug called to say that she's asleep. Susan half-re-

201

members something. We'll see if Dr. Garvitz can help us get to the bottom of it."

"I didn't believe her." He stopped as though struggling for words.

Myra could think of no words to help either of them.

"I thought they were nightmares." There was a plea in his voice.

"Yes. Well, I understand that, Peter." She took pity on his confusion. She owed it to him to connect the dots. "But now I think it was Roger. Back when she was a little girl."

"And he let Dad take the rap." His tone was heavy and certain.

"I don't know if Roger even knew, Peter. He was in Argentina when that happened."

"No, I think he did. Or at least Dad thinks so. He was clenching his fists, yelling at Roger. Like there's something more he knew—they all knew."

"Really?" She frowned, puzzled. "More than whatever he did to Susan?"

"I don't know. Maybe that was it. It was just a feeling I got. Jesus, what a mess."

"For sure. I'll call you when I know more, Peter. And you do the same. Talk to your Dad. Find out. It's too late to put things right, but—we need to know."

"Okay. And Mom? If I can help … with Susan, I mean."

"Just tell her you believe her."

"Yeah." His voice was still lost in the confusion of the day. "Okay."

She hung up and turned to face Randy. "She did scream like that in nightmares. Did say there were bodies on her—bears. And there was another nightmare of worms all over her. And it was long before Derek … Damn! Damn that horrid man. She was eight!" She slammed her hand down on the counter.

He watched without interfering as she swung away and began to pace, clenching and unclenching her fists. "I'll kill him. I swear … dear God I could." She stopped and put her hands to her head. "I never knew I could feel such rage. It's scary!"

He crossed the room and took her hand from her face. "Just let it out here, so it doesn't carry you away. You don't want to make a mistake."

"Another mistake, you mean." She wrapped her arms around herself and went to look at the rain beyond the window. "Derek went for him, today. Lunged at him, swearing. Do you suppose he's remembering, too? Peter said he was yelling at him."

"Maybe." He came up behind her and put his arms around her. "Don't beat yourself up."

She gave a laugh. "No? What do you do when you realize you've wrecked someone's life? Several someones."

"Yours, too?" He stepped away.

"I don't know. What do you do with your life after you've accused someone falsely … torn apart your family …" Too late, she turned and saw the veil that had dropped over his eyes. "You mean … no, no Randy. Not us. It's not going to wreck us." She held out a hand.

"Sure?" He took the proffered hand, but tentatively.

"Tonight that's about the only thing I am sure of. Everything else seems turned on its head."

Chapter 22

Myra sat in Dr. Garvitz's waiting room the next day, leafing through old magazines in a futile effort to silence her head. She hadn't slept. Revulsion at the molestation, rage at Roger, alternated with the plummeting of trust of herself. Horror at what she'd done to Derek replaced all else only to dissolve again in the unknowable. She needed an anchor.

Dr. Garvitz's early-morning response had given her hope for some measure of certainty, and when Susan had asked her to come with her, she'd jumped at the chance. Now she could do nothing but wait. She made another attempt to remember Susan's behavior after that day when she was eight, but couldn't. Disconnected images of the changed Susan emerged, but she couldn't put them in order.

She was deep in frustration when the inner office door opened and Dr. Garvitz appeared. "Would you come in, please, Myra?" His manner, usually relaxed and reassuring, was somber.

She leapt to her feet. Inside the therapy room, Susan sat on the couch, limp, her tear-stained face exhausted. Her eyes, as she stared at her mother, were drained of all expression.

Myra took a seat in the easy chair next to the couch and started to give her account of the day before, but Dr. Garvitz held up his hand, stopping her.

"Susan has been remembering a day back when she was eight ... a visit to her grandparents. She wants to share it with you to see if you remember anything."

"We were all at Grandma and Grandpas," Susan began, coming to life, now. "It was a party ... a celebration ... but I don't remember for what. The tree was up, so it was near Christmas, but not." Susan's voice was the child's, sending shivers down Myra's spine. "There was a man

I didn't know. He was nice. He asked me about my doll, Hilda. We played with her. And played checkers." Susan stopped and seemed to visibly shake free of the child who'd taken over the telling. "It was Roger. When I saw him yesterday, I felt it. Now, I remember. I told him I wanted to play with Grandma's rocks—the ones she'd collected on the shore and polished. He said he'd get them down for me." She stopped again, clearly finding it more and more difficult to continue. "So he did. Back in Grandma's closet where they were ..." Her energy seemed to give out. She leaned forward and sat wringing her hands.

"Go ahead, Susan," Dr. Garvitz urged, after letting her rest for a minute.

"We were sitting on the floor, looking at them," Susan began, "and he put his arm around me. I sort of jerked. It didn't feel right." She stopped, then forced herself to continue. "He laughed and said it was just what uncles do." She took a breath. "Then he ran his hand up under my dress and tickled me, and I tried to get away, and he put his other hand over my mouth. 'Shhh ...' he said. 'They'll find our secret place.'" Susan covered her face. "Then he put his fingers in my panties and I kicked him. He—he laid on top of me—I couldn't get out!" She stopped, breathing hard, as though trying to find the air to go on. "He heard something—I don't know what—and rolled off me. I scrambled to my feet to run, but the door was closed, and he caught me." She swallowed. "He pushed me against the wall. Told me if I told anyone, I'd get in trouble for what I let him do." Susan's last words were choked with shame. She started to cry. "But I didn't let him!" The child's voice returned, now. "I didn't."

Myra moved to the couch and put an arm around her.

"Yesterday, when Uncle Roger came in, I started to shake. He reminded me of something—but I didn't know what. Then he threw his arms around me when we were leaving ..." She broke off and clasped her own arms around herself. "The terror came back—and then my head pounded—as though it was swelling—and the rest of me—I was a monster!"

Myra could feel her trembling. "Oh, no, Susan. It wasn't you. Wasn't you, at all. Do you understand that?"

"Do you remember the day she's talking about?" Dr. Garvitz asked.

"I do. When she looked at Roger, yesterday, and cried, 'You!' it came back. It was the Bennings' fiftieth wedding anniversary—a party, as she said. Derek's brother Roger had come home from Argentina for it." She closed her eyes. "And I remember now, Roger sitting down next to Susan on the couch. Befriending her, I thought." She stopped, sickened by the words. "And later, I couldn't find her. Someone—Peter, I think—said Roger had taken her to look at Grandma's stones. She always loved playing with them, so it didn't bother me—except I guess, something did, because I went to find them." She shook her head. "They weren't in the bedroom, and I found Roger downstairs playing pool. I got upset then, and we all started looking for Susan. I found her in the closet—with the door closed, which was all wrong. She wouldn't say anything, except that she had a tummy ache and wanted to go home."

"And after that day? What was she like?" Dr. Garvitz had lost his casual manner. He was solemn, considering, a doctor now, collecting symptoms.

Myra shook her head. "I've been racking my brains, trying to remember."

"I was sick," Susan murmured. "I remember vomiting ... hugging my quilt. I drew black X's with magic marker all over Hilda. My doll," she explained to the doctor.

"Ahhh ..." Myra let her breath out as memory returned. "That's not all you did. You tore her head off. You told me you hated her ... that she was bad and to throw her away, but I thought—or you told me—I don't remember—that it was because you thought Hilda had made you sick. How did I get that idea, I wonder?"

"It wouldn't be unusual," Dr. Garvitz assured her, closing his notebook and pressing his nose between his fingers, "to project her shame onto the doll. Were there other changes in her behavior?"

Myra nodded. "After—after yesterday, I went looking at pictures, trying to remember when she changed. She just got quiet ... 'good,' her teachers called it." Myra gave a harsh laugh.

"Was I bad before?" Susan's voice showed the first signs of returning to normal.

"No. Just lively and noisy ... and curious. That's what I noticed most," she continued, turning back to Dr. Garvitz. "She'd always asked endless questions, especially when we were out walking on the mesa. And she stopped. I worried about her, but never connected it with ... oh, damn, Susan ..." She gave her daughter's shoulders a squeeze. "Why didn't you tell me?"

"Shame," Dr. Garvitz answered for her. "That's more usual than not. But the change was around that time?"

Myra nodded. "I think so. And I brought her class pictures from that year and the year before." She rose and handed him the folder. "When I found them, last night, the difference was shocking. Why didn't I see it?"

Dr. Garvitz looked at the pictures. "Hindsight is great stuff, but don't beat yourself up over it. As I remember my own school pictures, I was either sticking my tongue out or making buck teeth. When I outgrew being a clown, my mother could hardly find me in the picture. However," he continued, handing them back, "they corroborate her story, as does your account. I think we can say that this was the molestation that originally traumatized you, Susan."

Myra felt the words settle deep inside. "Thank God for some certainty. And may he burn …" She cut off the rage that threatened. "Can we charge him, Dr. Garvitz?"

"Susan can. You could have done so on her behalf back then, but she can now, as an adult."

"Susan?"

As they watched, the fear and revulsion on Susan's face changed to horror. "It wasn't Dad. And I blamed him—that night … oh, God, why did I do that?" She buried her head in her hands.

"Because whatever he did brought it back," Dr. Garvitz explained.

But Susan's head kept shaking back and forth. "I tore everything apart. I did it."

"No, Susan. Stop it." Myra pulled her chin up and held it, forcing Susan to look at her. "I kicked him out. Not you." The enormity of that act struck again, stopping her. "We'll put it right—somehow." She fought to regain traction on the icy slope. They both knew they couldn't fix it. "Right now, that isn't the question …"

"Yes, it is. What if I'm wrong again?"

"Susan, the crime is Roger's …" Dr. Garvitz leaned forward, his voice carrying more force than Myra had ever heard before.

"No, it isn't. It's mine." The finality of Susan's tone left no room for argument.

"All right," Myra said, matching her daughter's firmness. "Your father may be innocent …" She frowned, unable to pin down why she was unwilling to release him from all blame. "But you weren't the one who made him leave. In fact, you were furious with me."

Susan quieted, then started to cry.

"Let her," Dr. Garvitz advised, as Myra put an arm around her shoulders again.

Myra took a deep breath and let it out, finding nothing to say. She laid her head on her weeping daughter's shoulder and closed her eyes, finding release in Susan's tears. Tension drained out, then the image of Roger with his hand in her little girl's underpants jolted her upright. "Damn him, damn him, damn him!" She stood up and began to pace. "Look, if we don't do something, Roger's going to take off for Argentina."

"Is that where he's been all this time?" The doctor watched Susan, whose tears had subsided now. She lay back on the couch, eyes closed, her face slack. "She said she'd never seen him again until yesterday."

"According to his sister, Patricia, he took off after he was caught messing with an underage girl."

"Oh?" His eyes opened. "How underage, do you know? How old was she?"

Myra shook her head. "I don't know. I'll have to ask Patricia. But he wasn't at our wedding, so it was before that. He sent a gift." She saw again the heron sculpture and shuddered. "We have to stop him."

He raised a hand. "I'd be careful about pushing that right now, Myra. She needs a little time to absorb all of this."

"Can they bring him back?"

"I don't know. Extradition treaties come in endless varieties. But whatever happens to him, Susan's going to be a whole lot better for having unearthed the story. We need to settle for that, today. It's enormous—like expelling a cancer that's been eating away for years."

Myra sat down on the couch and put her hand on Susan's. "Do you feel that?"

Susan nodded and opened her eyes. She tried for a smile. "It's making me woozy. And light—like I don't dare stand up."

"Try it," the doctor urged.

She put a hand on the arm of the couch and pushed herself up. Then she gave another faint laugh. "I guess I'm okay."

Myra was struck by the sound of her voice. Tremulous and weak, but different. Clear. Unmuddied. A voice from the past. She laughed and drew her daughter to her, giving way to a lightheaded astonishment. "Thank you." She stepped back and turned to the smiling doctor. "You're right. It's incredible—the change."

As they drove down the highway toward home, Myra glanced at Susan. "He's right, honey. It's a terrible thing to remember, but it's out. It won't make you sick anymore."

"I do feel different." Susan rubbed her face. "But all I can think of is what I did to Dad."

"Then you need to know, Susan, that part of the reason I kicked him out—believed he molested you—was that he slept with other women ... young women ... students ..."

"Mother! Stop it. I don't want to hear it."

"He did, Susan, and we've had enough of not talking about things, haven't we?"

Susan sank back in her seat. "We've had enough of everything."

"I know. But it's over. We can leave it now, and move on. I'm telling you, so you'll stop blaming yourself." And I'm still not sure he's innocent, she finished to herself. I believe he put his weight on you. I still believe that. "I promised myself I'd divorce him as soon as Peter left for college and you got used to high school. So I would have kicked him out, anyway."

Susan frowned out the window. "But we were a good family. All I remember is ..." She broke off and turned her hands face up in her lap, helpless to make sense of it.

"Good times. And those were real. Very real. I know." She turned off of the freeway, then glanced at Susan, who stared out of the window as though seeking sense from the passing scene.

"I think I was happier with Dad than with you."

Myra winced, though she knew the words were mostly retaliation for her attack on Derek. "Toward the end, that was true," she conceded. "I was very angry."

Susan sighed and fell silent again.

"It's a lot to take in, darling. I know that. Just don't take it all onto yourself. Roger did it. Keep repeating that."

Susan didn't answer.

"You can make it right with your father," Myra said softly. "You can

209

fix that part." She turned into Fairchild drive, and Doug came out to meet them.

"How did it go?"

Susan climbed out of the car and clasped her arms around him. "It went ... okay. Huge." She took a breath. "Right now I need you and the baby."

Doug raised his eyes to Myra, who'd climbed out of the car.

"It was Roger," Myra told him. "The rest ..." She broke off, unwilling to repeat the repulsive details to Susan's husband. "She may tell you or not. Just convince her we need to get him." She gave a wave and headed for home.

She entered her own house to find Randy on the patio, sunning his face. "I thought you were on duty."

"Just got off. I was hoping for a free lunch but decided the sun would do."

"It's cold out here."

"True." He sat up then rose, leading her into the house. "So? What happened?"

"She remembered." She turned, once they were inside, and leaned against him. "He ..." the words choked her. "... touched her ... I don't want to say the words, but he molested her." She straightened and swung around toward the kitchen. "Roger." She yanked open the refrigerator. "And I'm so damn angry ..." She closed the refrigerator and leaned against it. "I could kill." She closed her eyes then opened them again. "We say that all of the time, don't we? Ruin it for when it's true. Because I could—really ..." She shook her head and rubbed her face, then started to pace back and forth to gain control of the energy. "I keep seeing his hands ..." She broke off to take deep breaths.

Randy watched, saying nothing.

"I'm sorry." She sank into a chair, limp now in the aftermath of the surge. "I think it just now hit me. I heard it and it sank to the pit of my belly, but—not like this."

He nodded. "Delayed reaction." He went to the refrigerator and started taking out lunch fixings. "And how's Susan?"

"Susan's wrung out—but relieved." She rose to help him then sat down again. She felt light and woozy—Susan's reaction in the office. "But horrified that she blamed her dad."

He raised his eyes from the bread he was buttering.

She met his gaze for a moment, then lowered her eyes to the table. "Yeah. Me too. But I was the grown-up. I was the one who told him to get out." She took a breath. "I was so angry at him … and at Peter … at the whole lot of them for saying it was all Susan's imagination and knowing damned well it wasn't. Calling her disturbed, which maybe I knew she was, by then, but …" She stopped to let the flow of words sink in. "Now I know why."

Randy brought sandwiches to the table and sat down next to her. "Good. You have an answer. Sometimes that's all you need—just knowing."

She looked at her sandwich but didn't pick it up. "Like the whole world coming into focus. Like being blind and seeing again. Worn out clichés. Nothing like … the weight of it. The 'so that's the way it is' moment." She took a breath and picked up her sandwich, looked at it, and put it down again. "And part of me won't let go. I still believed he put his weight on her."

He nodded. "Maybe he did and maybe he didn't. Once a suspect, always a suspect. They never quite come clean again."

"That's terrible."

He nodded. "But true."

They fell silent as the morning's events began to fade.

"What's Susan going to do?" he asked.

"I don't know. Dr. Garvitz said not to rush her … to let her absorb the shock of it all."

He nodded.

"But I'm afraid he'll get away. Go back to Argentina. Can we get him back, if he does?"

"I'd have to look it up, but extradition takes months, if not years. Let's hope it doesn't come to that." He put the meat and cheese back into the refrigerator and closed it. "Come. You need a walk on the beach."

It was a beautiful day, chilly but sparkling clear. The islands' blue-green outlines stood out against the sky as they never did in the summer. They walked holding hands, and Myra waited for her muscles and head to relax into the rhythm of her feet. Ease wouldn't come.

"You know," Randy mused, after a bit, "you're doing a wonderful job of holding onto your cool."

"Is that why it's churning me to bits inside?" Myra kicked a piece of driftwood in frustration.

"Probably. But I could tell you stories of parents who went berserk. I remember one woman … her daughter broke off her wedding … couldn't go through with it and finally told her mother her father had raped her when she was twelve." He stopped and jammed his hands into his pockets, then gazed out to sea for a moment without speaking. "That lady went and got her husband's hunting rifle and shot him in the head."

"Dear God."

He nodded. "A hunting rifle makes quite a mess of a human head. The problem was, there was no way to corroborate whether he'd really done it. And it turned out he hadn't. The girl had made it up to stop the wedding, which the mother was pushing her into over her protests."

Myra reached out and drew one of his hands from his pocket. "Not a nice story."

"No. She stood trial for murder."

"And had to live with that—forever." Myra closed her eyes and tried to imagine the weight.

"You give her too much credit, I'm afraid. She blames it all on her daughter."

Myra let her breath out. "Thank you, Randy. You've made me feel like a paragon of virtue."

He laughed and gave her hand a squeeze. "I don't know that I want you to be a paragon … just giving a little perspective. When people lose control the way that woman did, they start a chain reaction they can't stop. God help the daughter when that mother gets out of prison." They resumed walking, catching up with Rex and Lily who were making friends with a bulldog down the beach.

"Is she that dangerous? Still?"

"A lot of people are dangerous, Myra. Maybe all of us, when terrible things happen."

Myra watched her feet find their way among the rocks. He was right. The rage that had seized her repeatedly in the last twenty-four hours was dangerous. Could she have killed? If someone had put a gun or knife in her hands, what would she have done?

"That's why I've been impressed with the way you've kept control," Randy continued. "Susan is lucky. So is Derek, by the way."

She sighed. "I doubt very much he feels that way. You can't imagine how much he loved the children ... this beach ..." She stopped, then turned and picked her way over the slime-coated rocks to a tide pool. "Watch," she told him as he came up beside her.

Below, anemones waved their tentacles and a hermit crab crawled from an abandoned shell. "It's a quiet day," she said. "Derek would stand here for an hour, and he'd see things you and I wouldn't spot in a month. Like that limpet." She pointed to the little cone clinging to a rock. "Sooner or later it will move. Derek could tell the weather from a tide pool. He was willing to put up with all of the department jealousies, squabbling, and politics to live here and gaze into these pools."

"Among other things."

She burst into laughter, and in so doing lost the control Randy had so admired, releasing the tears she'd buried out of reach. She felt his arms come around her and cried all the harder, as though making up for the years she'd done her weeping alone. "I'm sorry!" she gasped a few minutes later.

"You needed that. It's high time." He lifted her head and kissed her.

"You don't know," she muttered. "Crying leaves me limp. I'll be lucky if I can climb that hill again." Casting dignity aside, what little she had left, she lifted her tee shirt to dry her face.

"Ready to go home?"

She nodded. The sea had done its work after all. The sea and Randy.

Back at the house, Randy pushed her gently into a chaise.

"It really isn't summer, you know," she commented when he returned. "It's too cold out here. What do you say to a fire, instead?"

"Good idea." He pulled her up. "And a pizza."

"When do you go back on duty?"

He closed the patio door behind them. "Not until nine, when the Christmas crowd starts going home from Grandma's house."

"Lucky you. How do you stand it, Randy, living in the middle of disasters all day—or night?" She sank down on the couch.

"Usually by staying an outsider. Thanking God it isn't my life."

"Which you aren't managing to do with me." The feeling of being one of those disasters hadn't quite left her, despite the walk and the tears.

"You're not a disaster, Myra. Stop thinking that way." He knelt before the fireplace and began setting kindling.

213

"No? Then what am I going to do to put this mess right?"

"You'll find a way. A lot of it depends on what Susan does."

"And what if she doesn't–won't—charge Roger? It's a terrible thing to ask of her ... to land that on Eleanor and Cornelius."

Randy laid a log on the fire and sank back on his heels. "Then he walks."

"And we live with that. Knowing some other eight-year-old, somewhere ..." her voice faded as her brain refused to finish the thought.

Randy came over to the couch and they sat, warming each other with their bodies, watching the fire. Derek was a lump of ice in her belly that the flames wouldn't warm. She couldn't ask Randy how to put that one right. The freedom she'd once claimed from her marriage was gone. Derek was a presence in the room, and when Randy pushed her down on the couch and ran his hand up under her shirt, it felt adulterous. She almost pushed him away, but desire won out, and she welcomed the power of sex to replace all else.

Chapter 23

The next morning, Myra awoke to the ringing of the telephone. Groggy, she released herself from Randy's arms and reached over to the nightstand. "Hello?"

Randy stirred at her voice.

"Myra? It's Cornelius." He sounded weak.

She sat upright, her grip on the receiver tightening. "Good morning."

"Eleanor died last night." The age of his voice didn't lessen the impact of the words.

Myra reached for Randy's hand. Overwhelmed by a combination of shock and a relief she didn't dare examine, she fought for words. "I'm sorry, Cornelius. I'm sorry." She squeezed the hand she'd found to anchor herself. "She put up a good fight … and it must have seemed a long one for both of you." She felt Randy rise to his elbows behind her.

Cornelius gave a grunt of agreement. "I suppose … but you keep hoping even when you know …"

"Is Tricia with you?"

"Yes. And the boys."

Myra winced at the macabre innocence of the last word. "Are you all right? Do you need anything?"

"All right. Yes." He paused. "And thank you for Christmas. A gift she …" He stopped, and Myra closed her eyes, imagining his struggle. "And for the sail, Myra."

The sail. So it had been that important. "You're welcome."

"It helped me work things out and … get ready." His voice broke.

"For me, too, I think." *What is it about death that brings this settling-up*, she wondered. *This unraveling of past tangles.*

"I'll go now. Patricia will be calling you … with arrangements."

215

"Yes. I'll tell Susan and Peter. Thank you for calling, Cornelius." The name sounded far too formal and distant, but suited the occasion far more than "Connie." She heard the receiver go down, but didn't move.

"Eleanor's gone." She sat back against the pillows and gave in to a relief she could now name. "She'll be spared whatever happens now." It also felt like the end of something—a resolution. Her initial reaction began to fade into the hollow emptiness of loss.

"Derek's mother."

"Yes." She opened her eyes to find him watching her, trying to read her reaction.

"You liked her," he guessed.

"Yes, in spite of it all, I suppose I did. I liked her dignity. Her warmth. Her sureness about what she had to do. There is … was … something admirable in her kind of strength." She got up and went to let the dogs in. Their bounding morning welcome broke through the shock.

Randy bent to give them a rub on his way to the coffeepot. He pushed the start button. "You forgive her?" He spoke to the wall.

"For protecting Derek? I don't know." She poured kibble into the dogs' dishes. "I suppose I understand it, at least." She added warm water and bent to put the dishes on the floor.

"And Roger?" His voice had a hard edge.

"Not Roger." She stood up, jolted by the name. "Do you think she knew? God, I hope not. How could she?"

"I don't know." His voice returned to normal. "You've never said how the rest of them reacted that day—to Susan's hiding in the closet."

Myra frowned, trying to remember. "Susan clung to me as we left Eleanor's bedroom. I remember that. I called downstairs to Derek that we had to go. She turned her face away when I asked her to say goodbye to her grandparents—like a-four-year-old. I remember being bothered by that. And she started to cry when Derek chided her. But Eleanor brushed it off, saying Susan just didn't feel good. 'Too much pie, I expect.'" Myra shook her head. "That's about it. I remember the smell of roast beef. The odor of too much food … and feeling a little sick myself … as though the party had turned sour. Wanting to go."

"But not Roger?"

She shook her head again. "Not Roger. I don't remember seeing him when we were looking for Susan, but I don't know where anyone was then." She rubbed her forehead. "It's a blur, I'm afraid."

"Well, that's no wonder. It was … what? Twenty years ago?"

"Eighteen." She took mugs down from the cupboard and stood watching the coffee drip. "Until yesterday at Dr. Garvitz' office. Susan's face … that came back crystal clear." She clenched her fists. "I'm going to get him. I swear …" She pounded her fists on the counter.

"Do you think his mother's death will keep him here? Until after the funeral, anyway?"

She turned and stared. "A ghoulish thought. Let's hope so."

"Unless someone raises an alarm."

Myra opened her mouth and closed it again. "Do policemen always think this way?" she asked, finally.

"I don't want that guy to get away this time." He crossed and took her in his arms. "And I can be ghoulish because I didn't know Eleanor." He looked at her face. "I'm sorry."

"That's okay. It's just—a funeral falling into the middle of this … it's mind boggling."

"Take a breath and slow the reel."

She gave a laugh. "Exactly what I used to tell Susan." She rested her head on his shoulder. "I have to call her now. And Peter."

"Ready to do that?"

"Don't know, but I haven't been ready for any of this." She didn't stir, however, but stayed, welcoming the warmth of his body until the coffee pot emitted its three dings of completion. "Coffee." She drew away and poured two mugs, then turned to the phone and dialed Susan's number.

Doug picked up the phone just as the answering machine cut in. "Hello? Wait …" He cut the machine out. "Sorry."

"It's me. Myra. How's Susan?"

"Ahh. Asleep, I think. I was out feeding dogs. Let me check." There was a long pause. "Yes. Asleep."

"How upset was she?"

"Mostly exhausted, Myra. Drained. She slept as though she was drugged."

"I guess that's understandable." Myra stopped to take a sip of coffee. "Did she tell you what she remembered?"

"In pieces. I'm trying to get my mind around it." Doug sounded shaken. "You gotta stop that guy. Can you?"

"Susan can. If she'll charge him. But Dr. Garvitz says not to push her right now."

"She has to … to take a little girl like that …" His voice rose and he cut himself off.

"Is disgusting. I know."

"I'll do it for her! Or you can."

"Nice thought, Doug, but it has to be Susan."

"I know, I know," he conceded. "Well, maybe when she wakes up, we can talk."

"No … I mean, wait. When she wakes up you need to tell her … Eleanor died last night, Doug. Cornelius just called." She took another gulp of coffee while she waited through the silence that followed.

"Now?" Doug managed, finally.

Myra almost laughed at the appropriateness of the irrational response. "Now, indeed."

"Sorry. That didn't make any sense."

"I understand perfectly. Everything does seem to be happening at once. How are those Christmas pups, by the way?"

"The pups are fine, as is their mother." He stopped. "Okay, I'll tell her. Maybe it will help."

"Help?"

"Well, she wouldn't charge him as long as her grandmother was alive, you know. She couldn't do that to her."

"Oh." Myra leaned against the counter as the truth of his statement sunk in.

Randy, sitting at the breakfast table in front of her, raised his eyebrows.

"That's true." She was glad someone else felt her relief.

"Does Peter know?"

"About Eleanor? No. I haven't called him yet."

"About Susan, I mean. That she remembered." Doug's tone had an urgency that surprised her.

"Only Randy. Things have happened so fast … why?"

"Because yesterday … no, I mean Christmas … at the party. He said he didn't like that guy … that there was something fishy about him."

"Really. I wonder what that's about?" Could Roger have approached Peter as a child, too? The thought turned her skin clammy. "I'll ask him about it, Doug."

"And Susan wanted to stay away from him. I told her he just looked like a guy who'd never done much with his life … if that makes sense."

"Yes." She brought up the image of Roger. "The weight of the years hangs on him like a sack."

"That's it. But Susan picked up something more. She really was repelled. I guess we know why now, huh?"

"I'm glad she remembered. I'll call Peter now. Let me know how Susan is when she wakes up."

"Will do. And I'll call you if she—you know—is ready to get him."

"No, don't bring that up, Doug. Let it wait. Her grandma's death comes first."

"Oh. Yes, I suppose." He sounded reluctant, but promised to go slow, then hung up.

"He says Peter didn't like Roger … said there was something fishy about him," she told Randy.

"Really. Interesting. Pedophiles don't usually put people off. I wish they did. Usually they are very charming to adults and children both. That's why they get away with it." His last words were rough.

The intrusion of the word "pedophile" shocked her afresh. She gazed at him, once again wondering about the scenes and people that filled his days. Scenes like this?

"You look exhausted. Want to take a break before you call Peter?"

"No, I want to get it over with." She turned back to the telephone and dialed.

"Peter?" His voice took her by surprise. She'd expected his answering machine.

"Mom. How's Susan?"

His voice was as urgent and anxious as Doug's had been—as though Christmas had left everyone waiting to take another breath. She was surprised, nevertheless. Something had gotten through Peter's usual self-assurance. "Sleeping, according to Doug. Exhausted, but okay, I think."

"Does Susan say anything—about what happened?"

"I took her to Dr. Garvitz yesterday, and it brought back quite a bit. It was at a party … Grandma and Grandpa's fiftieth anniversary. Do you remember? Susan was eight, so you must have been around twelve."

"Yeah?" His voice turned thoughtful. "Oh … she got sick. We took her home. That time?"

"Right. She disappeared, and we all went looking for her. I found her in Grandma's closet. She'd gone there to look at the stone collection."

"I sort of remember. I remember Roger was there, though. He—oh, shit—I remember now. He kept putting his hands on me—patting my shoulder and stuff."

So he *had* approached Peter. And been rebuffed. She gave a little sigh of relief. "Well, he did more than that with Susan."

"Shit." There was a long silence. "Damn. Dad went after him, yesterday … Christmas, I mean. Did you know that?"

"Yes. I remember Derek yelling at him, but I don't know what happened after we left. Do you?"

"No. I started to follow them, but Aunt Tricia said I should leave them to it. That it wasn't a time for spectators … with Grandma so sick and all."

"It's Grandma I'm calling about, Peter."

"What? Why?" His voice went high with apprehension.

"She died last night. Cornelius called."

"She …" His voice faded out.

"Peter?" she asked when he didn't respond.

"I'm here." His voice sounded muffled. "When? Last night, you said."

"Yes. It's a mercy, really, Peter. She's been sick for a long time, and she saw us all together, which was her greatest wish."

"It's just so weird. She was just there. I was talking to her." He sounded as though he was trying to find his bearings. "Is Grandpa okay?"

"Aunt Tricia and your dad are with him. And Roger, I guess."

"Does Grandpa know about Susan?"

"No. I don't think so. Why?"

"There was a look on his face … after Susan screamed and we all ran in. Roger just stood there and Grandpa … was sort of glazed over, if you know what I mean. And angry. As though he'd been struck."

She remembered the look, but had no more idea than Peter what it meant. She'd only felt confusion as the facade of normalcy crumbed. "I don't know, Peter. I guess we'll find out, but not now. I'm sure Grandma's death is all he can deal with."

"Yeah. Geez, it's too much."

Her competent lawyer son sounded like the ten-year-old he'd once been.

"Give it time to digest. I'll call when I know about the arrangements." She hung up and let the smell of coffee, the sound of Randy talking to the dogs, the winter birds outside the patio door, flow back in around her, filling the vast emptiness that had surrounded her as she talked. She turned and watched Randy kick a stuffed goof-ball for Rex to retrieve. "What's wrong?" he asked. "You look confused."

"I feel as though I've been in a time warp. I haven't had a conversation like that with Peter for fifteen years."

Randy cocked his head. "You don't suppose he's grown up, do you?"

"No, it's about Susan. He believes she was molested, now."

"Good for him. The Christmas scene did that for him?"

"So it seems." Myra picked up the pot to refill their cups. "How about that?"

Randy chuckled.

She put the pot down and sat herself on his lap. "Have I thanked you for being around during all of this? I think this family owes you a bundle."

The phone shrieked, jarring her back to her feet.

"Mother?" Peter's voice was too loud. "What are we going to do about Dad? All of that shit done to him, and it wasn't him!"

Myra closed her eyes. His tone said this part of the mess had just dropped on him. Randy, who had heard the tone if not the words, rose and came over to her. "We'll deal with it ... but later, Peter."

"How? How can you?"

Randy's arm came around her shoulder. "I don't know. I can't think about it yet, Peter."

"I never believed he could have ... done that."

She felt as though she'd been thrown back into the past to walk through every scene again. "I know. And you were right. Take comfort in that."

There was silence on the other end of the line.

"Peter, you're in law. You know people get accused falsely. How hard it is to be sure you're right. What suspicion does to people's lives."

"To clients' lives, yeah. Not mine. Guess I've always been sure. Too sure." His voice drifted, as though someone had cut his anchor line.

"Well, I was too sure about your dad. I owe you an apology ... and him. So this time—with Roger—we have to be certain."

221

"If that's possible."

Myra ached for the loss of faith—or self-confidence—she heard in his voice, even though she knew such wounds would strengthen him in the end. "Yes."

When he'd said goodbye, leaving his appalled discovery hanging in the air, she turned and put her arms around Randy. "Just hold me, will you?"

Chapter 24

The Sunday after New Year's, the family stood around Eleanor's open grave, the gray wet of the day sweetened only by the scent of the dripping eucalyptus behind them. For five days, her death had opened a space in the rush of events, stilling memory, rage and accusations, like a sentence cut off in mid-stride.

A syndicate deadline had taken Myra back to her tower room to stare at the panels of her comic strip, but the characters lay lifeless and nameless on the page, their usual antics a tasteless, if not cruel, mockery of life. She'd spun away and walked off, pacing all the way to the tanker pier and back.

Now, the mourners stood in suspended animation, like actors in a play that had been stilled. There were two newcomers, Eleanor's brother and Cornelius's sister, who were merely sad—characters in Eleanor's story. Only they and Cornelius, bareheaded in the rain, and the minister, standing at the far end, seemed truly present in the scene.

The church had been filled with the quiet dignity of academics, and the eulogies were a fitting farewell to one of their own. There was no hint of the turmoil held at bay by those around her grave. Myra kept her gaze on the coffin, all too aware of Derek beside her. Whether from anger or relief, the years of exile that had submerged his vitality when she'd last seen him, were gone. His presence was electric, and with it came the memory of Eleanor, as she'd been in those years—warm, welcoming, admiring. A friend. The sense of loss that had swept over Myra in intermittent waves during the last few days returned.

To counter it, she raised her head and looked across the grave at Roger, standing immobile on Cornelius's other side, his skin flaccid and grey. He kept his eyes fixed forward, as he had throughout the service, avoiding all of them. Patricia stood next to him with her arms folded over her breast, as though to minimize the chance of contact. Or as though to warm herself against the chill of his presence. Conrad, next to her, kept his arm around her shoulder. Beside Roger, Cornelius, a faint replica of the man who had met her at the door thirty years ago, looked as though he was already following his wife into oblivion.

Peter stood rigid on Myra's other side, clenching and unclenching his fists. Susan stood between him and Doug, her face averted. Myra saw her raise her gaze to Roger once, as though confirming his identity, then lower it again to the coffin. They'd tried to talk her out of coming, but with no success.

"You don't understand," she'd said. "I have to finish it. I have to say goodbye."

Only the baby, left with Doug's sister, was missing.

To her relief, the minister began the Lord's Prayer. Mouths moved, joining in, breaking the tension. Myra looked at Eleanor's brother and sister, strangers she'd met once or twice in the distant past. They looked like visitors to the scene, old and frail, gazing at the foreshadowing of their own demise. She wondered, briefly, what stories they moved about in, and hoped they were gentler, sweeter, than Eleanor's.

The prayer ended. After the casket was lowered, Cornelius cast the ceremonial handful of dirt. It landed with a thump on the polished walnut, and Myra winced for the woman inside who'd spent her life caring for beautiful things. Around her, they stood silent, each offering his or her own farewell, then turned away and scattered, picking up speed as they gained distance from the grave.

"Derek," Myra said as her once-husband turned to go to his father.

He turned. His dark eyes were opaque, as though walling her out.

"I was wrong." She saw his mouth move slightly, whether in a smile or bitter twist she couldn't tell. "I'm sorry—and I know that doesn't ..." She floundered, "begin to change what happened."

He gave a faint shrug, then turned away and walked off, quickening his pace to catch up with Cornelius.

Myra was left with the breath sucked out of her, watching him go. Well, she deserved that response, didn't she? What did she expect him to say? Eleanor's condemnation rose from the hole in front of her, and she could do nothing but stand, the last remaining mourner, and stare at the gold filigree that edged the walnut coffin. She felt a hand on her arm and turned to meet Peter's puzzled gaze.

"Are you all right?"

She nodded. "Just remembering," she muttered and moved away from the grave. The rain, which was increasing, served as an adequate cover for the tears she didn't deserve to shed, and she'd brushed them away before she reached the car.

She and her children had already excused themselves from the reception. Cornelius's eyes had turned a shade bleaker, and again Myra wondered how much he knew, but Tricia had put a reassuring hand on her arm. "I understand. Let's have lunch tomorrow."

Once inside her car, Myra cast off her rain hood and leaned back, relief replacing the memory of Derek's face. It was done. She pulled out of the cemetery, then onto the freeway accompanied only by the rhythmic beat of windshield wipers and the singing of tires on wet pavement. They'd buried a way of life, today. And Randy was waiting at her house with lunch.

Once there, they shed the morning's event along with their raincoats and warmed themselves at the open fire. The dogs circled, licking their wet hands. Beyond the patio doors, a curtain of rain obscured the mesa and the sea.

"Should I ask how it went?" Randy asked, bringing them coffee, "or would you rather forget it?"

"I vote to forget it," Peter said, his voice bitter.

Myra nodded in agreement. "There were no catastrophes—no scenes. And it's over."

"Amen," Susan murmured from the hearth rug, where she was hugging Lily. Doug had sunk down next to her and had Rex's head in his lap.

Randy, who had been studying Susan with concern, smiled at her response. "Whenever you're warm, we have food."

"I'm starved," Myra decided. "Can I help?"

"No." Randy patted her arm in passing. "You've done enough."

He disappeared into the kitchen.

Five minutes later, they gathered around a table laden with soup, fresh bread, and salad. "Ahhh," Myra breathed, "you are a true angel. Rex! Lily!" she scolded the two who'd accompanied Susan and Doug and now had their heads on their laps. "Go lie down." She snapped her fingers and pointed to the hearth.

The dogs obeyed, but only after the command was repeated by her daughter and son-in-law. For the next several minutes, there was no sound other than the clink of silverware. The release of tension had left them hungry, and Myra was relieved that no one felt the need for small talk. Randy, she noticed, kept pausing to study the faces around the table.

"You're dying to ask something," she said finally. "What is it?"

He smiled, chagrined. "Just wondered whether Roger was there."

"He was," Peter answered. "Every damnable inch of him."

"Meeting no one's eyes, including his father's," Myra added.

Susan looked from one to the other, then lowered her gaze to spear a piece of lettuce.

Conversation died around her.

"I'm charging him," she announced into the silence.

"You are?" Doug looked at her, surprised. "You've decided?"

Susan nodded. "When I looked at him, today, I saw him pulling some other little girl into a closet or a field or an empty building …" Her words stopped. "I knew if I didn't, I'd be to blame." She looked around the table. "So that's it."

Wordless, they stared at her, then everyone talked at once.

"Bless you," Myra gasped, her words buried in Randy's, "Good girl," Peter's "Super." Doug's hug made less noise but completed the change of mood. The dogs appeared at the table as though they'd read an invitation.

Myra sent them back, then turned to Randy. "Any chance he'll take off today? Before Susan can do it?"

"Dad took his passport," Peter declared.

"What?" Randy asked, astounded. "How do you know?"

"He told me. Yesterday. We had lunch." He looked around at their faces and shrugged, embarrassed. "Sort of a—vindication. A celebration of Dad's innocence." He cast an uncertain glance at Myra. "Anyway, he said he just lifted it from Roger's dresser."

"Well, well," Myra muttered.

"How much does Derek know?" Randy asked. "Did you tell him about—Susan's memory?"

"Yes, but not until lunch … which was after he took the passport. He got really furious then."

"As well he should. But if he didn't know," Myra mused, "why did he take it?"

Peter frowned and looked around at the bemused faces. "I don't know. Maybe …" He stopped, at a loss.

"Because Roger had done something like that before?" Randy offered.

Peter stared at him. "Geez."

"I'll bet he had!" Susan burst.

"Well, it's easy enough to find out—if he was charged, anyway. And we'll ask him." Randy rose to clear away the empty dishes.

The rest of them sat wondering at the new mystery that had opened before them.

"I'm having lunch with Tricia tomorrow," Myra offered, rising to help Randy. "Maybe she knows whether something happened before."

"I'll check the records," Randy said, heading into the kitchen.

Everyone left the table, then tumbled after him with dishes and theories about Roger's past.

"Stop!" Myra protested. "Let's not get carried away." She closed the refrigerator with a thump. "Just because we've found an agreeable target …" She let the thought complete itself and was pleased at the sudden silence.

They washed dishes in an abnormal quiet. Myra was content to let it be. Let them each create their own theories so long as they didn't combine—there was too much raw emotion in this family rushing to a vortex. It felt dangerous.

When the last dish was put away, they wandered into the living room, looking for something to distract them from the topic that consumed all.

"I don't want to wait until tomorrow," Susan announced after digging at the fire, then thumbing through an art book on the coffee table. "Now that I've decided, I want to do it. Today. Randy, can't you take care of it?"

Randy, who'd been tossing a goof ball for Rex, stopped. "No. You need to go to the city police, Susan, and it needs to be someone you don't know. To avoid conflict of interest problems. But Doug can go with you to the station. Ask for Sergeant Dwyer. He's good at—domestic situations. You can tell him I sent you."

Susan made a wry face

"You need a lawyer first, Susan." Peter sat down beside her. "To go with you. I'll talk to Manny Gonzaga. He's a friend. A lawyer. He works in the child protective unit—and he's great. He'll go with you and tell you what to do."

Susan straightened. "All right. Can you call him now?"

Peter smiled. "It's Sunday. I'll call him first thing tomorrow."

"Do you want me to go with you, too?" Myra asked.

"You should," Randy advised. "Your memory supports her story."

"All right," Susan agreed. "Tomorrow. Look!" She was staring out the patio door. "The sun's come out!"

Three hours later, the house emptied, and the newly emerged sun dipped behind the crest of Santa Cruz Island on its way into the sea. Myra lay deep in her leather chair with a glass of wine, too exhausted by the day to give worry about tomorrow any room. She wondered vaguely whether a time would come when she would grieve for Eleanor. The woman's reentry into her life after a twelve-year absence had brought back the warmth of their early years. She'd felt the loss of that in the church today, but it had faded back into the memory of a life she had no wish to relive.

She was dozing when the telephone rang.

"Mom?"

Myra sank back in relief at Susan's voice. "It's me."

"I called Dad. Peter said to. He wants to come."

"Your Dad does? To charge Roger, you mean?" She shook off sleep.

"Yes. I thought you should know …" Susan broke off in confusion.

"Thank you. I don't know why he wants to, but … why not?" Her mind was producing nothing in the way of answers to anything. Her head was filled with cotton wool. Had she been that deeply asleep?

"He says he won't say anything about … about your accusing him."

Myra let out her breath. "Good. That would certainly complicate things."

"Yes. We're meeting Peter's friend—the lawyer—at eight. Can you meet us on the courthouse steps at nine?"

"All right. Thanks for warning me, Susan. See if you can sleep now."

"Ha. Doug says he's going to make me take another sleeping pill, but I don't want to. I'll wake up with a fuzzy head."

"Take a half," Myra advised. "See you in the morning."

Myra put the phone down and shivered. Why did Derek want to be there? Why did she have this sense of knowing only a scant tip of what went on in the Benning household?

Chapter 25

Myra stared across the blue sea of Nile lilies trimmed in scarlet bougainvillea at the Moorish tower of the Santa Barbara Courthouse. What was she doing here? This was a tourist destination, with old tile floors, murals, open galleries, wrought-iron gateways, imposing historical courtrooms. Its clock tower was on every brochure of Santa Barbara. A Moorish gem, not to be missed. Not a place to so debase … were they really going to do this?

Susan, Peter, Doug and a man Myra didn't know—the lawyer no doubt—were waiting on the steps. Then Derek's familiar shape approached from the other side of the courtyard. He walked with a head-down determination, as though avoiding the sight of the grand old building. She shivered as her feet moved her toward the group. Derek was shaking the lawyer's hand as she came up.

"Peter called me." Derek addressed the words to her without preamble or explanation, and said no more. He turned to Susan, hesitated, then stepped forward and threw his arms around her—the embrace of a man released from purgatory—then stepped back. Susan stood speechless, biting her lip to restrain the tears in her eyes. Derek glanced at Myra, then turned away and stood staring at the concrete, looking at no one.

As the morning fog lightened, letting the sun through, they rehearsed their testimony for Manny Gonzaga. They listened in silence to his instructions, delivered with a casualness designed to reassure, and then crossed the street to the police department.

Tell only what you know. The lawyer's words repeated themselves in Myra's head as they left the imposing façade behind and entered the more businesslike adobe. Did that mean, 'only the facts,'? Things like, this is January 12th, 2009, or things you believe you know? And how do you know the difference?

Their feet still clattered on tile floors, raising echoes, but here they were surrounded by voices, photocopy machines, computers, and telephones. Myra relaxed a bit at the sound of merely human activity and by the lawyer's offhand request for Sergeant Dwyer.

The shirt-sleeved, jowly officer who appeared bore little resemblance to the Spanish explorers who adorned the walls of the hallways across the street. At his appearance, the appalling reality of what they were doing struck Myra anew.

Susan disappeared behind a door with Gonzaga, who put a reassuring hand on her back. Myra and Derek sat silent beside each other. If he'd given the lawyer his memory of that day, what more did he have to say? But his attitude forbade questions, and his very presence condemned her. They waited. For too long. The hands of the wall clock seemed stuck. Myra's dread returned.

Susan reappeared fifteen minutes later, white-faced and clasping her arms around herself as though cold. In a flash, the horror of what had been done to her returned, and Myra stood up and gave her a quick embrace as she went to take her turn.

"Ms. Benning?" Sergeant Dwyer shook her hand. "Have a seat. What do you know about this business?"

She glanced over to where Manny Gonzaga sat slouched in a corner, then recounted Susan's Christmas day collapse carefully, as though at an examination.

"All right. And what did you know at the time about the incident we're talking about—when she was eight?"

The sun burst out of the clouds and into Myra's eyes. She shifted her position so she could see him and began. Carefully, she recounted her memory of the fiftieth-anniversary party.

"You're sure of this? You sound a little …"

"No, no, I'm sure. I was just being careful."

"She didn't tell you what had happened?"

Myra shook her head. "She kept rubbing at herself, saying her tummy hurt. And she changed—started having nightmares. Of a body on her—not being able to get out."

The officer wrote without comment. Her words sounded like chaff in the wind. Were they charging Roger with felony child-molesting on the basis of nightmares? All of Peter's—and Eleanor's—skepticism rose, fresh and scathing. She looked at the lawyer for reassurance, but he was tapping away at his laptop, unaware. What would Peter tell them about those nightmares? Tell them only what you know. Gonzaga's words returned to nag at her. She fished in her purse for the school pictures, then laid them on the desk, pointing out the difference. Dwyer examined them without any noticeable change of expression.

"Dr. Garvitz, her psychiatrist, will testify," she insisted.

He nodded. "We'll be calling him. Why was Susan seeing a psychiatrist, Ms. Benning?"

Myra blinked. "She changed. I told you. I worried about her. Then—when she reached puberty and her friends started to talk about boys—she dropped them. Just came home from school and went to her room …" This wasn't working. She wasn't answering the question. She glanced again at Gonzaga and thought he nodded slightly. Was he simply giving encouragement, or did he know what she was about to say?

"When she was fourteen, her father leaned over her bed to give her a hug, and she screamed—as though he was attacking her." She stopped, then went on, choosing her words carefully. "I knew something was badly wrong. I took her to the doctor."

Sergeant Dwyer was watching her, waiting.

She spread her hands. "Actually, I thought it *was* her father … who had molested her. She screamed that it was him. I kicked him out." She stopped. "Now, Dr. Garvitz is sure it was Roger—and so am I." The lawyer, she noticed, didn't look either surprised or distressed. So he knew. Susan or Peter had told him.

"Could the brothers be mistaken for each other?" Sergeant Dwyer tapped his pen on the blotter.

She thought back to the man she'd met at that long-ago party. There was something loose, unformed in his carriage and his face was softer in its angles, but he was of Derek's height, and he wasn't carrying the weight he wore now. "At that time. In the moonlight, yes."

The pen made a mark. "All right. Is there anything else?"

She scanned her mind for something—anything—that would nail this down, make it sound like something other than female hysteria. There was nothing. She fought off the feeling that she'd made another dreadful mistake. "Dr. Garvitz says this is not her imagination. She'd been traumatized."

He nodded. "We'll bring Roger Benning in for questioning, Ms. Benning." He stood up and held out his hand. "We take pedophilia seriously."

A wave of relief almost put her back into her chair. "Thank you. Let us know, will you, when you pick him up?"

The sergeant nodded again, and walked her to the door. It was over. She dropped into a waiting-room chair and took Susan's hand. Together they watched Peter go in. What would he add? What would he say about Susan's nightmares, her imagination? He believed now, but how had his skepticism affected his memory of the past? He'd talked to Gonzaga, she told herself. Surely the lawyer wouldn't have Peter talk to the police if he'd weaken Susan's credibility. Would he?

When her son came out ten minutes later, he gave Susan a reassuring pat. Myra relaxed. Only Derek remained.

He rose and walked into Dwyer's office with the same frozen but determined bearing he'd worn—except for that one burst of affection—since he crossed the courtyard an hour earlier. He hadn't said a word to her—or any of them other than Gonzaga. The noise of the outer office had subsided to the clicking of computer keyboards, the hum of low voices, and the occasional ringing of a phone. She didn't dare ask Peter or Susan if they had any inkling what Derek was saying.

It was almost a half-hour later when Derek emerged, followed by Manny Gonzaga. They were finished. They'd done it. Cornelius Benning's face rose in Myra's mind and she blanched. Could he take another blow? This kind of blow? Then she remembered the look of hatred and rage, she'd seen on his face Christmas day and the unknowable depths of the family's history opened again.

Myra felt like a deflated balloon as she followed the others out of the office. They gathered at the door looking at the courtyard across the street, soaking in the colors that blazed in the sun.

"That went well," Manny Gonzaga told them.

"It did?" Susan asked. "It seemed so little. Will they believe me?"

"They will," her father assured her. He turned and cupped her chin in his hands. "And we do, too—now. That's what counts."

"You do? Why? I mean … after what I did …"

"I understand now." He gave her shoulder a squeeze then turned away

233

to shake the lawyer's hand. "I need to go. Thank you." He headed down the stairs and across the courtyard, leaving them all looking after him.

Gonzaga shook his head. "You'd never know it's his brother we're charging, would you? Is there bad blood there?"

"I don't know," Myra mused. "It's strange."

"I don't care," Susan proclaimed, "so long as he believes me—forgives me."

"I think he just wants it all to be over," Peter offered.

Myra saw her son glance at her. Did over, for Peter, mean putting their marriage together again, she wondered? She turned away. "Susan." She embraced her daughter. "You did a brave thing today. Don't second-guess it. Or start being ashamed all over again. It's over."

"As soon as they pick him up," Gonzaga agreed.

"And thank you." She shook Gonzaga's hand. "We needed you in there."

He smiled and shrugged. "All I did was watch."

"No, no. You were there. It mattered."

"How about lunch, everyone?" Peter asked.

Myra looked at her watch. "Not me, I'm afraid," she said, begging off, "I'm having lunch with Patricia, and I need to go."

She drove back across town to the Beachside Café and found Tricia staring out to sea, waiting for her. Her linen slacks and tunic were as well-tailored as always, but they hung limp, as though donned yesterday, and her hair was hastily pulled back and bound at the base of her neck.

"How can a day so beautiful seem so unreal that you reject it?" she asked as Myra came up.

"Because it doesn't fit with anything else that's going on," Myra offered.

Patricia laughed. "You've got that right. Hungry?"

"Starved."

They got a table next to the window without waiting, a sure sign school had not yet resumed. Most of the rest of the diners looked like academics enjoying the quiet of the inter-session.

"How are you doing?" she asked Patricia after they'd ordered salads and were munching hot bread. It was, after all, Patricia's mother they had buried yesterday and her brother they had just charged with pedophilia.

"I don't know." Patricia looked faintly surprised. "I hadn't thought about it. There's too much else ..." Her voice faded out.

"True. Why can't I remember anyone ever worrying about you?" Had Patricia's life always been blotted out by her brothers' escapades?

Patricia gave her a grateful smile. "My wheels didn't squeak much, and when they did ... well, there always seemed to be a bigger crisis going on. I was usually grateful for that."

Their salads arrived, creating a pause in their conversation.

"Crises with your brothers?" Myra asked, casually.

"Not always." She picked up her fork, then stared at it as though it had some message. "Sometimes it was my father—though I didn't know what that was about until I was older."

"You seemed such a perfect family to me," Myra mused. "I'm almost relieved to hear that you weren't. Less intimidating."

"Us? You were intimidated by us?" Patricia looked genuinely astounded.

Myra laughed. "You never knew that?"

"Myra." Patricia put her fork down and wiped her mouth with her napkin. "Do you have any idea what an imposing woman you are?"

"I'm tall. That's all." Myra waved it away.

"Is that it?" Patricia gave her a cock-eyed smile, and picked up her fork again. "You do a very good job of putting yourself down. Masterful, in fact."

They turned to their salads, letting the chatter of diners fill the silence. Then Patricia pushed her plate away, giving up on the pretense of eating. "I assume Susan charged him."

Myra was startled. She'd thought she would have to be the one to start this conversation. "This morning. Derek told you?"

Patricia nodded. "Why is it some people's lives send a shudder of premonition from the beginning ... as though they are programmed for disaster? How did it go?"

"All right, if you can say that about such a thing. At least the lawyer seemed to think so." Myra leaned back in her chair as the Hawaiian-shirted waiter brought coffee. "Tricia, why did Derek want to be there, do you know?"

Patricia stared out the window at the quiet surf rolling up the sand. "Yes." She turned back. "Or I think I do. I heard Derek yelling at Roger after you'd left Christmas day. Something about it's being the last time …" She turned her palms up. "I couldn't make out the rest, but I buttonholed Derek later." She put her hands together. "It seems that Roger, when he was in high school, was caught in the girls' bathroom of the elementary school." She forced the words out, then clamped her mouth in distaste. "How he got in there, nobody knew, but they weren't so alert in those days, and he'd gone there as a kid, so …" She shrugged. "Who'd think a thing about his being in the hallway?"

"What happened?"

"You mean what had he done? He hugged a little girl—and exposed himself." Patricia choked on the last words. "She got away and had the good sense to report it to her teacher." She gave the word a bitter finality. "They called our parents, of course, who managed to convince them not to carry it further—don't ask me how." Patricia took a breath and let it out. "I was away at college, so I never knew any of this. But Derek did. He said our mother decided it had all been some mistake. How she managed that …" Patricia flung her hands into the air. "I can't imagine. But my father—was broken by it. Derek says he closed himself in his study and wouldn't talk to anyone. He even cancelled classes—wouldn't go to the university. And he wouldn't—couldn't—look at Roger after that."

Myra remembered the outrage and hatred on Cornelius's face Christmas day. Her sense that there were unknown depths to the family's grief was being confirmed, but it only sickened her. "And the second incident—with the under-aged girl—how old was she?"

"Thirteen."

Myra's fingers tightened around her cup. She, too, turned to stare out at the sea as though it had the power to wash away this conversation.

"I know," Patricia said, reading her revulsion and rage. "And I do remember that. Roger was in college …"

"In college! When he was surrounded by girls his own age? Why on earth—dear God, what's the matter with him?"

"That's the question, isn't it?" Patricia took a gulp of coffee and signaled the waiter for more. "You can say a lot of things," she went on when he'd refilled their cups and departed. "That he was a middle kid and when Derek showed up, my father discovered the son he'd always wanted. I was Mom's star. Roger sort of disappeared between us. I remember him as a cuddly baby—I was four when he was born. I loved rocking him. He loved touching. Hugging. I gave him that. Mother wasn't much into physical affection, and Derek was born when Roger was only eighteen months or so. But none of that really explains it, does it?"

Myra shook her head. "Doesn't sound very abnormal. And he was okay, growing up—until the high school business?"

Tricia raised her shoulders and let them fall. "I don't remember anything that remarkable. He liked playing with younger kids—he'd play leader. Taking them down to the rec room to play school—or who knows what else, I guess. But that's hindsight."

She slumped. "I loved him, Myra." Her voice broke. "Maybe more than Mom did. Certainly more than Dad. I loved him for being a gentle soul. He didn't like rough stuff—football, or the sort of hostility-for-fun that boys engage in." Patricia put her elbows on the table and covered her eyes.

Myra reached a hand over to hers. "I'm sorry, Tricia. This is terrible for you."

"No, it's all right, Myra." She straightened and wiped her eyes with her napkin. "We need to clean it all out, now. I'm glad Susan charged him. It had to end. When you bury things they fester—rot. I'm glad Mother isn't here to see it—or force us to hide it, as the case may be. Really."

"Let's go walk on the beach, shall we?" Myra waved the waiter over for the check. She couldn't have described the cauldron of emotions that rocked her—sadness, revulsion, anguish for Patricia. She needed to move, to swing her arms and legs, to let the rhythm of her body and the expanse of the sea absorb them, reduce things to some sort of order.

"Good idea." Patricia took her purse from the back of her chair. "And this is on me."

"No, it isn't," Myra retorted as the waiter came up. "This is my thank you. For telling me what's going on." She put her credit card in the bill folder and handed it back to the waiter. "Because I knew there was something—that Derek was bent on some mission."

They finished paying the bill and left the restaurant, then walked around to the beach side of the building. "The pier or the sand?" Myra asked.

"The sand. I want to get my feet wet." Tricia kicked off her shoes.

237

"The water's pretty chilly for that. It's January."

Tricia laughed. "You can always tell a Minnesotan. It must be cold because it's January. Come on." She led the way off the boardwalk and away from the windows of the restaurant.

They walked a long way in silence, and Myra felt her initial reactions to Patricia's story begin to lose its edge. Acceptance and the satisfaction of questions answered began to emerge. Soon, however, Susan's face rose, and her revulsion returned, followed by Derek's anger and her complicity in his ruin. "How's Derek? He was very angry and sealed off this morning."

Patricia nodded and kicked at the water. "I think Derek doesn't know who he's angriest at, right now."

"And who can blame him?" Myra put her arms around herself, as though the temperature of the California day had dropped. "I keep trying to remember how Derek reacted that day we found Susan in the closet," Myra said, gazing out at the water. "When she was eight. You'd think he'd connect Roger to that, but I guess like everyone else, he just thought Susan had eaten too much pie."

"She didn't say anything that day?"

Myra shook her head. "Or ever—until last week. I remember talking to Derek about how she'd changed. He said something about her growing up. How could we both have missed it so badly?" Myra stepped back out of the lapping tide. Despite Patricia's assurances that this was California, her cold feet were sending chills up her spine. "Dr. Garvitz says it's not uncommon—so does Randy, but I'm never going to be right with it—or any of this."

Patricia put an arm around her shoulders. "Wrong. Forgive yourself, Myra, or it'll drag you down forever."

Myra gave a wry smile. "Easy to say. But thank you for the thought." She put an arm around Tricia's waist. "How is Roger dealing with all of this?" she asked, to change the subject. "Does he know the jig is up? Peter says Derek took his passport."

"I know. I could hear Roger storming about looking for it. He shut himself in his room. Which was fine because no one wanted to deal with him." Patricia turned and headed back toward the restaurant, walking in the water as though that cooled her. "We were with Mother right after. That was enough."

"He didn't join you?"

She shook her head. "And she didn't ask for him." Patricia gave a harsh laugh. "That says something, doesn't it? Tons, in fact."

"Dear God." If she'd felt erased from the family, what must Roger have felt? But her moment of compassion was fleeting—isolation was too small a price.

They walked together in silence, the tide lapping at their heels.

"Do you ever wonder what he did in Argentina?" Myra asked.

"No." Patricia's voice was firm. "I can't afford to. The here and now is bad enough." She took a breath and let it out. "Do you suppose they're picking him up right now?"

Myra stopped as the possibility hit her. "This soon?"

"Why not?" Patricia stopped beside her. "I'd better get home to Dad." She took Myra's arm and turned toward the restaurant parking lot.

As Myra drove toward Goleta, Patricia's face as she remembered her baby brother kept rising in her mind. She could feel nothing but revulsion for the man, but there was no doubting Patricia's grief. What had happened to twist his soul? Or had the perversity lain there all along, waiting for adolescence to spring forth? She shuddered and concentrated on traffic to divert her mind.

Chapter 26

Myra opened the door to Rex's and Lily's welcome, which blew away darker thoughts. But the dogs soon went off to their usual pursuits, taking the life of the house with them. No messages waited on her answering machine. Randy was on duty until seven. She called Susan, whose voice was tight.

"Oh," she breathed when Myra identified herself, "I thought you were the police … saying they had him."

"Ah. No, haven't heard from them. How are you doing?"

"Terrified, as though I've done something dreadful, but lightheaded—like a balloon set free—at the same time. And important." She gave a laugh. "Now tell me that makes sense."

Myra heard a lilt in the laugh that had been missing for years. Why hadn't she questioned its absence? "You did something huge for yourself."

Susan laughed again. "Yes. It feels that way. What did Aunt Patricia say? Did she know why Dad was there?"

"Yes. Or she thinks so. Derek told her Roger had been caught … in another incident, back when he was in high school." Patricia's grief made her hesitate to go into the details of Roger's crime.

"Another incident?" She gave an audible breath and stopped. "That makes me feel better … terrible but true. Tell me."

"Well … when he was in high school, he was found in the girl's bathroom at an elementary school—the same school he went to as a child." Myra forced the words, remembering Patricia's desire to clear the air, once and for all. Susan's silence was enough to confirm all of their disgust and outrage. Why was it, she wondered, that even speaking of such acts seemed taboo?

"If he was caught, why … what happened?" Susan asked.

"Somehow Eleanor and Cornelius managed to get it dropped."

Again the silence, as Susan took it in. "They shouldn't have done that," she said finally, her voice soft with disappointment in her childhood heroes. "Did they get him help, at least?"

Myra blinked. "I don't know. Aunt Tricia didn't say." Why hadn't she thought to ask? "She was away at college when all of this happened."

"I'll call Dad. He'll know if someone at least tried." Susan sounded indignant now, and determined, signs, to Myra, that she was overcoming the effect of all of this, regaining strength. And eager to reunite with her father.

"Let me know what you find out."

"Okay. But you call him, too, will you?" Susan's voice carried a plea now.

"I'm not sure he's ready to talk to me."

"Oh." The lightness dropped from her daughter's voice. "That's my fault. I'll fix it. I'll tell him …"

"No, you won't!" Myra cut her off. "You let me deal with your father, Susan. It's not your problem."

"I was just going to tell him how sorry you are," Susan mumbled.

"I already did that, Susan. Please—don't interfere with this. Promise?"

"If you insist." Susan sighed. "But I feel like I can work miracles right now."

Myra laughed. "Hold onto that. And let me know if they pick up Roger. They'll probably call you first."

She put the phone down and gazed out the patio door. Clouds blanketed the sun now, and it threatened rain. No walk for her. She sighed and climbed to her tower room to work.

Deprived of their usual occupations by their New Year's resolutions, the Rabbleville Varmints sat despondent in their leaky mud nest.

"Nothing ever happens," mourned Matilda.
"I'm hungry," Eustasia grumbled.
"Bored is more like it," Alphonse mumbled.
"What a bunch of losers!" Rufus burst, launching his quills into the scene.
The explosion brought them all to their feet, hopping about and pulling quills from their bellies.

Myra started a fresh strip.

> "You broke your resolution—already!" they cried in unison.
> "Got my starch back, too!" Rufus strutted about the nest. "Look at this place." He kicked at a twig—one of many that had fallen out of the wall. "Time you poultry types brought in some straw—since you've nothing better to do."
> "Are you calling me poultry?" Alphonse stretched to his full height and threatened Rufus from above.
> "Looks like a duck, quacks like a duck ..." Rufus began, unimpressed by the beak above his head.
> "And what's the matter with poultry?" Matilda stretched her long neck, putting her beak in Rufus's face.
> "So you think we're a bunch of ducks!" Eustasia cried, joining the fray.
> Rufus stood his ground under their outraged beaks, a pleased smirk on his face.
> "What is *he* doing here?" Eustasia demanded at the start of the next strip.
> The others looked at each other, then at Rufus.
> "Yeah!"
> "Rodent in the chicken house, that's what I say!" Matilda cried.
> Rufus's smirk died. "Rodent? You're calling me a rodent?"
> Chicken, heron, and gull stood in a circle with their back to him, noses in the air.
> Another barrage of quills filled the air, sending all but Eustasia flying out of the nest.
> Rufus looked down and found himself naked, now.
> "Serves you right," Eustasia gloated, then turned and hopped to the wall.

Myra pulled a blank strip from the stack.

> Matilda and Alphonse returned to the nest, carrying straw, Eustasia brought a rag sling full of mud in her beak. They stood on the rim of the nest, watching Rufus pack it all into the walls.

Myra leaned back, her burst of energy spent. Her watch said four o'clock. She called Susan's number again and got the answering machine. They were probably out in the kennel, but if so, how would they know if Sergeant Dwyer called? Maybe they were content to let the answering machine handle the news. What difference did it make? There was nothing any of them could do now. Maybe they had the right idea. "Susan, call me on my cell phone if you hear," she said into the answering machine. "I'm going for a walk."

She changed her shoes, whistled for the dogs, and set off into the fog now rolling in from the sea. The rhythm of her feet did their work, relaxing the tension that ate all else so her head could begin to function. It was over, but as Susan's plea had reminded her, they were still buried in the ruins. Susan had said she'd fix it. Myra gave a laugh at the eternal hope of the young. Everything could be fixed.

And it isn't over, a new voice said from the back of her brain. Just out of your hands, now. There would be a trial, lawyers, testimony. The words had little reality, and none of the vaporous sense of wrong that had infected their lives. They had captured that, encapsulated it and handed it over to the law. Done.

She'd reached the end of the mesa where the bird refuge began. Instead of turning landward, as was her habit, she decided to go down the more gradual path at this end to the beach. The fog grew damper as she descended, and she asked herself what need for punishment was driving her. There was no answer. At the bottom, she gazed down the slime-covered rocks of low tide and shivered in the freshening wind. It felt like January, and why not? Her feet marched her off down the strip of beach above the tidal rocks. By February, the winter tides would have taken the sand, leaving only rocks and rusty iron projections, the skeletons of piers left by the oil company that had once owned this land. Only in winter, when tides sucked away the sand, were they laid bare.

She walked fast, head down, regretting this misbegotten walk, so she was almost upon him before she saw him.

Derek knelt on the slippery rocks, fishing something from a tidal pool. "Derek."

He dropped whatever it was and raised his head. Then stood.

She could think of nothing to say.

"A trip into the past." He gestured to the length of beach.

She nodded, still without words. "Have they picked Roger up?" she managed finally.

He shook his head "Don't know. I decided not to hang around and wait." He looked down the strip of pool-dotted rocks. "I've missed this beach."

"Does Cornelius know? That we charged Roger?"

"Yes." Derek shoved his hands into his pockets. "I told him. I didn't want the police showing up without his knowing. He said he was going to campus. He still has an office there."

Myra frowned. So they'd all run away from the moment of Roger's arrest, once they'd set it in motion. Roger would have no defenders, when the police knocked at that lovely carved door. Unless Patricia was there. She would be, by now. They'd left Roger's nasty finale to the only one who would weep for him. Cowards. Still, the idea of Cornelius opening the door to the police was worse. "I had lunch with Patricia," she began as Derek turned his attention back to the tide pool. "She told me about Roger—when he was in high school."

Derek's jaw clenched. "But how the hell did he get to Susan? That's what …" His voice died.

"It was at your folks' fiftieth wedding …"

"I know." He cut her off before she could go on. "Peter told me." He frowned. "I just don't know why I can't remember it."

"She went missing, and we all looked for her. I found her in Eleanor's closet. She didn't tell us. Just said she had a tummy ache."

His eyes told her he remembered. "Christ. She was—what? Eight?" His voice was hoarse.

"Right." Myra wrapped her arms around herself. What had possessed her to come out without a coat? "She remembers now. She told Dr. Garvitz that …"

"Stop." He put a hand up. "I don't think I can stand details right now." He ran a hand through his hair. "Except—did he rape her, Myra? Did he?"

"No. Not quite, but too damn close."

His face seemed to age before her eyes. "I keep remembering … he used to walk me home from school, grab me if I got too close to the road … our dog had puppies once … he showed me how to hold them so they wouldn't get hurt …" His voice faded out.

Myra stood frozen, watching him as he remembered a big brother he'd never talked about. A boy who liked small tender things. "I'm sorry, Derek. I can't imagine how tough this is for you."

"Well, at least now Susan knows it wasn't me!" His voice expressed the long pain of his exile—every year of it.

"Yes. She knows that. Go see her, Derek."

He gave a smile that seemed to burst from nowhere—a smile she remembered, which brought one from her in turn. "I'll do that." He raised his head to the sea breeze. "Susan and this beach. They'll save this day from hell."

Myra gave a wave and swung away, leaving him to his reward. She only wanted to go home.

"Myra," he called after her.

She turned.

He seemed about to speak, then shook his head. "Later." He raised a hand in farewell.

She climbed the steep path to the mesa. Later, what? Where would any of them end, after this? They were caught in an eternal present, holding their breaths until Roger was arrested.

When she reached the house, the message light on her phone was blinking. She punched the button and heard Patricia's voice.

"Myra, call me. He's gone."

Did she mean Cornelius or Roger? Or Derek? Myra dialed the number she'd known by heart for years, and was relieved that it was Patricia who answered.

"Myra. Roger's gone. We all assumed he was in his room. I know I heard him rumbling around the kitchen last night after we went to bed—at least I think it was him. But the police came just after I got home, and he wasn't here."

Myra sat down. "Oh God, don't tell me he's escaped again. That would be—too much." She let her breath out in a noisy sigh. "He doesn't have a passport."

"Right. The police seemed to know that already."

"Where are they looking, do you know, Tricia?"

"No. I couldn't tell them where he might be. He has no friends here. No work. He was just home for Mother ..." Patricia's voice broke. "He must have sensed something."

"Maybe not. Maybe he just went out for something else—cigarettes or something."

"You mean he might just walk back in here? No one's here but me,

245

Myra." Her voice carried the realization of the job she'd been left to perform.

"Derek's down on the beach. I'll ask him to get home."

"Tell him to go get Dad first, will you? At his campus office. We need to tell him Roger's gone."

"Okay. Call me, Patricia, if anything ... Patricia," she said, as another thought hit her. "Call Doug, will you? Tell him to be on the lookout."

"You don't think he'd go there, do you? My God, Myra. Why?"

"I don't know. Because she charged him, I guess. To talk her out of it, maybe?" What would he do? Or would he disappear as his brother had? Become a specter, inhabiting the fog?

"I can't believe Roger would do anything but run away. But all right. Do you have Doug's number?" Patricia's voice had returned to its normal coping mode.

Myra gave it to her, listened to the receiver click, then pulled a sweatshirt from the hook and ran back across the meadow. "Derek!" she called from the top of the path. She started down to meet him.

A few minutes later, his head appeared below her on the beach.

"Roger's gone."

"What? Where?"

"No one knows. The police showed up, and he wasn't in his bedroom. Patricia wants you to go get your dad. He's at his campus office."

"Damn. You mean Roger's run off? Is she sure?"

"No one's sure of anything except that the police don't have him."

"Shit. Okay, tell her I'm on my way." He turned back toward the beach.

"Where's your car, Derek?" She called, realizing that it couldn't be very close.

"Cliff House," he called back.

Too far. It would take him ten minutes to get there at a dead run. "I'll drive you!"

He turned, hesitated, then came back and climbed the path.

When they reached the car, they were out of breath, saving them from further conversation. As she drove away from the house, Myra wondered if he, like she, was trying to avoid the familiarity of the situation. When she turned onto the road that ran along the slough, dry now, at low tide, memory overwhelmed her. This was a favorite walk, when the children were little. Osprey and cormorant, heron and coot, plover and curlew, blackbird and meadowlark all gathered here where sea, marsh, beach, and grassland came together. Myra glanced at Derek and saw that he was gazing eagerly at the scene, a smile playing on his face. For a moment, the pleasure of things shared wiped out the intervening years.

Shaking herself free of memory, she turned off onto the track that led to Cliff House, a one-room conference center owned by the university. It sat alone on a peninsula overlooking the water and was a favorite retreat spot for faculty groups. She wondered how he got permission to park out here, then realized that a ticket would be a cheap price to pay for the access he'd now won to his past. This had always been his favorite beach. The meeting center was dark, and only the Jag occupied the parking lot. To be sure, a white flag flapped on its windshield.

Derek read her smile and gave a tight one in return. "Some things never change." He opened the car door. "Thanks for the ride."

"Call me," she said as he got out of the car.

He nodded and waved.

As she waited for him to back out ahead of her, a dim memory returned, of watching the Jag come down this road toward her, a young girl sitting next to Derek. Had she been looking for him or out here on some errand of her own? She couldn't remember; the memory simply floated, free of encumbrance.

"Some things never change," she reminded herself.

A half-hour later, as the early winter dusk was falling, the telephone rang. Myra broke away from her futile pacing and ran for it.

"The Serendipity's gone." Derek's voice was both angry and victorious. "I've called the police. They'll send a boat out, but can't promise much until daylight."

A chill of foreboding sat Myra down. "Where could he go …? Are you sure Cornelius didn't take it?"

"Yes, I called. He answered the phone in his office."

She told herself there could be a dozen explanations. Maybe Roger had suspected nothing and simply gone for a sail. Maybe he'd planned his escape and provisioned the boat in advance. Neither explanation made a dent in her certainty that whatever was coming was bad. "Call Tricia. She's alone at the house and worried."

"I did," he said. "I'm on my way to pick up Dad. Then we'll go home."

"You'd better tell him—prepare him ..." She cut herself off from words that might confirm her fears.

"He knows."

Derek was thinking only of Roger's arrest—that much was clear from his tone. Myra hung up and looked at the clock. Six. Randy would be here in an hour. Until then ... She looked at the phone and rejected all of the calls that came to mind, unwilling to share her dread.

Rex's cold nose nuzzled into the palm of her hanging hand, reminding her that it was dinner time. "Okay, boy, a good idea." She dawdled over feeding the pair, then practiced some long unused yoga exercises to loosen her shoulders. Finally she set the table, made a salad, and started a pasta sauce she had no wish to eat.

Randy arrived to find her cursing a burned thumb, uttering a string of words that widened his eyes in mock shock. "Myra Benning, I would never have guessed!"

"Oh, hush," she mumbled. "Roger and the Serendipity are gone."

He crossed the kitchen and put his arms around her. "I know. Heard it on the radio."

"They can't do much until morning. By that time, he could be—who knows? Out of the Channel—ashore somewhere. Ventura ... LA ..."

"You can't dock a boat just anywhere, Myra. They'll find it. And the Coast Guard will send a helicopter, too, once it's light."

"Oh?" Her brain refused to work. She put her head against his shoulder for a minute, resting, letting her body enter this other world. "That's better." She stood up and gave a sigh. "My head's scrambled. When we left the courthouse, it felt like we'd finished something. Instead ..." she threw her hands up. "It's turned to chaos—or worse. Everything's torn loose." For the first time she noticed that his eyes were red-rimmed, his face lined with fatigue. "You're exhausted. How long have you been on duty?"

"Got called in last night. Someone starting the new year off by beating his girlfriend, then holding her kids hostage." He reached a hand up and brushed her cheek. "I'll be fine with a drink and a shower."

Myra opened the refrigerator and pulled out two beers. "You look like you need sleep more than anything else." She opened the bottles and handed him one. "Does every cozy-looking house on the street hide such ugliness, Randy? How do you do it?"

"I come here." He grinned. "For an antidote."

"Ha. Right." She closed her eyes. When she opened them she was calm. "Okay. We'll try. Dinner's about ready, and we'll eat—as though nothing is going on in the world."

"Except us." He drew her to him and kissed her. "Let's see that hand," he added, releasing her.

"It's nothing. I just needed to do a little swearing." She turned on the burner under the pasta water. "Go get yourself that shower. The clothes you left are in my closet."

Fifteen minutes later, they sat opposite, the blinds drawn against the night, the dogs asleep at their feet. Randy, freshly shaven and dressed in sweats and T-shirt, ate as though it was the first meal he'd had since he left yesterday. Was that just yesterday? Then she discovered she was hungry after all.

"You'd make a good cop's wife." Randy sat back with a sigh.

"I would? So you could come home from a twenty-four hour shift and find me falling apart over a burned finger?"

He laughed. "Because you pull yourself together and turn it all around." He took a sip of wine. "Now tell me. I talked with Bobby Dwyer, so I know Susan charged him."

"Did he tell you Derek was there? And about the school incident?"

Randy nodded, his face sobering. "The school filed a complaint, as it turned out. But then withdrew it."

She nodded. "That was Eleanor's and Cornelius's doing. I had lunch with Patricia. She told me." She took a breath. "She's really broken up about it. So is Derek, under all of that anger."

He watched her quizzically. "And you?"

"I had the good fortune not to know the man, really. He isn't *my* brother." Heavy with fatigue, she rose to collect the dishes. By the time she'd finished cleaning up the kitchen, he'd gone down the hall to the bedroom. She found him asleep on her bed, still in his clothes, and lay down beside him, pulling a quilt over both of them.

249

Chapter 27

They woke to the cackling of Randy's police radio on the bedside table. Randy reached for it without opening his eyes, then sat up and swung his feet off the bed. The sun of a cloudless winter day blazed in the window.

The voice from the instrument was blurred, or she was still half asleep. She struggled and failed to make out the words. By the time he clicked off the radio, she was wide awake.

"They found the Serendipity floating off Anacapa Island. Empty."

Myra stared at him. This was what she'd feared when Derek told her the boat was gone. Known, even. "He waited for his mother's funeral, then …"

"Couldn't find his passport," Randy finished for her.

Myra headed for the bathroom, shaking all over. She leaned against the wall, then sat, her back against it. "Don't tell Susan," she muttered as Randy came in and looked down at her. "Don't," she repeated, though she knew that was impossible. "There was nothing—no note?" What note, she couldn't imagine, just anything but a void.

"I don't know. They're towing her in." He reached down and pulled her to her feet.

"Could he have gotten off … on Anacapa … or somewhere …?"

"Don't know why he'd do that, Myra. There's nothing on that island but a ranger station. We'll know more when they get in."

She turned to wash her face. Randy was right. There would be no point in cornering himself on an island with a park ranger. "We'll never know. That's what I'm afraid of—we'll know but never know. I have to go to Susan." She picked up a brush and ran it through her hair.

Randy came up and put his arms around her from behind. "I want you to remember something." She stopped and looked at him in the mirror. "If he took this way out, it's not all bad. You think you'd feel better if a jury decides he's guilty, but juries—particularly in child molestation cases—can be in too much of a hurry to convict. They make mistakes. There's no certainty, either way."

"Unless he confessed. I guess I was hoping he'd put it to rest that way."

"Even that. Sometimes people—guilty or innocent—will do anything to avoid walking into that courtroom—facing the public's disgust and revulsion."

Myra nodded, remembering that Derek had fled family and career for fear of the same exposure. The thought only brought the horror of it closer. "I need to go."

"All right. I'll find out what I can and call you."

She drove, cursing the clog of rush-hour traffic. When she reached Susan's and Doug's house, a distraught Doug answered the door. "Manny Gonzaga called. He said Roger ..." He broke off, reading her face. "You know."

She nodded.

"Susan's in the bedroom." He waved her through.

Susan lay on her side, facing the window, staring blankly at the light. Myra sat down and reached for her. Susan raised an icy hand and took hold of her wrist but otherwise didn't move. "I feel as though someone threw me to the ground—smashed me to pieces. Only then I remember that it's me. I did this."

"Susan, you did what was right. What Roger did—and we don't know that yet—was his choice." She was forcing words she knew were right but didn't feel.

"Why did I do it? I pulled the pin on the grenade."

Myra rolled Susan toward her. "It does feel like that right now. But it was more like an abscess infecting the whole family—and you most of all."

She was quiet, but Myra felt her relax a little. "But to end like this, Mom. I didn't mean ..." Her words disappeared into a sob, and Myra felt her own tears rise.

An unmeasured time later, their shock dissolved, they lay together, quiet and drained. Myra gazed at the ceiling, letting the pieces settle.

None of them doubted that Roger was dead. Now that the shock had worn off, anger at his suicide—turning his accusers into persecutors, cheating them of any sense of justice—rose in its place. She groped for Randy's words about juries in molestation cases. Making mistakes was what he'd said. Unreliable was what he meant. Carried away by revulsion, taking revenge on the person in front of them, innocent or guilty. And yes. She wanted revenge. Wanted to see Roger standing in the dock, hear the verdict handed down. But she could find nothing in her heart that had wanted to see him dead.

Billy's cries roused them both from a half-doze. Susan rose and went to his crib. Myra watched as Susan shifted into the baby's universe, talking softly to him as she changed his diaper. She couldn't hear the words and didn't want to. The soft mutter gave off solace and peace. Susan lifted the baby and pressed his cheek to hers, still uttering the soothing nonsense. Then she went to the rocker and began to nurse him.

Myra rose and tried to shake herself into some semblance of life. Her body didn't respond. She looked down and discovered she was still wearing yesterday's clothes.

She needed a shower, before anything else. She found Doug in the kennels, filling water dishes. "Susan's better," she reported. "She's nursing Billy."

"Thanks, Myra." He straightened and ran a hand through his hair. "It isn't fair. Maybe that's a terrible thing to feel about someone—doing something like that, but I can't get past it. To put it on Susan—it just damn well is wrong!"

"You're right. And thank you for yelling it at the top of your lungs. It clears the air."

He looked abashed, then smiled. "Want me to do it again?"

She brushed a hand across his cheek. "Have I ever thanked you for loving my daughter?"

"You think it's that hard to do?" He gave her puzzled frown.

"Sometimes," Myra admitted. "And all of this—it can't have been easy on you."

He reached his hand over the kennel gate to rub the head of Brutus, the black Lab, who was begging his attention. "It felt like a doorway into a better time—until this happened. Now it feels like the door was slammed in our faces. So I'm pissed!"

"Good. Tell Susan to be pissed too, will you? Me, I'm heading home to the shower. Maybe I'll yell my head off at the walls."

"Good idea. And thanks for coming."

She nodded. "Did Gonzaga say whether he'd told Peter? When did he call, by the way?"

"Less than five minutes before you got here. He said the sheriff had just phoned him. He was going to call you and Peter next. I was wondering how you got here so fast."

"Randy got it on his radio. I guess there'll be a message on my answering machine."

"He wants to meet with us."

"Not until I've had my shower." Her skin turned clammy at the idea of all of them gathered around a table facing the consequences of their acts.

Doug smiled. "This afternoon around two. At his office. Do you think Susan can handle it?"

"Depends on what Gonzaga has in store, but I think so." She remembered Susan's face, drained but relaxed, as she nursed the baby. "She had a good cry and is nursing Billy. I think she's over the hump."

"I hope so." He opened the kennel to let the dog into the yard. "Go get your shower, then. We'll see you this afternoon."

For a minute, she stood watching him go down the row, talking to the dogs as he released them into the open. Susan would be okay.

The sun disappeared behind dark clouds as she reached the freeway. They would have rain soon, which suited her mood far better than sun. Once home, the message on her answering machine told her what she already knew. She returned the call and confirmed with the lawyer's secretary that she would be there at two, then phoned her son.

Peter answered almost immediately.

"Gonzaga phoned you, I gather," she began.

"He did." Peter sounded tired. "What a shitty way to end it. I feel cheated. Damn him."

"I know."

"Like leaving us stranded in ... nowhere."

"Maybe we'll find out more this afternoon." Even as she said it, she suspected they had as much as they were going to get.

Peter grunted, accepting the shred of hope. "See you then."

The unreality of this day stretched to infinity. Only the clamor of her unfed animals brought her back.

"Yes, you're here, and I love you." She knelt and put an arm around each. They licked her face. "You don't fool me a bit," she told them. "It's kibble you want. I'm just the means to an end." She obliged them with an extra portion apiece to make up for the lack of a morning walk, then headed upstairs to the shower.

As hot water poured over her, washing the morning from her hair and stale odors from her skin, she willed herself to yell at the walls as promised. But she couldn't manage Doug's clear untroubled outrage. Waves of guilt flattened hers. Finally, she yelled against the guilt. That helped. Blood flowed through her veins again. But by the time she'd toweled herself dry and dressed in clean jeans and sweater, she was exhausted. Unable to find traction to carry her forward, she could only lie down on the bed. Was this what suicide did to survivors? Lifting them up and dashing them against a wall, as Susan had said? She ran through the words she'd told her daughter with no effect. Finally, anger that a man like Roger had managed to so defeat her brought her to her feet. Damn him.

Myra was down the stairs and had opened the patio door before she realized it was pouring. They would have no walk today. She turned and went to the kitchen, but wasn't hungry. Finally, because there was nowhere else to go, she climbed the stairs to her studio. The rain beat on the roof and sluiced down the panes on three sides of her. She hadn't come to work. Satire was a mockery of life today. Instead she took up a drawing pad and charcoal.

A sailboat, its sheets sagging unfurled on the deck, rode the roiling waves. The rain beat on the cabin and on the lone figure at the helm whose arms were raised in a plea, appeasing the storm—or an angry God—or simply begging for release from the grip of the raging sea.

An hour later, Myra sat back, her blackened fingers at rest, and stared at what she'd done. She felt calm, as though she'd released some inexpressible knot of emotions onto the page. The drawing spoke of a man begging mercy not of man but of God, a man who had come to this end through his own actions. A dull headache was all that was left of the morning. She rose and washed her hands, giving the picture one final glance before she went downstairs. She was hungry now, and it was already one o'clock.

Held up by a traffic accident on the freeway, Myra arrived at Gonzaga's office late and in pouring rain. The rack inside the door was full of dripping raincoats—drenched by the same storm that swamped her charcoal boat. Susan, Doug, Peter, Derek, Patricia, and Cornelius sat around the lawyer's conference table.

Myra stopped, startled by Cornelius's presence, then realized that conversation had broken off when she entered.

"I'm sorry. There was an accident …" She waved away the rest of her sentence as irrelevant. She stopped behind her father-in-law's chair and put her hand on his shoulder. "I'm sorry, Conny. For all of this."

He raised a hand and laid it on hers.

"I was just telling the others," Gonzaga said as she took a seat, "that until we have some confirmation—until we know what happened to Roger—the case will be on hold. I'm sorry about that. I know you wanted it finished, but …" He spread his hands.

"It is as it has been for thirty years. Frozen in time." Cornelius's hollow intonation silenced the group and turned them all to the old man who sat, eyes riveted on a spot in the center of the table. "Forgive me," he said, as he noticed their stares. "Go on, please." He addressed the last to the lawyer.

"I was just going to say that Sergeant Dwyer wants to see you all across the street in about …" He consulted his watch. "Fifteen minutes. He'll make it official."

"Do they have a case against him, Manny?" Peter asked. "Can we know that much at least?"

"He can tell you that, but yes. As strong a case as these things ever are. Mr. Benning," he nodded toward Cornelius, "has corroborated the earlier incidents. And the warrant for his arrest will stand. That much is certain, I think."

Cornelius put his head in his hands, and Patricia reached for him. "No, no," he said, straightening. "It should have happened long ago. So long …" He looked at Susan, "and if I'd ever thought he'd take my grandchild, I'd …" He broke off and shook his head. "But I didn't. And I'll carry that to my grave, my dear. The rest …" He waved a bony hand and fell silent.

"You did it for Mom," Patricia responded. "We all know that, Dad." She looked up and met her brother's gaze. "And we were all blind—or willing ourselves to be."

"Does the sheriff believe …" Derek broke off and glanced at his father. "… he's alive?"

"Ask him. The chances are slim, I think." Gonzaga looked at his notes, then at his watch.

"Well, at least we know what happened," Peter insisted. "We know Dad's in the clear. We can be a family again." His gaze circled the table, rested on Susan, then moved on to Myra.

Myra felt the breath catch in her throat. "This is not the time …" she began.

"True!" Derek burst, cutting off her response. He put a hand on his son's shoulder. "We have a lot of years to make up."

"Folks, I think it's time to go across the street."

Myra closed her eyes in gratitude for the reprieve from this sudden turn in the conversation, but it stayed with her as they trooped over to the police department.

"Good morning," Sergeant Dwyer greeted them. "Thank you for coming. I wanted you all to hear the status of the case directly from me." He smiled. "Sometimes these things get muddied in translation."

They waited.

"We issued a warrant for Roger Benning's arrest yesterday morning."

The sentence, cold and flat, struck Myra dumb, and she realized that in the previous half hour with Manny Gonzaga, no one had uttered Roger's name. As though by referring to the man as "him", they avoided claiming them as their own. She had a sudden vision of a high-school boy left to wander nameless and of the resulting man, a faded unformed version of her husband. Dear God, why had no one helped him?

"They didn't find him at his home," the sergeant went on, "though his sister thought he was in his room." He paused. "None of the family vehicles was missing, and we find no evidence that anyone colluded in his escape."

Myra blinked. Such a notion had never occurred to her.

"An hour later, Mr. Derek Benning reported that the family sailboat, The Serendipity, was missing. We asked the Coast Guard to institute a sea search. Meanwhile, we determined that Roger took a Yellow Cab to the Santa Barbara Marina, corroborating Derek Benning's suspicion that he had taken the boat."

Myra listened, chilled, as the story divorced itself from their lived lives and took the form of a police investigation. It was both reassuring and intimidating.

"The Coast Guard found the boat at ten this morning off of Anacapa Island. No one was on board." Dwyer turned a page of his notebook. "We have asked the ranger's cooperation in searching the island, though we think it doubtful he would have gone ashore there, since there it doesn't offer an escape route, and we've found no evidence that he did so." He looked up, his gaze circling their faces. "We've consulted the Coast Guard to see whether the boat could have been carried to that location by the currents and winds, and they tell us it's highly unlikely, if not impossible. We are conducting a search of Santa Cruz Island just in case, but at this point we believe Roger Benning is lost at sea."

No one spoke. They simply stared at the sergeant, spent.

"The case will remain open on the books?" Gonzaga asked.

"Of course—with an outstanding warrant, but we don't think it's likely ..." A knock at the door interrupted him, and an officer came in and handed him a pair of notes. "All right," the sergeant began, reading the slip of paper. "There was a note in the cabin of the *Serendipity.*" He read from the second piece of paper.

"'This is the only way to end it. Roger.'"

The words brought the speaker into the room, then hung in the air until broken by a rough sob from his father. Myra, sitting next to him, put an arm around his shoulders, an act of forgiveness that surprised her, but was demanded by some force she couldn't name.

She looked up and saw that Susan's head was buried in Doug's chest. Patricia hugged herself, head down. Peter and Derek stared into some middle space as though defending themselves from the emotion that swept through the room.

Sergeant Dwyer cleared his throat. "We'll compare the handwriting, of course. But if that checks out, Roger Benning, in all probability, died by his own hand. You'll agree, counselor?"

"Right." Manny Gonzaga rose. He seemed about to speak, then changed his mind. He waited for them to follow his lead, then ushered them out.

Myra stopped to shake the sergeant's hand. "Thank you." She frowned, wondering what it was she was thankful for. "For bringing it all into the light of day—and closing the book."

He smiled, then held up the note. "Roger closed the book."

Myra took the slip of paper from him and read the words. "So few." As she stared at them, the certainty she'd felt when she first heard them faded away. Had he intended them as a confession or not? Surely they were. But the insistence of one side of her brain didn't dispel the shadow. She took a breath and handed the paper back and turned away.

They returned to Gonzaga's office, but the lawyer could find little to do but send them all home. "Believe me," he said, "and I know it doesn't seem that way now, but you'll come to see his death as merciful."

Only Cornelius nodded. Then he let Patricia help him to his feet and lead him out.

Myra followed Susan and Doug into the reception area and took her daughter in her arms. "We'll talk tomorrow. Right now, go on home and rest."

Susan shook her head. "I need to—I don't know—pound nails, clean kennels—something."

"Good. We'll haul manure—how's that?" Doug gave Myra a smile and turned Susan toward the street.

Myra watched them go off, then turned away. She wanted to be alone—had to be. Randy wasn't off duty until ten. Right now, she needed to walk the beach—rain or not.

She was numb as she drove toward Goleta and grateful for it. Once home, she lost no time in changing her clothes, donning boots and a slicker, collecting the dogs and setting off. She was alone in the cold damp of the mesa. The islands were hidden by drizzle and fog. Emotions surged, and the rhythm of her body dissipated them into the emptiness, unexamined. When they were gone, the image of Roger rose clear, and she willed herself to believe his death had released them from the curse of eternal doubt. Merciful. That's what Manny Gonzaga had said. He took the note as a confession then. God willing, Susan and Peter would, too. But for her, a shadow would remain. She remembered Randy's words, "there is no certainty." Would she ever achieve the acceptance she heard in his voice?

She gazed at the water sluicing down the path to the beach and decided not to risk it. The service road along the top of the cliff would do. She walked again, feeling the months and years unwind. She was crying, and it didn't matter. Nothing mattered except the rhythmic rocking of her gait. Dimly, she noticed another form taking shape ahead of her. Some other wanderer in the rain.

Then she stopped. It was Derek. He was waiting for her. When she didn't move, he headed toward her.

"Hello. I thought I'd find you out here." He smiled.

"What are you doing here?" Myra asked, though she guessed the answer. She started moving again, and he fell in step beside her.

"Susan and Peter asked me to come get you—bring you to supper."

Her heels hit the ground as Peter's cry, "We're a family again!" rang in her head.

"What sort of a dinner, Derek?"

"What do you mean? They just want us to be together. Maybe to celebrate it's being over."

"To celebrate a suicide? I'm not ready to do that."

"Of course not. No. But it *is* over. And I'm glad my brother doesn't have to appear in court, his name all over the papers. The whole nightmare did bring us back together."

She didn't answer.

"Cornelius spoke with the Chair of Marine Sciences. They have a position open—an on-going search. I may have a chance to get back in."

She stopped walking and looked at him for the first time. "Good. That would ... repair a lot of damage."

He nodded. "And we can repair more, you and I."

She looked him up and down, from his windbreaker, dripping in the fog, to his damp chinos and damper boat shoes. Except for the lines around his mouth and the graying beard, he was still the virile man she'd met in a campus coffee shop thirty years ago. But she wasn't the same girl. "You're serious aren't you?"

"I always loved you, Myra. Even when I hated you for what you did." His eyes proclaimed her guilt—his forgiveness—her obligation for restitution.

Something fell in place inside her, like the tumbler of a lock. "And that's the basis of our reconciliation?"

He looked down at his feet. "You loved me, once."

She turned and walked away. She needed space from the picture of a blissful past and the 'happy ever after' ending he was recreating. He was Eleanor's son after all, believing they could wave a magic wand

259

and eliminate the whole affair. For the children. And what of them? Had Susan and Peter told him about Randy? Evidently not. Was their loyalty to their childhood family so great? She remembered the light in Peter's eyes he said they were a family again. And Susan? She couldn't remember the expression on Susan's face, but knew there was no magician's spell that would lift the weight of either her accusations against Derek or Roger's death.

Again she heard Susan's screams in the middle of the night and Derek's explanation of his fatherly hug. "Because she looked so beautiful." Did anyone but Derek believe so totally in his innocence? She didn't. Was the weight Susan felt her imagination? Both Derek's innocence and Roger's guilt had turned as vaporous as the fog. She had an image of them together, every gesture conveying her accusations forgiven, his long, undeserved exile. She, weighted down by her mistake, he, released again into boyish innocence. She turned away from the sea that had hidden itself behind a curtain of gray and walked back toward him.

It was not hard to imagine her living room filled with bright young faces once again, her house haunted by breathy female voices. Some things never change. That was the only certainty she still believed in.

His eyes were eager for her assent.

"Tell Susan and Peter, no," she said as she came up to him. "Tell them the truth. That we have no basis for a marriage, Derek."

His face went still. "You can't mean that. We had all those years—the children …"

"Are you really using our children to get me into a marriage based on guilt—my guilt—restitution owed you?"

"Of course not. Why would you …?"

"Goodbye, Derek." She turned around and headed back toward the house—striding, stomping puddles to watch the water fly, feeling indignation and anger at someone other than herself that she hadn't felt in years.

Chapter 28

A week later, as Myra, surrounded by her family, was celebrating her birthday, the telephone rang.

"Myra." Patricia's voice carried the weight of the events from which this day was to be a reprieve.

"Where are you?" Myra asked. "We've been waiting for you."

"I won't be coming, Myra. I'm sorry. They found Roger this morning, washed up on the beach below the Brown Pelican."

Myra sat down. The buzz of conversation behind her went silent. "I … I don't know what to say, Tricia." For a week, she'd gone about the motions of her life, trying to convince herself the affair was finished. Now she realized how little she'd prepared herself for this.

"That's all right. It's all been said." Patricia's voice was exhausted. She'd spent the week, Myra knew, getting Cornelius out of bed each morning, moving him through days he had no wish to live.

"Maybe we can all put an end to it now." Her words caused a rustle in the room behind her, and she felt Randy come up close.

"I hope so. We've been waiting … for something like this. I'm just sorry it happened on your birthday."

"Oh, good grief, don't worry about that. Call me … with arrangements, will you?"

There was a long pause. "I hardly expect any of you to come, Myra."

"I know. But call." Even as she said it, she knew she would go. For Patricia. For the family whose tragedy had long since become her own. "And take care of yourself, Patricia. Okay?"

She turned to meet five pairs of eyes that awaited. "They found Roger, this morning, on the beach below the Brown Pelican."

Susan covered her face and let tears flow.

"Susie ..." Doug protested.

"Let her cry," Myra intervened, cutting him off. "We all need to ..." and she found herself weeping into Randy's chest.

"Don't know what's to cry about," Peter burst out, getting up to pace as though their tears irritated him. "Feel damned grateful, myself." He jammed his hands into his pockets and headed for the patio. He's not a ghost I want hanging around, thank you."

Myra gave a laugh, realizing that her shock was mixed with relief. "He's right. Patricia said it—we were all waiting." She released herself from Randy's arms and crossed the room to Susan.

"Look at me."

Susan raised her head.

"Promise me this is the last time you'll cry about this mess."

Susan gave a laugh. "Why?"

"Because Peter's right. It was Roger who set the ghosts in motion, and he's dead."

"But it's my fault he ..."

"Bullshit, Susan, you don't have that power," her brother, coming back into the living room, cut her off. "Roger did that. It was his choice."

"He did enough to you, Susan," Randy said, coming up. "Don't let him hang his death on you, too."

Susan looked at him, surprised. "You think that's what he was doing? Hanging it on us?"

Peter shrugged. "Actually, I think he just wanted a way out."

Susan nodded, her eyes thoughtful. "But there isn't one. Not for me—for us. Do you think he had any idea of the effect of what he did?"

"Doubtful." Myra came over and sat next to Susan, taking her hand. "From his last words, I'd guess he was overwhelmed by his own—sickness, monstrosity, perversity—whatever name he gave it." Was he? Myra asked herself silently. Was he terrorized by his guilt or their pursuit? But Susan sat back on the couch, calmed by her diagnosis. "We can never really know, Susan, and it doesn't matter. What matters is you. You need to leave him behind."

"You can do that," Randy assured her. "All you need is time."

A smile broke across Susan's new calm. "It feels so good to talk about it." She sat up straight. "To know it isn't—wasn't—something about me ..." An impatient cry from Billy, forgotten in his playpen across the room, brought her head around. She leapt up, went to him. "He says it's his turn," she said, picking him up.

Laughter bubbled through them releasing the tension in the room. One more dangerous pit traversed.

"And it's your Grandma's birthday," she told the baby in her arms. "Time for cake!"

Myra opened her mouth to protest, then changed her mind as Randy pulled her to her feet. She stared at the cake which Doug brought from the kitchen and unveiled. The four varmints from Rabbleville, formed of royal-icing, danced across the top. "Susan, they're wonderful!"

"Well, at least they're getting along for the moment." Susan handed her the server. "But you'd better hurry. I think Rufus's quills are beginning to droop."

Myra laughed and obliged, then sat listening to the chatter as her family sought to keep the mood aloft. She'd often wondered why people held funeral feasts. Now she knew. The determination of life to seek the light.

Three days later, she stood beside Patricia at Roger's open grave. Myra had not told the others the time and place, and they had not asked. Now, she gazed at the coffin, remembering Tricia's words about lives programmed for disaster. Cornelius's face was drained, emptied of all except the act of burying his son.

Other than a short prayer by the minister, commending his soul, the burial was held without ceremony. But for Myra, its very simplicity held a promise that the raw edges left by the man's life would eventually be dulled by the motion of the tides. Like the rusted iron stanchions revealed each winter, his life would return over and over to remind them of the tragedy of human evil.

CPSIA information can be obtained at www.ICGtesting.com
Printed in the USA
LVOW13s2340050114

368215LV00001B/1/P